EFFI BRIEST

THEODOR FONTANE was born in 1819 in North Germany, of a family which had originally emigrated to Prussia in the eighteenth century from France to avoid persecution as Protestants. Brought up in various towns around Berlin, Fontane left school early and became a pharmacist, like his father. His first publications were mostly ballads. In 1849 he became a full-time writer, which meant working as a journalist. From 1854 to 1859 he was based in London as an official correspondent for the Prussian government. In the following decade he wrote books about the Prussian wars against Denmark, Austria, and France. He also wrote a multi-volume travel book about the history and traditions of Prussia, *Wanderings Through the March of Brandenburg* (1862–92). He was nearly sixty when his first novel, a historical narrative inspired by Scott and Thackeray, appeared as *Before the Storm: A Novel from the Winter 1812–13* (1878). Thereafter he produced a series of novels, mostly set in the present and for the most part in Berlin, giving humorous, often critical, portrayals of middle- and upper-class society, and focusing especially on the problems of marriage. *Effi Briest* appeared in 1895. His last and in some ways most ambitious novel, *The Stechlin*, relying on conversation rather than action to give a broad picture of modern Germany in the context of Germany's changing place in the wider world, appeared a few months after Fontane's death in 1898. Popular in his own day, he is now recognized as Germany's leading contributor to the tradition of nineteenth-century realist fiction.

MIKE MITCHELL taught at the universities of Reading and Stirling before becoming a full-time translator. He is the co-author of *Harrap's German Grammar* and the translator of numerous works of German fiction. He has translated Kafka's *The Trial* for Oxford World's Classics.

RITCHIE ROBERTSON is Taylor Professor of German at the University of Oxford and a Fellow of Queen's College. He is the author of several works on German literature and has translated Kafka's *The Man who Disappeared* for Oxford World's Classics, as well as editing four other volumes of Kafka's fiction for the series, and two works by Sigmund Freud.

OXFORD WORLD'S CLASSICS

*For over 100 years Oxford World's Classics have brought
readers closer to the world's great literature. Now with over 700
titles—from the 4,000-year-old myths of Mesopotamia to the
twentieth century's greatest novels—the series makes available
lesser-known as well as celebrated writing.*

*The pocket-sized hardbacks of the early years contained
introductions by Virginia Woolf, T. S. Eliot, Graham Greene,
and other literary figures which enriched the experience of reading.
Today the series is recognized for its fine scholarship and
reliability in texts that span world literature, drama and poetry,
religion, philosophy, and politics. Each edition includes perceptive
commentary and essential background information to meet the
changing needs of readers.*

OXFORD WORLD'S CLASSICS

THEODOR FONTANE

Effi Briest

Translated by
MIKE MITCHELL

With an Introduction and Notes by
RITCHIE ROBERTSON

OXFORD
UNIVERSITY PRESS

OXFORD

UNIVERSITY PRESS

Great Clarendon Street, Oxford, OX2 6DP
United Kingdom

Oxford University Press is a department of the University of Oxford.
It furthers the University's objective of excellence in research, scholarship,
and education by publishing worldwide. Oxford is a registered trade mark of
Oxford University Press in the UK and in certain other countries

First published as an Oxford World's Classics paperback 2015

Impression: 9

Published in the United States of America by Oxford University Press
198 Madison Avenue, New York, NY 10016, United States of America

British Library Cataloguing in Publication Data

Data available

Library of Congress Control Number: 2014949670

ISBN 978–0–19–967564–7

Printed in Great Britain by
Clays Ltd, Elcograf S.p.A.

CONTENTS

INTRODUCTION

*Readers who do not wish to learn details of the plot will prefer to
treat the Introduction as an Afterword.*

OF the many novelists writing in nineteenth-century Germany,
Theodor Fontane is not only, by common consent, the greatest,
but also the most cosmopolitan. His ancestors were Huguenots,
Protestants from Nîmes, who fled from France after Louis XIV
denied them toleration by revoking the Edict of Nantes in 1685. Five
thousand Huguenots, skilled craftsmen with their families, were welcomed to Berlin by Friedrich I, the far-sighted ruler of Prussia, and
formed a colony whose church still stands on the Gendarmenmarkt
in the centre of Berlin. They included the Fontaine family, who pres-
ently changed the spelling of their name and modified its pronunci-
ation. The novelist pronounced his name Fóntan (two syllables, with
the stress on the first), though nowadays the name is generally pronounced as three syllables with the stress on the second.

   Although he was of French descent through both his father and
his mother, Theodor Fontane felt a particular affinity to the English
language and British culture. His first visit to England was a fortnight's stay in the summer of 1844. At this time Fontane, who had left
school at the age of fifteen, was following his father's profession as
a pharmacist. He was also writing poetry, especially ballads, and was
admitted in 1844 to a Berlin literary society called the Tunnel over the
Spree (the name of one of the rivers running through the city); this
society, of which he remained an active member till 1855, brought
him into contact with many prominent figures, including the important writers Theodor Storm and Paul Heyse (winner of the Nobel
Prize for Literature in 1910) and the painter Adolph Menzel. In
1849 he decided to become a full-time writer. This meant in practice
scraping a living as a journalist, often writing for newspapers whose
conservative politics Fontane disliked. But it had the advantage that
he was sometimes sent abroad. From April to September 1852 he was
in London as a correspondent for a Berlin paper, and from 1855 to
1859 he was there as an official correspondent for the government.
His residence in Britain gave rise to two travel books, *From England*

and *Beyond the Tweed*, the latter being an account of a tour through Scotland as far as Inverness that he undertook in the summer of 1858; both books are full of anecdotes associated with the stately homes, battlefields, and other historic sites that Fontane visited, and he tells them with the circumstantial detail, the gusto, and the friendly rapport with the reader that would later reappear in his novels. He also immersed himself in British realist fiction. He was already an admirer of Walter Scott, whose novels had a Europe-wide vogue, and his own first novel, *Before the Storm* (1878), is a work of historical fiction, inspired by Scott, dealing with the Prussian campaign against occupying French troops in the winter of 1812–13. During his stay in Britain, however, Fontane also discovered Thackeray, and was particularly enthusiastic about *Vanity Fair*. Thackeray is the principal model behind the series of social novels, beginning with *L'Adultera* (*The Woman Taken in Adultery*, 1882), and ranging in tone from gentle humour and satire to understated tragedy, that have earned Fontane a reputation as Germany's 'European' novelist.

Fontane's novels are most often set in late nineteenth-century Berlin. Various parts of the north German countryside, however, provide the setting for much of Fontane's fiction. *Effi Briest* begins and ends in the Havelland, west of Berlin, and Chapters 6 through 22 take place in a remote area of the Baltic coast. Other novels range further: *Unwiederbringlich* (*No Way Back*, 1891) is set in Denmark, *Graf Petöfy* (1884) in Vienna and Hungary, and much of *Quitt* (*Quits*, 1890) among German emigrants in the United States (though America, which Fontane had never visited, appears in this novel as a strange place inhabited solely by Germans).[1] Many especially of his later novels, including *Effi Briest*, contain significant references not only to America but to Asia and Africa. During the twenty years, 1878–98, in which Fontane's fiction appeared, Germany was intent on catching up with the older European powers by establishing its own colonies across the globe. Increasingly, and above all in his last novel, *Der Stechlin* (*The Stechlin*, 1898, named after a lake in northern Prussia), Fontane explores the connections between Germany and the rest of a world which is already becoming globally interconnected.

---

[1] See Jeffrey L. Sammons, 'Representing America Sight Unseen: Comparative Observations on Spielhagen, Raabe and Fontane', in Dirk Göttsche and Florian Krobb (eds.), *Wilhelm Raabe: Global Themes—International Perspectives* (London: Legenda, 2009), 87–99.

For the greater part of his life, however, Fontane was a citizen not of Germany but of Prussia. The state of Germany came into being only in 1871, when King Wilhelm I of Prussia was proclaimed the sovereign of the revived German Empire. Prussia was the dominant territory among those that were combined to form the Empire, and to appreciate Fontane's novels it is essential to know something of the Prussian history that is referred to in detail in the text and is vividly present to all the characters.

From Prussia to Germany

The historic core of Prussia is the region of Brandenburg in north-eastern Germany, with its capital at Berlin. In the early Middle Ages German colonists conquered this region from its original Slav inhabitants, known collectively as Wends, and settled it. Its status as the March of Brandenburg, indicating that it formed the eastern frontier of the Holy Roman Empire, is conventionally dated from 1157, when the town of Brandenburg was conquered by the margrave Albert the Bear.[2] Fontane used the German term 'Mark Brandenburg' for his series of travelogues, *Wanderungen durch die Mark Brandenburg* (*Wanderings Through the March of Brandenburg*, 1862–92), in which he recounted the traditions of the region. In 1417 Friedrich Hohenzollern bought Brandenburg outright from the then Emperor Sigismund. It cannot have seemed a desirable property, because Brandenburg was then, and long afterwards, a desolate, largely infertile region, sometimes sandy and sometimes swampy ('the sands of the March' became proverbial). A vigorous programme of land-reclamation and drainage, carried on in the seventeenth and eighteenth centuries, was required to create cultivable land.[3] The few naturally fertile districts included the Havelland, west of Berlin, where the Briest family have their estate at Hohen-Cremmen; Effi's father is in effect a farmer on a large scale, and his prosperity, never great, depends on the varying income from his crops. However, the ownership of Brandenburg included the status of Elector. The ruler of Brandenburg was one of the seven potentates who could vote on

[2] Robert Bartlett, *The Making of Europe: Conquest, Colonization and Cultural Change 950–1350* (London: Penguin, 1994), 34.
[3] This story is vividly told by David Blackbourn, *The Conquest of Nature: Water, Landscape, and the Making of Modern Germany* (London: Cape, 2006).

candidates for the office of Holy Roman Emperor. Although from the thirteenth century until the formal dissolution of the Empire in 1806 the position of Emperor was effectively hereditary in the House of Habsburg, the role of Elector conferred significant international standing.[4]

The Hohenzollern dynasty survived till 1918. One of its weaker representatives was the Elector Georg Wilhelm (reigned 1619–40), during whose reign, as Fontane tells us in the first sentence of *Effi Briest*, the Briest family came to live at Hohen-Cremmen. Georg Wilhelm was eclipsed by his successor, Friedrich Wilhelm (reigned 1640–88), who acquired the sobriquet 'the Great Elector'. He owed this name especially to his victory over a larger Swedish army at the Battle of Fehrbellin in 1675, where, as Effi proudly mentions in Chapter 8, a member of the Briest family played an honourable part. But Friedrich Wilhelm also illustrated two characteristics of the Hohenzollerns which secured their stability. One was a selfless devotion to government. He was a hands-on, full-time ruler, who once said: 'I shall manage my responsibility as prince in the knowledge that it is the affair of the people and not mine personally.'[5] He thus anticipated the more famous statement by his descendant, the enlightened despot Friedrich II, better known as Frederick the Great (reigned 1740–86): 'The sovereign, far from being the absolute master of the people under his dominion, is nothing else but their first servant.'[6] The other successful quality of the Hohenzollerns was their longevity. The Great Elector ruled for forty-eight years, Friedrich II for forty-six, his nephew Friedrich Wilhelm III for forty-three years (1797–1840), and the latter's son, Friedrich Wilhelm IV, for twenty-one years (1840–61). By this time the dynasty had replaced the title of Elector with that of King, which now carried more international prestige. The first King of Prussia was Friedrich, who had ruled as Elector from 1688 to 1701 and was King from 1701 till 1713.

Prussia, though a relatively poor country, soon established itself as a major international player. Friedrich II gained a personal and national reputation, first by enlarging his country through the illegal

---

[4] For the history of Prussia, I have drawn heavily on Christopher Clark, *Iron Kingdom: The Rise and Downfall of Prussia, 1600–1917* (London: Allen Lane, 2006).

[5] Quoted in Clark, *Iron Kingdom*, 41.

[6] Friedrich of Prussia, *The Refutation of Machiavelli's 'Prince' or Anti-Machiavel*, trans. and ed. Paul Sonnino (Athens, Ohio: Ohio University Press, 1981), 34.

seizure and incorporation of the rich territory of Silesia, and then through leading his nation to victory in the highly perilous Seven Years War (1756–63). Once Prussia had built up a reputation as a major military state, the shock was all the greater when, after the French Revolution and the advent of Napoleon, Prussia was decisively defeated in the battles of Jena and Auerstedt in 1806. The French occupation of Prussia brought about the birth of German nationalism. It also provided material for Fontane's first novel, *Before the Storm*, which culminates in an—unsuccessful—attempt by local landowners to capture the French stronghold at Frankfurt an der Oder in early 1813.

In the nineteenth century Fontane observed Prussian militarism with fascinated revulsion. As a young man he held radically liberal political views. He belonged to a society called the Herwegh-Club, ostensibly devoted to literature but in fact to promoting the revolutionary political ideals of the poet Georg Herwegh, after whom it was named. When revolution broke out in Berlin in March 1848, Fontane was not the bemused onlooker he depicts in his later autobiographical writings but an engaged participant. After the failure of the revolutions he found it painful to have to make a living by writing for conservative newspapers under the reactionary government of Otto von Manteuffel.

In the 1860s the Prussian minister-president and foreign minister, Otto von Bismarck, guided Prussia towards a dominant position in a united Germany via a series of wars. The first occasion was provided by the duchies of Schleswig and Holstein, which were claimed both by the Danish crown and by a German, Prince Friedrich of Augustenburg, while Bismarck hoped to annex both to Prussia. War with Denmark broke out in 1864. At Bismarck's insistence, Prussian forces stormed the Danish entrenchments at Düppel (Dybbøl) with heavy loss of life, and, after further successes, ended the war rapidly and victoriously. The twin duchies were occupied jointly by Prussia and Austria, but a dispute over their status led to the Austro-Prussian War, fought in northern Bohemia over seven weeks in the summer of 1866. The Prussians were victorious in the battle that is known to German historians as Königgrätz (after a Bohemian fortress) and to Austrian historians as Sadowa (after the nearby town). It was clear that any unification of Germany would no longer involve Austria. Prussia was far the largest state, and the unchallenged kingpin, in the

North German Confederation, but the south German states outside the Confederation still resisted proposals for German unification.

Bismarck saw that unification could be assisted by a threat from France. One soon came. France and Prussia were supporting rival claimants to the throne of Spain. Just when their differences were close to being reconciled, the French foreign minister unwisely demanded that Prussia should promise never again to support the candidate whom France disliked. King Wilhelm I of Prussia, who was on holiday at the resort of Bad Ems, drafted a polite refusal, but Bismarck got hold of the King's telegram and, by omitting a few words, made it seem like an insulting rebuff. Feeling their national honour offended, the French government declared war. It was a fatal mistake, leading to Prussia's crushing victory over France at Sedan on 1–2 September 1870, to the siege of Paris, the Paris Commune—events all vividly described in Émile Zola's great novel _La Débâcle_ (1892)—and to the proclamation of the German Empire at Versailles in January 1871.

These events deeply interested Fontane, who as a journalist visited the battlefields, wrote books about all three campaigns, and in France was taken prisoner, held in various prisons for two months, and released thanks to intervention by Bismarck. They are also imprinted both on the text of _Effi Briest_ and on the consciousness of the characters. The garden at Hohen-Cremmen contains a pyramid commemorating the Battle of Waterloo. Innstetten and Crampas have both fought in the Franco-Prussian War. An important conversation between Effi and her mother is interrupted by the celebration of Sedan Day on 1 September (Ch. 4). In Berlin, Effi and Innstetten go to see a panoramic picture of the storming of St Privat, one of the high points of the war (Ch. 6). The couple's child is born on 3 July, the anniversary of the Battle of Königgrätz, and christened, less auspiciously, on 15 August, the birthday of Napoleon Bonaparte. In their Berlin flat they have patriotic pictures illustrating victories in the Dano-Prussian and Austro-Prussian wars. Effi takes a holiday at Ems, the spa from which Wilhelm I sent the fateful Ems Telegram. Alone in Berlin, Effi lives in a boarding-house in the Königgrätzerstrasse with a view of Schinkel's monument on the Kreuzberg commemorating the dead of the Wars of Liberation (1813–14).

However, Fontane's portrayal of Imperial Germany is anything but triumphalist. Innstetten provides the focus for a critical picture of society. Although he is said to come from an ancient family,

Innstetten is contrasted with the rural aristocrats, known as 'Junkers', such as the Borcke, Grasenabb, and Güldenklee families near Kessin, who live on their estates and hold ultra-conservative views; Baron von Güldenklee of Papenhagen even thinks that God was on Prussia's side in the war against France. We learn that Innstetten, having found army life uncongenial, entered the civil service and worked fanatically. He has attained the position of 'Landrat' or local administrator. He is thinking of standing as a candidate for the Reichstag, in which case Effi, as a trophy wife, will be a useful asset. He enjoys the favour of Bismarck, who is by now Chancellor of Germany, and is often summoned by the latter to the hunting-lodge at Varzin which Bismarck received from a grateful nation after the victory over Austria in 1866. As it takes three hours in winter to reach Varzin from Kessin, by road and rail, these invitations are highly inconvenient. On being transferred to the ministry in Berlin, Innstetten goes to the Chancellery to sign the book of congratulations to Bismarck on his birthday. Although Bismarck never appears in person in the novel, he is an ominous off-stage presence. He inadvertently weakens the marriage between Innstetten and Effi because his invitations to Varzin (in which Effi is never included, perhaps because Innstetten, we are told, is a favourite of Bismarck's wife) require Innstetten to leave Effi on her own, feeling bored, lonely, and frightened.[7]

Despite the success of his career, Innstetten does not seem a happy man. His marriage to Effi, whose mother rejected him as a suitor twenty years earlier, is a rather unimaginative second attempt at a happiness which ultimately eludes him. On the very day when he receives news of his promotion, he tells his colleague Wüllersdorf how little such things mean to him. Fontane himself detested bureaucracy. His only experience of it, during his appointment as Secretary of the Royal Academy of Arts in Berlin, was so unpleasant that he resigned within three months, despite losing financial security and having to endure severe reproaches from his wife. He complains of the 'huge, tedious, and in my experience totally confused machinery that calls itself "the state" '.[8]

---

[7] On the fascinated ambivalence with which Fontane regarded Bismarck, see Gordon A. Craig, *Theodor Fontane: Literature and History in the Bismarck Reich* (New York: Oxford University Press, 1999), 116–17.

[8] Letter to Mathilde von Rohr, 30 Nov. 1876, quoted in Hans-Heinrich Reuter, *Fontane* (Berlin: Verlag der Nation, 1968), 532.

xiv

Innstetten's inner unease is manifested in his strange fascination with the supernatural.[9] He may have told ghost stories, as Crampas recalls, to impress his fellow soldiers, and he may cultivate the idea of living in a haunted house in Kessin to make himself seem special and to keep Effi under control, but he cannot control his own leaning towards superstition. When Effi's playfellows call her back, just after she and Innstetten have become engaged, he feels the incident is more than just chance (Ch. 3). He takes very seriously the discovery of the little picture of the Chinaman (Ch. 8), refuses to dismiss the idea of ghosts (Ch. 24), and later shares Effi's feelings of melancholy at the gloomy Lake Hertha (Ch. 24) and her sense that their house in Kessin is uncanny (Ch. 28). His love of Wagner is attributed by some people to his nervous disposition (an affliction shared by Effi, and characteristic of the period).[10] Others ascribe it to his sympathy with Wagner's anti-Semitism (Ch. 13). The narrator surmises that both are right.

Although we see no further evidence of Innstetten's anti-Semitism, we learn much about his distrust of Slavs. The inhabitants of the countryside round Kessin are Kashubs, a Slav people established in the region long before German settlers arrived. Since the Kashubs' territory is around Danzig (Gdańsk), in present-day Poland and a long way east of the Swinemünde on which Fontane partly based Kessin, we are to imagine a remote and somewhat precarious frontier area; Innstetten is rather like a colonial administrator governing an alien population.[11] The original inhabitants of northern Germany are often referred to as Wends (*Wenden*). Uvagla, near Kessin (adapted from the actual pre-Germanic place-name Pudagla), is said to be the site of a Wendish temple. On the island of Rügen Effi and Innstetten see the stones where the ancient Wends conducted human sacrifices. Here, as elsewhere in Fontane's novels, references

[9] On Innstetten's and other characters' unease, and its implications, see Erika Swales, 'Private Mythologies and Public Unease: On Fontane's *Effi Briest*', *Modern Language Review*, 75 (1980), 114–23.

[10] Cf. Effi's nervous trembling when she sees Innstetten (Ch. 2), her 'nervous tic' (Ch. 21), and the 'nervous disorder' detected by Dr Rummschüttel (Ch. 34). See Elaine Showalter, *Hystories: Hysterical Epidemics and Modern Culture* (London: Picador, 1997).

[11] The contradictions around the location of Kessin are examined by Mirosław Ossowski, 'Fragwürdige Identität? Zur national-territorialen Bestimmung der Figuren aus dem deutsch-slawischen Kulturgrenzraum in Fontanes Spätwerk', in Hanna Delf von Wolzogen (ed.), *Theodor Fontane: Am Ende des Jahrhunderts*, 3 vols. (Würzburg: Königshausen & Neumann, 2000), i. 255–67 (at 257–9).

to the ancient populations remind us that German rule is relatively recent and insecure, and also suggest an undercurrent of guilt at the violent conquests on which Prussia was founded: in his *Wanderings Through the March of Brandenburg* Fontane is forthright about the frequent treachery and cruelty practised by the Germans against the Wends.[12]

More recently, Prussia had annexed a large portion of the former kingdom of Poland. Each of the three partitions of Poland, in 1772, 1793, and 1795, enlarged Prussian territory, especially the Second Partition which gave it the extensive province of Posen (Poznań). Poles are viewed with guilty unease. Speaking of Golchowski, landlord of the inn 'Prince Bismarck', Innstetten remarks that he is 'half Polish', and that Poles are good-looking but untrustworthy. Similarly, he describes Crampas as 'half Polish, you can't really rely on him, not in anything, least of all with women' (Ch. 18)—a judgement that is confirmed by events. Curiously, being 'half Polish' seems worse than being a pure-blooded Pole, perhaps because such unclassifiable people are felt to be alien infiltrators passing as 'normal' Germans.

This subliminal paranoia about minorities reflects the reality of the German Empire. The new state followed the policy of creating solidarity among its citizens by organized discrimination against outgroups.[13] Throughout the 1870s Bismarck directed a campaign, with strong support from liberals, against the political and educational influence of the Roman Catholic Church, which was seen, especially since the proclamation of Papal Infallibility in 1870, as an illiberal, reactionary, anti-intellectual institution and as a rival to the new state for the allegiance of German Catholics.[14] Against this background, Effi's kindness to the Catholic Roswitha, whom she befriends and saves from destitution, has to be seen as a natural and humane gesture that goes against official ideology. The attempt by the anarchist Karl Eduard Nobiling to assassinate the Emperor on 2 June 1878 (mentioned in Chapter 9) provided a pretext for the legal prohibition later that year of the Social Democratic Party, a ban which remained

---

[12] Fontane, *Wanderungen durch die Mark Brandenburg*, ed. Walter Keitel and Helmuth Nürnberger, 3 vols., 2nd edn. (Munich: Hanser, 1977), ii. 25–6.

[13] See Hans-Ulrich Wehler, *The German Empire 1871–1918*, trans. Kim Traynor (Leamington Spa: Berg, 1985), 102–13.

[14] See Michael B. Gross, *The War Against Catholicism: Liberalism and the Anti-Catholic Imagination in Nineteenth-Century Germany* (Ann Arbor, Mich.: University of Michigan Press, 2004).

in force until 1890. Although anti-Semitism was never official policy
under the Empire (at least until the First World War), considerable
anti-Semitic activity was tolerated, while linguistic minorities such
as the Danes in Schleswig-Holstein, the French in Alsace-Lorraine,
and the Poles in the eastern Prussian territories were increasingly
compelled to use German in schools and law-courts.

Fontane's many references to continents beyond Europe also
intimate the position of Imperial Germany in a world of global
interconnections. Kessin is an international port whose businessmen often act as consuls serving the interests of foreign powers. Its
inhabitants are international. Besides natives of Scotland, Denmark,
and Sweden, we hear of a retired captain who sailed with the Chinese
river pirates of Vietnam. And as these pirates were also helping the
Vietnamese to resist French invaders, we are reminded of the conquests made by European powers. Trying to catch up with Britain
and France, Germany from the 1880s onwards acquired colonial territories by establishing protectorates in such regions as East Africa
(now Tanzania), and so we hear about African rulers such as Mirambo
and Mutesa. Innstetten half-jokingly advises Crampas to take service
in the Turkish or Chinese armies (Ch. 15). He himself is rumoured
(Ch. 21) to be leading a legation to Morocco, where Germany wanted
to extend her influence. In a despairing mood, Innstetten later
imagines emigrating to Africa to 'mingle with pitch-black fellows,
who know nothing of civilized behaviour and honour' (Ch. 35).

If Europe is penetrating remote parts of the globe, they in turn
are penetrating Europe. This is the context in which to see the
mysterious figure of the Chinaman. Innstetten reluctantly tells Effi
how a China merchant, Captain Thomsen, returned to Kessin with
a Chinese servant, and how Thomsen's granddaughter, on the eve of
her wedding to another captain, danced with the Chinaman and then
vanished, never to be seen again. The Chinaman soon afterwards died
and is buried among the dunes outside Kessin. This enigmatic story
is somehow connected with the little picture of a Chinaman that Effi
finds stuck to a chair in the upstairs room from which sinister noises
come, and which also turns up after their move to Berlin. Fontane
considered the motif of the Chinaman so important that he called it
the pivot of the novel. He wrote to a sympathetic reviewer, the Swiss
critic Joseph Victor Widmann: 'You are the first person to point to the
haunted house and the Chinaman; I don't understand how one can

overlook it, for first of all this ghost, or so I think at least, is interesting in its own right, and secondly, as you have emphasized, the matter
is not there just for amusement but is a pivot for the entire story.'[15]
The motif provides a focus for the uneasy relations between Germany
and the extra-European world which pervade the novel.[16] China was
important to German colonial policy. It provided a potential market
for German industrial products, but it was also felt to be untrustworthy, and popular stereotypes represented all Chinese as sinister.
In 1870 Bismarck authorized a naval expedition against Chinese
pirates; in 1897 Germany annexed an area on the Chinese coast,
Kiao-Chou, as a military base; and in 1900 the Emperor Wilhelm
II sent German troops in to help suppress the Boxer Rebellion in
Peking, adjuring them, in a notoriously bloodthirsty parting speech,
to behave like Huns and to take no prisoners. The image of the 'yellow
peril' is suggested in the many ominous appearances of the colour
yellow: in the upper rooms of Innstetten's house, on the yellow sands
where yellow flowers bloom, on the flag hanging from the hotel that
Effi sees as she leaves Kessin, and earlier—most suggestively—on
a yellow half-timbered house that Effi gazes at with unexplained
attentiveness (Ch. 20); is this the place where she and Crampas have
their illicit meetings? The motif of the Chinaman may be seen as
the Empire striking back in a form of 'reverse colonialism', as when
colonial peoples penetrate Britain in Victorian fiction—the Indians
in Wilkie Collins's *The Moonstone* (1868), the Andaman Islander in
Conan Doyle's *The Sign of Four* (1890), and the apparent references
to Thuggee in Dickens's *The Mystery of Edwin Drood* (1870).[17]

However, the motif of the Chinaman not only reminds us how
far the novel is a critique of imperial Germany; it also focuses the

[15] Letter to Widmann, 19 Nov. 1895, quoted in Fontane, *Romane, Erzählungen,
Gedichte*, ed. Walter Keitel, 6 vols. (Munich: Hanser, 1962), iv. 706.
[16] See Peter Utz, 'Effi Briest, der Chinese und der Imperialismus', *Zeitschrift für
deutsche Philologie*, 103 (1984), 212–25; Judith Ryan, 'The Chinese Ghost: Colonialism
and Subaltern Speech in Fontane's *Effi Briest*', in William Collins Donahue and Scott
Denham (eds.), *History and Literature: Essays in Honor of Karl S. Guthke* (Tübingen:
Stauffenburg, 2000), 327–40.
[17] See Stephen D. Arata, 'The Occidental Tourist: *Dracula* and the Anxiety of Reverse
Colonization', *Victorian Studies*, 33 (1990), 621–45; Ritchie Robertson, 'Jesuits, Jews,
and Thugs: Myths of Conspiracy and Infiltration from Dickens to Thomas Mann', in
Rüdiger Görner and Angus Nicholls (eds.), *In the Embrace of the Swan: Anglo-German
Mythologies in Literature, the Visual Arts and Cultural Theory* (Berlin: de Gruyter, 2010),
126–46.

question of power-relations, especially within marriage. For the Captain's granddaughter, Nina, resembles Effi in being the subject of an arranged marriage. She escapes from it, nobody knows how or where. The triangle of Nina, her intended husband, and the Chinaman who may have been her lover corresponds to the triangle of Effi, Innstetten, and Crampas. And this invites us to look closely at *Effi Briest* as a novel of marriage.

Marriage

In setting a story of marital breakdown against the background of Prussian traditions and Imperial German society, Fontane drew on the actual, recent, and much-discussed case of the Ardennes.[18] Elisabeth von Plotho (1853–1952), known as Else, a gifted, charming, and high-spirited young woman from an aristocratic family in the Havelland, married in 1873 an officer, Armand Léon von Ardenne (1848–1919), who belonged to the Zieten Hussars and was stationed in the garrison town of Rathenow (details alluded to early in Fontane's novel). Ardenne was five years older than Else; like Innstetten, he served in the Franco-Prussian War, received the Iron Cross, and inherited the title of Baron. When stationed with his regiment at Düsseldorf in north-west Germany (a location offering much more diversion than the remote 'Kessin'), he worked so hard, not only at his regimental duties but at writing for the military press and composing a history of his regiment (published in 1874), that Else felt neglected. Unlike Effi, she had a large social circle, consisting partly of officers but also including the lawyer Emil Hartwich, a cultivated person and talented painter, who was unhappily married. Quite how the intimacy between Else and Hartwich developed is hard to say, but in 1886, two years after Ardenne's transfer to the Ministry of War in Berlin, he became suspicious and broke open a box which turned out to contain letters from Hartwich planning how he and Else should each divorce their partners and get married. Else confessed to the liaison. Ardenne challenged Hartwich to a duel, which took place on 27 November

---

[18] This material was made known by Hans Werner Seiffert, 'Fontanes *Effi Briest* und Spielhagens *Zum Zeitvertreib*—Zeugnisse und Materialien', in Seiffert (ed.), *Studien zur neueren deutschen Literatur* (Berlin: Akademie-Verlag, 1964), 255–300. Fontane's treatment of it is examined by Jean A. Leventhal, 'Fact into Fiction: *Effi Briest* and the Ardenne Case', *Colloquia Germanica*, 24 (1991), 181–93.

1886. Hartwich was severely wounded and died four days later. The Ardennes got divorced; Ardenne, to Else's distress, received custody of the children. Like Innstetten, he was briefly imprisoned as a token punishment, but continued his career and reached the rank of lieutenant-general. Else von Ardenne devoted herself to charitable work. 'You may be interested to know', Fontane wrote to a friend, 'that the *real* Effi is still alive, as an excellent nurse in a large hospital. Innstetten, *in natura*, is about to become a general. I only made him abandon his military career so that the real persons should not be too obvious.'[19]

In turning this case into fiction, Fontane has made five obvious changes. First, he has increased the age difference from five to twenty-two years—Effi is sixteen when the novel begins, just before her seventeenth birthday, while Innstetten is thirty-eight; Fontane has also given much attention to how the marriage comes about.

To increase Effi's isolation, and make it more intelligible how she could fall for Crampas, Fontane has sent the newly married couple to 'Kessin' on the Baltic. For Effi, who has always lived near Berlin, Kessin feels like the back of beyond. It is closely based on Swinemünde, a town on the island of Usedom (now Świnoujście in Poland), where Fontane lived from 1827 to 1832, and which he had just described vividly in the first part of his autobiography, *My Childhood* (1894). But he has moved it to Hinterpommern (Farther Pomerania), a region which begins further east than Swinemünde, and the surrounding population are said to be Kashubs, who in fact lived around Danzig (Gdańsk). Świnoujście is nowadays a holiday resort with a fine bathing-beach and a promenade, whereas in Fontane's time, and in the novel, we must imagine a lonely coastal area covered with sand-dunes. Kessin too is a holiday resort, but the tourists come only in the summer; Effi arrives there in November, and her affair with Crampas takes place mostly in February, some fifteen months later, so we are to imagine Kessin as having the peculiar melancholy that afflicts a holiday resort outside the tourist season.

Fontane has left a gap of six years between the end of the affair and its discovery, so as to introduce the problem of 'Verjährung', or the statute of limitations. Is it necessary or right to punish an offence after the lapse of so much time?

[19] Letter to Clara Kühnast, 27 Oct. 1895, in Fontane, *Romane, Erzählungen, Gedichte*, iv. 704.

Crampas is not a civilian lawyer, as Hartwich was, but an officer himself, and a minor noble, so that aristocratic and military society in particular comes under Fontane's microscope.

Finally, whereas Elisabeth von Plotho survived into old age, Effi dies, for reasons that are kept somewhat unclear.

Unlike the Ardennes' marriage, that between Effi and Innstetten is largely arranged by the bride's parents. That is not necessarily fatal to the marriage. As Fontane pointed out in a testy review of Ibsen's *Ghosts*, most marriages throughout history have been based on convenience, not love: 'It is my firm conviction that if, since the beginning of history, marriages had been based, not on convenience and considerations of advantage, but solely on love, the state of the world would not be a jot better than it is.'[20] In this case, however, the marriage has been planned, ostensibly for practical reasons—Innstetten, heading for a distinguished career, is an excellent match—but really for unacknowledged emotional reasons. Over twenty years ago Effi's mother Luise received a proposal from the young Innstetten, but rejected him and soon afterwards married Briest, who is twelve years her senior, and whom she now clearly finds irritating. By marrying Innstetten to Effi, she is making her daughter enact the emotional life that she wishes she had had. Innstetten, for his part, is trying to compensate for Luise's rejection by marrying her daughter. As Russell Berman astutely points out, this makes Innstetten himself into a kind of ghost who belongs to Effi's past and now uncannily dominates her present.[21]

If we think about Innstetten's emotional history, we can see that there is more to him than a careerist. His emotional rejection twenty years before clearly inflicted a wound. It was to dull the pain that he plunged into his career. It is not surprising if now he treats Effi with some emotional reserve, nor if he involuntarily regards her somewhat like a daughter and assumes a sometimes excessively didactic manner towards her.[22] Near the end, Effi charges him with lacking genuine love. But his character has been shaped by Effi's mother's refusal to love him: 'Effi points to Innstetten, but the text points at Luise.

[20] 'Noch einmal Ibsen und seine "Gespenster"' (1887), in Fontane, *Aufsätze, Kritiken, Erinnerungen*, ed. Walter Keitel and others, 4 vols. (Munich: Hanser, 1969), ii. 712.

[21] Russell A. Berman, '*Effi Briest* and the End of Realism', in Todd Kontje (ed.), *A Companion to German Realism* (Rochester, NY: Camden House, 2002), 339–64 (at 356).

[22] See the sensitive analysis of Innstetten by Brian Holbeche, 'Innstetten's "Geschichte mit Entsagung" and its Significance in Fontane's *Effi Briest*', *German Life and Letters*, 41 (1987), 21–32.

Her daughter is dying because Innstetten would not love her, but his inability derives, so the text suggests, from an internalization of the denial he had experienced years ago at her hands.'[23]

Ironically, Innstetten is also a parallel figure to Luise von Briest. Both come to represent the internalized expectations of society which command one to act on principles and block the natural impulses of the heart. When Innstetten, having discovered Effi's unfaithfulness six years earlier, tells his colleague and confidant Wüllersdorf that the code of honour requires him to fight a duel on principle, he is clearly acting in bad faith. His conversation with Wüllersdorf, as John Walker has recently observed, is 'a study in self-deception'.[24] Innstetten may believe that Wüllersdorf has convinced him of the need to fight a duel with Crampas, but really he has confided in Wüllersdorf in order to render irrevocable a decision that he has already taken. His famous declaration, 'We're not just separate individuals, we're part of a whole, and we must always consider the whole, we're entirely dependent on it' (Ch. 27), is of course true insofar as we are social beings, but it becomes false in its final clause. Since he still loves Effi, feels no anger, yet is proposing to shoot Crampas in cold blood, he is entirely abandoning his own feelings and surrendering to a bloodless set of principles.[25] Luise von Briest acts similarly in refusing to accept her daughter back at Hohen-Cremmen, 'because we must nail our colours to the mast and show to all the world—I'm afraid I can't avoid the word—our condemnation of what you did' (Ch. 31).

What about Effi? Some commentators have been hard on her, treating her as an immature person who has thoughtlessly internalized the social norms with which she has been brought up. She does of course tell her girlfriends, with a spurious air of worldliness, 'Every man's the right one. Of course he has to belong to the nobility, have a position, and be presentable' (Ch. 2). But this remark can be interpreted more sympathetically as revealing not her shallowness, but her pardonable

[23] Berman, '*Effi Briest* and the End of Realism', 356. Cf. Valerie D. Greenberg, 'The Resistance of Effi Briest: An (Un)told Tale', *Publications of the Modern Language Association*, 103 (1988), 770–82 (esp. 777–8).

[24] John Walker, *The Truth of Realism: A Reassessment of the German Novel 1830–1900* (London: Legenda, 2011), 126.

[25] Among several studies of Innstetten's motivation in recent decades, one of the most searching is by a philosopher, and has been largely overlooked by literary critics: Julia Annas, 'Personal Love and Kantian Ethics in *Effi Briest*', *Philosophy and Literature*, 8 (1984), 15–31.

pride in being the first among her friends to become engaged, and her uneasy wish to reassure herself that she was right to accept the proposal.[26] And it is surely unjustified for J. P. Stern to assert that her 'experience of love remains immature', or John Walker that '[f]or most of the novel, she lacks any real sense of self'.[27] Rather, in the early phase of her marriage Effi looks for love, not just to have her social ambitions satisfied, and is disappointed by the lukewarm kindness she receives from Innstetten. Later, after their move to Berlin, they grow much closer, which makes the disruption of their marriage all the more distressing.

Effi is a fresh, lively, imaginative, playful, spontaneous person, thrust into a situation she can hardly cope with. Her charm is made clear in the delightful scene in which she wins the heart of the Kessin pharmacist Gieshübler (Ch. 8), and her genuine, active goodness is beyond doubt when she befriends the unfortunate Roswitha (Ch. 13). She embodies the natural humanity which was perhaps the supreme value in Fontane's eyes. 'The natural has appealed to me for a long time, it is the only thing that matters, the only thing that attracts me,' Fontane wrote in 1895, explaining why he created such heroines as Effi.[28] This natural feeling is shared by Effi's father, who unfortunately is mostly under his wife's thumb; by Roswitha, who stands by Effi when even her parents have rejected her; and by the faithful Newfoundland dog Rollo, who, at the end of the novel, is clearly about to die on Effi's grave.[29]

Such a natural being is bound to suffer under the restriction which the Prussian legal code imposed on married women. Dirk Mende provides a useful summary:

In matters of joint concern the husband's decision is always final. The wife shares the man's residence, name, and social rank, is obliged to run the household, and without his permission may neither practise a profession of her own

[26] See Charlotte Woodford, 'Fontane, *Effi Briest*', in Peter Hutchinson (ed.), *Landmarks in the German Novel (I)* (Oxford: Peter Lang, 2007), 83–98 (at 86).

[27] J. P. Stern, *Re-interpretations: Seven Studies in Nineteenth-Century German Literature* (London: Thames & Hudson, 1964), 318; Walker, *The Truth of Realism*, 137.

[28] Letter to Colmar Grünhagen, 10 Oct. 1895, quoted in *Romane, Erzählungen, Gedichte*, iv. 703.

[29] See Rolf Zuberbühler, *'Ja Luise, die Kreatur.' Zur Bedeutung der Neufundländer in Fontanes Romanen* (Tübingen: Niemeyer, 1991). One might not have thought that a whole book could be written about Newfoundland in Fontane, but Zuberbühler has done so most illuminatingly. I am grateful to the librarian of Lady Margaret Hall, Oxford, and to Dr Mary MacRobert, for providing me with a copy.

nor undertake any duties outside the home. The husband is entitled to open her letters. Physical violence against the wife . . . is not in itself any ground for complaint. In legal matters the husband represents the wife and is her legal guardian. The wife may not conduct a lawsuit without his agreement. The upbringing of the children is in the hands of the husband: daughters are freed from their father's authority only when they marry, unmarried ones only by his death. The father, who also controls the children's religious instruction, can remove a child from its mother's care as soon as it is four years old, can place it in an educational institution, and decide on its choice of profession.[30]

Hence, when Innstetten discovers that Effi was once unfaithful to him, all the rights are on his side, and there is not the slightest question of Effi's having custody of their child or even access to her. The laws, underpinned by moral condemnation, override all natural feelings.

In any case, natural feeling, in Fontane's view, was in danger of being extinguished by the rigid bureaucratization of Imperial German society. 'The more we are dominated by Assessors and Lieutenants of the Reserve, the worse things get,' he wrote to his friend Georg Friedlaender in 1896. 'The last remnant of natural feeling, which is always synonymous with poetic feeling, is disappearing.'[31] In the novel Fontane hints, more drastically, at an alliance between moral principle and sadistic cruelty, represented by the recurring image of sacrifice.[32] Effi recalls, in characteristically compassionate language, how 'poor, unfortunate women' in Constantinople used to be drowned for infidelity. Crampas shows his cruel streak by recounting unpleasant stories, taken from narrative poems by Heine, about Spanish prisoners being sacrificed to the Aztec idol 'Vitzliputzli', and Pedro the Cruel of Spain killing his unfaithful wife's lover (Ch. 17). Roswitha, who has borne an illegitimate child, tells how she was almost killed by her father, a blacksmith, who attacked her with a red-hot iron. On Rügen, near the village of Crampas, Effi sees stones where the ancient Wends used to perform human sacrifices (Ch. 24), and the horrible

[30] Dirk Mende, 'Frauenleben. Bemerkungen zu Fontanes *L'Adultera* nebst Exkursen zu *Cécile* und *Effi Briest*', in Hugo Aust (ed.), *Fontane aus heutiger Sicht* (Munich: Nymphenburger Verlagsbuchhandlung, 1980), 183–213 (at 184–5).

[31] Fontane, letter of 22 Mar. 1896, in *Briefe an Georg Friedlaender*, ed. Kurt Schreinert (Heidelberg: Quelle & Meyer, 1954), 295.

[32] See Alan Bance, *Theodor Fontane: The Major Novels* (Cambridge: Cambridge University Press, 1982), 66–7; Jennifer Cizik Marshall, *Betrothal, Violence, and the 'Beloved Sacrifice' in Nineteenth-Century German Literature* (New York: Peter Lang, 2001), 217–36.

image haunts her mind (Ch. 34). By now it is clear that Effi herself has been sacrificed to what her husband and Wüllersdorf explicitly call an 'idol': 'our cult of honour is worship of a false idol, but we have to submit as long as the idol rules' (Ch. 27).[33]

The details of Effi's sacrificial death are treated very discreetly. According to Dr Rummschüttel, a tendency to consumption, combined with a nervous disorder, is causing her to waste away. In late nineteenth-century fiction it is common for young women to die slowly but apparently painlessly from consumption or tuberculosis, as Milly Theale does in Henry James's *The Wings of the Dove* (1902), but such diseases are understood to be partly emotional in origin.[34] They may express the frustration of passionate feelings, or, as Dr Rummschüttel implies in Effi's case, the denial of love.

Realism

Commenting on his own fiction, Fontane always distanced himself from the Naturalists who aimed to represent the grimmer sides of life factually and unsparingly. He insisted that literature needed an element of poetry and 'transfiguration' (*Verklärung*). 'If he does not transfigure what is ugly,' he wrote, 'the poet has failed.'[35] Consequently, Fontane set great store by the poetic element in his fiction and by what he called the 'thousand subtleties' with which he developed it.[36] Here the poetic takes the form of repeated motifs, such as the invitation 'Effi, come', given by Hertha at the end of Chapter 2, and unwittingly repeated in the telegram from Effi's parents ten years later (Ch. 34) summoning her back to Hohen-Cremmen. There is the recurrent image of flight, suggesting Effi's dangerous adventurousness: her daring antics on the swing, for which her mother rebukes

[33] Cf. Fontane's letter of 3 Oct. 1893 to Friedlaender: 'there are only 6 idols in Prussia and the chief idol, the Vitzliputzli of Prussian worship, is the lieutenant, the officer of the reserve' (*Briefe an Friedlaender*, 236). Earlier in the letter Fontane lists five powers in Prussia: 'money, nobility, officer, assessor, professor' (235).

[34] Susan Sontag, *Illness as Metaphor* (published with *Aids and its Metaphors*, London: Penguin, 1991), 21–36. See also Anna Richards, *The Wasting Heroine in German Fiction by Women 1770–1914* (Oxford: Clarendon Press, 2004), where *Effi Briest* is discussed on pp. 81–5.

[35] Review of Hauptmann, *Vor Sonnenaufgang* (1889), in *Aufsätze, Kritiken, Erinnerungen*, ii. 820.

[36] Letter to Emil Dominik, 14 July 1887, in *Romane, Erzählungen, Gedichte*, ii. 913, referring specifically to *Irrungen Wirrungen* (*No Way Back*).

her (Ch. 1), and the speed with which she and Crampas 'flew along' in their sleigh, just before the fateful moment (Ch. 19).[37] The implications of the colour yellow, and of the imagery of sacrifice, have already been noticed. Many more examples could be added.[38]

However, if one focuses too intently on these symbolic overtones, as was customary in Fontane criticism a few decades ago, one runs several risks. One may succumb to what Karl Guthke has called 'symbolizing paranoia' and perceive all sorts of symbolic patterns that are not present, or only accidentally and pointlessly present, in the text.[39] One also risks endowing genuine symbolic overtones with a life of their own which they do not really have. They are nuances which serve to deepen and qualify Fontane's narrative, but they are very much subordinate to the story about people interacting in a specific society. This tendency to elevate the imagery into an autonomous aspect of the novel is apparent in some of the most intelligent essays on *Effi Briest*. When Russell Berman speaks of a 'dual regime of realism and allegory', the word 'allegory' itself exaggerates the independence of the imagery.[40] And when Michael Minden argues that the poetic element works against the realistic element, by making a story of social impression into a ballad-like, fate-driven narrative and thus evading its socially critical implications, it is tempting to reply that he is artificially separating two elements of the novel and then complaining that they are separate.[41] The imagery of sacrifice, running from the early allusion to the drowning of women in Constantinople and culminating in the sacrifice of Effi to the 'idol' of social expectations, is prominent, but not independent of the narrative, and it is an instrument of social criticism, not an evasion of criticism.

Alongside the symbolic overtones, it is important to remember and appreciate the solid, material reality of the world that Fontane creates. It is a world full of objects that are presented as being first and

---

[37] See Peter Demetz, 'Symbolische Motive: Flug und Flocke', in his *Formen des Realismus: Theodor Fontane* (Munich: Hanser, 1964), 204–16.

[38] See Reinhard H. Thum, 'Symbol, Motif and Leitmotif in Fontane's *Effi Briest*', *Germanic Review*, 54 (1979), 115–24.

[39] Karl S. Guthke, 'Fontanes "Finessen". Kunst oder Künstelei?', *Jahrbuch der Deutschen Schiller-Gesellschaft*, 26 (1982), 235–61 (at 237).

[40] Berman, '*Effi Briest* and the End of Realism', 344.

[41] Michael Minden, 'Realism versus Poetry: Theodor Fontane, *Effi Briest*', in David Midgley (ed.), *The German Novel in the Twentieth Century: Beyond Realism* (Edinburgh: Edinburgh University Press, 1993), 18–29.

foremost real, and symbolic (if at all) only afterwards, like the extensive description of the Briest house at Hohen-Cremmen with which
the novel begins. It is also a world full of people whose lives go on
independently of the main characters and often intersect with theirs
only momentarily. The novel is heavily populated: if my counting is
correct, forty-seven named characters appear in the action (to which
one should in fairness add the Minister and his wife), while forty-one
are mentioned but do not appear. This does not include characters
who are now dead, like Captain Thomsen and the Chinaman, nor
the undifferentiated noble families around Kessin—the Ahlemanns,
the Jatzkows—on whom Innstetten and Effi are obliged to call. Some
of these absent characters arouse an unsatisfied curiosity, like the
three aunts whom Effi avoids visiting in Berlin, or 'Madelung, the
decorator', who is said by Innstetten to be 'quite a character' but of
whom we hear nothing more (Ch. 4). A few are briefly brought to life,
such as the postman Böselager, whom the housemaid Afra despises
for coming from Siegen, lacking 'dash', and not combing his hair
(Ch. 30). Others, as Barbara Hardy points out, have tantalizingly
untold stories attached to them.[42] What occurred to plunge Frau
Kruse into her depression? Why did Wüllersdorf never marry? Is he
like the unnamed dignitary at Effi's wedding who is now 'in his fourth
"relationship" ' (Ch. 5)? By concisely suggesting a huge hinterland
of interconnected lives, Fontane persuades us that his story is rooted
in the real.

Despite occasional reservations, Fontane admired contemporary
realist and Naturalist writers, notably Henrik Ibsen, Émile Zola, and
Gerhart Hauptmann. 'In the introduction of exact reporting,' he
wrote in 1881, referring to Zola, 'I see an enormous literary advance,
which has liberated us at a stroke from the dreary verbiage of past
decades.'[43] He tried to get things right, though he admitted ruefully
that it was impossible to be accurate about every detail.[44] To give the
impression of exact reporting, Fontane appears to set the story of Effi
Briest in a precise temporal and geographical framework. If we look

[42] Barbara Hardy, 'Tellers and Listeners in *Effi Briest*', in Patricia Howe and Helen
Chambers (eds.), *Theodor Fontane and the European Context* (Amsterdam and Atlanta,
Ga.: Rodopi, 2001), 119–35 (at 119).

[43] Review of Kielland's *Arbeiter*, 1881, in *Aufsätze, Kritiken, Erinnerungen*, i. 527–32
(at 528).

[44] See Fontane's letter to Emil Schiff, 15 Feb. 1888, about the mistakes in *Irrungen
Wirrungen*: *Romane, Erzählungen, Gedichte*, ii. 919–20.

more closely, however, we find some sleight of hand. Fontane clearly intended the novel to begin in 1878. Böcklin's painting *The Elysian Fields*, which Effi sees in Berlin, was displayed only in that year. When Innstetten and Effi visit the Kessin nobility in November and early December, people are talking about Nobiling, the anarchist who tried to assassinate the Emperor on 2 June 1878. The novel equally clearly ends in 1888, since the penultimate chapter mentions the recent death of the Emperor Friedrich III, which occurred on 15 June 1888. Within that framework, Effi's affair with Crampas takes place some eighteen months after her marriage, late in the Innstettens' second winter in Kessin; Innstetten finds out about it some six-and-a-half years later; and after their separation Effi lives on her own for three years. That makes eleven years, not ten. Just before the discovery of the letters, Johanna says that Effi will soon have her twenty-sixth birthday (Ch. 29); but as she was sixteen when the novel began, and had her seventeenth birthday shortly before her marriage, this would mean that the marriage lasted nine years and Effi then survived for a further three. Fontane has simply lost count. There are other, minor anomalies. In Berlin, before going to Kessin, Effi and Innstetten visit the St Privat Panorama, which opened only in 1881. At Kessin, in 1878, people plan to perform the comedy *War in Peace*, published in 1881. But one can hardly expect Fontane, or any novelist, to worry about such details. The inconsistent time-frame is a more serious matter—but again, one can hardly call it a defect, since it has seldom if ever been noticed.

Geography is similarly treated with a deceptive air of precision. Kessin is based on Swinemünde on the Baltic, where Fontane spent part of his childhood. He has also given Kessin some features that belong to Rostock, a city further west along the coast: the river Kessine broadens into a lake called the Breitling, and has a wood beside it called the Schnatermann, both of which are taken from the river Warnow which enters the sea near Rostock. However, Fontane always intended Kessin to be understood as much more easterly and hence as intimidatingly remote. To reach Kessin by train one travels via Stettin, a city in Farther Pomerania (now in Poland) and gets out at Klein-Tantow (an actual place which Fontane has moved). Close to Klein-Tantow station the road forks, one fork leading to Kessin, the other to Varzin, where Bismarck has his hunting-lodge. However, Varzin is also said to be an hour away by train (Ch. 9), so presumably some forty miles by road. The fork in the road expresses symbolic rather than actual geography: like Hercules choosing between virtue and pleasure, Innstetten has the alternatives of consolidating his marriage with Effi in Kessin or pursuing his career by attending on Bismarck in Varzin. Even the most solid-looking realism, therefore, is at a remove from documentary accuracy.

Nineteenth-century Germany, contrary to a lingering literary myth, produced a large body of realistic fiction.[45] However, Fontane, as the leading exponent of German realism, and *Effi Briest* as (in many people's opinion) his outstanding novel, need to be seen in a wider literary and historical setting. *Effi Briest* can be considered as a 'novel of adultery' alongside Flaubert's *Madame Bovary* and Tolstoy's *Anna Karenina*.[46] While the comparison recognizes three great treatments of the subject, it also reminds us of the striking differences among them. The cynicism with which Flaubert regards Emma Bovary is remote from the emotional warmth associated with Effi, while *Anna Karenina* not only dwarfs most other novels, making comparison unfair, but is governed by an Old Testament moralism announced in its epigraph, 'Vengeance is mine: I will repay', which recalls the rigid social mores that condemn Effi.

We may bring *Effi Briest* into sharper focus if we compare it to German and non-German fiction of the turn of the nineteenth and twentieth centuries. Barbara Everett briefly suggests a comparison with the novels of Henry James, from *The Portrait of a Lady* (1881) to *The Wings of the Dove*, which 'all tell of the destruction of women as young and innocent as Effi, if more virginal and more deeply self-aware'.[47] Or we may think of the prolonged and undeserved sufferings undergone by Hardy's Tess of the D'Urbervilles, in a novel subtitled 'A Pure Woman' (1891).[48] Nearer to home, in Austria, there

[45] See Jeffrey L. Sammons, 'The Nineteenth-Century German Novel', in Clayton Koelb and Eric Downing (eds.), *German Literature of the Nineteenth Century, 1832–1899*, The Camden House History of German Literature, 9 (Rochester, NY: Camden House, 2005), 183–206.

[46] See J. P. Stern, '*Effi Briest: Madame Bovary: Anna Karenina*', *Modern Language Review*, 52 (1957), 363–75, substantially reprinted in his *Re-interpretations*, ch. 7. A much wider range of comparisons appears in Bill Overton, *The Novel of Female Adultery: Love and Gender in Continental European Fiction, 1830–1900* (London: Macmillan, 1996), which includes a good discussion of Fontane (pp. 167–86).

[47] Barbara Everett, 'Night Air: *Effi Briest* and other Novels by Fontane', in Howe and Chambers (eds.), *Theodor Fontane and the European Context*, 85–94 (at 86).

[48] This comparison is suggested by Greenberg, 'The Resistance of Effi Briest', 770.

are remarkable similarities between *Effi Briest* and the challenging novel *Unsühnbar* (*Inexpiable*, 1890) by the veteran novelist Marie von Ebner-Eschenbach (1830–1916), which also deals with the consequences of an arranged marriage in an aristocratic milieu. The heroine, pressured by her father into marriage with a worthy but unloved man, lets herself be seduced by a Crampas-like figure; she returns to her husband, grows to love him, and reveals her misdemeanour voluntarily after his death. And of course Fontane himself first treated the theme in *The Woman Taken in Adultery*, where the heroine, unable to stand her coarse-grained husband, is able, despite much suffering, to divorce him and enjoy a much happier second marriage.

At this period we find the theme of marriage treated in a serious manner. Previously marriage often marked the end-point of a novel or play. In the late nineteenth century it increasingly becomes the starting-point. We are shown fictional characters living through marriage, with its emotional ups and downs, its intermittent crises, and sometimes its definitive breakdown. If any one writer can be credited with bringing marriage into focus, it must be Ibsen. In his plays we see marriages being threatened, saved, or destroyed. In *A Doll's House* the heroine walks out of a suffocating conventional marriage; in *The Wild Duck* a marriage built on dubious foundations is held together by the wife's good sense, but ruined by the intervention of a head-in-the-clouds idealist; in *The Lady from the Sea* and *Little Eyolf* shaky marriages are finally saved.

However, there is one element in marriage that receives too little attention from Ibsen, namely children. The Allmers in *Little Eyolf* recover from the death of their nine-year-old son with implausible speed. Nora in *A Doll's House* abandons her children altogether. This was found so hard to accept that two versions were played alternately in Berlin, one with the original ending and one with a conciliatory end in which her husband leads Nora to the door of the children's bedroom, she faints, and agrees to stay at home. The latter is the so-called 'German ending' which Ibsen is said to have written at the behest of an actress, Hedwig Niemann-Raabe, who declared: 'I would never leave *my* children!'[49] Other writers not only acknowledged the importance of children but allowed them to express their own point of view. In *Anna Karenina* we see Anna's son Seryozha unhappy and

[49] Michael Meyer, *Ibsen* (Stroud: Sutton, 2004), 331.

puzzled about his mother. Henry James goes further, and in *What Maisie Knew* (1897) recounts a complicated history of divorce and remarriage from the perspective of a little girl of uncertain age.[50]

When Fontane addresses the themes of marriage and adultery, he gives due attention to children. In *The Woman Taken in Adultery* the heroine abandons not only her husband but her two daughters. This invites comparison with Ibsen's Nora.[51] However, she is desperate to see her children, but when she meets them again the elder, aged ten, harshly rebuffs her. This painful scene foreshadows the unfortunate reunion between Effi and Annie. We may notice that three years of being brought up only by her father have changed Annie: as a young child she is 'wild' like her mother, 'always dashing around like a whirlwind' (Ch. 26), but by the age of ten she is serious and almost preternaturally self-controlled. No doubt Innstetten has taught her to reject her mother, but, as Brian Holbeche argues, she has probably been brought up quite as much by the servant Johanna, who is secretly in love with Innstetten and hence jealous of Effi.[52]

The presence of Effi's child at a climactic moment of her story testifies to Fontane's realism. Fontane is not only a realist in writing a novel which can be assigned to the literary mode of realism, or the period of realism in literary history; he is also realistic in the related, everyday sense of facing without illusions the consequences that an action—marriage, adultery, or divorce—is bound to have. A marriage cannot end, for example, without some effect on the children. This 'realism of assessment', as J. P. Stern called it, strengthens our confidence in the realist writer.[53] We can feel that he or she is also realistic in knowing and displaying how the world actually works.

At the same time, Fontane is realistic in not overestimating how much he, or we, can know about other people. On a few occasions the omniscient narrator supplies an authoritative remark about one of the characters: about Effi's 'demanding' nature (Ch. 3), about Innstetten's enthusiasm for Wagner (Ch. 13), or about Crampas's

---

[50] On Maisie's age, see Sally Shuttleworth, *The Mind of the Child: Child Development in Literature, Science, and Medicine, 1840–1900* (Oxford: Oxford University Press, 2010), 330. Shuttleworth's detailed account of how Maisie is introduced prematurely to a corrupt adult world (pp. 325–34) suggests many parallels with *Effi Briest*, although Maisie is an observer and Effi a participant.

[51] Made e.g. by Overton, *The Novel of Female Adultery*, 170.

[52] Holbeche, 'Innstetten's "Geschichte mit Entsagung"', 29.

[53] J. P. Stern, *On Realism* (London: Routledge & Kegan Paul, 1973), 140.

casual betrayals (Ch. 17). Often, however, he suggests emotional layers in the characters about which we are left to speculate. When Effi and Crampas see each other for the last time, how do we interpret his being 'visibly moved', while Effi's look has 'something pleading about it' (Ch. 22)? It is very rare for characters to bare their souls, as Effi does in her final outburst against society's icy virtue, or Innstetten when he declares, at the height of his professional success, 'I've made a mess of my life' (Ch. 35). Much of the time the characters are opaque. This applies especially to Annie. We can only guess what the little girl has gone through in turning from a lively child to an automaton-like product of discipline. And this opacity also forms part of the story of the Chinaman, which Fontane, as we have seen, called the pivot of the novel. We know next to nothing about him, and even less about the vanished Nina; but this opaque relationship haunts the novel, spreading its influence over the lives of Effi, Innstetten, Crampas, and eventually Annie. It is part of Fontane's achievement to find room in a realist setting for areas of emotional life that resist the realist's analysis.

NOTE ON THE TEXT

FONTANE wrote *Effi Briest* between 1891 and 1893. It was serialized in the journal *Deutsche Rundschau* between October 1894 and March 1895 and published in book form by F. Fontane & Co., Berlin, in October 1895. This text forms the basis for the present translation. The novel was first translated into English in 1914 by William A. Cooper in an abridged edition as part of a twenty-volume series of German Classics published by the German Publication Society in New York. It has been filmed several times, including a 1974 version directed by Rainer Werner Fassbinder and starring Hanna Schygulla as Effi.

SELECT BIBLIOGRAPHY

(CONFINED TO WORKS IN ENGLISH)

Translations of Other Works by Fontane

Before the Storm [*Vor dem Sturm*], trans. R. J. Hollingdale, World's Classics (Oxford: Oxford University Press, 1985).

Cécile, trans. Stanley Radcliffe (London: Angel Books, 1992).

No Way Back [*Unwiederbringlich*], trans. Hugh Rorrison and Helen Chambers (London: Angel Books, 2010).

On Tangled Paths [*Irrungen Wirrungen*], trans. Peter James Bowman (London: Angel Books, 2010).

The Stechlin, trans. William L. Zwiebel (Rochester, NY: Camden House, 2013).

Two Novellas: The Woman Taken in Adultery [*L'Adultera*] and *The Poggenpuhl Family*, trans. Gabriele Annan (London: Penguin, 1979).

Critical Studies

Annas, Julia, 'Personal Love and Kantian Ethics in *Effi Briest*', *Philosophy and Literature*, 8 (1984), 15–31.

Bade, James N., *Fontane's Landscapes* (Würzburg: Königshausen & Neumann, 2009).

Bance, Alan, *Theodor Fontane: The Major Novels* (Cambridge: Cambridge University Press, 1982).

Berman, Russell A., '*Effi Briest* and the End of Realism', in Todd Kontje (ed.), *A Companion to German Realism* (Rochester, NY: Camden House, 2002), 339–64.

Chambers, Helen, *The Changing Image of Theodor Fontane* (Columbia, SC: Camden House, 1997).

Everett, Barbara, 'Night Air: *Effi Briest* and Other Novels by Fontane', in Patricia Howe and Helen Chambers (eds.), *Theodor Fontane and the European Context* (Amsterdam and Atlanta, Ga.: Rodopi, 2001), 85–94.

Ewbank, Inga-Stina, '*Hedda Gabler, Effi Briest* and "The Ibsen-effect"', in Patricia Howe and Helen Chambers (eds.), *Theodor Fontane and the European Context* (Amsterdam and Atlanta, Ga.: Rodopi, 2001), 95–104.

Garland, H. B., *The Berlin Novels of Theodor Fontane* (Oxford: Clarendon Press, 1980).

Gilbert, Anna Marie, 'A New Look at *Effi Briest*: Genesis and Interpretation', *Deutsche Vierteljahresschrift*, 53 (1979), 96–114.

Greenberg, Valerie D., 'The Resistance of Effi Briest: An (Un)told Tale', *Publications of the Modern Language Association*, 103 (1988), 770–82.

Hardy, Barbara, 'Tellers and Listeners in *Effi Briest*', in Patricia Howe and Helen Chambers (eds.), *Theodor Fontane and the European Context* (Amsterdam and Atlanta, Ga.: Rodopi, 2001), 119–35.

Holbeche, Brian, 'Innstetten's "Geschichte mit Entsagung" and its Significance in Fontane's *Effi Briest*', *German Life and Letters*, 41 (1987), 21–32

Hotho-Jackson, Sabine, ' "Dazu muss man selber intakt sein": Innstetten and the Portrayal of a Male Mind in Fontane's *Effi Briest*', *Forum for Modern Language Studies*, 32 (1996), 264–76.

Howe, Patricia, 'Manly Men and Womanly Women: Aesthetics and Gender in Fontane's *Effi Briest* and *Der Stechlin*', in Mary Orr and Lesley Sharpe (eds.), *From Goethe to Gide: Feminism, Aesthetics and the French and German Literary Canon 1770–1936* (Exeter: University of Exeter Press, 2005), 129–44.

Jamison, Robert, 'The Fearful Education of Effi Briest', *Monatshefte*, 74 (1982), 20–32.

Leventhal, Jean A., 'Fact into Fiction: *Effi Briest* and the Ardenne Case', *Colloquia Germanica*, 24 (1991), 181–93.

Miller, Leslie E., 'Fontane's *Effi Briest*: Innstetten's Decision', *German Studies Review*, 4 (1981), 383–402.

Minden, Michael, '*Effi Briest* and "Die historische Stunde des Takts" ', *Modern Language Review*, 76 (1981), 871–9.

—— 'Realism versus poetry: Theodor Fontane, *Effi Briest*', in David Midgley (ed.), *The German Novel in the Twentieth Century: Beyond Realism* (Edinburgh: Edinburgh University Press, 1993), 18–29.

Riechel, Donald C., '*Effi Briest* and the Calendar of Fate', *Germanic Review*, 48 (1973), 189–211.

Robinson, A. R., *Theodor Fontane: An Introduction to the Man and his Work* (Cardiff: University of Wales Press, 1976).

Ryan, Judith, 'The Chinese Ghost: Colonialism and Subaltern Speech in Fontane's *Effi Briest*', in William Collins Donahue and Scott Denham (eds.), *History and Literature: Essays in Honor of Karl S. Guthke* (Tübingen: Stauffenburg, 2000), 327–40.

Schneider, Jeffrey, 'Masculinity, Male Friendship, and the Paranoid Logic of Honor in Theodor Fontane's *Effi Briest*', *German Quarterly*, 75 (2002), 265–81.

Stern, J. P., '*Effi Briest: Madame Bovary: Anna Karenina*', *Modern Language Review*, 52 (1957), 363–75.

—— 'Realism and Tolerance: Theodor Fontane', in *Re-interpretations: Seven Studies in Nineteenth-Century German Literature* (London: Thames & Hudson, 1964), 301–47.

Subiotto, Frances M., 'The Ghost in *Effi Briest*', *Forum for Modern Language Studies*, 21 (1985), 137–50.

Swales, Erika, 'Private Mythologies and Public Unease: on Fontane's *Effi Briest*', *Modern Language Review*, 75 (1980), 114–23.

Thum, Reinhard H., 'Symbol, Motif and Leitmotif in Fontane's *Effi Briest*', *Germanic Review*, 54 (1979), 115–24.

Turner, David, 'Theodor Fontane: *Effi Briest* (1865)', in D. A. Williams (ed.), *The Monster in the Mirror: Studies in Nineteenth-Century Realism* (Oxford: Oxford University Press, 1978), 234–56.

Walker, John, 'Theodor Fontane, *Effi Briest*: Realism, Empathy, and Identity', in *The Truth of Realism: A Reassessment of the German Novel 1830–1900* (London: Legenda, 2011); 125–47.

Woodford, Charlotte, 'Fontane, *Effi Briest*', in Peter Hutchinson (ed.), *Landmarks in the German Novel (I)* (Oxford: Peter Lang, 2007), 83–98.

Historical Context

Blackbourn, David, *The Long Nineteenth Century 1780–1918*, The Fontana History of Germany (London: HarperCollins, 1997).

Clark, Christopher, *Iron Kingdom: The Rise and Downfall of Prussia, 1600–1917* (London: Allen Lane, 2006).

Craig, Gordon A., *Germany 1866–1945* (Oxford: Clarendon Press, 1978).

—— *Theodor Fontane: Literature and History in the Bismarck Reich* (New York: Oxford University Press, 1999).

Eyck, Erich, *Bismarck and the German Empire* (London: Allen & Unwin, 1950).

Frevert, Ute, *Women in German History: From Bourgeois Emancipation to Sexual Liberation*, trans. Stuart McKinnon-Evans (Oxford: Berg, 1989).

—— *Men of Honour: A Social and Cultural History of the Duel*, trans. Anthony Williams (Cambridge: Polity, 1995).

Steinberg, Jonathan, *Bismarck: A Life* (Oxford: Oxford University Press, 2011).

Wehler, Hans-Ulrich, *The German Empire 1871–1918*, trans. Kim Traynor (Leamington Spa: Berg, 1985).

Further Reading in Oxford World's Classics

Flaubert, Gustave, *Madame Bovary*, trans. Margaret Mauldon, ed. Malcolm Bowie.

Ibsen, Henrik, *An Enemy of the People, The Wild Duck, Rosmersholm*, trans. and ed. James McFarlane.
—— *Four Major Plays* (*A Doll's House, Ghosts, Hedda Gabler, The Master Builder*), trans. and ed. James McFarlane.
Scott, Sir Walter, *Wæverley*, ed. Claire Lamont.
Tolstoy, Leo, *Anna Karenina*, trans. and ed. Rosamund Bartlett.

A CHRONOLOGY OF THEODOR FONTANE

1819 (30 December) Theodor Fontane born at Neuruppin in northern Prussia, son of the pharmacist Louis Henri Fontane (1791–1867) and Emilie Fontane, née Labry (1797–1869).

1827 The Fontane family moves to Swinemünde on the Baltic coast (the original of Kessin; now Świnoujście in Poland).

1836 Fontane begins his apprenticeship as a pharmacist in Berlin. From then till 1849 he works for pharmacists in various towns, taking his professional exams in 1847.

1840 The ultra-conservative Friedrich Wilhelm IV becomes King of Prussia.

1844 Joins the literary club 'Der Tunnel über dem Spree' ('The Tunnel over the Spree', named after one of the rivers at Berlin). Writes ballads, especially on events from Prussian history; (May–June) pays his first visit to England.

1848 Revolutions in Paris, Berlin, Vienna, and elsewhere. Fontane takes part in the Berlin revolution in March.

1849 Becomes a freelance writer, working for various, often conservative, newspapers.

1850 Marries Emilie Rouanet-Kummer (1824–1902).

1851 Birth of eldest son, George (1851–87).

1852 (April–September) Lives in London as newspaper correspondent.

1854 Publishes his first prose work, *A Summer in London*.

1855 Moves to London as correspondent on British affairs for the Prussian government led by the prime minister Otto von Manteuffel. His family joins him in 1857.

1856 Birth of second son, Theodor (1856–1933).

1858 Journey to Scotland. The fall of the Manteuffel ministry deprives Fontane of a major source of income. He scrapes a living from scattered journalism.

1859 Settles permanently in Berlin.

1860 Birth of daughter, Martha, known as Mete (1860–1917). Publishes travel books about England and Scotland.

1861 Wilhelm I becomes King of Prussia.

1862 Bismarck becomes prime minister of Prussia. Fontane begins publishing his series of historical travelogues, *Wanderings Through the March of Brandenburg* (5 vols.; the last appears in 1892).

1864 Birth of youngest son, Friedrich (1864–1941). War between Prussia and Denmark over Schleswig-Holstein. Prussian troops capture the Danish fortifications at Düppel (Dybbøl) in April; Schleswig is annexed by Prussia; (May) Fontane visits the battlefield of Düppel; (September) Fontane revisits the war locations, travels through the whole of Denmark, and immerses himself in Danish history and culture.

1865 Publishes a book, *The Schleswig-Holstein War of 1864*.

1866 War between Prussia and Austria, concluded by the Prussian victory at Königgrätz on 3 July and Austrian capitulation on 22 July. Fontane visits the battle locations in Bohemia.

1869 Publishes *The German War of 1866*.

1870 Franco-Prussian War; (1–2 September) decisive Prussian victory at Sedan. Fontane, visiting battlefields, is taken prisoner by the French on 5 October and confined in various prisons, including Oléron off the coast of Gascony, until released in December thanks to intervention by Bismarck.

1871 (18 January) German Empire proclaimed in the Hall of Mirrors at Versailles; Wilhelm I of Prussia becomes Emperor. Fontane publishes a book about his captivity, *Taken Prisoner*.

1874 (October–November) Visits Italy with his wife.

1875 (August) Second visit to Italy.

1876 Fontane becomes Secretary of the Academy of Arts in Berlin, but so hates his bureaucratic tasks that he resigns his post, and with it financial security, within three months, thereby upsetting his wife and putting their marriage under severe but temporary strain.

1878 Publishes his first novel, *Vor dem Sturm* (*Before the Storm*), about Prussian resistance to French occupation in the winter of 1812–13.

1882 *L'Adultera* (*The Woman Taken in Adultery*), his first novel set in contemporary society, with a theme anticipating that of *Effi Briest*.

1884 Foundation of the Society for German Colonization to encourage Germany to copy other European powers in acquiring overseas colonies. Germany establishes protectorates in East Africa (now Tanzania) and South-West Africa (now Namibia).

1887 *Cécile*, a novel about a 'fallen woman'.

1888 The 'Year of Three Emperors': Wilhelm I dies on 9 March; is succeeded by Friedrich III (son-in-law of Queen Victoria), who dies of throat cancer on 15 June, and is in turn succeeded by his son Wilhelm II (1859–1941), whose reign ends with the fall of the Empire in November 1918. *Irrungen Wirrungen* (*On Tangled Paths*), a Berlin novel about a cross-class relationship.

1890 Bismarck is dismissed from his post as Imperial Chancellor.

1891 *Quitt* (*Quits*), a novel set largely in America.

1892 *Unwiederbringlich* (*No Way Back*), a novel of marriage, set in Denmark.

1893 *Frau Jenny Treibel*, a humorous social novel set in Berlin.

1894 *Meine Kinderjahre* (*My Childhood*), the first volume of Fontane's autobiography.

1895 *Effi Briest*.

1896 *Die Poggenpuhls* (*The Poggenpuhl Family*), another Berlin novel.

1898 *Von Zwanzig bis Dreißig* (*From Twenty to Thirty*), a further instalment of Fontane's autobiography. Another volume, *Kritische Jahre—Kritikerjahre* (*Critical Years–Years as Critic*), covering the decade from his fiftieth to his sixtieth year, remained a fragment. (20 September) Fontane dies. *Der Stechlin* (*The Stechlin*), by common consent one of Fontane's finest novels, is published posthumously.

EFFI BRIEST

EFFI BRIEST

CHAPTER 1

OUTSIDE the manor house in Hohen-Cremmen,* where the Briests
had lived since the days when Georg Wilhelm* had been elector of
Brandenburg, the village street, quiet at midday, lay in bright sunshine, whilst on the park and garden side a wing built on at right
angles threw a long shadow over a path of white and green flagstones
and then across a large, circular flowerbed with a sundial in the middle
and *Canna indica** and giant rhubarb planted round the edge. Some
twenty yards away, running precisely parallel to the side wing, was
a churchyard wall, entirely covered in small-leaved ivy and only interrupted by a little, white-painted iron door, beyond which the shingle
tower of Hohen-Cremmen church rose up, its weathercock gleaming
gold, since it had only recently been repainted. The main building,
the wing, and the churchyard wall formed a horseshoe round a little
flower-garden, at the open side of which a pond with a jetty and a boat
tied up could be seen and, by the edge, a swing, its seat a horizontal
board hanging from two ropes on either side—the posts supporting
the cross-beam were already sagging a little. Between the pond and
the flowerbed, however, and half-concealing the swing, stood a pair of
massive old plane trees.

The front of the manor house—a terrace with tubs of aloe and
a few garden chairs—was also a pleasant place to be and to amuse
oneself when it was overcast; on days when the sun was burning
down, however, the garden side was infinitely preferable, especially
for the lady of the house and her daughter, who on this day were once
more sitting in the shade on the flagged path, with a few open windows with Virginia creeper twining round behind them and, beside
them, a small staircase of four stone steps leading up from the garden
to the mezzanine of the wing. Both of them, mother and daughter,
were busy at work on an altar-cloth made up from separate squares;
countless hanks of wool and skeins of silk were scattered over a big
table, with a few side-plates left over from lunch and a majolica bowl
full of lovely big gooseberries. The tapestry needles went in and out,
swiftly and precisely, but while the mother kept her eyes fixed on her
work, her daughter, who was known as Effi,* would put her needle
down from time to time to get up and, bending and stretching this

way and that, go through the whole series of callisthenic exercises. It was clear to see that she was particularly fond of these movements, which she deliberately exaggerated a little for comic effect, and when she stood there, slowly raising her arms and putting the palms of her hands together high above her head, her mother would look up from her needlework, though always briefly and surreptitiously because she did not want to show how charming she found her own daughter, a feeling of maternal pride that was entirely justified. Effi was wearing a blue-and-white striped linen dress, a bit like a smock, that needed its tight bronze leather belt to give it a waist; a wide sailor collar thrown back over her shoulders left her neck free.

Everything she did combined high spirits and gracefulness, and her laughing brown eyes revealed a great deal of natural intelligence and much *joie de vivre* and warm-heartedness. She was called 'little Effi', which she had to put up with simply because her beautiful, slim mother was still at least a couple of inches taller.

Effi had just stood up once more to do her twists and turns to the left and right when her mother, looking up from her embroidery again, called out to her, 'You really ought to have been a circus artiste, Effi. Always on the trapeze, always flying through the air. I can almost imagine you'd enjoy something like that.'

'Perhaps, Mama. But if that's the case, whose fault is it? Where do I get it from? It has to be from you. Or do you think I get it from Papa? You see, the very idea makes even you laugh. And then why do you stick me in this pinafore dress, in this boy's smock? Sometimes I think I'm going to be back in short clothes again. And once I'm wearing *those*, I'll start curtseying like a little girl again, and when the Rathenow Hussars* come riding past I'll ride a cock-horse in Colonel Goetze's lap.* And why not? He's three-quarters an uncle and only one-quarter a beau. It's your fault. Why don't I get any fine gowns? Why don't you make a lady out of me?'

'Is that what you'd like?'

'No.' And with that she dashed over to her Mama, flung her arms round her, and kissed her.

'Not so wild, Effi, you mustn't get into such a passion. It always makes me uneasy when I see you like that . . .' Her mother seemed determined to continue to express her worries and fears, but it didn't come to that, for at that very moment three young girls came into the garden through the little iron door in the churchyard wall and set off along a gravel path towards the circular flowerbed and sundial. All three waved their parasols as a greeting to Effi then hurried over to Frau von Briest to kiss her hand. She asked them a few questions then invited the girls to keep them, or at least Effi, company for half an hour. 'I've got enough to do as it is, and anyway, young folk prefer to be amongst themselves. Good-day to you.' And saying which, she went up the stone steps into the wing of the house.

And with that the young folk were truly left to themselves.

Two of the girls—short, plump lasses whose freckles and good humour went very well with their auburn hair—were the daughters of Jahnke,* the church organist and village schoolmaster, who swore by the Hanseatic League,* everything Scandinavian, and his favourite writer and fellow Mecklenburger, Fritz Reuter;* on the model of the twins, Mining and Lining, from Reuter's popular novel, he had given his own twins the names Bertha and Hertha.* The third young lady was Hulda Niemeyer, Pastor Niemeyer's only child; she was more ladylike than the other two, but boring and conceited, a pale, puffy blonde with weak, slightly protuberant eyes that still seemed to be constantly seeking something, which had induced Klitzing* of the Hussars to say: 'Doesn't she look as if she's expecting the Angel Gabriel* to arrive at any moment?'

Effi thought that the rather censorious Klitzing was only too right, but still took care not to make any distinction between her three friends. She felt least like doing that at this moment and, leaning her arms on the table, she said, 'This tedious embroidery. Thank God you're here.'

'But we drove your Mama away,' said Hulda.

'No you didn't. As she said, she would have gone anyway; she's expecting a visitor, you see, an old friend from before she was married. I must tell you about it later, a love story with a hero and a heroine and ending with renunciation. You'll be amazed, you really will. I've already met Mama's old friend, over in Schwantikow;* he's a Landrat,* a fine figure of a man.'

'That's the main thing,' Hertha said.

'Of course it's the main thing. "Women womanly, men manly"—as you know that's one of Papa's favourite sayings. And now help me get this table tidied up, otherwise I'll be in for a telling-off again.'

In no time at all the hanks of silk and wool were packed in the basket, and when they were all sitting down Hulda said, 'Come on Effi, it's time now: the love story with renunciation. Or was it not that bad?'

'A story with renunciation is never bad. But I can't start until Hertha's had some of the gooseberries—she can't take her eyes off them. Anyway, take as many as you like, we can pick some more afterwards; only throw the hulls well away or, better still, put them on the newspaper supplement here, then we'll wrap them up in it and clear everything away. Mama hates it when the husks are lying all over the place, she's always saying you could slip on them and break your leg.'

'I don't believe that,' Hertha said, tucking into the gooseberries.

'Me neither,' Effi said. 'Just think, I fall over at least two or three times every day and I've never broken anything. A proper leg doesn't break that easily, certainly not mine, nor yours, Hertha. What do you think, Hulda?'

'One shouldn't tempt fate; pride comes before a fall.'

'Always the governess; you're a born old spinster.'

'And still hope to get married. And perhaps before you.'

'Doesn't bother me. Do you think I'm just waiting for that? That's the last thing I need. Anyway, I'm going to get a husband, and that perhaps soon. I'm not worried. Only recently little Ventivegni from Rathenow said to me: "What will you bet, Fräulein Effi, that we'll be here again in a year's time listening to them smashing crockery for an eve-of-wedding party." '*

'And what did you say to that?'

'Could well be, I said, could well be; Hulda's the oldest, she could get married any time. But he brushed that aside and said, "No, for another young lady who's as brunette as Fräulein Hulda's blond." And as he spoke he gave me such an earnest look . . . But there I go, rambling on and forgetting the story.'

'Yes, you keep digressing; perhaps you don't want to tell us the story after all.'

'Oh, I do, but it's true I keep digressing because it's all a bit strange, yes, almost romantic.'

'But you said he was a Landrat.'

'A Landrat, true. And he's called Geert von Innstetten, Baron von Innstetten.'

All three laughed.

'Why are you laughing?' Effi said, put out. 'What's all this about?'

'Oh, Effi, we're not trying to insult you, nor the Baron either. Innstetten, you said? And Geert? No one round here has that kind of name. Though, of course, there's often something funny about the names of nobles.'

'Yes, my dear, there is. That's why they're nobles. They can afford it, and the farther back they go, in time I mean, the more they can afford it. You know nothing about that, but don't take it amiss, we'll still stay good friends. Geert von Innstetten, then, and a baron. He's the same age as Mama, to the very day.'

'And how old is your Mama, actually?'

'Thirty-eight.'

'A fine age.'

'It is that, especially when you still look like my Mama. She's a beautiful woman, don't you agree? And the way she can do everything, always so assured and so refined and never says inappropriate things like Papa. If I were a young lieutenant I'd fall in love with Mama.'

'But how can you say something like that, Effi?' Hulda said. 'It's against the fourth commandment.'*

'Nonsense. How can it be against the fourth commandment? I think Mama would be pleased if she knew I'd said something like that.'

'That may well be,' Hertha broke in, 'but do get on with the story.'

'All right, calm down, I'm starting . . . Baron Innstetten, then. When he wasn't yet twenty he was stationed over there, with the Rathenow Hussars, and used to visit the estates round here a lot, but best of all he liked to be over in Schwantikow, with Grandfather Belling.* Of course, it wasn't because of Grandfather that he was over there so often, and when Mama talks about it anyone can tell whom he went to see. And I think it was mutual.'

'So what happened?'

'Well, what was bound to happen, what always does happen. He was far too young, and when my father appeared on the scene, already a Ritterschaftsrat* and having inherited Hohen-Cremmen, it didn't take long for her to make up her mind. She accepted him and became Frau von Briest . . . And the rest, well, you know that . . . the rest is me.'

'Yes, the rest, that's you, Effi,' Bertha said. 'Thank God. We wouldn't have you if things had turned out differently. But now tell us, what did Innstetten do, what became of him? He can't have taken his own life, otherwise you wouldn't be expecting him today.'

'No, he didn't take his own life. But it was something a bit along those lines.'

'Did he try to?'

'Not that either. But he didn't want to stay near here, and soldiering in general seems to have been spoilt for him. It was peacetime, of course. To put it in a nutshell, he resigned his commission and started to study law, in "deadly earnest", as Papa says; only he joined up again when war broke out* in '70, but with the Perleberg Lancers,* not with his old regiment, and he was awarded the Iron Cross—of course, he's very dashing. And as soon as the war was over, he went back to his files and they say Bismarck* thinks highly of him and the Emperor as well, and so it was that he was made a Landrat, Landrat in the Kessin* district.'

'What's this Kessin? I've never heard of a Kessin round here.'

'No, it's not in our area, it's a fair way away from here, in Pomerania, in Eastern Pomerania even, though that doesn't mean anything, since it's a seaside resort (everything round there's one of those), and this holiday he's taking is actually a family visit, or something like that. He wants to look up old friends and relatives.'

'Does he have relatives round here?'

'Yes and no, it depends how you look at it. There are no Innstettens round here, in fact I don't think there are any at all, anywhere now. But he does have distant cousins on his mother's side, and I presume that above all he wanted to see Schwantikow and the Bellings' house that holds so many memories for him. He was over there the day before yesterday, and he wants to spend today here in Hohen-Cremmen.'

'And what does your father say about that?'

'Nothing at all. He's not like that. And then of course he knows Mama, he just teases her.'

At that moment midday struck, and before the chimes had finished Wilke, the Briests' old factotum who looked after the house and family, came to tell Effi, 'The Mistress would remind the Fräulein to get dressed in good time; the Herr Baron will presumably arrive at one precisely.'

And even as he was passing on this message, Wilke had already started to clear up the ladies' sewing table, first of all picking up the sheet of newspaper with the gooseberry hulls.

'No, Wilke, not that; the remains of the gooseberries are our business . . . Hertha, you wrap them up and put a stone in with them so that everything will sink better. Then we'll go off in a long funeral procession and bury the package on the high sea.'

Wilke smirked. 'She's a real little devil, is our young Mistress,' was what he was thinking. And Effi, as she placed the package on the tablecloth that had been quickly gathered up, said, 'Now all take a hold of it, each to a corner, and we'll sing something sad.'

'It's all very well to say that, Effi, but what are we to sing?'

'Anything, it doesn't matter what, only it has to rhyme in "oo", "oo" is always the vowel of mourning. So let's sing, "Stay true, true and bid the world adieu . . .",' and as Effi started her litany all four of them set off for the jetty, got into the boat that was tied up there, and let the package, that was weighted with a pebble, slide slowly down into the pond.

'Now your guilt has been sent to the bottom, Hertha,' Effi said, 'and that reminds me that in olden times poor, unfortunate women used to be sent to the bottom too. Because of infidelity, of course.'

'But not here.'

'No, not here,' Effi laughed, 'things like that don't happen here. But they do in Constantinople and, as I recall, you ought to know that too, you were there when that probationer teacher, Holzapfel, told us about it in Geography.'

'Yes,' Hulda said, 'he was always telling us that kind of thing. But one quickly forgets it.'

'Not me. I remember that kind of thing.'

CHAPTER 2

They continued talking for a while, recalling with outrage and pleasure their classes together and a whole series of Holzapfel's unsuitable topics. They couldn't stop until Hulda suddenly said, 'It's high time, Effi; you look, well, how can I put it, you look as if you've just come from picking cherries, everything crushed and crumpled; linen always gets so creased and your big, white turn-down collar . . . yes, oh, now I've got it, you look like a cabin boy.'

'Midshipman, if you please. My noble name must be worth something. Apropos midshipman or cabin boy, only recently Papa promised me a flagpole again, here by the swing, with yardarms and a rope-ladder. I'd really like that and I'd insist on fixing the pennant up there myself. And you, Hulda, you can come up the other side and at the top we'll shout "Hurrah" and give each other a kiss. By Jove, that would be something.'

' "By Jove"—there you go again . . . You sound like a midshipman already. But I'm certainly not climbing up after you, I'm not such a daredevil. Jahnke's quite right when he says there's too much of the Bellings in you, from your mother's side. I'm just a child of the parsonage.'

'Oh, get away. Still waters run deep. Do you remember that time when my Briest cousin was here? He was still a cadet, but grown-up enough, and you crawled along the barn roof. And why? All right, I'm not going to tell. But come on, let's go on the swing, two on each side; I'm sure it won't break, but if you don't feel like it, for I can see you're pulling long faces, let's play tig. I've still got a quarter of an hour. I don't want to go inside yet and all just to say hello to a Landrat, and a Landrat from Eastern Pomerania at that. He's pretty old, too, he could almost be my father, and if he really does live in a seaside town, and Kessin's supposed to be something like that, then I ought to please him best in this sailor's costume, he must almost see it as a kind of compliment. When royalty receive someone—I have this from Papa—they always put on a uniform from the place the other person comes from. So no holding back . . . quick, quick, I'm away and beside the bench here's home.'

Hulda wanted to introduce a couple of restrictions, but Effi was already heading up the nearest gravel path, once to the left, once to the right, then all at once she disappeared. 'That doesn't count, Effi; where are you? We're not playing hide and seek, we're playing tig,' and with these and other objections her friends rushed off after her, well beyond the circular flowerbed and the two plane trees beside it, until Effi suddenly burst out from her hiding-place and, being behind her pursuers, easily made it to 'home' beside the bench in no time at all.

'Where were you?'

'Behind the rhubarb. It has such huge leaves, even bigger than a figleaf . . .'*

'Shame on you . . .'

'No, shame on the three of you because you lost. Hulda with her big eyes didn't see anything again, hopeless as ever.' And with that Effi was flying off once more, beyond the flowerbed towards the pond, perhaps because she intended to hide first of all behind a thick hazel hedge growing there and then make a long detour round the church-yard and the front of the house and thus reach the wing and 'home'. It was a good idea, but even before she was halfway round the pond she heard her name being called from the house and, as she turned, saw her Mama on the stone steps waving her handkerchief. Another moment and Effi was standing beside her.

'You're still in your smock and our visitor's here. You're never on time.'

'I am on time, it's our visitor who isn't. It's not one o'clock yet; it's ages to go,' and, turning to the twins (Hulda was farther behind) called out to them, 'You keep on playing, I'll be back soon.'

*

One moment later Effi was going with her mother into the large gar-den room that took up almost the whole of the wing. 'You shouldn't tell me off, Mama. It really is only half-past. Why has he come so early? A proper gentleman doesn't arrive late, but even less too early.'

Frau von Briest was visibly embarrassed, but Effi snuggled up against her in a show of affection, saying, 'Sorry, I will hurry up now; you know I can be quick as well, in five minutes Cinderella will be transformed into a princess. He can wait that long or chat to Papa.'

And nodding to her Mama, she was about to skip up a little iron staircase that went from the garden room to the upper floor. But Frau von Briest, who could, on occasion, be unconventional, suddenly held Effi back as she was about to dash off, looked at the charmingly youth-ful creature that, still flushed from the excitement of playing, stood before her, the very picture of living freshness, and said, almost con-fidingly, 'Perhaps it would be best if you stayed as you are. Yes, stay like that. You look very nice. And even if it weren't so, you look quite unprepared, not at all as if you'd been specially dressed up, and that's the important thing at this point. You see, I have to tell you, Effi dear . . .' and she took both her daughter's hands in hers, 'I have to tell you . . .'

'Whatever's the matter with you, Mama? I feel quite frightened.'

' . . . I have to tell you, Effi, that Baron Innstetten has just asked for your hand in marriage.'

'Asked for my hand in marriage? Seriously?'

'It's not a matter to joke about. You saw him yesterday and I think you liked him very much as well. True, he's older than you, which, all things considered, is a good thing. Added to that, he's a man of character, good breeding, and with a good position, and if you don't say no, which I can hardly imagine my clever little Effi will, at twenty you'll be where other women are at forty. You'll rise much higher than your Mama.'

Effi remained silent, wondering what to say, but before anything occurred to her she heard her father's voice from the neighbouring room, still at the front of the house, and immediately afterwards Ritterschaftsrat von Briest, a well-preserved and particularly genial man in his fifties, came into the garden parlour—and with him Baron Innstetten, slim, brown-haired, and with a military bearing.

When she saw him, Effi started to tremble nervously; but not for long, for at almost the same moment as Innstetten was approaching her with a friendly bow, the heads of the auburn-haired twins appeared in the middle one of the wide-open windows, half overgrown with Virginia creeper, and Hertha, the more exuberant of the two, called, 'Come, Effi.'

Then her head disappeared and the two sisters jumped from the back-rest of the bench they'd been standing on down into the garden, and all that could be heard was their soft giggles and laughter.

CHAPTER 3

On that very same day Baron Innstetten had become engaged to Effi Briest. At the following meal to celebrate the engagement the affable father of the bride, who had some difficulty summoning up the required solemnity, proposed a toast to the young couple, which tugged a little at Frau von Briest's heartstrings as she thought back to a time that was hardly eighteen years ago. But not for long; *she* hadn't been the one, now it was her daughter instead of her—just as good, all in all, if not perhaps even better. Life with Briest was tolerable, even though he was somewhat down-to-earth and could at times make suggestive remarks. Towards the end of the meal, the ice-cream was already being served, the old Ritterschaftsrat stood up to address them again and proposed that they should use the familiar *du* to each other. He embraced Innstetten and gave him a kiss on the left cheek. But that wasn't the end of it, he went on to suggest, along with the *du*, more intimate names and titles for use among themselves, setting up a kind of informal list, naturally retaining well-established individual appellations. For his wife, he said, it would presumably be best to continue to call her 'Mama' (for there were young mamas as well), while for himself, renouncing his claim to the honourable title of 'Papa', he had a decided preference for the simple 'Briest', not least because it was nice and short. And as far as the children were concerned—at that word, eye to eye with Innstetten, who was only about twelve years his junior, he had to pull himself together—well, Effi was Effi and Geert Geert. Geert, if he was not mistaken, meant a tall, slim trunk, which would make Effi the ivy that was to twine itself round it. At this the engaged couple gave each other rather embarrassed looks, Effi's with a touch of childlike merriment, but Frau von Briest said, 'Say what you have to say, Briest, and formulate your toasts as you like, only I would ask you to avoid poetic metaphors, they're outside your sphere of competence.' To which rebuke Briest responded with acceptance rather than dissent. 'You might possibly be right there, Luise.'*

Immediately after they left the table Effi excused herself in order to go to the parsonage to see the Niemeyers. On the way there she said to herself, 'I think Hulda will be annoyed. Now I've beaten her to it after all—she was always too vain and stuck-up.' But Effi was not quite right in this; Hulda kept her composure and behaved very well, leaving the expression of annoyance and resentment to her mother, who then made some very odd remarks. 'Oh yes, that's the way things are. Of course. If it couldn't be the mother, it had to be the daughter. We know all about that. Old families always stick together, and to those that have shall be given.' Pastor Niemeyer was extremely embarrassed at this stream of caustic remarks, with no sense of refinement or propriety, and once more regretted having married his housekeeper.

From the parsonage Effi naturally went to the Jahnkes, where the twins were already looking out for her and came to meet her in the front garden.

'Well, Effi,' Hertha said as the three of them walked up and down between the beds of marigolds in flower on either side, 'well, Effi, how do you feel?'

'How do I feel? Oh, very well. We're already on first-name terms and calling each other *du*. He's called Geert—as I've already told you, of course.'

'Yes, you have. But it makes me feel so worried. Is he the right man for you?'

'Of course he's the right man. You don't understand, Hertha. Every man's the right one. Of course he has to belong to the nobility, have a position, and be presentable.'

'God, Effi, the way you're talking. You used to talk quite differently.'

'Used to, yes.'

'And do you feel very happy now?'

'You're always very happy when you've been engaged for just two hours. At least I imagine you must be.'

'But don't you feel, well, how shall I put it, a bit awkward?'

'Yes, I do feel a bit awkward but not very much. And I think I'll be able to get over it.'

After these calls at the parsonage and the organist's, that hadn't taken even half an hour, Effi had gone back to the manor house, where they were about to have coffee on the garden veranda. Father-in-law and son-in-law were walking up and down the gravel path between the two plane trees.

Briest talked about the difficult side of a Landrat's position; various ones had been offered to him, but each time he had declined. 'I've always preferred to do things my own way, at least—sorry, Innstetten—rather than having to keep an eye on the powers that be all the time. Then you're always looking out for those above you and those above them. Here I can live my own life, taking pleasure in every green leaf, in the Virginia creeper growing round the windows over there.'

He went on like that, with all manner of anti-officialdom comments, excusing himself now and then with a brief, 'sorry, Innstetten'. Innstetten nodded mechanically, but his mind wasn't really on the topic; rather, he kept on looking across to the Virginia creeper entwined round the window that Briest had just mentioned, and as he pursued these thoughts it was as if he could see the heads of the two auburn-haired girls among the creeper and hear their high-spirited 'Come, Effi.'

He didn't believe in omens and that sort of thing, on the contrary, he rejected any kind of superstition. But, despite that, he could not get the two words out of his mind, and while Briest rattled on, he kept feeling that the little incident had been more than mere chance.

*

Innstetten, who had only taken short leave, left the next day, after having promised he would write every day. 'Yes, you must do that,'

Effi had said, a response that truly came from the heart, since for years there had been nothing she liked better than to get lots of letters, for example on her birthday. Everyone had to write to her on that day. Remarks like 'and Gertrud and Klara also send you their best wishes' casually included in a letter were frowned on; if Gertrud and Klara wanted to remain her friends, then they had to see that a letter came with its own stamp on it, a foreign one if possible, from Switzerland or Carlsbad, since Effi's birthday fell during the summer holidays.

Innstetten actually did write every day, as promised; what made this correspondence particularly pleasant, however, was the fact that he only expected one short letter of reply a week. And these he did receive, full of charmingly important news that never failed to delight him. It was Frau von Briest who dealt with the more serious business that had to be discussed with her future son-in-law: arrangements regarding the wedding, questions of the dowry and the running of the household. The furnishings in Innstetten's house in Kessin were, if not sumptuous, at least very much befitting a man of his status, and it made sense for her to get a good idea of what was there through their correspondence so that they didn't buy anything that wouldn't be needed. Once Frau von Briest had sufficient information about all these things, it was decided that mother and daughter should go to Berlin to acquire what Briest called 'Princess Effi's trousseau'. Effi was very much looking forward to their stay in Berlin, especially since her father had agreed that they could stay at the Hotel du Nord.* The cost could be deducted from her dowry, Briest said, since Innstetten had everything anyway. Unconcerned whether he meant it seriously or in jest, Effi—unlike her mother, who told him sharply to forget such *mesquineries** once and for all—joyfully agreed with her father, her thoughts much, much more concerned with the impression the two of them, mother and daughter, would make in the dining-room than with Spinn & Menke, Goschenhofer,* and other similar firms that were on their provisional list. And once their great Berlin week had arrived, she acted out these delightful imaginings. Her cousin Dagobert, an uncommonly lively lieutenant in the Tsar Alexander Guards Regiment*—he took *Die Fliegenden Blätter** and kept a note of the latest jokes—placed himself at their disposal for every hour when he was not on duty, and so they had a table with him in the corner window of Café Kranzler or, at an appropriate time, in

Café Bauer* as well, and in the afternoon they went to the Zoo to see the giraffes, of which her cousin—Cousin Dagobert—liked to say that they looked like aristocratic old maids. They had a programme they followed every day, and thus on the third or fourth they went to the National Gallery, because Dagobert wanted to show his cousin the *Island of the Blest.** His cousin, he said, was on the point of getting married, but it would perhaps be a good idea if she became acquainted with the *Island of the Blest* beforehand. His aunt gave him a little slap with her fan, but accompanied it with such a gracious look that he saw no reason to change his tone. They were divine days for all three of them, not least for Effi's cousin, who was such an excellent chaperone and always quick to resolve any little disagreements. There was no lack of differences of opinion between mother and daughter, but that was just the way things are and fortunately they never cropped up over the purchases they needed to make. Effi was happy with everything, whether they bought six or three-dozen of a particular item, and when they talked about the price of the things they had just purchased on the way back to the hotel, she regularly confused the figures. Frau von Briest, who was usually very critical, even towards her beloved child, not only took this apparent lack of interest lightly, she even regarded it as an advantage. 'All these things', she told herself, 'mean very little to Effi. She's undemanding as far as worldly goods are concerned; she lives in the world of her imagination, and if Princess Maria Anna* drives past and gives her a friendly wave from her carriage, that means more to her than a whole chestful of linen.'

All this was true, but only half true. The possession of more or less everyday objects didn't matter much to Effi, but when she walked up and down Unter den Linden with her Mama and, after examining the most splendid window displays, went into Demuth's* to buy all sorts of things for their honeymoon trip to Italy, then her true character came out. Only the most elegant items were good enough for her, and if she couldn't have the best, then she refused to make do with second-best, because it meant nothing to her. Yes, she had the ability to do without things, her mother was right about that, and there was something undemanding about that ability; but on the occasions when there was something she did have to acquire, then it had to be something very special. And in that she was demanding.

CHAPTER 4

Cousin Dagobert was at the station when the ladies set off back for Hohen-Cremmen. They had been happy days, above all in that they had not had to suffer the company of an awkward relative, one almost beneath their social station. 'This time,' Effi had said as soon as they arrived, 'we must remain incognito as far as Aunt Therese is concerned. It's either the Hotel du Nord or Aunt Therese, the two don't go together.' Eventually her mother had agreed to that, and had even sealed her agreement with a kiss on her darling's forehead.

It was, of course, quite different with Cousin Dagobert. He not only had the Guards' bearing, above all he had the good humour that was almost traditional among Tsar Alexander officers, and that from the very beginning had enabled him to stimulate and amuse both mother and daughter, and this mood had lasted to the very end of their stay. 'Well, Dagobert,' Effi said as they took their leave, 'you must come to my eve-of-wedding party, and with a retinue, of course. After the sketches* (but don't turn up as a porter or a mouse-trap seller) there'll be a ball. And, you must remember, it's going to be my first ball and possibly also my last. No entry with less than six of your comrades—excellent dancers, of course. And you can all go back on the early train.' Her cousin promised to comply and so they parted.

The two arrived at their station in the Havelland Marshes round midday and were back in Hohen-Cremmen after a half-hour drive. Briest was glad to have his wife and daughter at home again and asked question after question, mostly without waiting for an answer, telling them instead what had happened in Hohen-Cremmen in the meantime. 'You told me just now about the National Gallery and the *Island of the Blest*—well, we had something of the sort here, while you were away: our farm manager Pink and the gardener's wife. I had to dismiss Pink, of course, though unwillingly. It's very awkward that such things almost always happen at harvest time. And in all other respects Pink was an uncommonly capable man, just in the wrong place here, unfortunately. But that's enough of that, Wilke's getting restless.'

Over lunch Briest concentrated more on what they were saying; he was happy that they had got on so well with Effi's cousin, about whom they had much to tell him, less so about their behaviour towards Aunt Therese. But it was clear that, behind all his disapproval, he was actually pleased with it; a little bit of mischief was something that appealed to him, and Aunt Therese really did cut a ridiculous figure. And when, after lunch, they unpacked some of the nicest of their purchases for him to say what he thought of them, he showed great interest, which didn't even flag, or at least didn't entirely disappear, when he glanced through the bill. 'A bit expensive, or rather, let's say, very expensive. Everything so chic, I mean so stimulating, that I definitely feel that if you were to give me a suitcase and a travelling rug like these we'd end up in Rome at Easter as well, on our own honeymoon after eighteen years. What d'you think, Luise? "Late ye come, but ye have come,"* as Schiller has it.'

Frau von Briest waved her hand as if to say, 'He's incorrigible,' and left him to his own sense of shame, which wasn't all that great.

*

August had ended, the wedding day (the 3rd of October) was approaching, and in the parsonage and the schoolhouse, as well as in the manor house, the preparations for the eve-of-wedding party were in full swing. Jahnke, true to his enthusiasm for Fritz Reuter, had thought up something particularly apposite, letting Bertha and Hertha appear as Lining and Mining, in Low German dialect of course, while Hulda was to play Kleist's Käthchen von Heilbronn,* the scene under the elder tree, with Lieutenant Engelbrecht of the Hussars as Wetter vom Strahl. Niemeyer, from whom the idea came, had insisted on writing a sly reference to Innstetten and Effi into the scene. He himself was very pleased with his work and received much praise from all involved after the first rehearsal, with the exception, however, of his patron and old friend Briest, who, after listening to the mixture of Kleist and Niemeyer, protested vigorously, though not for literary reasons. ' "My lord" here and "my lord" there—what's the point? It's misleading, it distorts everything. Innstetten is a capital specimen of humanity, no question, a man of character and very dashing, but the Briests—forgive the colloquialism, Luise—the Briests are not to be sneezed at either. After all, we're a family who've played a part in history, thank God, let me add, and the Innstettens* are *not*; the Innstettens are merely old—ancient nobility, if you like, but what does that mean? And I don't want a Briest, or at least a character in an eve-of-wedding party sketch in whom everyone can see a reflection of our Effi—I don't want a Briest saying "my lord" all the time. For that Innstetten would have to be at least a by-blow* of the Hohenzollerns, and there are some of those around. But he isn't that, and I repeat, it distorts the situation.'

And indeed, for a while Briest stuck particularly doggedly to that view. Only after the second rehearsal, in which 'Käthchen', already half in costume, wore a very close-fitting bodice, was he—who anyway was not slow in making complimentary remarks to Hulda— sufficiently carried away to remark that Käthchen was very well done, which was as good as a surrender, or at least led to one. That all these things were kept secret from Effi doesn't need to be said. Had she shown more curiosity that would of course have been impossible, but Effi had so little desire to find out about the arrangements and planned surprises that she told her mother emphatically that she was happy to wait and see and when her mother expressed doubts about that, Effi would repeat her assertion that that really was the case, her mother could believe it. And why not? she added, it was all just play-acting, and it couldn't be nicer and more poetic than *Cinderella** that they'd seen on their last evening in Berlin. She'd really have loved to act in that, if only to make a chalk-mark on the back of the silly boarding-school teacher. 'And how delightful the last act was, "Cinderella's awakening as a princess," or at least as a countess, really, it was just like a fairy-tale.' She often spoke like that, and was mostly more high-spirited than before, though she did find her friends' constant whispering and secretiveness irritating. 'I wish they'd put on less important airs and pay more attention to me. Afterwards they're going to be stuck here and I'll have to worry about them and be ashamed that they're my friends.'

That was Effi's mocking tongue, and there was no doubt that she was unconcerned about the party and wedding. It did give Frau von Briest some pause for thought, but she wasn't worried, because Effi was much preoccupied with her future, which was a good sign, and with her lively imagination could go on for a whole quarter of an hour describing her life in Kessin, descriptions which incidentally expressed a strange idea of Eastern Pomerania or, perhaps, were cleverly calculated to express that idea. She made a point of seeing Kessin as a semi-Siberian town that was never entirely free of ice and snow.

'Goschendorfer's have sent the last things today,' Frau von Briest said when, as usual, she was sitting with Effi outside the wing, at their work-table on which the piles of linen were growing while there were fewer and fewer newspapers, they simply took up space. 'I hope you've got everything now, Effi. However, if there are any more little things you'd like, you'll need to say so now, best of all at this very moment. Papa got a very good price for the rape and is in an uncommonly good mood.'

'Uncommonly? He's always in a good mood.'

'In an uncommonly good mood,' her mother repeated. 'And we must exploit that. So tell me. When we were in Berlin I sometimes had the feeling there was this or that object that you particularly wanted.'

'What can I say, Mama dear, I do really have everything one needs, I mean everything one needs *here*. But since it is my fate to end up so far to the north—I must add that I've nothing against that, on the contrary, I'm looking forward to the Northern Lights and the stars shining more brightly—but since that is my fate, I would like to have a fur.'

'But Effi, child, that's all foolishness. You're not going to St Petersburg or Archangel.'

'No. But I'll be on the way there . . .'

'Of course, child. You'll be on the way there, but what does that mean? If you go from here to Nauen you'll be on the way to Russia. But anyway, if that's what you want you shall have your fur. Only let me tell you first that I advise against it. A fur is for older women, even your old Mama's still too young for one, and if you, at seventeen, turn up in mink or marten the Kessiners will think you're in fancy dress.'

*

It was the 2nd of September when they had this conversation, and it would have continued if it hadn't happened to be Sedan Day.* As it was, they were interrupted by the sound of fifes and drums, and Effi, who had heard of the procession that was to take place but then forgotten about it, at once rushed off from the work-table, past the circular flowerbed and the pond, to a little balcony on the churchyard wall with six steps, no wider than the rungs of a ladder, leading up to it. She was up there in a flash and, yes, all the pupils from the school were approaching, Jahnke marching solemnly on the right flank whilst a little drum-major, well in front, was leading the procession with an expression that looked as if he intended to fight the Battle of

Sedan again. Effi waved her handkerchief and, thus acknowledged, the drum-major did not fail to salute her with his shining mace.

*

A week later mother and daughter were sitting at the same place again and busy with their work. It was a beautiful day; the heliotrope in its neat little bed round the sundial was still in bloom and the scent was carried over to them on the gentle breeze.

'Oh, I do feel happy,' Effi said, 'so happy that I can't imagine heaven is any better. And then, who knows if they have such wonderful heliotrope in heaven.'

'But Effi, you mustn't say things like that; you get it from your father, for whom nothing's sacred. He recently said Niemeyer looked like Lot.* Outrageous. And what's that supposed to mean? In the first place he doesn't know what Lot looked like, and in the second it shows an immense lack of consideration for Hulda. It's a good job Niemeyer only has one daughter, which means the comparison doesn't work. In just one respect he was only too right, in everything he said about "Lot's wife" and our good parson's lady, who once again ruined our Sedan Day with her stupidity and presumptuousness. Which reminds me. We were interrupted in our conversation when Jahnke came past with the schoolchildren—at least I can't imagine that the fur you spoke about then is the only thing you'd like. So tell me, my treasure, what else do you have in mind?'

'Nothing, Mama.'

'Really nothing?'

'No, really nothing; quite seriously . . . though if there does have to be something after all . . .'

'Well then . . .'

' . . . it would be a Japanese bed-screen, black, with golden birds on it, all with a long crane's beak . . . and then perhaps another lamp for our bedroom, with a red glow.'

Frau von Briest said nothing.

'There, you see, Mama, you're saying nothing and looking as if I've said something particularly improper.'

'No, Effi, not improper—and certainly not to your mother. I know what you're like. You're a very imaginative little person, you most like to visualize scenes from your future, and the more colourful they are, the more beautiful and desirable they seem to you. I could see that when we were buying the things for your journey. And now you think it will be really wonderful to have a bed-screen with all kinds of fabulous animals on it, all in the half-light of a red lamp. It seems like a fairy-tale to you, and you'd like to be the princess.'

Effi took her mother's hand and kissed it. 'Yes, Mama, that's the way I am.'

'Yes, that's the way you are. I'm well aware of that. But, Effi dear, in life we have to be careful, especially we women. And when you get to Kessin, a little place where there's hardly a street-light on at night, people will laugh at that kind of thing. And laughing will be the least of it. Those who are ill-disposed towards you, and there are always some people like that, will talk about you being badly brought up, and perhaps even worse.'

'So nothing Japanese and no lamp. But I have to admit, I imagined it would be very beautiful and poetic to see everything in a red glow.'

Frau von Briest was moved. She stood up and gave Effi a kiss. 'You're a child. Beautiful and poetic. These are imaginings. The real world is different, and it's often good that there can be darkness instead of light and a soft glow.'

Effi seemed about to reply, but at that moment Wilke came with the post. One letter was from Innstetten in Kessin. 'Oh, from Geert,' Effi said, and putting the letter on one side, she went on in a calm tone, 'But you will allow me to have the grand piano at an angle in the drawing-room, won't you. That's more important to me than the fireplace Geert's promised. And the portrait of you, I'm going to put that on an easel; I can't be completely without you. Oh, how I'll miss you all, perhaps even on the journey there and definitely when we're in Kessin. They say there's no garrison there, not even a surgeon-major, it's a good thing it's at least a seaside resort. Cousin Dagobert—I'll take heart from this, his mother and sister always go to Warnemünde, and I really don't see why he shouldn't dispatch his relatives off to Kessin for once. "Dispatch," that sounds very general staff, which is where I believe his ambitions lie. And then, of course, he'll accompany them and stay with us. Moreover, the Kessiners, someone was telling me recently, have a pretty big steamer that goes over to Sweden twice a week. And there's a ball on the ship (they have a band, of course) and he's a very good dancer . . .'

'Who?'

'Well, Dagobert.'

'I thought you meant Innstetten. Anyway, it's time we knew what he's got to say . . . The letter's still in your pocket.'

'Oh, yes. I'd almost forgotten it.' She opened the letter and glanced through it.

'Well, Effi, nothing to say? You're not beaming and not laughing. And his letters are always so cheerful and amusing and not at all full of fatherly wisdom.'

'I wouldn't have that. He has his age and I have my youth. And I'd wag my finger at him and say, "Just think which is better, Geert."'

'And then he'd reply, "What you have, Effi, that's what is better." He not only has perfect manners, he's fair and understanding and knows very well what youth means. He keeps telling himself that, and is attuning himself to youth. And if he stays like that after you're wed, you'll have an ideal marriage.'

'Yes, I think so too, Mama. But can you imagine, I'm almost ashamed to say it, but I'm not very keen on what people call an ideal marriage.'

'That's just like you. So tell me, what are you actually keen on?'

'I'm . . . well, I'm all for having the same interests, and affection and love as well. And if affection and love aren't possible, because love, as Papa says, is stuff and nonsense (which I don't believe), then I'm all for wealth and a grand house, a *very* grand house, where Prince Friedrich Karl will come for the hunting, elk or capercaillies, and the old emperor will drive up and have a gracious word for all the ladies, even the young ones. And then when we're in Berlin I'm for the court ball and a gala performance at the opera, always right next to the royal box.'

'Are you making that up and letting yourself get carried away?'

'No, Mama, I'm really serious. Love comes first, but immediately after that comes esteem and honour, and then comes diversion, always something new, always something to make me laugh or cry. What I can't stand is boredom.'

'Then how did you manage with us?'

'Oh, how can you say that, Mama! Of course, when our charming relations drive over in the winter and stay for six hours, sometimes even longer, and Aunt Gundel and Aunt Olga look me over and think I'm a pert young miss—Aunt Gundel told me that once—yes, then it can be pretty dreary, I have to admit. But otherwise I've always been happy here, very happy . . .'

And as she said that, she threw herself down on her knees and, bursting into tears, kissed her mother's hands

'Get up, Effi. These are just moods that take you when you're as young as you are and about to be wed and don't know what the future holds. But now read the letter out to me, unless there's something very special in it, or secrets.'

'Secrets!' Effi laughed and jumped up, her mood suddenly changing again. 'Secrets! Well, yes, he does try now and again, but I could put most of his letters up on the board with the Landrat's ordinances outside the mayor's office. Well, Geert is a Landrat himself, of course.'

'Read it, read it.'

'"Dear Effi . . ."—that's how they always start, and sometimes he also calls me his "little Eve".'

'Read it . . . you're to read it out.'

'Right then:

'DEAR EFFI,

The closer our wedding day comes, the less frequent your letters are. When the post arrives, I always look for your handwriting first of all but, as you know (and I have to say that it was what I wanted), generally in vain. At the moment the tradesmen are in the house, making the rooms (though only a few) ready for when you come. The best will presumably only be done while we are away. Madelung, the decorator who is delivering everything, is quite a character, I'll tell you about him in my next letter, but above all how happy I am with you, my sweet little Effi. I can't wait to get away from here and our little town is getting quieter and lonelier. The last holidaymaker left yesterday; in the end he was bathing in the sea at nine degrees and the attendants were always glad when he came out safe and sound. They were afraid he might have a stroke, that would have damaged our reputation as a bathing resort, as if the waves were worse here than elsewhere. I rejoice when I think that in four weeks' time I'll be going from the Piazzetta to the Lido with you or out to Murano, where they make glass pearls and beautiful jewellery. And the most beautiful piece will be for you.

Best wishes to your parents and a most tender kiss for you from

your Geert.'

Effi folded the letter up to put it back in the envelope.

'That's a very nice letter,' said Frau von Briest, 'and that he strikes the right balance in everything is one more virtue.'

'The right balance, yes, he does strike that.'

'Effi, dear, let me ask you one thing: would you prefer it if his letter *didn't* strike the right balance, would you rather he were more affectionate, perhaps rapturously affectionate?'

'No, no, Mama. Really and truly no, I wouldn't want that. It's better as it is.'

'It's better as it is. What does that sound like? You're so strange. And crying just now. Is there something bothering you? There's still time. Is it that you don't love Geert?'

'Why shouldn't I love him? I love Hulda and I love Bertha and I love Hertha. And I love old Niemeyer as well. And I don't need to say that I love you and Papa. I love everyone who means well by me, who's kind to me, who spoils me. And I expect Geert will spoil me as well. In his own way, of course. He's already said he's going to give me some jewellery in Venice. He has no idea that jewellery means nothing to me. I prefer climbing and swinging, most of all when it makes me afraid that something might tear or break and I might fall down. It wouldn't be the end of the world.'

'And do you perhaps also love your cousin Dagobert?'

'Yes, very much. He always cheers me up.'

'And would you have liked to marry him?'

'Marry him? For goodness sake, no. He's still not much more than a boy. Geert's a man, a fine figure of a man, a man with whom I can put on a show, a man who will be somebody. What an idea, Mama.'

'Well that's right, Effi, I'm pleased about that. But there's still something you have on your mind.'

'Perhaps.'

'Tell me.'

'You see, Mama, there's nothing wrong with the fact that he's older than me, it could perhaps be a good thing. He isn't old and he's fit and healthy and very soldierly and dashing. And I could almost say I'd have absolutely nothing against him if only . . . yes, if only he were a little different.'

'In what way, Effi?'

'Yes, in what way. Now you mustn't laugh at me. There are some things I've only recently picked up, over in the parsonage. We were talking about Innstetten, and suddenly Niemeyer furrowed his brow, but it was out of respect, out of admiration, and he said, "Yes, the Baron! He's a man of character, a man with principles."'

'He is that, Effi.'

'Certainly. Niemeyer even went on to say high principles. Oh, and
I . . . I haven't got any. And you see, Mama, that's what worries me
and torments me. He's so kind and good to me and considerate but
. . . I'm afraid of him.'

CHAPTER 5

The celebrations in Hohen-Cremmen were over; everyone had left,
including the young couple, who went on the evening of their wedding day.

Everyone had been happy with the eve-of-wedding party, especially
those who had played a part, and Hulda had been the toast of all the
young officers, both the Rathenow Hussars and their somewhat more
demanding comrades of Tsar Alexander's Regiment. Yes, everything
had gone well and smoothly, almost better than expected. Only Bertha
and Hertha had sobbed so much that Jahnke's Low German lines had
been as good as inaudible. But even that had done nothing to spoil
the occasion. Some of the more discriminating were even of the opinion that that was what really counted; forgetting lines, sobbing, being
incomprehensible—in *that* sign* (especially when it was such pretty
auburn heads) one always conquered most decisively. Cousin Dagobert
enjoyed a special triumph in the role he had written for himself. He
appeared as an assistant from Demuth's who had heard that the young
bride intended to leave for Italy immediately after the wedding and
was delivering a suitcase—which of course turned out to be a gigantic
box of chocolates from Hövel's.* The dancing went on until three in
the morning, during which old Briest, who had talked himself more
and more into a champagne mood, made all sorts of remarks about the
torch dance that was still the tradition at certain courts and the bizarre
custom of dancing for the garter,* neverending remarks that got worse
and worse, eventually going so far that a stop had to be put to them.
'Pull yourself together, Briest,' his wife had whispered to him in fairly
emphatic tones, 'you're not here to make risqué jokes but to look after
your guests. This is a wedding, not a hunting party.' To which Briest
replied that he didn't see much difference and, anyway, he was happy.

The wedding itself had also gone well. Niemeyer had given an
excellent sermon, and on the way back from the church to the manor

house one of the older gentlemen from Berlin, who was on the fringes of court society, had gone so far as to say how rich in talent a country such as ours was. 'I see that as a triumph of our schools and perhaps even more of our philosophy. When I think that this Niemeyer, an old village pastor who at first looked like someone from the poorhouse . . . yes, my friend, you tell me, did he not speak like a court chaplain? Such tact and his mastery of the use of antithesis, just like Kögel,* and more deeply felt than him. Kögel's too cold. Of course a man in Kögel's position has to be cold. What is it that causes disaster in people's lives? Heat, always heat.' The dignitary, still unmarried but, presumably because of that, in his fourth 'relationship', to whom these words were addressed, couldn't have agreed more. 'Too much heat! . . . Excellent . . . Oh, and remind me to tell you a story afterwards.'

*

The day after the wedding was a bright October day. The morning sun was shining but there was still an autumnal freshness on the air, and Briest, who had just taken breakfast with his wife, rose and, hands behind his back, stood in front of the open fire that was gradually dying down. Frau von Briest, a piece of needlework in her hands, also moved closer to the fire and said to Wilke, who had just come in to clear away the breakfast things, 'And now, Wilke, once you've cleared up the dining-room, that must be done first, then see to it that the cakes get carried out, the hazelnut tart to the parsonage and the bowl with the little cakes to the Jahnkes. And be careful with the glasses. I mean the thin crystal ones.'

Briest, already on his third cigarette, looked very well and declared that nothing did you so much good as a wedding, your own excepted, of course.

'I don't know how you can say that, Briest. It's news to me that it made you suffer. And I couldn't say why either.'

'You are a spoilsport, Luise. But I don't take anything amiss, not even that kind of thing. Anyway, who are we to talk, when we didn't even go away on honeymoon? Your father was against it. But now Effi's on her honeymoon. She's to be envied. Left on the ten o'clock train, they must be in Regensburg by now, and I assume he'll be showing her the artistic treasures of the Valhalla*—without getting off, of course. Innstetten's an excellent fellow but he is something of an art enthusiast, and Effi, our poor Effi's a child of nature. I fear he's going to torment Effi somewhat with his mania for art.'

'Every man torments his wife. And an enthusiasm for art is far from being the worst thing.'

'No, of course not; at least it's not something to quarrel about; it's a big question. And then people are all so different. You, yes, you would have been the right person for that. In fact you'd have been more suited to Innstetten than Effi. Pity, it's too late now.'

'What a compliment, apart from the fact that it's unsuitable. But however that may be, what's gone is gone. Now he's my son-in-law, and to keep harping on about our young days will get us nowhere.'

'I just wanted to get you in a lively mood.'

'How very kind. But not necessary. I *am* in a lively mood.'

'In a good mood too?'

'You could say that. But you mustn't spoil it. So what is it? I can see you've got something on your mind.'

'What did you think of Effi? What did you think about the whole business? She was so strange, half like a child and then so self-assured and not at all as unassuming as she ought to be towards a man like that. That can only be connected with the fact that she doesn't really know what she has in him. Or is it simply that she's not really in love with him? That would be bad. For all his good qualities, he's not a man with the easy manner to win her love.'

Frau von Briest remained silent and counted the stitches on her tapestry. Eventually she said, 'What you've just said, Briest, is the most sensible thing I've heard from you for the last three days, including your speech at the wedding dinner. I had misgivings too. But I think we can set our minds at rest.'

'She's poured out her heart to you?'

'I wouldn't put it like that. She does need to talk, but she doesn't feel the need to say what's really on her mind and deals with many things on her own. She's communicative and reserved at the same time, almost secretive; all in all, a very particular combination.'

'I agree with you entirely. So if she didn't tell you anything, how do you know?'

'I only said she didn't pour out her heart to me. That kind of general confession, getting everything off your chest, that's not her way. Everything came out in snatches and suddenly, and then it was all over just as quickly. But it seemed important to me precisely because it was so unintentional and seemed to come out, straight from the heart, by chance.'

'And when was this and what was the occasion?'

'It will have been three weeks ago now. We were in the garden busy with all sorts of things, large and small, for her trousseau, when Wilke brought a letter from Innstetten. She put it in her pocket and a quarter of an hour later I had to remind her that she had it. Then she read it but showed no sign of emotion at all. I was really concerned, I have to admit, in fact so concerned that I wanted to be sure, as far as you can be sure in these matters.'

'Too true, too true.'

'What do you mean by that?'

'Well, all I was saying was . . . But that doesn't matter. You go on, I'm all ears.'

'So I asked her straight out how things were, and since, given her character, I wanted to avoid a solemn tone and take everything lightly, almost making a joke of it, I casually asked whether she'd perhaps rather marry her cousin Dagobert, who'd been so attentive in Berlin.'

'And?'

'You should have seen her. Her immediate response was a snort of laughter. Her cousin, she said, was nothing but a big cadet in a lieutenant's uniform. And she couldn't even fall in love with a cadet, never mind marry one. And then she talked about Innstetten, whom she suddenly saw as the incarnation of all manly virtues.'

'And how do you explain that?'

'It's quite simple. However alert and vivacious and almost passionate she is, or perhaps because of that, she's not one of those people who are really focused on love, at least not on what truly deserves that name. She'll talk about it, even with emphasis and a tone of conviction, but only because she's read somewhere that love is the highest thing there is, the most beautiful, the most wonderful. Perhaps it's just something she got from that sentimental young woman Hulda, and is only repeating what she heard from her. But there's very little feeling in it. Perhaps that will all come, God forbid, but it's not there at the moment.'

'And what is there? What does she have?'

'From what I've observed myself and from what she's said, two things: a love of pleasure and ambition.'

'Well, that can happen. I find that reassuring.'

'I don't. Innstetten is determined to make a career for himself; he's not a pushy place-hunter, he's too well bred for that, but determined to make a career, and that will satisfy Effi's ambition.'

'Well then, that's all to the good.'

'Yes, it is good, but that's only the half of it. Her ambition will be satisfied, but will her inclination for play and adventure also be? I doubt it. Innstetten is ill-equipped to provide the hourly little diversion, the stimulus, anything that counters boredom, that mortal enemy of a bright young woman. He won't leave her without things to occupy her mind, he's too intelligent, too astute for that, but he won't make a great effort to amuse her. And the worst thing is that he won't even really consider the question of how to go about it. For a while that will be all right, no great harm will be done, but eventually she'll realize that and will feel hurt. And I don't know what will happen then. For, soft and yielding as she is, there's also something intemperate about her and she can take chances and damn the consequences.'

At that moment Wilke came in and told them he'd counted everything and nothing was missing; just one of the thin wine-glasses had been broken, but that had happened the previous day, when there'd been three cheers for the bride and groom—and Fräulein Hulda had clinked glasses too vigorously with Lieutenant Nienkerken.

'Of course, always asleep, even before she played Käthchen von Heilbronn, and of course it didn't get any better under the elder tree. A silly girl; I can't understand Nienkerken.'

'I can understand him perfectly.'

'But he can't marry her.'

'No.'

'So why then?'

'That's a big question, Luise.'

*

That was the day after the wedding. Three days later a little scribbled card arrived from Munich, the names just indicated by two letters.

'DEAR MAMA,

Went to the Pinakothek* this morning. Geert also wanted to go across to the other one—I've not written the name because I'm not sure how to spell it and I don't like to ask him. I have to say he's very kind and patient with me and explains everything. Anyway, everything's very beautiful, but exhausting. Things will probably ease off in Italy and get better. We're in the *Four Seasons*,* which made Geert say it was autumn outside but with me he had spring. I found that very thoughtful. He's very attentive anyway. Of course, I have to be that *as well*, particularly when he tells me something or explains something. He knows *everything*, so I don't need to look anything up. He goes into raptures about you two, especially Mama. He thought Hulda was a bit affected but was very taken with old Niemeyer.

A thousand kisses from your exhilarated but rather tired Effi.'

From then on cards like that arrived every day, from Innsbruck, from Verona, from Vicenza, from Padua, each one beginning: 'This morning we went to the famous gallery here,' or, if it wasn't the gallery, it was an arena or some 'Santa Maria' church with a name added. From Padua a proper letter came, along with the card.

'Yesterday we were in Vicenza. You have to see Vicenza because of Palladio;* Geert told me that everything modern had its roots in him. Only modern architecture, of course. In the hotel carriage here in Padua (where we arrived this morning) he muttered "In Padua there he buried lies,"* several times and was surprised when I told him I'd never heard those words before. Finally, however, he said that actually it was good, an advantage, that I didn't know anything about that. He's very fair. And above all he's really kind and patient with me and not at all superior and not at all old either. My feet are still aching and I find all the looking things up and standing for a long time very strenuous. But it has to be. I'm very much looking forward to Venice. We're staying there for five days, perhaps a whole week. Geert has already been going on to me about the pigeons in St Mark's Square and that you can buy bags of peas to feed the beautiful birds. There are supposed to be pictures of that, beautiful blond girls, "the same type as Hulda," he said. Which brings the Jahnke girls back to mind. Oh, what I would give to be sitting on a cart-shaft on our farm feeding *our* pigeons. But you mustn't kill the fantail with the big crop, I want to see him again. Oh, it's so lovely here. They say it's the loveliest place in the world.

Your happy but rather tired Effi.'

After she'd read the letter out, Frau von Briest said, 'The poor child, she's homesick.'

'Yes,' Briest said, 'she's homesick. All this confounded travelling round.'

'Why are you saying that now? You could have prevented it. But that's the way you are, being wise after the event. Locking the stable door after the horse has bolted.'

'Oh, Luise, don't go on at me like that. Effi's our daughter, but since the 3rd of October she's Baroness Innstetten. And if her husband, our son-in-law, wants to go on a honeymoon and take the opportunity to draw up a new catalogue of every gallery, I can't stop him. That's what's called being married.'

'So now you admit it. To me you've always denied, always denied, that the woman is in a situation where she has no choice.'

'Yes, Luise, I have. But what's the point of going into that now? It really is too big a question.'

CHAPTER 6

In the middle of November—they had got as far as Capri and Sorrento—Innstetten's leave ran out, and it was in his character and habits to be back on time to the day and the hour. So on the morning of the 14th he arrived in Berlin on the express, where cousin Dagobert was there to welcome him and Effi, and to suggest they should spend the two hours until the Stettin train left viewing the St Privat panorama* and then taking a light snack. Both suggestions were gratefully accepted. By midday they were back at the station, and after both Effi and Innstetten had delivered the usual invitation, that was fortunately never taken seriously, to 'come over and see us some time', they said farewell with friendly handshakes. As the train set off, Effi waved from the carriage. Then she made herself comfortable and closed her eyes, just straightening up from time to time and giving Innstetten her hand.

It was a pleasant journey, and the train arrived on time at Klein-Tantow,* from where a highway went to Kessin, that was about nine miles away. In the summer, during the holiday months, people preferred to go by water, taking an old paddle-steamer down the Kessine, a little river from which Kessin took its name; on the 1st of October, however, the *Phoenix*—of which people had long and vainly hoped it would remember its name and, when there were no passengers on board, go up in flames—stopped running, which was why Innstetten had sent a telegram to Kruse, his coachman, from Stettin: 'Klein-Tantow station five p.m. Open carriage if fine.'

And it *was* fine, and Kruse pulled up at the station with the open carriage and greeted the arrivals with the regulation formality of a baron's coachman.

'Well, Kruse, everything in order?'

'Yes, Herr Landrat.'

'Then get in please, Effi.' And while Effi was doing so and one of the station people was stowing a small suitcase with the coachman at the front, Innstetten gave instructions for the rest of their luggage to be sent on by the omnibus. Then he took his seat in the coach, asked—ingratiating himself with the locals—one of the bystanders for a light, and shouted to Kruse, 'Off we go, then, Kruse.' And off they went, over all the rails at the level-crossing, at an angle down the railway embankment, then immediately past an inn on the highway called the Prince Bismarck, since at that point the road branched, the left fork going to Varzin* and Bismarck's estate, the right to Kessin. Outside the inn was a man, broad-shouldered and of average height, wearing a fur coat and a fur cap that he took off in a very dignified manner when the Herr Landrat drove past. 'Who was that?' Effi asked. She was extremely interested in everything she could see, and therefore in the best of moods. 'He looked like a *starosta*,* though I have to admit I've never seen a *starosta* before.'

'That doesn't matter, Effi, you've hit the nail on the head. He really does look like a *starosta* and is something of the kind. He's half Polish, called Golchowski, and when we have an election or a hunt here he's really in his element. Actually he's a dubious customer I wouldn't trust an inch, and I suspect he has a lot to answer for. But he makes a great show of being loyal to the government, and when the Prince and his wife come over from Varzin he looks as if he'd like to throw himself down in front of their carriage. I know that the Prince finds him repulsive too. But what can one do? We can't fall out with him. He's got the whole area in his pocket, and there's no match for him at arranging an election. He's also said to be well off. And he lends money at usurious interest, which Poles don't normally do; in fact, the opposite as a rule.'

'But he looked good.'

'Yes, he looks good. Most of the people round here look good. A handsome type of people, but that's the most you can say about them. Your people from the Mark look more unprepossessing and morose, and they show less respect, in fact none at all, but their "yes" means yes and their "no" means no, and you can rely on them. Here everything's uncertain.'

'Why are you telling me this? I have to live among them here.'

'You won't, you won't hear or see much of them. Here town and country are very different, and you will only become acquainted with our good Kessiners.'

'Our good Kessiners. Is that ironic or are they really that good?'

'I wouldn't say they really are good, but they're different from the others; indeed, there's no similarity at all between them and the country-folk here.'

'How is that?'

'Because they're quite different people as regards both their origins and their connections. The people you will see inland from here are what are called Kashubs;* you may have heard of them, they're Slavs who've been settled here for a thousand years, probably even longer. But all those who live on the coast in the little seaports and trading towns are immigrants from far away, who have no concern for the Kashub hinterland because there's little they get from it and they're dependent on something quite different. What they're dependent on are the areas with which they trade, and since they trade the whole world over and are in contact with the whole world, you'll find people among them who come from all parts of the world. Even in our Kessin, despite the fact that it's just a small town.'

'But that's delightful, Geert. You keep talking about a small town, and now, if you haven't been exaggerating, I'm going to find a whole new world here. All sorts of exotic things. You did mean something like that, didn't you?'

He nodded.

'A whole new world, perhaps a negro or a Turk or even a Chinaman perhaps.'

'Even a Chinaman. How good you are at guessing. It's possible we do really still have one, but at least we used to; he's dead now and buried in a little railed-off plot beside the churchyard. If you're not frightened I'll show you his grave some time; it's among the dunes, nothing but marram grass round it, a few immortelles here and there, and all the time you can hear the sea. It's very beautiful and very eerie.'

'Yes, eerie, and I'd like to know more about it. But perhaps I'd better not, after all, I always get visions and dreams, and if, as I hope, I'm fast asleep tonight, I don't want a Chinaman appearing beside my bed.'

'No, he won't do that.'

'No, he won't do that. But listen, that sounds as if it were possible.

You're trying to make Kessin sound interesting, but you're going a bit too far. Are there lots of foreigners like that in Kessin?'

'A lot. The whole town consists of foreigners, people whose parents or grandparents lived somewhere else.'

'How very strange. Tell me more about it, please. But not something creepy this time. I think there's always something creepy about a Chinaman.'

'Yes, there is, isn't there,' Geert laughed. 'But all the rest are quite different, thank God, nothing but respectable people, perhaps with a bit too much of the merchant about them, a bit too much on the look-out for a profit, and always there with a dubious bill of exchange. Yes, you have to watch out with them. But otherwise very agreeable. And just to show you that I'm not pulling your leg, I'll give you a little sample, a kind of register, a list of characters.'

'Yes, Geert, do that.'

'Well, for example, not fifty yards from us—our gardens butt onto each other—there's Macpherson,* who hires out all sorts of machinery and excavators; he's a genuine Scot, a Highlander.'

'And does he wear the dress?'

'No, thank God. He's a wizened little manikin that neither his clan nor Walter Scott would be proud of. Then there's an old surgeon, Beza* by name, really he's only a barber; he's from Lisbon, the place the famous General de Meza* comes from—Meza, Beza, you can hear they're fellow countrymen. And then on the Embankment upstream—that's the quay where the boats tie up—we have a goldsmith called Stedingk, who comes from an old Swedish family; I even believe there are imperial counts of that name, and to go on, and this will be the last one on my list for the moment, there's good old Dr Hannemann, who is Danish of course, and was in Iceland for a long time and even wrote a little book about the most recent eruption of Hekla or Krabla.'

'But that's wonderful, Geert. That's like six novels, you can't even take it all in. First of all it sounds quite humdrum but then it turns out to be very special. And then, given that it's a seaport, there must be people who're not just surgeons or barbers or things like that. There must be captains here, a Flying Dutchman* or . . .'

'You're quite right there. We even have a captain who was a pirate with the Black Flags.'*

'Never heard of them. What are the Black Flags?'

'They're people on the other side of the world, in Tonkin and on the South Sea . . . But since he's back among people again he has perfect manners and is very amusing.'

'But I'd still be afraid of him.'

'Which is quite unnecessary, at any time, even when I'm out in the country or taking tea with the Prince, for, along with everything else, we've got our Rollo,* thank God . . .'

'Rollo?'

'Yes, Rollo. You'll be thinking, assuming you've heard about these things from Niemeyer or Jahnke, of the Norman duke, and there's something of that about our Rollo. But he's just a Newfoundland, a lovely dog that loves me and will love you, for Rollo's a connoisseur of people. And as long as you have him with you you'll be safe, and nothing will get close to you, neither living nor dead. But just look at that moon up there. Isn't it lovely?'

Effi, who was sitting there lost in thought, sat up and looked out to the right, where the moon had just risen, veiled in white cloud that was rapidly dispersing. The great copper disc was behind a copse of alders and cast its light over a wide stretch of water the Kessine formed there. Or perhaps it was already the lagoon that was fed by the open sea.

Effi was in a daze. 'Yes, you're right, Geert, it is lovely; but there's something eerie about it as well. I never had that impression in Italy, not even when we crossed from Mestre to Venice. There was water there too, and marshes and moonlight, and I thought the bridge might collapse, but it wasn't as ghostly. Why is it? Is that the Northern Lights?'

Innstetten laughed. 'We're seventy miles to the north of Hohen-Cremmen here and you'll have to wait a while before the first polar bear comes. I think it's all been too much for your nerves, the long journey and then the St Privat panorama and the story of the Chinaman.'

'But you didn't tell me the story.'

'No, I only mentioned him. But just the mention of a Chinaman's a story all on its own . . .'

'Yes,' she laughed.

'And, anyway, you'll soon be over it . . . Do you see that house with the light in front? That's the smithy. The road curves there. And once we're round the curve you'll see the tower of Kessin or rather, both of them . . .'

'It has two?'

'Yes. Kessin's taking off. It has a Catholic church as well now.'

*

Half-an-hour later the carriage stopped at the Landrat's house, that was right at the other end of the town. It was a simple, rather old-fashioned half-timbered house; its façade faced the main street leading out to the bathing places, while the gable looked out on a little wood, between the town and the dunes, that they called the Plantation. This old-fashioned, half-timbered house was Innstetten's private dwelling, not the Landrat's office; that was on the other side of the street.

Kruse's announcement of their arrival with three cracks of the whip was unnecessary, the occupants had long been looking out of the door and windows, and even before the carriage drew up they had all gathered on the stone threshold that took in the whole width of the pavement. Rollo was at the front, and as soon as the carriage halted he started to run round it. First of all Innstetten helped his young wife to alight, and then, giving her his arm, walked with a friendly greeting past the servants, who followed the young couple into the hall with its splendid old cupboards. The parlourmaid, a pretty woman past the first flush of youth, whose buxom figure suited her almost as well as the dainty little cap on her blond hair, helped her new mistress take off her muff and was bending down to take off her fur-lined rubber boots. But before she could do so Innstetten said, 'It will be best if I introduce you to the whole household here, apart from Frau Kruse, who—I presume she's with her inevitable black hen—doesn't like to appear in public.' They all smiled. 'But let's forget Frau Kruse . . . this here is my old Friedrich, who was already with me when I was at university . . . Weren't you, Friedrich, the good old days . . . and this here is Johanna, a fellow countrywoman from the Mark, if you're willing to count people from the Pasewalk area as such, and this is Christel, to whom we entrust our bodily well-being at lunchtime and in the evening and who, I can assure you, really knows how to cook. And this here is Rollo. Well, Rollo, how are things?'

Rollo seemed to have been waiting to be addressed personally, for the moment he heard his name he gave a yelp of pleasure, stood up, and put his paws on his master's shoulders.

'All right, Rollo, all right. But look, this is the woman; I told you about her and I told her that you were a handsome beast and would protect her.' And now Rollo took his paws away and sat down in front of Innstetten, at the same time looking up appraisingly at the young woman. And when she held out her hand to him, he gave it a friendly lick.

During all these introductions Effi had had time to look around. She was spellbound by everything she saw and at the same time dazzled by the profusion of light. Two paraffin lamps with red shades, a wedding present from Niemeyer, were on a folding table between two oak wardrobes, in front of them the tea things with the flame under the kettle already lit. But there were many, many other things, some very strange, as well as all this. There were three beams running across the hall, dividing the ceiling up into separate sections; from the one nearest the front door a ship under full sail with a high afterdeck and gun-ports was hanging, whilst farther back a huge fish seemed to be swimming through the air. Taking her umbrella, that she was still holding, she gave the monster a gentle prod so that it started to swing slowly. 'What is that, Geert?' she asked.

'That's a shark.'

'And what's that right at the back there, that looks like a huge cigar outside a tobacconist's?'

'That's a young crocodile. But you'll be able to see everything better and more clearly in the morning; come, let's have a cup of tea now. Despite all the travelling-rugs you'll have been freezing. It was bitterly cold at the end.'

He offered Effi his arm and, while the two maids withdrew and only Friedrich and Rollo followed them, they went to the left, into the master's living room-cum-study. Effi was just as surprised there as in the hall, but before she could say anything about it Innstetten drew back the curtain over a door beyond which there was another, larger room with a view out to the courtyard and garden.

'So this is yours now, Effi. Friedrich and Johanna have arranged it as far as possible according to my instructions. I think it's tolerable and I'll be happy if you like it as well.'

She took her arm out of his and stood on tiptoe to give him a heartfelt kiss.

'How you pamper me, poor little thing that I am. The piano there and that carpet, I think it must be Turkish, and that bowl with the fish, and then the table with those flowers. Pampering, pampering everywhere.'

'Yes, Effi dear, that's something you're going to have to get used to, being young and pretty and charming, as the Kessiners must already have heard, though God knows from where. The flowers on that table at least have nothing to do with me. Where did they come from, Friedrich?'

'From Herr Gieshübler, the chemist . . . There's a card with them.'

'Ah, Gieshübler, Alonzo Gieshübler,'* Innstetten said, handing the card with the rather foreign-sounding Christian name to Effi with an almost unreserved laugh. 'Gieshübler, I forgot to tell you about him—he has a doctorate, by the way, but doesn't like people using the title, it just annoys the real doctors, he says, and he's probably right about that. Well, I think you'll get to know him, and that very soon; he's a capital fellow, the best we have round here, cultured, a real character, and above all a perfect dear, which is always the main thing. But that's enough of that, let's sit down and drink our tea. But where? Here in your room or over there in mine? There's no other choice. Small and cramped is my cottage.'*

Without giving the question any thought, she sat down on a little corner sofa. 'Today we'll stay here, today you're my guest. Or should we do it this way: tea regularly in my room, breakfast in yours? Then each of us will have a turn, and I'm curious to know which I'm going to like best.'

'That's a question of morning and evening.'

'Of course. But how it arises or, rather, how we rise to it, that's the point.'

And she laughed and cuddled up to him and tried to kiss his hand.

'No, Effi, for heaven's sake, no, not like that. I don't want to be someone who commands your respect, that's what I am for the Kessiners. For you I'm . . .'

'What, then?'

'Oh, leave it. There's no way I'm going to tell you that.'

CHAPTER 7

It was already broad daylight when Effi woke the next morning. She had difficulty finding her bearings. Where was she? Of course, in Kessin, in the house of the Landrat, von Innstetten, and she was his wife, Baroness Innstetten. Sitting up, she looked round, full of curiosity; the previous evening she'd been too tired to take in properly all the things, part strange, part old-fashioned, around her. There were two pillars supporting the ceiling beams and green curtains separated off the alcove-like bed-closet from the rest of the room; the middle curtain was missing, or had been drawn back, allowing her to orientate herself from the comfort of her bed. There, between the two windows, was the tall pier-glass, while to the right of it, against the wall separating the bedroom from the entrance hall, the big black stove towered up which (that much she had noticed the previous evening) was fuelled in the old way from outside. She could feel the heat from it pouring across the room. How lovely it was to be in your own house; she'd never felt so at ease during the whole of their trip, not even in Sorrento.

But where was Innstetten? Everything was quiet, no one around. All she could hear was the tick-tock of a little pendulum clock and now and then a dull thud from the stove, from which she assumed a few more logs were being put in from the hall. It gradually came back to mind that the previous evening Geert had talked about an electric bell that it then didn't take her long to locate; right beside her pillow was a little ivory button that she now pressed gently.

Immediately Johanna appeared. 'You rang, Madam?'

'Oh, Johanna, I think I must have overslept. It must be quite late.'

'Just struck nine.'

'And . . .'—she simply couldn't bring herself to say, 'my husband'—'the Master, he must have been very quiet; I didn't hear anything.'

'He definitely was. And Madam will have slept soundly. After that long journey . . .'

'Yes, I certainly did. And the Master, does he always get up that early?'

'Always, Ma'am. He's very strict about that; he can't bear sleeping in, and when he goes to his room the stove must be warm and his coffee mustn't be long in coming either.'

'So he's already had his breakfast?'

'Oh, no, Ma'am . . . the Master . . .'

Effi sensed that she shouldn't have asked that, shouldn't have suggested that Innstetten might not have waited for her. She felt she ought to make up for her mistake, as far as possible, and once she was out of bed and sitting at the mirror she took up the conversation again and said, 'And the Master's right. Early to rise, that was the rule in my parents' house. When people sleep until late in the morning the whole day's topsy-turvy. But he won't be so severe on me. I couldn't get to sleep for quite a while last night and I was even a little frightened.'

'What a thing to say, Ma'am! What was it?'

'There was a very odd noise above me. At first it sounded like long dresses with trains dragging across the floorboards, and I was so worked up I thought I could see little white satin shoes a couple of times. It was as if people were dancing upstairs, but very quietly.'

While she was saying this, Johanna kept looking over the young woman's shoulder at the high, narrow mirror in order to be able to observe Effi's expression better. Then she said, 'Yes, that's the upstairs chamber. We used to hear it in the kitchen as well. But we don't any more, we've got used to it.'

'Is there anything special about it?'

'Oh, God forbid, no. For a while we couldn't really say where it came from and the Pastor looked embarrassed, even though Dr Gieshübler just laughed. But now we know it's the curtains. The chamber's a bit musty and mouldy, so the windows are always left open, except when there happens to be a storm blowing. So there's almost always a strong draught there and the old white curtains, that are much too long anyway, sweep back and forward across the floorboards. It sounds like silk dresses or satin shoes, as Madam just said.'

'Of course it'll be that. But I don't understand why the curtains haven't been taken down. Or they could be shortened. It's such a strange noise, it gets on your nerves. But now get that little cloth, Johanna, and dab my forehead. Or, no, get the cologne spray out of my suitcase . . . Oh, that's lovely, that is refreshing. Now I'll go through. He's still here, isn't he, or has he gone out already?'

'The Master has been out already, over in the office, I think. But he's been back for a quarter of an hour now. I'll tell Friedrich he can bring breakfast.'

With that Johanna left the room and Effi, after another glance in the mirror, went across the entrance hall, that had lost a lot of the previous evening's magic in the light of day, to Geert's room.

He was sitting at his roll-top desk. It was rather cumbersome, but he was attached to it as it came from the family home. Effi stood behind him and embraced and kissed him before he could get up from his chair.

'Already?'

'Already you say. Just to make fun of me, of course.'

Innstetten shook his head. 'Why would I do that?' But Effi was enjoying accusing herself and refused to accept that his 'already' wasn't meant ironically. 'You must remember from our journey that I never kept you waiting in the morning. During the day, well, yes, but that's different. It's true that I'm not very punctual, but I'm not a late riser. In that respect I think my parents brought me up very well.'

'In that respect? In all respects, my sweet little Effi.'

'You're just saying that because it's still our honeymoon ... but no, we're past that now. Good heavens, Geert, I've only just realized that we've already been married for over six weeks, for six weeks and a day. Ah, now that is different; in that case I don't look on it as flattery, I look on it as the truth.'

At that moment Friedrich came in, bringing the coffee. The break-fast table was placed diagonally in front of a little, right-angled sofa that filled one corner of the room. They both sat down there.

'The coffee's excellent,' Effi said, at the same time examining the room and furnishings. 'That's hotel coffee or like what we had at Bottegone* ... you remember, in Florence, with a view of the cath-edral. I must tell Mama about it when I write to her, we don't have coffee like this in Hohen-Cremmen. And anyway, Geert, now I can see what a superior household I've married into. At home everything just gets done any old way.'

'Don't be silly, Effi. I've never seen a better-run household than yours.'

'And then your house. When Papa bought himself a new rifle cabi-net and hung a buffalo head over his desk with a portrait of Wrangel* underneath it (he'd been the old man's adjutant) I thought what he'd done was marvellous; but compared with what I see when I look round here, all the glories of Hohen-Cremmen are just paltry and ordinary. I don't know what to compare all this with; only yesterday evening, when I just gave it a cursory glance, all kinds of thoughts came to me.'

'What thoughts, if I may ask?'

'Yes, what thoughts? But you mustn't laugh at them. I once had a picture-book with a Persian or Indian prince (he was wearing a tur-ban) sitting cross-legged on a red silk cushion, and behind him there was a big roll of silk as well, billowing out on either side, and the wall behind the Indian prince was bristling with swords and daggers, with leopard-skins and shields and long Turkish rifles. That's just what it looks like here, and if you cross your legs the similarity will be complete.'

'Effi, you're a delightful, darling creature. You've no idea how much I think that, and how I'd like to show you all the time that I think that.'

'Well, there's plenty of time for that; I'm only seventeen and don't intend to die just yet.'

'Not before I do, at the very least. Of course, were I to die I'd most like to take you with me. I don't want to leave you to anyone else; what do you say to that?'

'I'll have to think about that. Or, rather, let's just forget it. I don't like talking about death, I'm all for life. On the way here you told me all sorts of strange things about the town and the countryside. I can see that everything here's different from in Hohen-Cremmen and Schwantikow, but in your "good old Kessin", as you keep on calling it, we must have some social life. Are there our kind of people in the town?'

'No, Effi dear; in that respect you're going to be very disappointed. There are a few noble families in the vicinity whom you will get to know, but nothing at all in the town.'

'Nothing at all? I can't believe that. There are three thousand people here, and among those three thousand there must be, apart from ordinary people like Beza the barber (that was his name, wasn't it?), an elite, notables, that kind of thing.'

Innstetten laughed. 'Yes, notables, we have some of those. But when you have a good look at them, they don't amount to much. We have a pastor, of course, and a district judge and a headmaster and a pilot commander, in all there must be a dozen such people with official positions, but most of them are, as the saying goes, good people but poor musicians.* And all that leaves is just consuls.'*

'Just consuls. Oh, come now, Geert, how can you say "just consuls"? Consul, that's something very high, very great, I'd almost say something awesome, they're the people carrying the bundles of rods with, I think, an axe sticking out.'

'Not quite, Effi. They're called lictors.'

'That's right, they're called lictors. But consuls, that's also something very grand to do with the law. Brutus was a consul.'

'Yes, Brutus was a consul. But ours aren't at all like him, all they do is deal in sugar and coffee, or break open a crate of oranges and sell them to you at ten pfennigs each.'

'That's not possible.'

'It's certain, even. They're sharp little merchants who give advice to foreign ships that arrive here and don't know how to sort out some commercial matter, and when they've given this advice and assisted some Dutch or Portuguese ship they eventually become the accredited representatives of those foreign states, with the result that here in Kessin we have just as many consuls as they have ambassadors in Berlin, and when there's some special day, and there are lots of those here, all the flags are raised, and if it's a morning with bright sunshine you'll see the flags of the whole of Europe flying from our roofs, and the Stars and Stripes and the Chinese dragon as well.'

'You're in the mood for mockery this morning, Geert. You may well be right, but I for my part, simple young woman that I am, have to admit that I find all that delightful, and our towns in the Havelland are nothing compared to it. When they celebrate the Emperor's birthday it's always just black-and-white flags,* with at most a little bit of red here and there, but that's no comparison with the world of flags you've told me about. Anyway, as I've already said, I keep finding that there's something foreign in everything here, and so far there's nothing I've heard or seen that I haven't found in a way amazing, that strange ship in the hall yesterday evening with the shark and the crocodile behind it, and your own room here. Everything so oriental and, I repeat, like some Indian prince's . . .'

'If you insist. Congratulations, Princess . . .'

'And then that upper chamber with the long curtains that sweep over the floorboards.'

'But what do you know about the upper chamber, Effi?'

'Nothing apart from what I've just told you. I woke up during the night, and for what must have been an hour it seemed as if I could hear shoes sliding across the ground, and as if people were dancing and almost like music as well. But all very quiet. And I told Johanna about it this morning, just as an excuse for sleeping in so long. And she then said it came from the long curtains in the upper chamber. I think we should simply cut something off the curtains, or at least close the windows; the weather's going to be pretty stormy soon anyway. The middle of November's the time for that.'

Innstetten stared into space, slightly embarrassed, apparently unsure whether to reply to all this. Eventually he decided not to go into it. 'You're right, Effi, we'll shorten the long curtains up there.

But there's no hurry, especially since it's not certain it'll make any difference. It could be something else, in the chimney, or woodworm, or a polecat. We do have polecats here. But before we start making changes you must have a look round at the way things are in the house, under my guidance, of course; it'll only take us a quarter of an hour. And then you must get dressed up, just a little bit, you're at your most charming as you are—get dressed up for our friend Gieshübler; it's past ten now, and if I know him he'll report here at eleven, or at the latest midday, to lay his most humble respects at your feet. That, you see, is the kind of language he indulges in. For all that he is, as I told you, an excellent fellow who will become your friend, if I know anything about you and him.'

CHAPTER 8

It was well past eleven, but Gieshübler had still not arrived. 'I can't wait any longer,' Geert had said, 'duty calls. If Gieshübler does come, be as accommodating as you can and everything will be fine. He mustn't feel embarrassed, once he's confused he can find it impossible to get a word out, or he says the strangest things; but if you can gain his confidence and get him in a good mood he can talk the hind legs off a donkey. You'll manage that, I'm sure. Don't expect me back before three, there's all sorts of things I have to do over there. As for the room upstairs, we'll think about that; it'll probably be best if we leave things as they are.'

With that Innstetten went and left his young wife by herself. She sat, leaning back slightly, in a snug corner by the window, supporting herself, as she looked out, with her left arm on a little shelf that had been drawn out of the roll-top desk. The street was the main way to the beach, which meant there was plenty going on there in the summer but now, in the middle of November, it was empty and quiet, and just a few poor children, whose parents lived in some thatched houses on the edge of the Plantation, clattered past the Innstettens' house in their wooden clogs. But Effi was unaffected by this solitude, for her imagination was still occupied with the strange things she'd just seen on her tour of inspection round the house. The inspection had started with the kitchen that had a modern stove and an electric cable running across the ceiling, going as far as the maid's room—both only recently installed. Effi had been pleased when Innstetten told her about these improvements, but then they had gone into the hall and from there out into the courtyard, the nearer part of which wasn't much more than a fairly narrow passageway between two wings. These wings housed everything appertaining to the management of the household: on the right the maid's room, the servant's room, the scullery, on the left the Kruses' flat between the stable and the coach-house. The chickens were kept in a shed above the Kruses', and there was a flap in the roof of the stable allowing the pigeons to fly in and out. Effi had looked at all this with interest, but that interest was nothing compared with what she felt when, going back into the house, Innstetten led the way up the stairs. They were crooked and dark; the landing to which they led, on the other hand, was almost cheerful, since it had plenty of light and enjoyed a good view out over the countryside: on the one side, of a Dutch windmill high on one of the dunes beyond the Plantation and the roofs at the edge of the town; on the other side, of the Kessine that here, immediately before it joined the sea, was pretty wide and imposing. It made an impression that couldn't be ignored, and Effi hadn't hesitated to express her pleasure in it. 'Yes, very beautiful, very picturesque,' was all Innstetten had said in reply, and then opened some rather crooked double doors on the right that led into the so-called upper chamber. This took in the whole of that storey; the front and back windows were open and the aforementioned curtains were flapping to and fro in the strong draught. A chimney with a large stone slab jutted out from one of the long walls, while there were a few tin lamps on the wall opposite, each with two openings, just as in the hall below, but all tarnished and uncared-for. Effi was somewhat disappointed and said so, declaring that instead of the shabby, desolate chamber she'd rather see the rooms on the other side of the landing. 'They're really nothing at all,' Innstetten had replied, but still opened the doors. There were four one-windowed rooms, all painted yellow, like the chamber, and equally empty. Only in the one there were three wicker chairs with the seats worn through, and a little picture, half the length of a finger, had been stuck on the arm of one; it represented a Chinaman, in a blue coat with baggy yellow pantaloons and a flat hat on his head. Effi looked at it and said, 'What's the Chinaman doing here?' Innstetten seemed surprised by the picture himself and assured her he knew nothing about it. 'Christel will have stuck it there, or Johanna. Just

for fun. You can see it's been cut out of a children's picture-book.'
Effi thought so too, and was only puzzled that Innstetten took it all
so seriously, as if there were something to it after all. After that she'd
had another look at the chamber and said what a pity it was that it
was all so empty. 'We only have three rooms downstairs, and if someone comes to visit us we won't know what to do with them. Don't
you think we could make two nice guest-rooms out of the chamber?
That would be something for Mama; she could sleep at the back and
she'd have the view of the river and the two breakwaters, and in front
there'd be the town and the Dutch windmill. In Hohen-Cremmen
we still have just a post windmill. Come on, tell me what you think of
that? I imagine Mama will be visiting us next May.'

Innstetten agreed to everything and finally said, 'That's all very well,
but I think that after all it will be better if we put your Mama up across
the road in the Landrat's office; the whole of the first floor's empty
there, just as it is here, and she'd have more space to herself over there.'

*

That was the result of the first tour of the house; then Effi had
made herself presentable, though not quite as quickly as Innstetten
had assumed, and now she was sitting in her husband's room, her
thoughts occupied alternately with the little Chinaman upstairs and
Gieshübler, who still hadn't arrived. A quarter of an hour ago a little
gentleman with shoulders so crooked he was almost deformed, and
wearing a short, elegant fur coat and a high top-hat brushed very
smooth, had walked past on the other side of the street and looked
across at her window. But that couldn't have been Herr Gieshübler!
No, the man with the crooked shoulders, who at the same time had
something so distinguished about him, must have been the high-
court judge, and she recalled actually seeing one at a soirée of her
Aunt Therese's, until she suddenly remembered that Kessin only had
a district court.

While she was still pursuing these reflections their subject, who
had clearly just been taking a morning stroll—or plucking up his
courage—round the Plantation, came into view again, and one minute
later Friedrich appeared to announce Herr Doktor Gieshübler, the
chemist.

'Show him in, please.'

The poor young woman's heart was pounding. It was the first time she had to appear as the lady of the house, and as the first lady of the town at that.

Having helped Gieshübler out of his fur coat, Friedrich opened the door again.

Effi held out her hand to the man as he came in, looking embarrassed, and he grasped and kissed it with some fervour. The young woman seemed to have made a great and immediate impression on him.

'My husband has already told me . . . but I'm receiving you in his room . . . he's over in the office and can be back any moment . . . May I ask you to be so good as to come to my room?'

Gieshübler followed Effi as she led the way to the neighbouring room and pointed to one of the armchairs, sitting down on the sofa herself. 'I'm delighted to have the opportunity to tell you what pleasure your lovely flowers and your card gave me yesterday. I immediately stopped feeling a stranger here, and when I told Innstetten that, he said we were sure to be good friends.'

'He said that, did he? The Herr Landrat is very kind. Yes, the Herr Landrat and you, Frau Baronin, there are two dear people who have come together, if you will allow me to say so. For what your husband is like I know, and what you are like, Frau Baronin, I can see.'

'I only hope you're not looking on me with too kindly an eye. I'm so very young, and young people . . .'

'Oh, my dear Madam, say nothing against young people. With all their faults, young people are still fine and charming, and old people, for all their virtues, are not up to much. Though in fact I'm not qualified to say much about this from personal experience; about being old, yes, but not about being young, for I've never really been young. People like me never are young. And that, I think I may say, is the saddest aspect of the whole business. You lack real courage, you have no confidence in yourself, you hardly dare ask a lady to dance because you want to save her the embarrassment, and so the years pass and you grow old and your life has been poor and empty.'

Effi took his hand. 'Oh, you mustn't say things like that. We women aren't that bad.'

'Oh no, certainly not . . .'

'And when I think back', Effi went on, 'to all the experiences I've had . . . they don't amount to a lot, since I haven't got round very much and have always lived out in the country . . . then it seems to me that we like what is likeable. And I can see at once that you're different from other people, we women have a sharp eye for that. Perhaps your name is part of that, in your case. That was something our old Pastor Niemeyer used to maintain; there was, he used to say, something mysteriously defining about a name, especially a person's Christian name, and for me Alonzo Gieshübler opens up a whole new world, yes, I'd almost say, if you'll allow, that Alonzo is a romantic name; it comes in *Preziosa*.'*

Gieshübler smiled with a quite uncommon feeling of pleasure, and found the courage to put down the top-hat, that was much too tall in relation to its owner and that he'd been holding in his hand until then. 'Yes, my dear lady, you're quite right there.'

'Oh, I understand. I've heard about all these consuls there are supposed to be in Kessin, and I suspect your father met the daughter of a seafaring *capitano* in the house of the Spanish consul, some beautiful woman from Andalusia, I assume. Women from Andalusia are always beautiful.'

'You assume quite correctly, my dear Madam. And my mother truly was a beautiful woman, poor proof of it that I am. But she was still alive when your husband came here three years ago, and still had her fiery looks. He will confirm what I've just said. Personally I'm more of a Gieshübler, their looks aren't much but they're a respectable family. We've been here for four generations now, a good hundred years, and if there were a nobility for chemists . . .'

'You would belong to it. And I, for my part, take it as proven, and even as proven without qualification. That is easiest for us who come from the old families, because we—at least this is how I was brought up by my father, and by my mother too—are happy to acknowledge any true way of thinking, whoever it comes from. I was born a Briest and I'm descended from the Briest who, on the day before the Battle of Fehrbellin,* carried out the attack on Rathenow that you have perhaps heard of . . .'

'Oh, certainly, Frau Baronin, that's my speciality.'

'So I'm a Briest. And my father, it must have been more than a hundred times he's said to me, Effi (that's what I'm called), Effi, this is where it is, *here*, and when Froben* swapped his horse for the Elector's, he belonged to the nobility, and when Luther* said "Here I stand," he truly did belong to the nobility. And I think Innstetten,

Herr Gieshübler, was quite right when he assured me that we would
be good friends.'

What Gieshübler would now most have liked to do would have
been to make a declaration of love and ask to be allowed to fight
and die for her, as El Cid or some other *campeador*. Since all of that
was out of the question, and his heart could stand it no longer, he
stood up, looked for his hat, that he fortunately found, and, after
kissing her hand once more, quickly withdrew without uttering
another word.

CHAPTER 9

Such was Effi's first day in Kessin. Innstetten allowed her half a week
to give her time to get settled in and write her various letters to
Hohen-Cremmen, to her Mama, to Hulda and the twins; but then the
visits in the town had to begin, some of which were made (unusually,
but it happened to be raining, so it was permissible) in a closed carriage. Once they were completed, it was the turn of the gentry in the
surrounding countryside. That took longer since, given the distances,
mostly only a single visit could be made on any one day. First they
went to the Borckes* in Rothenmoor, then to Morgnitz, Dabergotz,
and Kroschentin, where they made duty-calls on the Ahlemanns,
Jatzkows, and Grasenabbs.* A few further visits came later, including
one to old Baron Güldenklee* in Papenhagen. The impression they
made on Effi was the same everywhere: mediocre people, mostly of
dubious friendliness, who, while pretending to talk about Bismarck
and the Crown Princess,* were actually just scrutinizing Effi's outfit,
that some thought too pretentious for such a young lady and others
too showy for a lady of standing. In everything, they told each other,
you could see the influence of Berlin: a penchant for outward appearances, and remarkable embarrassment and uncertainty when it came
to dealing with big questions. At the Borckes' in Rothenmoor, and
the families in Morgnitz and Dabergotz as well, she was adjudged
to be 'afflicted with rationalism', at the Grasenabbs' in Kroschentin,
however, she was immediately declared an 'atheist'. Old Frau von
Grasenabb, a south German (née Stiefel von Stiefelstein),* did at
least make a feeble attempt to rescue Effi as a deist; however, Sidonie
von Grasenabb, an old maid of forty-three, had brusquely broken in,

'Simply an atheist I tell you, Mother, not one iota less, and that's that,' at which the old woman, who was afraid of her own daughter, held her tongue.

*

The whole round had lasted more or less two weeks, and it was the 2nd of December and already late in the day when they returned to Kessin from the final visit. That had been to the Güldenklees in Papenhagen, and Innstetten had found it impossible to avoid having a political discussion with old Güldenklee. 'Yes, my dear Landrat, when I think how times have changed. A whole generation ago, or something like that, there was another 2nd of December,* and Louis, Napoleon's nephew—*if* that's what he was and he didn't come from somewhere quite different—fired grapeshot on the Paris mob. Well, we can forgive him that, he was the right fellow for that kind of thing, and I stick by the motto, "Every man does as well or as badly as he deserves." But losing all sense of proportion later on and picking a quarrel out of the blue with *us* in '70, well, Baron, that was, how shall I put it, that was an impertinence. And he paid for it. The old man up there won't be mocked, *he's* on our side.'

'Yes,' Innstetten said, being sensible enough to appear to take that kind of blinkered nationalism seriously. 'The hero and conqueror of Saarbrücken* didn't know what he was doing. But you mustn't judge him too harshly as a person. After all, who was master in his house? No one. I'm already preparing to put the reins in other hands myself, and Louis Napoleon, well, he was putty in the hands of his Catholic—or should we say Jesuit—wife.'

'Putty in the hands of his wife, who then cocked a snook at him. Of course he was *that*, Innstetten. But surely you're not saying this to try and rescue the reputation of that marionette? History has pronounced its verdict on him. Though in fact it has never been proved'—as he spoke, his eye somewhat anxiously sought that of his better half—'whether petticoat government can't actually be seen as something positive; always assuming the woman's right for it, of course. But who was this woman? She wasn't a woman at all, at best she was a lady, and that tells us everything; when you say "lady" the word always smacks of something else. This Eugénie*—I'll pass over her relation-ship with that Jewish banker, I can't stand arrogant moralizers—had something of the cabaret artiste about her, and if the city where she lived was Babylon, then she was the woman of Babylon. I won't put it any more clearly than that, for I know'—he bowed to Effi—'what is due to German women. And please forgive me, dear Madam, for even having touched on these matters in your presence at all.'

Such had been the way the conversation had gone, after they'd talked about the elections, Nobiling's attempt* on the Emperor's life, and the price of oilseed rape, and now Innstetten and Effi were back home chatting for half an hour. The two housemaids were already in bed, for it was close on midnight.

Innstetten, in a smoking jacket and morocco-leather slippers, was walking up and down; Effi was still in her formal attire, fan and gloves beside her.

'Yes,' Innstetten said, coming to a halt, 'I think this is a day we really ought to celebrate, though how I couldn't say. Should I play you a victory march or set the shark out there swinging or carry you across the hall in triumph? Something ought to happen for, as I'm sure you're aware, that was our last visit.'

'It was, thank God,' Effi said. 'But the feeling that we shall have some peace and quiet from now on is, I think, celebration enough. You could give me a kiss, though, but that never occurs to you. Not a single caress on all that long way, you just sat there, cold as a snowman. Puffing away at your cigar.'

'That's enough of that, I'll mend my ways soon enough, what I want to know at the moment is what you think about the whole question of the people with whom we should mix. Do you feel attracted to one or other of the families? Have the Borckes defeated the Grasenabbs or vice versa, or do you go for old Güldenklee? What he said about Eugénie sounded very noble and pure.'

'Well, well, Herr von Innstetten, you can be catty too. That's quite a different Geert from the one I know.'

'And if the local gentry aren't up to it,' Innstetten went on unperturbed, 'how do you feel about the notables here in Kessin? How do you feel about the Club? That, when it comes down to it, is the vital question. Recently I saw you chatting to our reserve-lieutenant district judge, a neat little man one could perhaps get on with, if only he would abandon the idea that it was his appearance on the flank that led to the capture of Le Bourget.* And his wife! She's supposed to be the best player of boston* and also has the prettiest chips. But again, Effi, how are things going to be in Kessin? Will you settle in? Will you become a popular figure and secure me a majority if I want to get into the Reichstag? Or are you in favour of the life of a recluse, of shutting yourself off from Kessin society, both town and country?'

'I'll probably go for the life of a recluse, if the Moor Pharmacy doesn't draw me out of it. In which case I'll probably sink even lower in Sidonie's estimation, but I'll just have to accept that; it's a battle that still has to be fought. I put everything on Gieshübler. It does sound a bit odd, but he really is the only person worth talking to, the only real human being here.'

'He is that,' Innstetten said. 'How good you are at choosing!'

'Would I have got you otherwise?' Effi said, clinging on to his arm.

*

That was on the 2nd of December. One week later Bismarck was in Varzin, and Innstetten knew that until Christmas and perhaps beyond the quiet days were over for him.

The Prince had a liking for him that went back to the time when they had both been in Versailles, and frequently invited him to dine when he had visitors, but also by himself, for the youthful Landrat, with his presence and intelligence, was also a favourite of the Princess.

The first invitation came on the fourteenth. Snow was lying, so Innstetten decided to do the almost two-hour journey to the station by sleigh; from there it was an hour by train to Varzin. 'Don't wait up for me, Effi. I won't be back before midnight; it'll probably be two or even later. But I won't disturb you. Farewell, I'll see you tomorrow morning.' And with that he got into the sleigh and the two dun Graditzers* flew off through the town and then out into the country, heading for the station.

That was their first long separation, almost twelve hours. Poor Effi. How should she spend the evening? Early to bed, that was dangerous, then she would wake up and not be able to get back to sleep again, listening for every sound. No, first of all get really tired and then sleep soundly, that was best. She wrote a letter to her Mama and then went to see Frau Kruse, for whose melancholia—she often sat late into the night with the black hen in her lap—she felt great sympathy. But not for one moment did the woman sitting still in her overheated room, silently brooding, respond to the friendly gesture, so that Effi, as soon as she realized her visit was felt more as a disturbance than as something to be enjoyed, left again, merely asking if there was anything she could get the poor woman. She, however, refused the offer.

By now it was evening and the lamp was already on. Effi stood at the window of her room and looked out at the little wood, the branches glittering with snow. She was quite engrossed by the scene and didn't concern herself with what was happening in the room behind her. When she looked round again she saw that Friedrich had softly and silently laid the table by the sofa. 'Oh yes, supper . . . I suppose I'll have to sit down.' But she found she just didn't have the appetite for it, so she got up and read through the letter she'd written to her Mama again. If she'd felt lonely before, she now felt twice as lonely. What wouldn't she have given for the two Jahnke redheads to come in, or even Hulda. She was always so sentimental, of course, and mostly preoccupied with her triumphs, but however dubious those triumphs were, at that moment Effi would have been happy to listen to her telling her about them. Finally she opened the lid of the piano in order to play; but that didn't work. 'No, that would make me completely melancholy; better to read.' So she looked for a book. The first that came to hand was a fat tome, an old travel guide, perhaps from Innstetten's days as a lieutenant. 'Yes, that's what I'll read; there's nothing more calming than that kind of book. The dangerous parts are always just the maps, but never fear, I'll make sure I avoid that tiny print that I hate.' So she opened the book at random: page 153. From the next room she could hear the tick-tock of the clock, and from outside Rollo who, once it was dark, had abandoned his place in the coach-house and, as on every evening, stretched out on the large, woven mat outside the bedroom. The awareness that he was near lessened her feeling of abandonment, indeed, she almost felt in good spirits again and so immediately started to read. The page the book happened to be open at dealt with the Hermitage, the well-known Margrave's palace near Bayreuth;* that attracted her, Bayreuth, Richard Wagner, and so she read on: 'One further picture in the Hermitage deserves mention, if not for its beauty then for its age and the figure it represents. It is a female portrait, very much darkened, a small head with severe, slightly sinister features and a ruff that looks as if it is carrying the head. Some maintain it is an old margravine from the end of the fifteenth century, others are of the opinon that it is Countess Orlamünde; both, however, agree that it is the portrait of the lady who since then has achieved a certain notoriety in the history of the Hohenzollerns under the name of the "white woman".'*

'Well, I really happened on the right thing, didn't I?' Effi said, pushing the book to one side. 'I want to calm my nerves, and the first thing I read is the story of the "white woman" I've been afraid of for as long as I can remember. However, since I've got the creeps already, I might as well read it right through.'

She opened the book again and read on, '. . . and precisely this old portrait (the *original* of which plays an important role in the history of the Hohenzollerns) plays a role as a *picture* in the history of Hermitage Palace itself, which is probably connected with the fact that it is hung on a concealed door, not visible to outsiders, behind which there is a staircase coming up from the basement. It is said that when Napoleon spent the night there, the "white woman" came out of the frame and walked towards his bed. The Emperor, starting in horror, called his adjutant, and to the end of his life used to talk indignantly of that "maudit château".'*

'I'll have to give up trying to calm myself down with this sort of reading,' Effi said. 'If I go on I'm sure to come to a dungeon where the devil rode off on a wine barrel. I believe there's a lot of that kind of thing in Germany, and a travel guide has to gather it all together. I think instead I'll close my eyes and try to remember my eve-of-wedding party: the twins who couldn't carry on for tears, and Cousin Dagobert who, when all the others were looking at each other in embarrassment, declared in astonishingly dignified tones that tears like that opened up the gates of paradise for one. He really was charming and so full of high spirits . . . And now me! And here of all places. Oh, I'm not fitted to be a grand lady. Mama, yes, she would have been in the right place here, she would have set the tone, as is right and proper for the Landrat's wife, and Sidonie Grasenabb would have been all deference and not particularly concerned about her belief or unbelief. But me . . . I'm a child, and that's what I'll probably stay. I once heard it said that that was a piece of good fortune, but I don't know if it's true. You always have to fit in where you happen to be put.'

At that point Friedrich came in to clear the table.

'What's the time, Friedrich?'

'Coming up to nine, Madam.'

'Well thank God for that. Send Johanna in.'

*

'Madam sent for me.'

'Yes, Johanna. I'm going to go to bed. It's actually still early, but I'm so alone. Please put the letter in with the post first, and when you're back I suppose it'll be time. And even if it isn't.'

Effi took the lamp and went across to her bedroom. Yes, there lying on the rush mat was Rollo. When he saw Effi coming, he stood up to make room for her and brushed against her hand with his ear. Then he lay down again.

In the meantime Johanna had gone across to the Landrat's office to put the letter in with the post there. She hadn't particularly hurried while she was doing this, instead she'd had a chat with Frau Paaschen, the wife of the clerk. About the Landrat's young wife, of course.

'What's she like?' Frau Paaschen asked.

'She's very young.'

'Well there's nothing wrong with that, the opposite, rather. The young ones, and that's the good thing about them, spend all their time in front of the mirror primping and preening themselves and don't see or hear much, and they're not the kind who're always counting the candle-ends in the hall and don't object if someone gives you a kiss just because they never get any.'

'Yes,' Johanna said, 'that's what my old mistress was like, even though she had no reason to be. But there's nothing of that in our mistress.'

'Is she very affectionate, then?'

'Oh, very much so, as you can well imagine.'

'But then he leaves her alone like this . . .'

'Yes, Paaschen, but you mustn't forget . . . the Prince. And then, he is the Landrat after all. And perhaps he's set his sights on higher things.'

'I'm sure he has. And he will get there. There is something about him. Paaschen's always saying that, and he understands people.'

Johanna's errand to the office must have taken a quarter of an hour, and when she came back Effi was already sitting at the mirror, waiting.

'You took a long time, Johanna.'

'Yes, Ma'am . . . You must excuse me . . . I met Frau Paaschen over there and I got caught up a little. It's so quiet here, you're always glad when you meet someone you can have a bit of a chat with. Christel's a very nice person but she doesn't talk, and Friedrich's so dozy and so cautious and won't really say much. Of course, there are times when you have to know how to hold your tongue, and Frau Paaschen, she's so nosey and so common, not really my taste, but it's good to hear and see something now and then.'

Effi sighed. 'Yes, Johanna, that's best . . .'

'Madam has such lovely hair, so long and silky soft.'

'Yes, it's very soft. But that's not a good thing, Johanna. The way your hair is, so's your character.'

'True, Ma'am. And a soft character's better than a hard one. I've got soft hair too.'

'Yes, Johanna. And your hair's blond as well. That's what men like best.'

'Oh, that varies a lot, Ma'am. There are some who go for dark hair as well.'

'Of course,' Effi laughed, 'I've found that too. There will probably be something else behind it. But women who are blond always have a fair complexion, you have, Johanna, and I'm willing to bet you get lots of men after you. I'm still very young but I know about that too. And then I have a friend, she was blond as well, even blonder than you, really flaxen, and she was a pastor's daughter . . .'

'Oh, in that case . . .'

'Oh, come on, Johanna, what do you mean by "Oh, in that case". It sounds quite strange and suggestive, I'm sure you can't have anything against pastor's daughters . . . She was a very pretty girl, even our officers thought that—where we lived there were officers around, and red hussars at that—and she knew how to make the most of it: a black velvet bodice and a flower, a rose or a heliotrope, and if she hadn't had such large, protuberant eyes . . . oh, you should have seen them, Johanna, at least this big'—and with a laugh Effi pulled her right eyelid down—'she would have been a real beauty. She was called Hulda, Hulda Niemeyer, and we weren't even really that close; but if she were here now, sitting there on the little corner sofa, I'd chat to her till midnight, or even longer. I've such a yearning, and . . .' as she said this, she drew Johanna's head close to her, 'I'm so afraid.'

'Oh, you'll get over it, Ma'am, we've all felt that.'

'You've all felt that? What is that supposed to mean, Johanna?'

' . . . And if Madam really is that afraid, I can bed down here. I'll use the straw mat and lay a chair down for a headrest and sleep here till the morning, or until the Master's back.'

'He's not going to disturb me, he promised me that.'

'Or I'll just sit on the corner sofa.'

'Yes, that might be alright. But then, no, it won't. The Master mustn't know I'm afraid, he doesn't like that. He always wants me to be brave and resolute, the way he is. But I just can't manage it, I was always a little timorous . . . But I can see I'll have to make an effort and comply with his wishes in such matters . . . and then I have Rollo, of course. He's lying across the threshold.'

Johanna nodded at everything she said, and then lit the candle on Effi's bedside table. Then she took the lamp. 'Is there anything else Madam requires?'

'No, Johanna. The shutters are properly fastened?'

'Just pulled to, Madam. Otherwise it's very dark and stuffy.'

'That's alright.'

And now Johanna left; Effi went over to her bed and wrapped herself up in the blankets.

She left the candle burning because she didn't want to go to sleep straight away; rather, she intended, as she had previously with her eve-of-wedding party, to think about the honeymoon and go through everything again in her mind's eye. But things turned out differently, and when she was in Verona,* looking for Juliet's house, her eyes were already closing. The stub of the candle in the little silver candlestick gradually burnt down, then flickered up and went out.

For a while Effi slept soundly. But all at once she woke from her sleep with a loud cry—indeed, she heard the cry herself and also Rollo barking outside; 'woof, woof' echoed down the corridor, a hollow sound, almost as if he were afraid himself. She felt as if her heart were standing still; she found it impossible to call out, and just then something scurried past her and the door out into the corridor flew open. But that moment of intense fear was also the one that freed her from it for, instead of some horror, it was Rollo who now came to her, his head searching for her hand, and, once he'd found it, he lay down on the rug beside her bed. But with her other hand Effi had already pressed the button of the bell three times, and less than thirty seconds later Johanna was there, barefoot, her coat over her arm and a large checkered scarf round her head and shoulders.

'Thank God you're here, Johanna.'

'What was it, Ma'am? Madam must have been dreaming.'

'Yes, dreaming. It must have been something like that . . . but there was something else as well.'

'What, Ma'am?'

'I was fast asleep and suddenly I woke up with a scream . . . perhaps it was a nightmare . . . they do run in the family, my Papa gets them too and frightens us with them, only Mama always says he should have more self-control; but that's easily said . . . So I woke with a start and screamed, and as I was looking round, as far as that was possible in the darkness, something brushed past my bed, just there, where you're standing, Johanna, and then it was gone. And when I ask myself what it was . . .'

'Well what was it, Ma'am?'

'And when I ask myself what it was . . . I don't like to say it, Johanna . . . but I think it was the Chinaman.'

'The one from upstairs?' Johanna tried to laugh. 'The little Chinaman that Christel and I stuck to the arm of that chair? Oh, Madam will have been dreaming, and even if you were awake, all that will have come from your dream.'

'I'd gladly believe it. But it was exactly the same moment as when Rollo barked outside, so he must have seen it too, then the door flew open and the dear, brave thing came bounding towards me, as if he were coming to save me. Oh, my dear Johanna, it was terrible. And me all alone, and so young. Oh, if only I had someone here whose shoulder I could cry on. But so far from home . . . Oh, from home . . .'

'The Master might come back any moment.'

'No, he mustn't come, he mustn't see me like this. He might laugh at me, and I could never forgive him that. It was so horrible, Johanna . . . You must stay here now . . . But let Christel and Friedrich sleep on. No one must know.'

'Or perhaps I could fetch Frau Kruse; she doesn't sleep, she sits there the whole night through.'

'No, no, she's something like that herself. All that with the black hen, that's something like it as well; she mustn't come. No, Johanna, just you stay here. And what a good thing you didn't fasten the shutters. Push them open and make a loud noise about it, so that I can hear a sound, a human sound . . . that's what I must call it, even if it does seem odd . . . and then open the window a little so that I can have some air and light.'

Johanna did what she had been told to do, and Effi sank back onto the pillows and soon into a profound sleep.

CHAPTER 10

It wasn't until six in the morning that Innstetten came back from Varzin and, warding off Rollo's attentions, withdrew as quietly as possible to his room. He made himself comfortable and allowed Friedrich to do no more than cover him with a travelling-rug. 'Wake me at nine.' And at that time he was woken. He got up quickly and said, 'Bring breakfast.'

'Madam's still asleep.'

'But it's late already. Has something happened?'

'I don't know; all I do know is that Johanna had to spend the night in Madam's room.'

'Well, send in Johanna.'

She came. She had the same rosy complexion as ever, so didn't seem to have been particularly affected by the events of the night.

'What's the matter with your mistress? Friedrich tells me something happened and you slept over there.'

'Yes, Herr Baron. The mistress rang three times, one after the other, so I thought right away it must mean something. And it did. She'll have been dreaming, or perhaps it was the other thing.'

'What other thing?'

'Oh, you know, sir.'

'I know nothing. At all events we have to put a stop to it. And what was my wife like when you went to her?'

'She seemed beside herself with fear and was clinging on to Rollo's collar; he was standing by Madam's bed and was frightened himself.'

'And what had she dreamt or, if you insist, what had she heard or seen? What did she say?'

'Something had crept across, close by her.'

'What? Who?'

'The one from upstairs. The one from the upper chamber or the little bedroom.'

'Nonsense, I say. The same silly stuff again and again. I don't want to hear any more about it. And then you stayed with my wife?'

'Yes, sir. I made myself a place to sleep close by her. And I had to hold her hand, then she fell asleep.'

'And she's still asleep?'

'Fast asleep.'

'That concerns me, Johanna. You can make yourself well again by sleeping, but also ill. We must wake her, taking care not to frighten her, of course. And Friedrich's not to bring the breakfast now, I'll wait until the mistress is here. And be careful how you go about it.'

*

Half-an-hour later Effi came. She looked charming, quite pale and leaning on Johanna. But when she saw Innstetten she rushed over, threw her arms round him and kissed him; the tears were pouring down her cheeks as she did so.

'Oh, Geert, thank God you're back. Now everything will be all right again. You mustn't go away again, you mustn't leave me alone again.'

'My dear Effi . . . put it there, Friedrich, I'll see to it myself . . . my dear Effi, I'm not leaving you alone out of lack of consideration or because the mood takes me, but because I have to; I have no choice, I have an official position, I can't say to Prince Bismarck, or to the Princess for that matter, "I can't come, your Highness, my wife feels so alone," or "my wife's afraid". If I were to say that, we'd look rather ridiculous, I certainly would and you as well. But first of all have a cup of coffee.'

Effi had a drink and it clearly revived her. She took her husband's hand again. 'You're quite right, I can see that's not possible. And we want to get on in the world. I say we, since I actually want it more than you . . .'

'That's the way you women are,' Innstetten said with a laugh.

'So that's agreed then: you can continue to accept your invitations and I'll stay and wait for "my lord", which reminds me of Hulda under the elder tree. I wonder how she's getting on?'

'Ladies such as Hulda always get on fine. But what else was it were you going to say?'

'I was going to say that I'll stay here, and alone if it has to be. But not in this house. Let's move. There are some very nice houses on the Embankment, one between Consul Martens's and Consul Grützmacher's and one on the market square, opposite Gieshübler's. Why can't we live there? Why does it have to be here? When we had friends or relations visiting I often used to hear them talk about families in Berlin moving out because of piano-playing or cockroaches or an unfriendly concierge; if people do it because of such trivial matters . . .'

'Trivial matters? A concierge? You can't say that . . .'

'If it's possible for things like that, it surely must be possible here, given that you're the Landrat and the people do as you say, some even owe you a debt of gratitude. I'm sure Gieshübler would help us, if only for my sake, since he'll feel sorry for me. So tell me, Geert, shall we give up this house with a curse on it, this house with the . . .'

'Chinaman, you were going to say. There, you see, Effi, it's possible to say the dreaded word without him appearing. What you saw or what, as you said, crept past your bed, was the little Chinaman the maids stuck to the arm of a chair upstairs; I bet he was wearing a blue gown and a very flat hat with a shining button on top.'

She nodded.

'You see now, a dream, hallucination. And then I suppose Johanna will have told you some story yesterday evening, about the wedding, about the wedding up there . . .'

'No.'

'All the better.'

'She didn't tell me anything. But I can see from all this that there's something special here. And then the crocodile; everything's so eerie here.'

'But that first evening, when you saw the crocodile, you thought it was like a fairy-tale . . .'

'Yes, then . . .'

'And then, Effi, I can't really move out of here, even if it were possible to sell the house or do an exchange. It's the same as with declining an invitation to Varzin. I can't have people here in the town saying, Landrat Innstetten's selling his house because his wife saw the stuck-on picture of a Chinaman as a ghost by her bed. That would be the end of it for me, Effi. You can never get over looking so ridiculous.'

'Well, Geert, are you so sure that kind of thing doesn't exist?'

'I wouldn't say that. It's something one can believe in or, better, not believe in. But assuming such things do exist, what's the harm? The fact that there are bacilli, you'll have heard about them, flying round in the air is much worse and more dangerous than all these rollicking ghosts. Assuming that they do rollick, that they do really exist. And then I'm surprised to see this fear and aversion in you of all people, a Briest. It's as if you came from some ordinary middle-class home. A ghost is a distinction, like a pedigree and suchlike, and there are families I know who would no more like to lose their "white woman", that can also be a black one of course, than their coat of arms.'

Effi remained silent.

'Well, Effi, nothing to say to that?'

'What can I say? I've shown willing and let you have your way, but I still think that for your part you could show more sympathy. If you only knew how I long for that. I've suffered, really suffered, and when I saw you I thought I'd be released from my fear. But all you tell me is that you don't want to look ridiculous, not in the eyes of the Prince nor in those of the town. That's pretty cold comfort. I don't think that's much, and all the less when you end up contradicting yourself, and not only seem to believe in these things yourself but expect some noble pride in our ghost from me. And as regards families who value their ghost as highly as their coat of arms, that's all a matter of taste; my coat of arms is more important to me. We Briests don't have a ghost, thank God. We Briests have always been good people, and that's probably the reason.'

*

The argument would probably have gone on, perhaps even have led to a serious disagreement, if Friedrich hadn't come in to hand a letter to his mistress. 'From Herr Gieshübler. The messenger's waiting for your reply.'

The ill-humour immediately vanished from Effi's face; just to hear Gieshübler's name did her good, and the feeling increased as she scrutinized the letter. In the first place, it wasn't a letter but a note, with the address, 'Frau Baronin von Innstetten, née von Briest', wonderfully written in copperplate and, instead of a seal, a little round picture stuck on, a lyre with a rod through it, or it could have been an arrow. She handed the card to her husband, who also admired it.

'Well read it.'

Now Effi unstuck the wafer sealing it and read:

'Most esteemed Madam, most gracious Baroness,

I beg you to permit me to be so bold as to add a request to my most dutiful greetings this morning. A dear friend of many years, a daughter of our fair town of Kessin, Fräulein Marietta Trippelli, is due to arrive on the midday train and will stay here until tomorrow morning. On the 17th she has to be in Petersburg, where she is to give a concert in the middle of January. Prince Kotchukoff has most kindly agreed to offer her hospitality again this year. As ever, Fräulein Trippelli has been good enough to agree to spend the evening in my house and to perform a few songs, that I may choose at will, since nothing is too difficult for her. Would you, Frau Baronin, condescend to grace this musical soirée with your presence? At seven. I am sure your good husband, whose attendance I confidently expect, will support my submissive request. Present will be just Pastor Lindequist (as accompanist) and Frau Trippel, the widow of his predecessor.

Your devoted servant,

A. Gieshübler.'

'Well—' Innstetten said, 'yes or no?'

'Yes, of course. It will take me out of myself. And then I can't turn down my dear Gieshübler's very first invitation.'

'Agreed. Right then, Friedrich, tell Mirambo—presumably it's he who brought the note—we'll be delighted.'

Friedrich left. Once he'd gone, Effi asked, 'Who is Mirambo?'

'The real Mirambo* is the chief of a band of brigands in Africa . . . Lake Tanganyika, if your geography goes that far . . . our Mirambo, however, is merely Gieshübler's chief dispenser of coal and general factotum; he'll probably be in attendance this evening, in white gloves and tails.'

It was clear that the little interlude had had a good effect on Effi and had helped to restore much of her natural lightheartedness, but Innstetten was determined to do his bit to speed her recovery. 'I'm glad you said yes, and that so quickly and without having to ponder, and now I'd like to make a further suggestion to revive your spirits completely. I can see that there's still something left over from the night that isn't part of my Effi; we really must get rid of it, and for that there's nothing better than fresh air. It's a splendid day, both fresh and mild with hardly a breath of wind; what would you say to going out for a drive, in my sleigh of course, and a long one, not just round the Plantation, with the bells and the white blanket of snow, and when we get back at four you can have a rest, and at seven we'll go to Gieshübler's and listen to Fräulein Trippelli.'

Effi took his hand. 'You are good to me, Geert, and considerate. I must have seemed childish to you, or at least very childlike; first of all with my fear and then demanding we sell the house and, what was worse, that about the Prince. To suggest you make yourself unavailable to him, it's ridiculous. After all, he's the man on whom our future depends. Mine as well. You wouldn't believe how ambitious I am. Actually, I only married you out of ambition. Now don't put on that serious look. I do love you . . . what do they say when they pluck petals off a flower? She loves me, she loves me not, she loves me, she loves me a lot.'

And she laughed out loud. 'And now tell me,' she went on, as Innstetten still said nothing, 'where shall we go?'

'I thought we'd go to the station, but by a roundabout route, and then back along the highway. And we'll have something to eat at the station or, better, at the Prince Bismarck tavern, if you remember we went past it on the day we arrived. Dropping in like that always makes a good impression, and I need to talk to the owner—Golchowski, *starosta* by the grace of Effi—about the elections; even if I don't think much of him personally, he keeps a decent inn and the food's even better than that. The people here know about food and drink.'

It was around eleven when they had this conversation. At twelve Kruse pulled up outside the door with the sleigh and Effi got in. Johanna wanted to get a foot-muff and furs, but after all she'd been through Effi felt such a need for fresh air that she said no to everything and just took a double rug. Innstetten said to Kruse, 'We're going to the railway station now, Kruse; we were both there this morning and people will be surprised, but no matter. I think we should drive along the Plantation and then head off to the left, towards the church tower in Kroschentin. Give the horses their heads. We must be at the station by one.'

So off they drove. Smoke was hanging over the white roofs of the town, for there was hardly any movement in the air. Utpatel's mill was only turning slowly, and they flew past, close to the churchyard; Berberis was growing over the railings and the tips of the bushes brushed against Effi, sending the snow down on her travel-rug. On the other side of the road was a fenced-in square, not much bigger than a flowerbed, and nothing could be seen in it apart from a young pine tree rising up from the middle.

'Is someone buried there as well?' Effi asked.

'Yes, the Chinaman.'

Effi started; it was like a stab of pain. But she had the strength to control herself and asked, with apparent calm: 'Ours?'

'Yes, ours. Of course he couldn't be put in the communal grave-yard, so then Captain Thomsen, who was what you might call his friend, bought that plot and had him buried there. There's also a stone with an inscription. All before my time, of course, but people still talk about it.'

'So there is something after all. A story. You said something like that this morning. In the end it'll be best if I'm told what it is. As long as I don't know, despite all my good intentions, I'll be the victim of my own imaginings. Tell me what really happened. The reality of it can't torment me as much as my imagination.'

'Well done, Effi. I wasn't going to say anything about it, but now it's come out naturally and that's a good thing. It's nothing, really.'

'Doesn't matter; nothing or a lot or a little. Just begin.'

'Well, that's more easily said than done. The beginning's always the most difficult part of anything, stories included. I think, then, I'll start with Captain Thomsen.'

'Yes, do.'

'For many years Thomsen captained a so-called China trader, always sailing between Shanghai and Singapore with a cargo of rice, and would have been around sixty when he arrived here. I don't know whether he'd been born here or had other connections, but the long and short of it is that he came here and sold his ship, an old hulk that didn't bring in much, and bought a house, the one in which we now live. Out there he'd become a wealthy man. And that's the reason for the crocodile and the shark, and the ship, of course . . . So Thomsen settled here, he was always pleasant and neatly turned out (or so I've been told) and well-liked by all, including Kirstein, the burgomaster, and above all by the pastor at the time, a Berliner who had also come here, shortly before Thomsen, and aroused much animosity.'

'I can believe it. I've noticed that too; they're all so severe and self-righteous. I think that's Pomerania.'

'Yes and no, it all depends. There are areas where they're not so strict at all, where everything's higgledy-piggledy . . . But just look, Effi, there's the tower of Kroschentin church right in front of us. Shall we abandon the idea of the station and go and visit old Frau von Grasenabb? Sidonie, if I've been rightly informed, is not at home, so we can risk it . . .'

'Oh come now, Geert, what are you thinking of? It's heavenly flying along like this, and I feel really free, all my fears are melting away. And now I'm to give all that up just to make a flying visit to some old folk, and very probably put them to some embarrassment as well. For God's sake, no. And then above all, I want to hear the story. So we were with Captain Thomsen, whom I see in my mind as a Dane or an Englishman, very neat and tidy, with a white stand-up collar and very white linen . . .'

'Quite right. That's what he's supposed to have been like. And with him was a young woman of around twenty; some say she was his niece, but most say his granddaughter which, given their ages, seems unlikely. And apart from his granddaughter, or niece, there was also a Chinaman, the one who's buried in the dunes and whose grave we just drove past.'

'Yes. And then?'

'Well, this Chinaman was Thomsen's servant, but Thomsen thought so highly of him that he was actually more of a friend than a servant. And so it went on for some years. Then all at once word went round that Thomsen's granddaughter, she was called Nina, I think, was to get married, according to the old man's wishes, to another sea-captain. And that was what happened. There was a big wedding in the house, the pastor from Berlin joined them in wedlock, and Utpatel, the miller who belonged to some nonconformist sect, and Gieshübler, whom people in the town thought unreliable in church matters, were both invited, and above all lots of captains with their wives and daughters. Things were pretty lively, as you can imagine. In the evening there was dancing, and the bride danced with everyone, eventually with the Chinaman as well. Then all at once word went round that she had gone, the bride that is. And she really had gone, somewhere or other, and no one knew what had happened. And fourteen days later the Chinaman died; Thomsen bought the patch of ground I showed you and he was buried there. The pastor from Berlin is supposed to have said he could just as well have been buried in the Christian churchyard, for the Chinaman had been a very good man and just as good as the others. Gieshübler told me no one quite knew whom he was referring to with "the others".'

'Well, there I disagree entirely with the pastor; one shouldn't say things like that, because it's challenging and inappropriate. Even Niemeyer wouldn't have said that.'

'And it was very much held against the poor pastor—he was called Trippel, by the way—so that it was actually fortunate that it led to his death, otherwise he would have lost his position. For the town was against him, even though they'd appointed him, just as you are, not to mention the Church Council of course.'

'Trippel, you said? Then he must be connected with Frau Trippel, whom we're to see this evening?'

'Of course he's connected with her. He was her husband, and the father of Marietta Trippelli.'

Effi laughed. 'Of Marietta Trippelli! Ah, now I see it all clearly. In his note Gieshübler said she was born in Kessin, but I assumed she was the daughter of some Italian consul. There are so many foreign names here. But it turns out she's German through and through, and the name comes from Trippel. Is she then so outstanding that she could risk Italianizing her name?'

'Fortune favours the brave. But she is very good as well. She spent a few years in Paris with the famous opera-singer Pauline Viardot;* there she also met the Russian prince, for Russian princes are very enlightened, not tied by petty class prejudice, and Kotchukoff and Gieshübler—she calls him "Uncle" by the way, you could almost say he's a born uncle—it's really the two of them who made little Marie Trippel what she is today. It was through Gieshübler that she went to Paris, and then Kotchukoff turned her into Marietta Trippelli.'

'Oh, Geert, how delightful all that is and what an ordinary life I led in Hohen-Cremmen. Never anything special.'

Innstetten took her hand and said, 'You mustn't say that, Effi. As far as ghosts are concerned, you can take whatever attitude you like. But beware of wanting something special, or what people call special. These things that seem so appealing to you—and I include in that the kind of life Marietta Trippelli leads—have to be paid for, usually with your happiness. I know very well how you love your Hohen-Cremmen, how attached to it you are, but you often make fun of it and have no idea what quiet days, such as you have in Hohen-Cremmen, can mean.'

'Oh but I do,' she said. 'I know that very well. It's just that I like hearing about something different from time to time, and then I get the feeling I'd like to be part of it. But you're quite right. And what I actually long for is peace and quiet.'

Innstetten wagged his finger at her. 'My dear, dear Effi, there you go imagining things again. Idle fancies all the time, sometimes going one way, sometimes the other.'

CHAPTER 11

The drive went as planned. At one the sleigh pulled up by the railway embankment outside the 'Prince Bismarck', and Golchowski, delighted to see the Landrat in his inn, took pains to prepare an excellent lunch. When the dessert and the Tokay had been served, Innstetten called over the landlord, who had appeared at the table from time to time to see that everything was in order, and asked him to join them at the table and tell them the news. Golchowski was the right man for that; not an egg could be laid for ten miles all round but he knew about it. And that was the case again that day. Sidonie Grasenabb, as Innstetten had rightly assumed, had gone to spend four weeks staying with the court chaplain's family, as she had the previous Christmas; Frau von Palleske, he went on, had had to dismiss her maid on the spot because of a regrettable incident, and old Herr Fraude was in a bad way—they'd given out that he'd merely slipped, but it was a stroke and his son, who was in Lissa* with the Hussars, was expected back at any moment. After this chitchat they turned to more serious matters and got on to Varzin. 'Yes,' Golchowski said, 'when you think of the Prince running a paper mill! It's all very strange; he can't actually stand paperwork, least of all printed paper, and now he's setting up a paper mill of his own.'

'True, my dear Golchowski,' Innstetten said, 'but you can't avoid such contradictions in life, not even if you're a prince or a great man.'

'No, no,' Golchowski said, 'not even if you're a great man.'

The conversation about the Prince would probably have continued, had not the signal bell sounded from the station announcing the imminent arrival of a train. Innstetten looked at the clock.

'What train is that, Golchowski?'

'That's the Danzig express; it doesn't stop here, but I always go up and count the carriages; now and then there's someone I know at the window. There are some steps up the embankment here, right behind the courtyard, signal box 417 . . .'

'Oh, let's take advantage of that,' Effi said. 'I love watching trains . . .'

'Then it's high time we went, Madam.'

And so the three of them set off and stood, once they were up there, in a vegetable bed beside the box; it was covered in snow, of course, but there was a patch that had been cleared. The signalman was already there, flag in hand. And then the train was thundering across the station track and the next moment past the box and the vegetable patch. Effi was so excited she didn't see anything and just watched, as if dazed, the last carriage disappear, a brakeman sitting on top.

'It'll be in Berlin at six-fifty,' Innstetten said, 'and an hour after that, if the wind holds, the people in Hohen-Cremmen will be able to hear it rattling past in the distance. Would you like to be on it, Effi?'

She said nothing. When he looked at her, he saw that there was a tear welling up in the corner of her eye.

*

As the train thundered past, Effi was seized with heartfelt yearning. However comfortable her situation, she still felt as if she were in an alien world. Whenever she found something that delighted her, she immediately afterwards became aware of what she was missing. Over there was Varzin, and there, in the other direction, the church tower of Kroschentin was shining, and far beyond it that of Morgnitz, and that was where the Grasenabbs and the Borckes lived, not the Bellings and not the Briests. 'Yes, *them!*' Innstetten had been quite right about her swift change of mood, and now she saw everything that lay behind her as if transfigured. But however strong the yearning with which she watched the train disappear, she was of far too flexible a disposition to dwell on it for long, and on the drive home, as the red ball of the setting sun poured out its shimmering light over the snow, she felt free again; everything looked fresh and beautiful, and when, after their return to Kessin, she entered the hall of Gieshübler's house on the stroke of seven, she was not merely contented but almost in high spirits, to which the scent of valerian and orris-root permeating it probably contributed.

Innstetten and his wife arrived on time, but despite that were still later than the other guests; Pastor Lindequist, old Frau Trippel, and

Marietta herself were already there. Gieshübler—in a blue tail-coat with dull gold buttons, and his pince-nez on a broad, black ribbon that looked like the ribbon of some medal across his white piqué waist-coat—could only control his excitement with difficulty. 'May I intro-duce you, ladies and gentlemen: Baron and Baroness Innstetten, Frau Pastor Trippel, Fräulein Trippelli.' Pastor Lindequist, whom they all knew, stood on one side, smiling.

Until the introductions Marietta Trippelli, early thirties, very mannish, with a pronounced humorous air, had been sitting in the place of honour on the sofa. After the introductions, however, she went over to a high-backed chair, saying, 'I beg you, Madam, hence-forth to assume the burdens and hazards of your office, for I think the word hazards'—she indicated the sofa—'is not out of place here. I pointed this out to Gieshübler years ago but in vain; he is, I'm afraid, as stubborn as he is kind.'

'But Marietta . . .'

'The sofa you see here, that first saw the light of day at least fifty years ago, has been constructed according to some old-fashioned countersunk principle, and anyone who ventures to sit on it without first reinforcing the seat with a veritable mountain of cushions will sink into a bottomless pit, or at least so far down that their knees will tower up like a monument.' All of this Marietta Trippelli said in a tone that was both good-humoured and self-assured, as if to say, 'You're Baroness Innstetten and I'm Marietta Trippelli.'

Gieshübler was full of enthusiasm for his beloved singer and thought very highly of her talent, but all his enthusiasm did not blind him to the fact that she lacked some of the social graces. And those were precisely what he himself cultivated. 'My dear Marietta,' he said, 'you have a delightfully amusing way of treating such questions; but as far as my sofa's concerned, you are truly mistaken and I'd be happy to have any expert decide between us. Even a man such as Prince Kotchukoff . . .'

'Oh, please, Gieshübler, leave *him* out of this. Always Kotchukoff. The way you go on, the Frau Baronin here will be thinking that this prince—who, anyway, is only one of the smaller ones and doesn't have more than a thousand souls, that is *had* (in the past, when their wealth was counted in souls*)—that I was proud that this prince had made me his thousand-and-first. No, the situation is quite different; you know me, Gieshübler, always free-spoken. Kotchukoff is a good companion and he's my friend, but he knows nothing at all about art and that kind of thing, certainly not about music, even though he composes masses and oratorios—most Russian princes, if they're active artistically, tend to the religious or orthodox side somewhat—and questions of furnishings and decoration belong to the many things he knows nothing about. He's just about sufficiently aristocratic to be easily persuaded to buy anything that's brightly coloured and costs a lot of money.'

Innstetten was amused, and Pastor Lindequist was very clearly enjoying this as well. For poor old Frau Trippel, however, her daughter's free-and-easy tone was a source of constant embarrassment, and Gieshübler thought it was time to cut short a conversation that was becoming awkward. The best way of doing that was with a few vocal pieces. It was unlikely Marietta would choose songs of questionable content, and even if she were to, her art was so great that the content would be ennobled. So he said, 'My dear Marietta, I've ordered our little collation for eight. So we have three-quarters of an hour, unless you would perhaps prefer to regale us with a cheerful song at table, or perhaps after we've finished . . .'

'Oh, come now, Gieshübler. You, the aesthete! There's nothing less aesthetic than a song performed on a full stomach. Moreover—and I know you're a man of choice cuisine, yes, a gourmet—moreover, it tastes better when you've the business of the evening behind you. First art, then hazelnut ice-cream, that's the right order.'

'So I may bring you the music now, Marietta?'

'Bring the music. What do you mean by that, Gieshübler? If I know you, you'll have whole cabinets full of music, and I can't sing you the whole of Bock & Bote.* Music! What *kind* of music, Gieshübler, that's the important thing. And then it has to be in my range. Alto.'

'Don't worry, I'll bring something suitable.'

And he started rooting through a cabinet, pulling out one drawer after another while Marietta pushed her chair round the table to the left so that she was right next to Effi. 'I'm curious to see what he brings,' she said. Effi didn't quite know what to say.

'I'd assume,' she started hesitantly, 'something by Gluck,* something particularly dramatic . . . In fact, Fräulein Trippelli, if you don't mind my saying so, I'm surprised to hear that you only do recitals. I would have thought that you, more than most, were made for the stage. Your figure, your power, your voice . . . So far I've seen so little of that kind of thing, only during short visits to Berlin . . . and I wasn't much more than a child. But I would have thought *Orpheus* or *Chrimhild* or the *Vestal*.'*

Marietta Trippelli shook her head from side to side and stared into space, but didn't get round to replying because Gieshübler returned and handed her half-a-dozen scores she quickly glanced at. '"Erlkönig"* . . . ugh; and *Die schöne Müllerin** . . . Oh, come now, Gieshübler, you're a dormouse, you must have been asleep for seven years. And then Loewe's ballads, not exactly the latest thing either: "Die Glocken von Speier".* Oh, that eternal ding-dong, it's laying it on with a trowel, tasteless and hackneyed. But here: "Ritter Olaf"* . . . yes, that's all right.'

So she stood up and, the pastor accompanying, sang 'Olaf' with great assurance and bravura, to general applause.

After that more songs in a similar Romantic vein were found, some excerpts from *The Flying Dutchman* and *Zampa*, and 'Heideknabe',* all pieces that she sang with equal calmness and virtuosity, while Effi was stunned by both the words and the music.

When Marietta Trippelli had finished 'Heideknabe' she said, 'That's enough,' a declaration she made so firmly that neither Gieshübler nor any of the others had the courage to press her for more. Least of all Effi. When Gieshübler's friend was sitting beside her again she simply said, 'If only I could tell you, my dear Fräulein, how grateful I am for that. Everything was so beautiful, so assured, so accomplished. But, if you'll forgive me, there's one thing I admire even more and that's the calm way you perform these pieces. I'm so easily carried away by impressions, and when I hear the merest ghost story I start trembling and can hardly get myself back under control. And your singing is so powerful and profoundly moving, yet you yourself are quite serene and unperturbed.'

'Yes, my dear Frau Baronin, that's the way it is in art. And above all in the theatre, from which I have fortunately been preserved. For, however much I feel personally immune to its temptations—it ruins one's reputation, the best thing one has, that is. What is more, one's art becomes deadened, as colleagues have assured me a hundred times. People are being poisoned and stabbed, and the dead Juliet whispers a pun to Romeo, or perhaps a malicious remark, or he presses a billet-doux into her hand.'

'I just can't understand that. But to stick with what I have to thank you for this evening, for example the ghostly atmosphere in "Olaf", I can assure you that if I have a frightening dream, or if I think I can hear quiet dancing and music above when there's no one there, or someone creeping past my bed, I'm beside myself with fear and can't forget it for days on end.'

'Well, yes, my dear Madam, what you are talking about there is different, it's something that's real or at least could be real. A ghost walking in a ballad, that doesn't give me the shivers at all, but like other people I find a ghost walking across my room very unpleasant. In that our feelings are the same.'

'Have you ever experienced something like that?'

'Certainly. And that when I was staying with Kotchukoff. And I've insisted I shall sleep somewhere else this time, perhaps with the English governess. She's a Quaker, I'll be safe with her.'

'So you think that kind of thing is possible?'

'My dear Madam, when you're my age and have been around a lot, in Russia, and even spent six months in Romania, you think anything's possible. There are so many bad people, and that other stuff as well, it's part of it, in a manner of speaking.'

Effi pricked up her ears.

'I come', Marietta Trippelli went on, 'from a very enlightened family (only Mother had some problems with that), and yet my father said to me, when there was all that talk about the psychograph,* "There's something in it, Marie." And he was right, there is something in it. We're surrounded, we're being watched from all sides. That's something you'll find out for yourself.'

At that moment Gieshübler came up to them and gave Effi his arm, Innstetten took Marietta, then came Pastor Lindequist and Frau Trippel. And so they sat down to dine.

CHAPTER 12

It was late when they set off home. Already at ten o'clock Effi had said to Gieshübler that it must be time, Fräulein Trippelli had a train she mustn't miss and would have to leave Kessin at six. However, Marietta, who was standing beside them and heard this, had protested against this show of consideration in her characteristically forthright manner. 'Oh, Madam, you think people such as me need regular sleep, but that's not the case; what we need regularly is applause and high fees. You may well laugh. Moreover, I can sleep in the carriage (that's the kind of thing you learn), in any situation, and even on the left side, and I don't even need to unbutton my dress. Of course I'm never tightly laced up; my chest and lungs must always be free, and above all my heart. Yes, that's the main thing, my dear Madam. And, anyway, as far as sleep is concerned, it's not the quantity that counts but the quality; a good five-minute snooze is better than five hours tossing and turning, now this way, now that. In fact you sleep wonderfully well in Russia, despite the strong tea. It must be the air, or dining late or because you're so pampered. You have no worries in Russia, in that respect Russia's even better than America, though as far as the money's concerned they're the same.'

After Marietta Trippelli had explained all this, Effi had made no more suggestions about it being time to go, and so midnight came. Their farewells were happy and heartfelt, and not without a certain familiarity.

It was quite a long way from the Moor Pharmacy to the Landrat's house, but it was made shorter by the fact that Lindequist asked to be allowed to accompany Innstetten and his wife for part of it; a walk under the stars, he said, was the best way of getting over the effect of Gieshübler's Rhine wine. Naturally they passed the time talking about various items of Trippelliana; Effi started with what she could remember and the pastor immediately took it up. Much given to irony, he had asked her about many very worldly matters, but then finally enquired about her position regarding the church, to which she had replied that, as far as she was concerned, there was only *one* position, the strictly orthodox one. Her father, she went on, had been a rationalist, almost a freethinker, which was why he would most of all have liked to have the Chinaman buried in the churchyard. For her part she took the opposite view, despite the fact that personally she had the great advantage of not believing in anything. But in her absolute non-belief she was every moment aware that that was a luxury one could only allow oneself as a private person. That was something the state could not countenance, and if she were in charge of the Ministry of Public Worship and Instruction or the Church Council she would deal with such matters extremely rigorously. 'I can feel something of a Torquemada* inside me.'

Innstetten was in a very mellow mood and told them that he, for his part, had deliberately avoided such a tricky subject as matters of dogma and emphasized the moral aspect more. His main point had been the seductive nature of public appearances, that such a person must be constantly in danger, to which Marietta Trippelli had replied lightly, with the emphasis on the second half of the sentence, 'Yes, constantly in danger; mostly one's voice.'

Chatting thus, they relived their Trippelli evening before they separated, and only three days later Gieshübler's friend once more brought it back to mind with a telegram to Effi from St Petersburg. It read, 'Madame la Baronne d'Innstetten, née de Briest. Bien arrivée. Prince K. à la gare. Plus épris de moi que jamais. Mille fois merci de votre bon accueil. Compliments empressés à Monsieur le Baron.* Marietta Trippelli.'

Innstetten was delighted, but why he expressed his delight in such lively terms was beyond Effi.

'I can't understand you, Geert.'

'Because you don't understand Marietta Trippelli. I'm delighted at the way she's the real thing; it's all there, right down to the last jot and tittle.'

'So you see all this as play-acting?'

'What else? Everything calculated for over there and for here, for Kotchukoff and Gieshübler. Gieshübler will probably make her a gift, perhaps just a bequest.'

Gieshübler's musical soirée had been in the middle of December; immediately afterwards the preparations for Christmas began, and Effi, who would otherwise have found those days difficult to get through, was glad she had a household that made demands on her. She had to ponder, ask, purchase, and all that stifled any gloomy thoughts. On the day before Christmas Eve presents arrived from her parents in Hohen-Cremmen, with all sorts of little gifts from the Jahnkes included in the box: lovely pippins from a tree Effi and Jahnke had grafted several years previously, and brown wrist- and knee-warmers from Bertha and Hertha. Hulda just wrote a few lines because, as she said in excuse, she had to knit a travel-rug for X. 'Which simply won't be true,' Effi said. 'I bet X doesn't exist. She just can't stop surrounding herself with admirers who aren't there.'

And thus Christmas Eve arrived.

Innstetten decorated the tree for his young wife himself, there were candles burning on it and a little angel hovering on the top. There was also a crib with pretty little streamers and inscriptions, one of which gave a subtle hint of an event to take place in the Innstetten household during the following year. Effi read it and blushed. Then she went over to Innstetten to thank him, but before she could a Yuletide gift, as was the tradition in Pomerania, was thrown into the hall: a crate with a whole host of things in it. Finally they found the most important item, an elegant little box of comfits with all kinds of little Japanese pictures stuck on it; among the contents was a note. It read:

> Three kings came to Christ in days of yore,
> And one of those eastern kings was a Moor.
> On this day a Moor pharmacist
> Begs to offer this spicy gift:
> Not frankincense and, no, not myrrh
> But comfits filled with sweet *liqueur*.

Effi read it two or three times and was delighted with it. 'There's something particularly comforting about a good person paying his respects. Don't you agree, Geert?'

'I certainly do. It's actually the only thing that gives us pleasure, or at least ought to give us pleasure. For every one of us is involved in all kinds of stupid stuff. Me too. But then that's the way we are.'

On Christmas Day there was a church service, on the next day they were out at the Borckes'; everyone was there apart from the Grasenabbs, who didn't want to come because Sidonie wasn't there, which everyone thought a rather strange excuse. Some even whispered, 'It's the other way round, that's precisely why they ought to have come.' On New Year's Eve there was the Club ball, at which Effi's attendance was obligatory and also what she wanted, for the ball would give her the opportunity finally to see the whole upper crust of the town gathered together. Johanna was fully occupied preparing her mistress's finery; Gieshübler, who had a hothouse as he had everything else, sent some camellias; and Innstetten, despite the shortage of time, drove out on the afternoon of the ball to Papenhagen, where three barns had burnt down.

It was very quiet in the house. Christel, with nothing to occupy her and sleepy, had pulled a footstool over to the stove, and Effi withdrew to her bedroom, where she sat at a little desk between the mirror and the sofa to write to her Mama. She'd only sent a card to thank her for her Christmas letter and Christmas presents, otherwise she hadn't sent any news for weeks.

'Kessin, 31st December.

DEAR MAMA,

It looks as if this is going to be a long letter as I haven't written for ages—the card doesn't count. The last time I wrote I was busy with the preparations for Christmas and now that's over. Innstetten and my good friend Gieshübler did everything they could to make Christmas Eve as nice as possible for me, but I still felt a little lonely and longed for you and Papa. In fact, however much cause I have to be grateful and content and happy, I can't entirely get rid of the feeling of loneliness and if I used to mock, perhaps more than necessary, the tears of emotion that were constantly welling up in Hulda's eyes, I'm being punished for it now and have to fight back such tears myself. For Innstetten mustn't see them. I'm sure, however, that all that will get better when things liven up in our house and that will be the case, my dear Mama. What I hinted at recently is now certain and Innstetten lets me know every day how pleased he is about it. I don't need to say how happy I am about this myself, not least because then I'll have more life around me and diversion or, as Geert puts it, a "darling toy". He's probably right with that expression but I'd rather he didn't use it, since it always gives me a little twinge, reminding me how young I still am and not much more than a child myself. I can't get over this idea (Geert says it's unhealthy) and it makes what ought to be my greatest happiness into a constant source of embarrassment. Yes, my dear Mama, when the good Flemming ladies recently asked me about all sorts of things, I felt as if I was poorly prepared for an examination and I think I must have given some really stupid answers. I was in a bad mood as well, because some things that sound like expressions of sympathy are merely curiosity and seem all the more importunate because I still have a long wait, until the summer, for the happy event. The beginning of July, I think. You must come here then or, even better, once I've more or less recovered I'll arrange to go to Hohen-Cremmen. Oh, I really do look forward to it, and to the Havelland air—here it's almost always raw and cold—and every day we'll have a drive out into the Marshes and all the trees will be red and yellow and I can already see the child stretching out its hands for them, for I'm sure it will feel that's where it really belongs. But I'm just writing that for *you*. Innstetten mustn't know and I also feel as if I ought to apologize to you for announcing as early as this my intention to go to Hohen-Cremmen with the child, instead of sending you the warmest of invitations to come to Kessin, that has fifteen hundred summer visitors every year and ships with the flags of all sorts of nations and even a hotel on the dunes. But the reason for my lack of hospitality is not that I wouldn't welcome visitors, I am a Briest after all, it's simply our house here that, although there's so much about it that's attractive and special, is not really a proper house, just a home for two people and not really even that, we haven't got a dining-room, which is an embarrassment when a few visitors turn up. True, there are rooms on the first floor, a large one and four smaller ones, but none of them is very inviting. I'd call them lumber-rooms, if there was any lumber in them, but they're quite empty apart from a few wicker chairs, and make a very strange impression, to say the least. Now I'm sure you'll be saying that's easily changed, but the house we live in is . . . is haunted. There, it's out. By the way, I must beg you not to mention that in your reply; I always show your letters to Innstetten and he'd be furious if he knew I'd told you that. I wouldn't have done it, either, especially since I haven't been troubled by it for weeks and have stopped feeling frightened, but Johanna told me it keeps reappearing, in particular when there's someone new in the house. And I couldn't expose you to such a danger or, if that's going too far, to such a peculiar and unpleasant disturbance. I won't bother you with the story behind it today, at least not at any great length. It concerns an old captain of a so-called China trader and his granddaughter who, after a short engagement to a young captain from here, disappeared on her wedding-day. But let that pass. What's more important is a young Chinaman her father had brought back from China, at first as a servant but then he became the old man's friend and he died shortly afterwards and is buried in a lonely place beside the churchyard. I drove past it recently but quickly turned aside and looked the other way because I thought that otherwise I'd see him sitting on his grave. For oh, dear Mama, I really did see him once, or at least that's what I thought, when I was sound asleep and Innstetten was away visiting the Prince. It was terrible, I wouldn't want to go through anything like that again. And I really can't invite you to a house like that, however attractive it is (in a strange way it's both cosy and eerie at the same time). And I would go as far as to say that in this matter Innstetten, although I agreed with him in many aspects, didn't behave quite correctly. He wanted me to look on it as women's nonsense and laugh at it, but then all at once he seemed to believe in it himself and rather oddly expected me to regard a family ghost like that as something superior and aristocratic. But I neither can nor want to do that. Indulgent as he is towards me in general, in this matter he's not indulgent or considerate enough. For I know from Johanna that there's something to it and also from our Frau Kruse. She's the coachman's wife and she spends all the time sitting in an over-heated room with a black hen. That in itself is frightening enough. And now you know why I want to come and stay with you when the time comes.

Oh, if only it were already here. There are so many reasons why I wish it were. This evening it's the New Year's Eve Ball and Gieshübler—the only nice person here, despite the fact that he has a high shoulder, or actually something more—Gieshübler's sent me some camellias. I might perhaps dance after all. Our doctor says it won't do any harm, on the contrary. And Innstetten agreed as well, which surprised me. And now give my best wishes and kisses to Papa and all the other dear ones. And a Happy New Year.

Your Effi.'

CHAPTER 13

The New Year's Eve Ball had lasted until late in the morning, and Effi had been extensively admired, though not quite as uncritically as her bouquet of camellias, that everyone knew came from Gieshübler's hothouse. In general, though, things remained as they were after the ball, hardly any attempts were made to establish social contact, with the result that the winter felt as if it went on for a long, long time. Visits from the neighbouring gentry were rare and the duty return visit was always preceded by a weary, 'Yes, Geert, if we really have to, but I'm dying of boredom.' A comment that Innstetten always just accepted. The things that were said about the family and children, farming as well, were tolerable; but when matters of religion cropped up and the pastors who were present were treated as little popes, or regarded themselves as such, then it was with melancholy that her thoughts went back to Niemeyer, who had always been reserved and modest, despite the fact that at every important church occasion people would say he had what it took to be called to the 'cathedral'. Although, with the exception of Sidonie Grasenabb, people were friendly, she never felt comfortable with the Borckes, Flemmings, and Grasenabbs, and she would have been in a pretty bad way as far as pleasure, amusement, even just feeling reasonably content were concerned had it not been for Gieshübler. He was a kind of human Providence in the way he looked after Effi, and she was grateful to him for it. Amongst all his other qualities, he was naturally a keen and attentive newspaper reader, not to mention the fact that he ran the local reading group, so that hardly a day passed without Mirambo bringing a large white envelope with all kinds of magazines and newspapers in which the important passages were marked, mostly with a fine pencil line, sometimes in heavy blue crayon, with an exclamation- or question-mark beside them. And that wasn't all, he also sent figs and dates, bars of chocolate in glossy paper tied with a red ribbon, and if something particularly beautiful came into bloom in his hothouse, he would bring it himself and would then spend a happy hour chatting to the young woman he liked so much and for whom he felt a mixture of all the finer feelings of love at once: those of a father and uncle, a teacher and admirer. Effi was touched by all this and often wrote about it in her letters to Hohen-Cremmen, so that her mother started to tease her with her 'love of the alchemist'; but this well-meant teasing missed its mark, indeed it touched an almost painful spot because it made her aware, if only vaguely, of what was actually lacking in her marriage: avowals, suggestions, little attentions. Innstetten was kind and good, but he wasn't a lover. He had the feeling that he loved Effi and the clear conscience that fact gave him meant that he didn't feel the need to make any special effort. It had almost become the rule that when Friedrich brought the lamp he would leave his wife's room and go to his own. 'I've got an awkward matter to sort out.' And with that he would go. He did leave the curtain between the rooms drawn back so that Effi could hear him leafing through a file or the scratch of his pen as he wrote, but that was all. Sometimes Rollo would come and lie down in front of her on the fireside rug, as if to say, 'Just have to check up on you again, no one else's going to do it.' Then she would bend down and say quietly, 'Yes, Rollo, we're alone.' At nine Innstetten would reappear, mostly with the newspaper, to take tea, and would talk about Bismarck, who had annoying problems again, especially with that Eugen Richter* whose attitude and language were unacceptable, and then go through the appointments and honours, most of which he criticized. Finally he would talk about the elections and how fortunate it was to be in charge of a district where people still had respect. Once he'd been through all that, he would ask Effi to play something, from *Lohengrin* or *Die Walküre*, for he was a Wagner enthusiast. It was unclear what had brought Innstetten to him; some said his nerves, for however down-to-earth he seemed to be, he was actually highly strung; others put it down to Wagner's attitude to the Jewish question.* Both were probably right. By ten Innstetten was relaxed and would indulge in a few well-meaning but somewhat weary caresses, that Effi tolerated without really responding to them.

*

Thus the winter passed, April arrived, and green shoots appeared in the garden behind the yard, which pleased Effi; she couldn't wait for summer, with its walks along the beach and the holidaymakers. When she looked back, the Trippelli evening at Gieshübler's and the New Year's Eve ball, yes, that had been all right, they had even been enjoyable, but the months that had followed had left much to be desired, and above all they had been so monotonous that she had even written to her mother:

'Can you imagine, Mama, that I'm almost reconciled to our ghost? Of course I wouldn't want to go through that terrible night again, when Geert was over at the Prince's, no, I certainly wouldn't; but always being alone with nothing happening, that has its difficult side too and then when I wake up in the night I sometimes listen to see if I can't hear the shoes sliding across the floor up there, and when everything stays quiet, I'm almost disappointed and think, if only it would come back, only not too bad and not too close.'

It was in February that Effi had written that, and now it was almost May. Over in the Plantation things were livening up already, you could hear the finches singing. That week was also the one when the storks returned, and one floated over her house and settled on a barn beside Utpatel's mill. It was its old resting-place. Effi, who was now writing frequently to Hohen-Cremmen, reported that as well and it was in the same letter that she went on:

'There's one thing I almost forgot, Mama dear: the new commander of the district army reserve, whom we've had here for almost four weeks now. Well, yes, do we really have him here? That is the question and an important question as well, however much you laugh, you can't help laughing at that because you don't know how desperate the social situation still is here. At least for me who doesn't get on with the local gentry. Perhaps it's my fault, but that doesn't alter the fact that the situation is desperate and for that reason I was putting all my hopes of relief on the new district commander. His predecessor was a horror, with poor manners and even worse habits and, to crown it all, always short of cash. He made us suffer all the time, Innstetten even more than me, and when, at the beginning of April, we heard that Major von Crampas—that's the name of the new one—was here, we fell into each other's arms as if all our troubles here in Kessin were over. However, as I suggested, it seems that although he is here, nothing's going to come of it again. Crampas is married, two children of ten and eight, his wife one year older than him, let's say forty-five. Now in principle that wouldn't be a problem, why shouldn't I be able to have wonderful chats with a motherly friend? Marietta Trippelli was close to thirty and we got on very well together. But there's no joy to be had with Frau von Crampas (she wasn't born a "von", by the way). She's always depressed, almost melancholy (like our Frau Kruse, whom in fact she reminds me of) and all that out of jealousy. He, Crampas, is said to be a man who's had many affairs, a ladies' man, something that's always seemed ridiculous to me and would be ridiculous in this case too if he hadn't had a duel with a comrade because of these matters. His arm had been smashed just below the left shoulder and you can see it straight away even though the operation, as Innstetten told me (I think they call it resection; it was Wilms* who carried it out), is said to be a masterpiece of the surgeon's art. Both Herr and Frau von Crampas came to make their call on us a fortnight ago; it was a very awkward situation since Frau von Crampas kept her eye on her husband in such a way that he was moderately and I very embarrassed. Three days later, when he was alone with Innstetten and I could follow the course of their conversation from my room, I discovered that he can be very different, relaxed and high-spirited. I talked to him myself afterwards. A perfect gentleman, exceptionally urbane. Innstetten was in the same brigade as him during the war and they quite often saw each other at Count Gröben's* in the north of Paris. Yes, Mama dear, that would have been something to start new life in Kessin; he, the Major, doesn't suffer from the Pomeranian prejudices, even though they say he comes from Swedish Pomerania.* But his wife! It's impossible without her and absolutely impossible with her.'

*

Effi was quite right, no real closer friendship developed between them and the Crampases. They occasionally saw each other out at the Borckes', another time briefly at the station, and a few days later during an excursion by boat to a large oak and beech wood called the 'Schnatermann', by the Breitling estuary, but contact never went beyond cursory greetings, and Effi was glad when June arrived and the season approached. There was still a lack of summer visitors, of course, only odd ones would appear before Midsummer Day, but the preparations themselves provided a diversion. Roundabouts and stalls with shooting-targets were being set up in the Plantation, the boatmen were caulking and painting their boats, every little house had new curtains, and the rooms that were damp and therefore had rot under the floorboards were fumigated and then aired.

There was a certain excitement in Effi's house as well, though for a different expected arrival than that of the summer visitors, of course; even Frau Kruse wanted to join in as far as possible. But Effi was horrified at the idea, and said, 'Geert, see that Frau Kruse doesn't touch anything; it won't do any good and I'm frightened enough as it is.' Innstetten promised her everything, Christel and Johanna, he said, had plenty of time, and to put such thoughts out of his young wife's mind he dropped the subject of the preparations entirely, and asked her instead if she'd noticed that a summer visitor had already moved in across the road, not the very first, but one of the first.

'A gentleman?'

'No, a lady. She's been here before, always taking the same apartment. And she always comes this early in the season because she can't bear it when everything's full.'

'I can't blame her for that. Who is she?'

'Frau Rohde, the widow of a filing-clerk.'

'Strange. I've always imagined clerks' widows as poor.'

'Yes,' Innstetten laughed, 'as a rule they are. But in this case you have an exception. She must have more than just her widow's pension. She always brings a lot of luggage, much, much more than she uses, in fact she's quite a singular woman, eccentric, infirm, and not very steady on her feet. She doesn't trust herself to go out alone and always has an oldish servant with her who's strong enough to protect her or to carry her if something happens. She's got a new one this year, but this one's very stocky as well, like Marietta Trippelli only even more robust.'

'Oh, I've already seen her. Nice brown eyes with a loyal, trusting look. But just a little stupid as well.'

'Yes, that's her.'

*

That conversation between Effi and Innstetten took place in the middle of June. From then on new visitors were coming every day, and a walk out to the quay to watch the steamer arriving was a kind of daily occupation for the Kessiners. Of course Effi was unable to join them, since Innstetten couldn't accompany her, but at least she could enjoy seeing the usually empty street fill with crowds heading out to the beach and the beach hotel, and to do that she spent much more time than usual in her bedroom, the window of which gave her the best view. Johanna would then stand beside her and could tell her almost everything she wanted to know. Most of the passers-by were people who came every year, and so the maid could not just tell her their names but often had a little story to go with them.

That was an entertainment for Effi and cheered her up. But on Midsummer Day of all days it so happened that, shortly before eleven when the stream of traffic from the steamer was usually at its most lively, instead of cabs loaded with parents, children, and trunks a carriage draped in black (followed by two cabs with mourning housings) came down the street leading from the centre of town to the Plantation and stopped outside the house opposite. Frau Rohde had died three days before, and her Berlin relations, who had arrived at short notice, had decided not to have the body taken to Berlin but buried in the Kessin churchyard on the dunes. Effi stood at the window watching the strangely solemn scene being played out across the road with keen interest. The people who had come from Berlin were two nephews and their wives, all around forty and with enviably healthy complexions. The nephews, in neatly fitting dress-coats, were acceptable, and the matter-of-fact, businesslike way they went about everything was seemly rather than out of place. But their two wives! They were visibly determined to show the Kessiners what real mourning was and so wore long, black-crape veils that went down to the ground and also covered their faces. And now the coffin, on which there were a few wreaths and even one palm-leaf, was placed on the hearse and the two couples took their seats in the carriages. Lindequist got into the first with one of the couples, but behind the second was the landlady and, walking beside her, the imposing figure of the attendant Frau Rohde had brought with her to Kessin. The latter was very agitated, and her agitation seemed to be genuine, even if it wasn't exactly mourning; on the other hand, one could tell all too clearly that the landlady, a widow who was sobbing loudly, was on the look-out for a gratuity, even though she had the advantage, for which all the other landladies envied her, of being able to re-let the apartment that had been taken for the whole summer.

Once the procession had set off Effi went to her garden behind the courtyard in order to clear from her mind, between the boxwood hedges, the impression, so devoid of love and life, that the scene across the road had left her with. When this was unsuccessful, she decided she felt like going for a longer walk rather than continuing to plod round the garden, especially since the doctor had told her that plenty of exercise in the open air was the best way to prepare for what lay ahead. Johanna, who was with her in the garden, brought her a shawl, hat, and parasol, that could also serve as an umbrella, and with a friendly 'Goodbye', Effi went out and set off for the little wood that, alongside the broad, macadamized road, had a narrower footpath leading to the dunes and the hotel by the beach. There were benches along it and she used every one, for she found it tiring to walk now, in the midday heat. But once she was sitting down and watching the carriages with people in their finery driving past she brightened up again, for seeing cheerful scenes was the stuff of life for her. The worst part of the walk came when the wood ended: sand and more sand and not a scrap of shade, but fortunately the path had been surfaced with boards and planks, so she arrived at the beach hotel in good spirits, if somewhat hot and tired. People were already eating in the dining-room inside, but outside everything around was quiet and empty, which at that moment was what she liked best. She got the waiter to bring her a sherry and a glass of Biliner mineral water,* and watched the sea shimmering in the bright sunlight as little waves broke on the shore. 'Bornholm's* over there and beyond it Visby,* that Jahnke was always going into raptures about years ago. Visby was almost more important to him than Lübeck and Wullenweber.* And beyond Visby there's Stockholm, where they had the Stockholm Bloodbath,* and after that the great rivers, then the North Pole and the midnight sun.' And she was gripped by a longing to see all of that. But then, almost with a start, she remembered the event that was so close at hand. 'It's a sin for me to be faraway, dreaming such frivolous thoughts, when my mind ought to be on the immediate future. Perhaps I'll be punished for it and we'll both die, the child and me. And the hearse and the two carriages won't be stopping across the road, they'll stop outside our house . . . No, no, I don't want to die here, I don't want to be buried here, I want to go back to Hohen-Cremmen. And Lindequist, good that he is—I still prefer Niemeyer, he christened and confirmed and married me, and Niemeyer's to bury me as well.' And at that a tear fell on her hand. Then she laughed again. 'But I'm still alive, I'm only seventeen and Niemeyer's fifty-seven.'

She could hear the clatter of crockery from the dining-room, but all at once she thought she heard the sound of chairs being pushed back. Perhaps people were already getting up, and she wanted to avoid meeting anyone, so she quickly stood up herself to go back into the town by a roundabout route. This passed close by the graveyard on the dunes, and since the gate was open she went in. Everything was in bloom, butterflies were flying over the graves, and there were a few gulls hanging high up in the air. It was so quiet and beautiful there she would have liked to linger by the first graves, but as the sun burning down was getting hotter by the minute, she went up to where the path was shaded by weeping willows and ash planted by the graves. When she came to the end of the shade she saw on the right a fresh mound of sand with four or five wreaths on it and, close by, a bench. It was beyond the row of trees, and sitting there was the good, robust woman who had been the last mourner following Frau Rohde's coffin beside the landlady. Effi immediately recognized her and was moved to see this good, faithful woman, for that is what she felt sure she was, there in the scorching heat of the sun. It must have been two hours since the burial.

'It's a hot spot you've chosen here,' Effi said, 'much too hot. And if you're unlucky you'll get sunstroke.'

'And that would be best.'

'Why so?'

'Then I'd be finished with all this.'

'I don't think one should say that kind of thing, even if you're unhappy or someone you like has died. I presume you liked her very much?'

'Me? *Her?* God forbid.'

'But you're very sad. There must be some reason for that.'

'There certainly is, Ma'am.'

'You know who I am?'

'Yes. You're the Landrat's wife from across the road. I was always talking about you with the old woman. At the end she couldn't, because she couldn't get her breath properly, she had it on her chest, it must have been water. But for as long as she could still speak she talked all the time. She was a real Berliner . . .'

'A good mistress?'

'No, I'd be lying if I said that. She's under the ground now and you shouldn't speak ill of the dead, especially when they're only just at rest. Yes, she'll certainly be that at last. But she was a bad lot, nagging and mean, and she made no provision for me. And her relations who came from Berlin yesterday . . . they were bickering until late into the night . . . no, they're a bad lot too, a really bad lot. Greedy and grasping and hard-hearted: they did pay me my wages, but in a surly, unfriendly manner and with all sorts of nasty comments, just because they had to and because it was only six days to the end of the quarter. Otherwise I wouldn't have got anything, or just half or just a quarter. Nothing but what they were obliged to give me. And they gave me a torn five-mark note so that I can get back to Berlin; well, that should be just about enough for fourth class and I suppose I'll have to sit on my suitcase. But I'm not going to; I'm going to stay sitting here until I die . . . God, I thought I'd be settled for a bit and I could have put up with the old woman. And now nothing's come of it and I'm going to be pushed around again. And I'm Catholic into the bargain. Oh, I'm fed up, most of all I'd like to swap places with the old woman, as far as I'm concerned she could go on living . . . She'd have liked that; those kind of people who enjoy tormenting others, even when they can't get their breath, are always the ones who like living most.'

Rollo, who had come with Effi, was now sitting in front of the woman with his tongue hanging right out, and looking at her. When she stopped talking he stood up, took a step forward, and laid his head on her knee.

Suddenly the woman was transformed. 'God, that's something! A creature that can stand me, gives me a friendly look, and puts its head on my knee. God, it's a long time since I've had something like that. Well then, old boy, what are you called? Aren't you a beauty.'

'Rollo,' Effi said.

'Rollo, that's a funny name, but it doesn't matter. I've got a funny name as well. Christian name, that is, and that's the only name people like us have.'

'So what is your name?'

'I'm called Roswitha.'

'Yes, that's unusual, that must be . . .'

'Yes, Ma'am, it's a Catholic name. And on top of that I am a Catholic. From Eichsfeld.* And being Catholic always makes things more difficult, makes life a misery. A lot of people refuse to hire Catholics because they're off to church so often. "Always going to confession and still they keep quiet about the most important thing"—God, how often have I heard that, first of all when I was in service in Giebichenstein* and then in Berlin. But I'm a poor Catholic, I've quite got out of the habit, perhaps that's why I'm in such a bad way; no, you shouldn't abandon your faith, you should do everything you're supposed to.'

'Roswitha.' Effi repeated the name and sat down beside her on the bench. 'What do you plan to do now?'

'Plan to do, Ma'am? I plan to do nothing at all. Really and truly I'd like to stay sitting here till I drop down dead. Then people would think I loved the old woman like a faithful dog, and couldn't leave her grave and so died there. But that's wrong, you don't die for an old woman like that; I just want to die because there's no way I can live.'

'Let me ask you something, Roswitha. Are you fond of children? Have you ever worked where they had young children?'

'I certainly have. Those are the best, the nicest positions I've had. An old Berliner like her—God forgive me, she's dead now, she'll be before the throne of God and can accuse me—with old women like that, well, it's terrible all the things you have to do, it really makes you feel sick, but a sweet little thing, a little mite like a doll, looking at you out of those big, round eyes, that really is something, it really does your heart good. When I was in Halle I was nurse to the wife of the manager of the salt-works, and in Giebichenstein, where I was later, I brought up twins on the bottle. Yes, Ma'am, I know about that, it's all second nature to me.'

'Now I'll tell you something, Roswitha, you're a good, faithful woman, I can see that just by looking at you, a bit outspoken but that's no harm, some of the best are like that, and I immediately felt I could trust you. Will you come and work for me? I'm expecting a child soon, God grant me his aid, and once the baby's here it will have to be looked after and attended to and perhaps even bottle-fed, you never know, though I hope that won't happen. What do you think, will you come and help me? I can't imagine I'm wrong about you.'

Roswitha leapt up, grasped the young woman's hand, and kissed it impulsively. 'So there is a God after all. The night is darkest just before dawn. You'll see, Ma'am, it will be all right; I'm a respectable woman and I have good testimonials. You'll see that when I bring you my record of employment. The very first time I saw Madam I thought, if only you could work for someone like that. And now I can. O dear Lord, O holy Virgin Mary, who would have thought this would happen after we'd buried the old woman, and her relations saw to it that they got away and left me stuck here.'

'Yes, Roswitha, good things can come like a bolt from the blue as well. Now it's time to go. Rollo's getting impatient, he keeps running over to the gate.'

Roswitha was ready, but first she went over to the grave again, mumbled something and crossed herself, then they went back down the shady path to the graveyard gate. Across the road was the patch surrounded by railings, its white stone gleaming and glinting in the sun. Now Effi could look at it more calmly. For a while the path continued between the dunes until, shortly before Utpatel's mill, they reached the edge of the little wood. There they turned left and, taking an avenue called the Reeperbahn* that ran diagonally through the wood, Effi headed for her house together with Roswitha.

CHAPTER 14

In less than quarter of an hour they were at the house. When they went into the cool hall Roswitha's attention was caught by all the strange things hanging there, but before she could start thinking about them Effi said, 'Go in there, Roswitha. That's the room where we sleep. First of all I'm going to go and see my husband in the Landrat's office over there—the big house next to the little one where you were—to tell him I'd like to take you on to look after the child. I'm sure he'll be happy with that, but I have to get his agreement first. And once that's done we'll have to move his things out and you can sleep in the alcove in my room. I'm sure we'll get along with each other.'

When Innstetten heard what it was about he took it in good part, and quickly said, 'You were quite right to do that, Effi, and if there's nothing too bad in her record of employment we'll take her on the basis of her honest face. It's very rare that one is wrong about that.'

Effi was pleased to encounter so little in the way of problems, and said, 'Now things will be all right. I'm not afraid any more.'

'Of what, Effi?'

'Oh, you know . . . But things you imagine are the worst, sometimes worse than anything else.'

*

With her few belongings Roswitha moved across into the house straight away and settled into the little alcove. At the end of the day she went to bed early and, weary as she was, fell asleep immediately.

The next morning Effi, who for a while had been suffering from her fears again (it was the time of the full moon), asked Roswitha how she had slept and whether she had heard anything.

'What?' Roswitha asked.

'Oh, nothing. I was just asking; something going across the floor-boards, like a brush sweeping or a person sliding.'

Roswitha laughed, which made a particularly good impression on her new mistress. Effi's upbringing had been firmly Protestant, and she would have been horrified if anyone had seen anything Catholic about her; despite that, she believed that Catholicism was better at protecting us against such things as 'those up there'; indeed, that idea had had considerable influence on her plan to make Roswitha part of the household.

They quickly settled in together, for Effi, like most young ladies from the country areas of Brandenburg, enjoyed hearing little anecdotes, and the late Frau Rohde and her miserliness, as well as her nephews and their wives, provided an inexhaustible source of those.

Johanna liked to listen in as well. She would smile when Effi, as she often did, laughed out loud at Roswitha's graphic descriptions, quietly surprised that her mistress enjoyed all that silly stuff so much. Her surprise, however, which went together with a sense of superiority, was a good thing in that it ensured there were no quarrels about precedence. Roswitha was simply seen as a clown, and to envy her would for Johanna have been no different from being jealous of Rollo's position as a special friend.

Thus a week passed in pleasant chat, and Effi felt almost at ease as she was less apprehensive than she had been about what was to come. Nor did she feel it was that close, but two days later there was an end to the cosy chats; people were running and dashing to and fro, even Innstetten abandoned his habitual reserve, and on the morning of the 3rd of July there was a cradle beside Effi's bed.

Dr Hannemann patted her hand and said, 'Today's the anniversary of the Battle of Königgrätz,* pity it's a girl. But you can always have one of the other kind next and the Prussians have lots of victories to celebrate.' Roswitha could well have had similar ideas, but in the meantime her delight at the child that was there was completely unreserved, and without further ado she called her 'Wee Annie', which her young mother took as a sign, saying Roswitha must have chanced on that name by inspiration. Even Innstetten could think of no objections, and so they were talking of little Annie long before she was baptized. Effi, who intended to be at her parents' in Hohen-Cremmen from the middle of August on, would have liked to have put off the baptism until then, but that was impossible. Innstetten couldn't take leave, so it was arranged that the baptism would take place, in the church of course, on the 15th of August, even though that was the anniversary of Napoleon's birthday* (which did indeed raise objections from some families). Since their house had no room large enough, the subsequent meal was held in the large hotel on the Embankment; all the neighbouring gentry had been invited and came. Pastor Lindequist proposed a charming toast, that everyone admired, to mother and child, which led Sidonie von Grasenabb to remark to her neighbour, a young civil servant from a noble family with strict views on religion, 'Yes, he's all right as far as that kind of speech goes, but his sermons are fit for neither God nor man; he's half-hearted about religion, one of those who will be rejected because they are lukewarm. I think this is not the right place to quote the actual words from the Bible.'* Immediately afterwards Herr von Borcke stood up to propose a toast to Innstetten. 'Ladies and gentlemen, these are difficult times in which we live, rebellion, defiance, insubordination wherever you look. But as long as we still have men and, might I add, women and mothers . . .' (and with that he made a bow with an elegant gesture in Effi's direction), 'as long as we still have men like Baron Innstetten, whom I am proud to call my friend, things will be all right, old Prussia will still survive. Yes, my friends, Pomerania and Brandenburg, that's what will do it, that's what will crush the head of the pernicious dragon of revolution. If we remain loyal and steadfast, we will win through. Our brother Catholics, whom we must respect, even though we are fighting against them, have their rock of St Peter, but we have our *rocher de bronze*.* Ladies and gentlemen, raise your glasses to Baron Innstetten.'

Innstetten gave a very brief reply of thanks. Turning to Major von Crampas, who was sitting next to her, Effi said that all that about the rock of St Peter was probably a compliment to Roswitha; later on she'd go over to Justizrat Gadebusch and ask if he agreed with her. For some reason or other Crampas took this remark seriously and advised her not to ask the Justizrat,* which amused Effi no end.

'I thought you were a better judge of character.'

'But, my dear Frau Baronin, no judgement gets one anywhere with beautiful young women who aren't even eighteen.'

'You really are ruining your chances, Major. Call me a grand-mother, if you like, but allusions to the fact that I'm not yet eighteen are unforgivable.'

After the meal was finished the late-afternoon steamer came down the Kessine and moored at the pier opposite the hotel. All the windows were open, and Effi, who was taking coffee with Crampas and Gieshübler, watched the scene on the other side of the river. 'Tomorrow at nine the same ship's going to take me up the river, by midday I'll be in Berlin, in the evening in Hohen-Cremmen, and Roswitha will be alongside me, carrying the child. I hope she won't cry. Oh, I'm already looking forward to it so much. My dear Gieshübler, have you ever felt so happy at seeing your parental home again?'

'Yes, I've felt that too, Frau Baronin. Only I didn't have a little Annie to take home with me.'

'It's never too late,' Crampas said. 'Your good health, Gieshübler, you're the only sensible person here.'

'But there's only brandy left, Major.'

'All the better.'

CHAPTER 15

Effi left in the middle of August; by the end of September she was back in Kessin. Several times during those six weeks she had felt a desire to be back, but when she was home again and entered the dark hallway, that was only lit by the rather pale light from the stairs, she all at once felt afraid again and said quietly, 'There's no such pale light anywhere in Hohen-Cremmen.'

Yes, a few times during the weeks in Hohen-Cremmen she had longed to be back in the 'eerie house', but all in all her days at home and been happy and contented. True, she found things difficult with Hulda, who couldn't get over the fact that she was still waiting for a husband or fiancé, but they were all the better with the twins, and more than once, when she was playing ball or croquet with them, she completely forgot she was married. Those had been happy moments. But what she enjoyed most of all was standing the way she used to on the swing as it flew through the air, feeling a strange tingling, a pleasurable shudder of danger, as she thought, 'Now I'm going to fall.' When she finally jumped down she would go with the two girls to the bench outside the schoolhouse and, once they were sitting there, tell Jahnke, who soon came to join them, about her life in Kessin, that was half Hanseatic, half Scandinavian, but at any rate very different from that in Schwantikow and Hohen-Cremmen.

Such were her daily amusements, with the occasional trip out into the summer Marshes, mostly in the phaeton; but what Effi enjoyed most of all were the chats she had almost every morning with her Mama. They would sit upstairs in the large, airy drawing-room, with Roswitha rocking the child and singing all sorts of cradle-songs in Thuringian dialect that no one could understand, perhaps not even Roswitha herself. Effi and Frau von Briest would go and sit by the open window, looking down on the park while they spoke, at the sundial or the dragonflies hovering almost motionless over the pond, or at the flagstones where Herr von Briest would be sitting by the outside staircase, reading the newspaper. Every time he turned a page he would first take off his pince-nez and wave to his wife and daughter. Once he was on the last page, that was usually the *Anzeiger fürs Havelland*, the one with local news, Effi would go down, either to sit with him or to take a stroll together round the garden and park. On one such occasion they turned off from the gravel path to a little monument Briest's grandfather had erected in memory of the Battle of Waterloo, a rusty pyramid with a cast-iron figure of Blücher* at the front and a similar one of Wellington at the back. 'Have you walks like this in Kessin,' Briest said, 'and does Innstetten accompany you and tell you all kinds of things?'

'No, Papa, I don't have that kind of walk. It's impossible, we've only got a little garden behind the house, it's hardly even a garden, just a few beds bordered with box and some vegetable plots with two or three fruit-trees in them. Innstetten's not interested in that and probably doesn't think he's going to stay in Kessin for long.'

'But you must get some exercise and fresh air, child, you're used to that.'

'But I do. Our house is next to a little wood they call the Plantation. I go for walks there a lot and take Rollo with me.'

'Always Rollo,' Briest laughed. 'If one didn't know otherwise, one could almost think Rollo meant more to you than your husband and child.'

'Oh, that would be terrible, Papa, though actually—this much I have to admit—there was a time when life there wouldn't have been possible without Rollo. That was at the time when . . . you know . . . He as good as saved me, or at least I imagined he did, and since then he's been my friend, one I know I can always rely on. But he's only a dog, people come first, of course.'

'Yes, people always say that, but I have my doubts. It's a funny thing about dumb animals, what's right or wrong, the jury's still out on that one. Believe me, Effi, that's another big question. Just imagine someone has an accident in the water or, what's worse, on thin ice, and there's a dog there, one like your Rollo, let's say, well it won't give up until it's got the poor person back on land. And if they're dead it'll lie down beside the body and bark or whine until someone comes, and if no one comes it'll stay there until it's dead itself. That's what a dumb animal like that will always do. Mankind, on the other hand! God forgive me, but sometimes I think dumb animals are better than humans.'

'But, Papa, what if I were to tell Innstetten that . . .'

'No, you'd better not do that, Effi.'

'Of course Rollo would save me, but Innstetten would save me too. He has his honour.'

'He certainly does.'

'And he loves me.'

'Of course, it goes without saying. And where there's love, it's returned. That's the way things are. The only thing that surprises me is that he hasn't taken a couple of days off and nipped over. When you've got such a young wife . . .'

Effi blushed because the same thought had occurred to her, but she didn't want to admit it. 'Innstetten's so conscientious and, I think, wants to be well regarded and has his plans for the future; Kessin's just a stepping-stone. And I'm not going to run off. He's sure of me. If you're too affectionate . . . and with the difference in age . . . people would just grin.'

'Yes, they do do that, Effi. But you have to accept it. And don't say anything about this. Not even to your Mama. It's so difficult to decide what you should or should not do. That's another big question.'

*

There had been more than one conversation like that during Effi's stay with her parents, but fortunately the effect never lasted long. Similarly, the somewhat melancholy feeling that had immediately overcome Effi on her return to the house in Kessin quickly dissipated. Innstetten was full of attentions, and once they had taken their tea over animated gossip about what had been going on in the town and who was in love with whom, Effi affectionately took his arm to continue their chat in her room and to hear a few more anecdotes about Fräulein Trippelli, who had recently been in lively correspondence with Gieshübler which, as always, meant there was a new charge to her account that was permanently in the red. During this conversation Effi was in very high spirits, felt she truly was a young woman, and was glad to be rid of Roswitha's presence for the immediate future, the maid having been moved to the servant's quarters.

In the morning she said, 'It's fine today and mild, and I hope the veranda looking out onto the Plantation's still sound and we can go and sit outside and have breakfast there. We'll be back in our rooms soon enough, and the winter in Kessin really is four weeks too long.'

Innstetten was happy with that. The veranda Effi was talking about, perhaps 'tent' would be a better word, had been repaired during the summer, three or four weeks before Effi had gone to Hohen-Cremmen, and consisted of a large wooden deck with a huge canvas canopy above it and, on either side, broad linen curtains on iron rings that could be pushed back and forward along iron rods. It was a delightful spot, admired throughout the summer by the holiday-makers who had to pass it on their way to the beach.

Effi, leaning back in a rocking-chair, pushed the coffee tray over from the side of the table to her husband and said, 'You could be mother today, Geert; I feel so comfortable in this rocking-chair, I don't feel like getting up. So make an effort, and if you're really glad to have me back I'll soon find ways of making it up to you.' As she spoke she straightened the damask tablecloth and left her hand there, that Innstetten picked up and kissed.

'How did you ever manage to cope without me?'

'Not very well, Effi.'

'You're just saying that and looking downcast, while it's not true at all.'

'But Effi . . .'

'As I will prove to you. If you'd felt the slightest longing to see your child—I'm not going to talk about myself, after all, what is one to such a noble lord who was a bachelor for so long and wasn't in a hurry to . . .'

'Well?'

'Yes, Geert, if you'd felt just the slightest longing, you wouldn't have left me all on my own in Hohen-Cremmen, like a widow, with no company apart from Niemeyer and Jahnke and the Bellings in Schwantikow. And none of the Rathenow hussars came over, it was as if they were afraid of me or that I was too old now.'

'The way you talk, Effi. You're a little coquette, did you know that?'

'Thank God you said that. For you men, that's the best we can be. And you're no different from all the rest, despite your solemn, staid airs. I'm well aware of that, Geert . . . Actually you're . . .'

'I'm what?'

'Well, I'd rather not say. But I know you very well; actually, as my uncle from Schwantikow once said, you're an affectionate type, born under Venus, and Uncle Belling was quite right when he said that. You just don't want to show it, you think it's not proper and might ruin your career. Am I right?'

Innstetten laughed. 'You're not entirely wrong. Do you know what, Effi, you seem to be quite different. Until little Annie arrived you were a child. But all at once . . .'

'Well?'

'Suddenly you're a different person. But it suits you, I like you very much like that. Do you know what?'

'What?'

'There's something seductive about you.'

'Oh Geert, my one and only, that's marvellous what you've just said; it really does my heart good to hear it . . . Pour me another half-cup . . . Do you know, that's something I've always wished for? We have to be seductive, otherwise we're nothing at all . . .'

'Is that your own idea?'

'It could be my own, but I got it from Niemeyer.'

'From Niemeyer! God in heaven, what a pastor! No, there aren't any like that round here. But how did he come to say that? It's more like a Don Juan or ladies' man talking.'

'Yes, who knows,' Effi laughed . . . 'But isn't that Crampas? Coming from the beach? He surely can't have been for a dip? On the 27th of September . . .'

'He does that kind of thing quite often. Just showing off.'

By this time Crampas was close by and wished them a good morning.

'Good morning,' Innstetten called back. 'Come over, come over.'

Crampas, who was in civilian clothes, did so, and kissed Effi's hand. Effi continued to rock in her chair. 'You must excuse me, Major, for not playing the lady of the house, but ten in the morning's not the time for it, nor is the veranda a house. Things are quite informal here or, if you like, intimate. Now sit down and tell me what you've been doing and why. From your hair—and for your sake, I wish you had more of it—it's clear you've been for a dip in the sea.'

He nodded.

'Irresponsible,' Innstetten said, half seriously, half joking. 'Only four weeks ago you saw yourself the business with Heinersdorf,* the banker, who thought the sea and the magnificent breakers would show him respect because of his millions. But the gods are jealous of each other, and Neptune immediately rose up against Pluto,* or at least against Heinersdorf.'

Crampas laughed. 'Yes, a million marks! If I had that, my dear Innstetten, I wouldn't have risked it at all; the weather may be fine, but the water was only nine degrees. But people like yours truly, with his million overdraft—forgive me for boasting—can risk it without fear of arousing the jealousy of the gods. And I take comfort in the proverb: a man destined for the gallows will never drown.'

'But, Major, surely you wouldn't . . . how shall I put it? . . . bring something as banal as that on yourself by idle talk. Though there are people who think that everyone more or less deserves what you were talking about. Still, Major . . . for a major . . .'

'. . . it's not a traditional way of meeting one's end, agreed, Frau Baronin. Not traditional and in my case not even probable, so it was all just a quotation or, to be more precise, a *façon de parler*. But when I said just now that the sea wouldn't harm me, there was something that was honestly meant behind it. The fact is that I will die a true and, I hope, honourable soldier's death. It was only a gypsy prophecy, but it struck a chord in my own conscience.'

Innstetten laughed. 'There'll be some difficulty with that, Crampas, unless you intend to serve under the Grand Turk or the Chinese dragon.* They're still fighting out there but, believe you me, history's over and done with here for the next thirty years, so anyone who wants to die a soldier's death . . .'

'. . . has to order a war from Bismarck. I know all that, Innstetten. But that would be no problem for you. It's the end of September now; in ten weeks at the latest the Prince will be back in Varzin, and since he's taken a liking to you—not to put it any stronger, I don't want to end up facing the barrel of your pistol—I'm sure you can get just a little war for an old comrade from Vionville.* After all, the Prince is only human, and a persuasive tongue can help.'

During this conversation Effi had been rolling bits of bread into balls, tossing them on to the table, and arranging them in patterns in order to indicate that she would like a change of topic. Despite that, Innstetten seemed about to reply to Crampas's jocular remarks, so she decided to intervene directly. 'I don't see why we should concern ourselves with your manner of death, Major; life is closer and, at the moment, a much more serious business.'

Crampas nodded.

'It's right for you to admit I'm right. How should one live here? *That* is the question, *that* is more important than all the rest. Gieshübler wrote to me about it. I'd show you the letter, except that would be indiscreet and vain of me, for there's all sorts of other incidental remarks in it . . . Innstetten doesn't need to read it, he has no appreciation of that kind of thing . . . beautifully neat copperplate, and turns of phrase as if our friend had grown up at an old French court rather than on the old market square in Kessin. And that he's deformed and wears white cravats such as no one else does any more—where he gets them ironed I've no idea—all that fits together perfectly. Well, Gieshübler wrote to me about the Club evenings and mentioned an organizer by the name of Crampas. So you see, Major, I'd be happier to hear about that rather than a soldier's death or the other kind.'

'Me too, I assure you. And the winter season is bound to be a splendid one if we can be assured of the support of the Frau Baronin. Marietta Trippelli's coming . . .'

'Fräulein Trippelli? That makes me superfluous.'

'Not at all, my dear Frau Baronin. Marietta Trippelli can't sing from one Sunday to the next, that would be too much for her and too much for us; variety is the spice of life, a truth that seems to be contradicted by every happy marriage.'

'If there are happy marriages, mine excepted . . .' and she took Innstetten's hand.

'Variety, then,' Crampas went on. 'And to provide that for the Club, whose vice-president I have the honour to be at the moment, we need to get all our experienced members together. If we can do that I'm sure we can turn the town upside-down. The plays have already been chosen: *War in Peace*, *Monsieur Hercules*, Wilbrandt's *Young Love*, perhaps also Gensichen's *Euphrosyne*.* You as Euphrosyne, I as the old Goethe. You'll be amazed how well I can play the old Goethe.'

'I'm sure I will. I learnt from the letter of my alchemical secret correspondent that you are also an occasional poet. At first I was surprised . . .'

'For I didn't look the part.'

'No. But since I know that you bathe at nine degrees, I've changed my mind . . . the Baltic at nine degrees, that surpasses the Castalian spring . . .'*

'The temperature of which is unknown.'

'Not to me; at least no one will contradict me. But I have to get up now, here comes Roswitha with Wee Annie.'

She stood up quickly and went over to Roswitha, took the child from her, and held it up, with a proud and happy look.

CHAPTER 16

The weather was fine, and remained so well into October. One result of this was that the tent-like veranda came into its own, so much so that they regularly spent the mornings there. Towards eleven the Major would usually turn up, first to ask how the Frau Baronin was and to indulge in a little scandal-mongering with her, which he was exceptionally good at, then to arrange a ride with Innstetten, often heading inland, up the Kessine as far as the Breitling estuary or, even more often, out to the breakwaters. Once the men had gone Effi would play with the child or leaf through the newspapers and magazines Gieshübler continued to send her; now and then she wrote a letter to her Mama or would say, 'Roswitha, let's take Annie for a walk,' and Roswitha would take the bassinet and push it, with Effi walking behind, the few hundred yards into the little wood, to a place with chestnuts scattered over the ground that they would pick up and give to the child to play with. Effi didn't go into the town much, there was no one there she could have a real chat with after her second attempt to establish closer relations with Frau von Crampas had failed. The Major's wife was, and remained, unsociable.

This went on for several weeks, until Effi suddenly expressed the wish to go out riding with them; she was passionately fond of it, she said, and it was asking too much to expect her to abstain from something that meant so much to her simply because of what the townsfolk would say. The Major thought it was a capital idea, and Innstetten, who was clearly unhappy with it—so unhappy that he kept saying it would be impossible to find a horse suitable for a woman—had to give way when Crampas assured him that he would see to that. And, indeed, the required mount was found and Effi was in seventh heaven at being able to tear along the beach now that the divisive injunctions, 'Ladies' Bathing' and 'Gentlemen's Bathing', no longer applied. Rollo usually joined them, and since it had occasionally happened that they wanted to rest on the beach or go for a short walk, they decided they would have servants to accompany them, to which end the Major's batman, an old Treptow uhlan called Knut, and Kruse, Innstetten's coachman, were transformed into grooms, though only to a certain degree: they were garbed in a rather motley livery which, much to Effi's disappointment, still bore visible traces of their actual functions.

It was already the middle of October when this whole cavalcade set off for the first time, Innstetten and Crampas in front with Effi between them, then Kruse and Knut and, bringing up the rear, Rollo, who however, fed up with trotting along behind, was soon in front of everyone. After they'd passed the now empty beach hotel and, keeping to the right on the beach path with a moderate sea washing over it, soon afterwards reached the breakwater, they decided they'd like to dismount and walk to the end of it. Effi was the first out of the saddle. Between the two stone walls the broad Kessine flowed calmly out to the sea that lay before them, a sunlit expanse ruffled just here and there by a slight wave.

Effi had never been out there yet, for when she arrived in Kessin the previous November the weather was already stormy, and when summer came she was no longer in a state to undertake long walks. Now she was delighted, thought everything was grand and splendid, indulged in derisive comparisons of the Havelland Marshes with the sea, and whenever she came across a piece of driftwood she picked it up and threw it, either to the left into the sea or to the right into the Kessine. As always, Rollo was happy to oblige his mistress by plunging in; all at once, however, his attention was caught by something in a different direction and, creeping forward carefully, indeed almost fearfully, he suddenly leapt at some object they could see in front. But his leap was in vain, for at the same moment a seal slipped smoothly and silently off a seaweed-covered rock down to the sea that was only five yards away. Its head could be seen for a short while, then that also disappeared under the surface.

They were all excited, and Crampas had visions of a seal-hunt and said they should bring their guns the next time, 'those blighters have a solid pelt'.

'Impossible,' Innstetten said. 'Harbour police.'

'The things you say,' the Major laughed. 'The harbour police! Surely the three authorities we have here can all turn a blind eye. Does everything have to be so terribly lawful? All lawful activities are boring.'

Effi clapped.

'Yes, Crampas, that suits you and, as you can see, Effi is applauding. Of course. Women always shout for the police straight away, but the law can go hang as far as they're concerned.'

'A woman's right since time immemorial and we can do nothing to change it, Innstetten.'

'No,' Innstetten laughed, 'and I don't want to, either. There's no point in attempting the impossible. But a man like you, Crampas, who has grown up under the flag of discipline and knows very well that without it, without order, life would be impossible, a man like you shouldn't talk like that, not even in jest. You have a worldly, couldn't-care-less attitude and assume the world won't come crashing down round your ears. It won't, not immediately. But one day it will.'

For a moment Crampas was embarrassed, because he thought that had been said with a particular intention in mind, though that wasn't the case. Innstetten was just giving one of his little lectures, as he was wont to do. 'Take Gieshübler, for example,' he went on to bridge the awkwardness, 'ever the gallant, but he still has his principles.'

The Major had recovered his composure and said in his old tone, 'Oh yes, Gieshübler; the best fellow in the world and, if possible, with even better principles. But then where does he get them from? And why? Because he has an "affliction". Anyone who's well-formed is for frivolity. Without frivolity life's not worth the powder and shot.'

'Now listen, Crampas, that's precisely what one sometimes gets.' As he spoke he fixed his gaze on the Major's slightly shortened left arm.

Effi heard little of this conversation. She had gone close to the spot where the seal had been, and Rollo was beside her. Then both of them looked up from the stone at the sea, waiting to see whether the 'mermaid' would reappear.

*

At the end of October the election campaign began, making it impossible for Innstetten to continue to take part in their excursions; Effi and Crampas would presumably have also been forced to give them up, because of the reaction of the townsfolk, had Knut and Kruse not formed a kind of guard of honour. Thus it was that their rides continued into November.

The weather had changed, a constant wind from the north-west brought banks of cloud and white-topped waves crashed against the shore, but it wasn't cold yet and remained dry, so that these rides beneath a grey sky to the thunder of the breakers were almost better than they had been in the sunshine beside a calm sea. Rollo would tear along in front of them, occasionally spattered by the foam, and the veil of Effi's riding-hat streamed out behind her. Talking was almost impossible, but when they turned off into the protection of the dunes or, even better, into the pine-wood that was farther back, everything became still, Effi's veil no longer blew in the wind, and the narrowness of the track forced the two riders close together. That was the time when, of necessity going at a walk because of the gnarled tree-roots, they could resume the conversations interrupted by the noise of the waves. Crampas had a fund of small-talk and recounted stories of his time in the war or with the regiment, also little anecdotes revealing traits of Innstetten's character who, with his earnestness and reserve, had never really fitted in with his high-spirited comrades, so that he was actually more respected than liked.

'I can imagine that,' Effi said. 'Fortunately respect's the most important thing.'

'Yes, at the right time. But it's not always appropriate. And along with all that there was his mystical side that sometimes caused offence, on the one hand because soldiers don't have much time for that kind of thing, and on the other because we had the—perhaps mistaken—idea that he didn't really believe in what he was trying to convince us of.'

'Mystical side?' Effi said. 'What do you mean by that, Major?

Surely he can't have held conventicles and played at being a prophet. Not even the one from that opera . . . I've forgotten the name.'

'No, he didn't go that far. But perhaps we ought to stop there. I don't want to say something behind his back that could be misinterpreted. Especially since they're things that could well be discussed in his presence, things that, whether we mean to or not, would only be blown up into something special if he's not there to intervene all the time, to refute us or even laugh us to scorn.'

'But that's cruel, Major. How can you arouse my curiosity like that and then keep me in an agony of suspense? First there's something, then it's nothing. And mysticism! Does he see ghosts?'

'See ghosts! I'm not saying that, but he did like to tell us ghost stories. And once he'd got us really worked up and some probably even frightened, it suddenly seemed as if he simply wanted to make fun of his credulous comrades. To put it in a nutshell, it once happened that I told him straight out, "Oh, come on, Innstetten, you're just putting on an act. You can't fool me. You're just having us on. In fact you don't believe in this any more than we do, you're just trying to cut a figure; you have this idea that a reputation for being unusual goes down well with our superiors. They don't want ordinary men in higher posts, and since that's your ambition, you've looked for something distinctive and that's how you came up with ghosts." '

Effi didn't say a word, which the Major eventually found oppressive. 'You're saying nothing, Frau Baronin?'

'No.'

'May I ask why? Have I offended you? Or do you think it ungentlemanly of me to make what I have to admit, despite my protestations, are slightly mocking remarks about an absent friend? But despite all that, you're doing me an injustice. All of this will be continued in his presence, when I will repeat to him every word I've just said.'

'I can believe that.' Now Effi broke her silence and told him all that she had experienced in their house and Innstetten's strange reaction. 'He didn't say yes and he didn't say no, and I didn't know what to make of him.'

'Still the same old Innstetten, then,' Crampas laughed. 'That's what he was like in the old days when we were quartered with him in Liancourt and then later on in Beauvais.* He was in an old bishop's palace there—incidentally, this might interest you: it was a bishop of

Beauvais, who rejoiced in the name of "Cochon", who condemned the Maid of Orleans to death—and not a day, that is not a night, passed without Innstetten having incredible experiences. Though there was always a "perhaps" about them; it could have been nothing. And he still works on the same principle, as I see.'

'Yes, right. But now I have a serious question, Crampas, and I expect a serious answer: how do you explain all that?'

'Well, my dear Frau Baronin . . .'

'Don't try to wriggle out of it, Major. This is all very important for me and I'm your friend. I want to know what this means. What does he think he's doing?'

'Well, Frau Baronin, God can see into our hearts, but a major in command of the district army reserve sees nothing at all. How can I solve a psychological puzzle like that? I'm a simple man.'

'Oh, don't be silly, Crampas. I'm too young to have a great knowledge of human nature, but I'd have to be a little girl not yet confirmed, almost not yet baptized, to think you a simple man. You're the opposite, you're dangerous . . .'

'The most flattering thing you can say to a man well into his forties with a "retired" after his title. So, what does Innstetten think he's doing . . .'

Effi nodded.

'Well, if I have to say something I'd say that a man like Landrat Baron Innstetten, who could become head of a government department or something like that any day (believe me, he's heading for the top), that a man like Baron Innstetten thinks he can't live in an ordinary house, not in a cottage like the Landrat's residence—forgive me, Frau Baronin, but that's what it is. So he does his bit. A haunted house isn't an ordinary house . . . That's one thing.'

'One thing? My God, have you something to add?'

'Yes.'

'Go on then, I'm all ears. But, if at all possible, make it something good.'

'I'm not too sure about that. It's a delicate matter, almost unseemly, especially for your ears, Frau Baronin.'

'That only makes me all the more curious.'

'Right then. Apart from his burning desire to get to the top, whatever the cost, even if it means bringing in a haunted house, Innstetten has a further passion: his actions always have an educational purpose behind them. He's a born educator, he's somewhere between Basedow* and Pestalozzi* (but closer to the Church than either), and he really belongs in Schnepfenthal or Bunzlau.'*

'And he wants to educate me as well. Educate me with a ghost?'

'Educate's perhaps not the right word. But educate in a round-about way.'

'I don't understand what you mean.'

'A young wife's a young wife and a Landrat's a Landrat. He's often driving round the district, and then the house is empty and unguarded. But a ghost like that is like a cherub with a flaming sword . . .'*

'Oh, we're out of the wood now,' Effi said. 'And there's Utpatel's mill. We just have to go past the churchyard.'

Soon they were riding through the sunken lane between the churchyard and the railed-off plot, and Effi looked over to the stone and the fir tree where the Chinaman was buried.

CHAPTER 17

It was two when they got back. Crampas took his leave and rode off into the town, to his home on the market square. Effi, for her part, changed her clothes and tried to get some sleep, but without success; her bad mood was worse than her tiredness. She could accept that Innstetten should have a ghost to hand so that he didn't live in an ordinary house, it fitted in with his tendency to set himself off from the crowd, but the other aspect, that he was using the ghost as a means of educating her, that was too much, was almost insulting. And 'means of education' was only the half of it, the lesser half, she was clear about that; what Crampas had suggested was much, much more, a device deliberately calculated to create fear. It was totally devoid of feeling, almost border-ing on cruelty. She felt a rush of anger and clenched her little fist, determined to make plans; but all at once she had to laugh. 'Silly girl that I am. What guarantee do I have that Crampas is right? Crampas is amusing because he has a wicked tongue, but he's unreliable, just a coxcomb, and not a patch on Innstetten.'

At that moment Innstetten drove up, arriving back home earlier than usual. Effi jumped to her feet to be in the hall to greet him, and did so all the more affectionately as she felt she had something to make up for. But she couldn't quite get what Crampas had said out of her mind, and as she embraced him tenderly and listened to him with apparent interest, she kept hearing, 'So a ghost to serve his own purposes, a ghost to keep you in order,' going round and round inside her head.

Eventually she forgot that and listened to his stories without looking for some hidden insinuation.

*

By now it was the middle of November, and the north-westerly, that increased to gale force, blew against the breakwaters for a day and a half with such strength that the Kessine rose, overflowed the embankment, and poured down into the streets. But once it had had its fling the storm abated and there were a few more sunny, late-autumn days. 'Who knows how long they're going to last,' Effi said to Crampas, and so they decided to go out for a ride the next morning; Innstetten, who had a free day, decided to join them. They intended to go as far as the breakwater again, then dismount, have a short walk on the beach, and finally breakfast in the dunes, where they would be out of the wind.

Crampas arrived at the house at the agreed time. Kruse was already holding his mistress's horse; Effi quickly mounted, excusing Innstetten as she did so: he couldn't come, the previous night there had been a great fire in Morgnitz, the third in three weeks so it must be arson and he had to go out there, much to his disappointment, for he had really been looking forward to this ride that would probably be the last of the autumn.

Crampas expressed his regret, perhaps just for the sake of saying so or perhaps he really meant it, for however ruthless he could be in the matter of amorous adventures, he was equally a good comrade. Though that was quite superficial, of course. To help a friend and then cuckold him five minutes later caused no problem for his concept of honour. He would do both with unbelievable bonhomie.

As usual the ride took them through the Plantation. Rollo was in front again, then came Effi and Crampas, then Kruse.

'Where did you leave Knut?'

'He's got mumps.'

'How odd,' Effi laughed. 'Actually he always looks like that.'

'True. But you should see him now! Or better not. Mumps is infectious, you can catch it just by looking.'

'I don't believe it.'

'There are lots of things young women don't believe.'

'And then they believe lots of things it would be better they didn't.'

'Is that aimed at me?'

'No.'

'Pity.'

'That "pity" is so typical of you. I really believe you would think it quite in order if I made you a declaration of love, Major.'

'I wouldn't go that far. But I'd like to see the man who wouldn't hope for something like that. You can't legislate for thoughts and wishes.'

'That's open to question. And then there's a difference between thoughts and wishes. Thoughts are generally things that stay in the background, but wishes are mostly already on a person's lips.'

'Oh, don't put it like *that*, please.'

'Oh, Crampas, you're . . . you're . . .'

'A fool.'

'No. You're exaggerating again there. But you are something else. In Hohen-Cremmen we—me included—always used to say that the vainest thing on earth was an eighteen-year-old hussar ensign . . .'

'And now?'

'And now I say that the vainest thing on earth is a forty-two-year-old major in the district army reserve.'

'. . . and the two years you are kind enough to take off my age compensate me for all the rest. I kiss your hand—'

'As they say in Vienna. Yes, that's an expression that suits you. I got to know the Viennese in Carlsbad four years ago, where they flirted with me, a girl of fourteen. The things I heard!'

'I'm sure it was no more than was justified.'

'If that were the case, then the things that were meant to flatter me were pretty impudent . . . But look at the buoys there, the way they bob and sway. The little red flags on them have been taken down. Whenever I saw the red flags, the few times this summer when I managed to get down to the beach, I said to myself: that's where Vineta* is, that's where it *must* be, those are the tops of the towers . . .'

'That's because you know Heine's poem.'*

'Which one?'

'The one about Vineta.'

'No, I don't know it; I only know a few. Unfortunately.'

'And that with Gieshübler and the journal-reading group! Though Heine did give the poem a different name, sea-ghost, or something like that. But he had Vineta in mind. And he himself—forgive me if I go on and tell you the story here and now—the poet that is, is lying on the deck of a ship as he passes the place and looks down and sees the narrow, medieval streets and women trotting along in poke bonnets, and they're all carrying a hymn-book and going to church and all the bells are ringing. And when he hears that he's filled with a yearning to go to church with them, if only because of the bonnets, and he cries out with longing and is about to throw himself into the sea. But at that moment the captain grabs his leg, saying, "Doctor, are you out of your mind?" '

'That sounds delightful. I'd like to read it. Is it long?'

'No, it's actually short, a little longer than "Diamonds and pearls thou hast" and "Your fingers white as lilies . . ." ' so saying, he brushed her hand with his fingers. 'But long or short, what descriptive power, what vividness! He's my favourite poet and I know him off by heart, even though, apart from a few aberrations, I don't much care for poetry. But it's different with Heine: everything's full of life, and above all he knows about love, which is, after all, the most important thing. Though he's not one-sided about it . . .'

'How do you mean?'

'I mean he's not just concerned with love . . .'

'Well, even if he were one-sided in that way, it wouldn't be the end of the world. What else does he concern himself with?'

'He's very much concerned with the romantic side of life, which of course comes immediately after love, indeed some people think it's the same. I don't agree there, for his later poems, the ones people have also called "romantic"—or actually he did so himself—these romantic poems are full of people being executed, though often enough for love. But mostly for other, cruder reasons; in that I include politics, that is almost always crude. In one of these romances, for example, Charles Stuart* is carrying his head underneath his arm, and the story of Vitzliputzli* is even worse . . .'

'Of whom?'

'Of Vitzliputzli. Vitzliputzli's a Mexican god, and when the Mexicans captured twenty or thirty Spaniards those twenty or thirty had to be sacrificed to Vitzliputzli. There was no alternative, local customs, religion, and everything happened in an instant, belly open, heart out . . .'

'No, Crampas, you mustn't go on. That's both unseemly and disgusting. And all that, more or less at the moment when we're about to take breakfast.'

'Personally I'm not influenced by it; my appetite is entirely dependent on the menu.'

During this exchange they had, according to plan, turned off from the beach to a bench, set up half in the shelter of the dunes, by an extremely primitive table, two posts supporting a board. Kruse, who had ridden on ahead, had already set the table; rolls and slices of cold roast meat, red wine to go with it, and beside the bottle two pretty, delicate, gold-rimmed glasses such as people buy at holiday resorts or take home as a souvenir from glassworks.

Now they dismounted. Kruse, who had wrapped the reins of his own horse round a dwarf pine, walked the two other horses up and down while Effi and Crampas sat down at the table that allowed them a view of the beach and breakwater through a narrow gap in the dunes.

The somewhat wintry November sun cast its pale light over a sea still rough from the storms, and the waves were high. Now and then a gust of wind blew the foam close to them. There was marram grass all around and, despite the similarity in colour, the bright yellow of the immortelles stood out sharply from the yellow sand in which they were growing. Effi did the honours. 'I'm afraid I can only give you this cold roast beef, Major . . .'

'At least it's not the cold shoulder . . .'

'. . . but Kruse forgot the cheese. Oh, there you are, Rollo. I'm afraid we haven't brought anything for you. What are we going to do with Rollo?'

'I think we should give him the lot; out of gratitude, as far as I'm concerned. For you see, dearest Effi . . .'

Effi gave him a look.

'. . . for you see, my dear Frau Baronin, Rollo has reminded me of what I was going to tell you as a follow-up to Vitzliputzli—only, being a love story, it's much more piquant. Have you ever heard of a certain Pedro the Cruel?'*

'Vaguely.'

'A kind of Bluebeard king.'

'That sounds good. We like hearing about that kind of person best of all; I can remember that we always used to say about my friend Hulda Niemeyer—you will have heard her name—that she knew nothing about history apart from the six wives of Henry VIII, that English Bluebeard, if the word is strong enough for him. And, really, she knew every last detail about them. And then you should have heard how she pronounced their names, especially the name of Elizabeth's mother*—she was so very embarrassed, as if *she* were the next on the list . . . But now the story of Don Pedro, please.'

'Right then: at Don Pedro's court there was a handsome, black-haired Spanish knight who bore the Cross of Calatrava on his chest—which is as good as the Black Eagle and the Pour le Mérite* put together. The cross was part of it, they had to wear it all the time, and this Knight of the Order of Calatrava, with whom the queen was naturally secretly in love . . .'

'Why naturally?'

'Because we're in Spain.'

'Oh, I see.'

'And this knight had an incredibly beautiful dog, a Newfoundland, although they didn't exist at the time, it was exactly a hundred years before the discovery of America. A beautiful dog, like Rollo, let's say . . .'

Hearing his name, Rollo barked and wagged his tail.

'So things went on for a while. But eventually the matter of the secret love, which probably wasn't entirely secret, became too much for the king, and because he couldn't really stand the knight—for he wasn't just cruel, he was also a jealous type—he decided to have the knight secretly executed because of his secret love.'

'I can't say I blame him.'

'I'm not sure about that, my dear. Listen. Some things are acceptable, but this was too much; to my mind the king went too far by a considerable distance. You see, he pretended he was going to arrange a banquet for the knight, because of his heroic deeds in the wars, and there was a long, long table with all the grandees sitting at it and the king in the middle; opposite him was the place for the man in whose honour it was being held, for the knight of the Order of Calatrava, that is. And because he still hadn't come, even though they'd waited quite a while, the festivities had to begin without him and there remained one empty seat—an empty seat opposite the king.'

'And then?'

'And now, my dear Frau Baronin, just imagine the king, this Pedro, standing up to express his hypocritical regret that his "beloved guest" had still not appeared, when shouts from the horrified servants could be heard on the stairs outside and, before anyone realized what was happening, something tore along the banquet table then jumped up on to the chair and put a head that had been chopped off on the empty place, and Rollo stared over the head at the man opposite, the king. Rollo had accompanied his master to the block, and the moment the axe came down the faithful hound had grasped the head as it fell, and there was our friend Rollo at the long table accusing the royal murderer.'

Effi had gone very still. Finally she said, 'In its way that's very beautiful, Crampas, and because it's beautiful, I forgive you. But it would be better, and more to my liking, if you told me different stories. Also by Heine. Heine won't have only written poems about Vitzliputzli and Don Pedro and *your* Rollo—for mine wouldn't have done something like that. Here, Rollo. You poor thing, I can't look at you without thinking of the knight of the Order of Calatrava, with whom the queen was secretly in love . . . Will you call Kruse, please, and get him to put these things back in the saddlebag, and as we ride back you must tell me something different, something very different . . .'

Kruse came. But as he was about to take the glasses Crampas said, 'Leave that glass, Kruse, that glass there. I'll take that one myself.'

'As you wish, Herr Major.'

Effi, who had heard this, shook her head. Then she laughed. 'What do you think you're doing, Crampas? Kruse's stupid enough not to give the matter further thought, and if he does, he'll see nothing in it, fortunately. But that doesn't give you the right to take this glass . . . this thirty-pfennig glass from the Josephine Glass Works . . .'

'That you give the price in such a mocking tone only increases its value for me all the more.'

'Ever the same. There's a lot of the jester about you, but a strange kind of one. If I understand correctly—it's ridiculous, and I'm almost too embarrassed to say it—you aim to play Goethe's King of Thule.'*

He nodded, with an arch expression.

'Well, as far as I'm concerned, you can. If the cap fits, wear it; you know which one I have in mind. But I must tell you that the role you have in mind for *me* doesn't suit me at all. I refuse to go round as a rhyme to the King of Thule. Keep the glass but, please, don't draw any conclusions that might compromise me from that. I shall tell Innstetten about it.'

'That you will not do, my dear Frau Baronin.'

'Why not?'

'Innstetten is not the man to see such things the way they should be seen.'

She gave him a brief, sharp look. But then, confused and almost embarrassed, she lowered her gaze.

CHAPTER 18

Effi was dissatisfied with herself, and was glad that it had been decided the rides together should be discontinued for the whole of the winter. When she thought over the things that had been said, touched on, hinted at during all those weeks and days, she could find nothing for which she should actually reproach herself. Crampas was a clever man, experienced, amusing, free, free in a good sense as well, and it would have been petty and tedious if she had been stiff towards him and stuck strictly to the rules of propriety all the time. No, she couldn't blame herself for having fallen in with his tone, and yet she had a faint sense of having overcome a danger and congratulated herself that all of that was now presumably behind her. For it was unthinkable that they would see each other fairly frequently at home, the nature of the Crampas household made that as good as impossible, and meetings in the houses of the neighbouring noble families that were, of course, planned for the winter would be very rare and cursory. Effi worked all this out with growing satisfaction, eventually coming to the conclusion that giving up what she got out of her association with the Major would not be too great a loss. In addition to that, Innstetten told her his trips to Varzin would not take place that year, since the Prince was going to Friedrichsruh,* that he seemed to prefer more and more. From the one point of view, Innstetten said, he regretted that, from the other he was happy about it—he could now devote himself entirely to his family, and if she was agreeable, they could go through their Italian journey again with the notes he had made. To recapitulate it like that was the most important thing about a journey, only in that way could one assimilate it for good, only such later studies could make one fully and permanently aware of even things that one had only seen briefly, that one hardly realized had made any impression on one. He explained this in greater detail, adding that Gieshübler, who knew the 'Italian boot' right down to Palermo, had asked to be allowed to join them. Effi's response—she would have far, far preferred a perfectly ordinary evening's chat with-out the 'Italian boot' (even photographs were to be handed round)—was rather forced, but Innstetten, full of his plans, noticed nothing of that and went on, 'Of course there won't just be Gieshübler with us, Roswitha and Annie must be there too, and when I imagine that we're going up the Canal Grande and can hear the gondolieri singing in the distance, while not ten feet away Roswitha is bending over Annie and singing "Buhküken von Halberstadt"* or something like that, they'll be such lovely winter evenings, and you'll be sitting there knitting me a big winter nightcap. What do you say to that, Effi?'

These evenings were not merely planned, they actually started and would, in all probability, have gone on for many weeks had not poor innocent, harmless Gieshübler, despite his great aversion to anything of an equivocal nature, been the servant of two masters. One of them was Innstetten, the other Crampas. He had accepted the invitation to Innstetten's Italian evenings with genuine pleasure, if only for Effi's sake, but the pleasure with which he obeyed Crampas was even greater. Crampas had a plan to put on a production of the play *One False Step** before Christmas, and as the third Italian evening was approaching Gieshübler took the opportunity to discuss it with Effi, who had been chosen to play the role of Ella.

The effect on Effi was electrifying; what was Vicenza, Padua com-pared with that! Reheated fare meant nothing to Effi, it was fresh experiences, variety she longed for. But as if a voice were telling her 'Take care', she asked, elated as she was: 'Is it the Major who sug-gested this?'

'Yes. As you will know, Frau Baronin, he was voted unanimously on to the entertainments committee. We can finally look forward to a nice winter in the Club. He's just made for the role.'

'And will he have a part too?'

'No, he refused that. Unfortunately, I have to say. He can do any-thing, and would have made an excellent Arthur von Schmettwitz. He's just taken on the direction.'

'All the worse.'

'All the worse?' Gieshübler repeated.

'Oh, you mustn't take it so seriously. It's just a manner of speaking, that actually means the opposite. On the other hand, though, there is something overpowering about the Major, he does like to decide things without consulting you. And then you have to act the way he wants, not the way you want.'

She went on speaking, getting more and more tangled up in contradictions.

*

One False Step really did come about, and since they only had a fort-night (the last week before Christmas was ruled out), everyone made an effort and it went excellently; the actors, above all Effi, received loud applause. And Crampas did limit himself to directing and, however strict he was with all the others, interfered very little with Effi's interpretation during the rehearsals. Either Gieshübler must have said things to him about his conversation with Effi, or he had noticed himself the effort Effi made to keep apart from him. And he was intelligent enough, as one who understood women, not to disturb the natural development, of which, from all his experience, he was all too well aware.

The theatre evening in the club went on until late, and it was past midnight when Innstetten and Effi got home. Johanna was still up, in order to help, and Innstetten, who was more than a little proud of his young wife, told Johanna how lovely her mistress had looked and how well she had acted. Pity he hadn't thought of it earlier, but she and Christel and also the old toad, Frau Kruse, could have watched from the musicians' gallery; there had been a lot of people there. Then Johanna left, and Effi, who was tired, went to bed. Innstetten, how-ever, who still wanted to chat, pulled over a chair and sat by his wife's bed, giving her a warm look and holding her hand.

'Yes, Effi, that was a lovely evening. It was a nice little play and I found it very amusing. And just imagine, the author's a Kammergerichtsrat,* it's hardly believable. And from Königsberg at that! But what pleased me most of all was my delightful little wife who charmed everyone.'

'Oh, don't say things like that, Geert, I'm vain enough as it is.'

'Vain enough, that's about right. But nowhere near as vain as the others. And that in addition to your seven charms* . . .'

'All women have seven charms.'

'A slip of the tongue; you can multiply the number by itself.'

'How gallant you are, Geert. If I didn't know you, I'd feel afraid. Or is there really something lurking behind it?'

'Have you got a guilty conscience? Been listening at the door yourself?'

'Oh, Geert, now I really am afraid.' She sat up in bed and stared at him. 'Should I ring for Johanna to bring us some tea? You do so like a cup before going to bed.'

He kissed her hand. 'No, Effi. Even the Kaiser can't demand a cup of tea after midnight, and you know I don't like making more demands on people than necessary. No, all I want to do is to look at you and feel happy that I have you. There are times when one is more strongly aware of what a treasure one has. You could be someone like poor Frau Crampas; an awful woman, can't be friendly to anyone, and she would have liked to wipe you off the face of the earth.'

'Oh, I beg you, Geert. You're imagining things again. The poor woman. I didn't notice anything.'

'Because you haven't got an eye for that kind of thing. But it was as I said, and poor Crampas was inhibited by it and kept avoiding you and hardly looked at you. Which was quite natural, for in the first place he's a real ladies' man, and then ladies like you are his particular passion. Which I'm willing to bet no one knows better than my little wife herself. When I think of the way the pair of you jabbered on— sorry—when he came on to the veranda in the mornings or when we rode along the beach or went for a walk on the breakwater. He's the kind of man I'm telling you, and today he'd lost his assurance, he was afraid of his wife. And I can't blame him. Frau Crampas is something like our Frau Kruse, and if I had to choose between the two of them I don't know which one it would be.'

'I would. There is a difference between the two of them. Poor Frau Crampas is unhappy, Frau Kruse is uncanny.'

'So you'd go for the unhappy one?'

'Definitely.'

'Now that's all a matter of taste. One can tell you've never been unhappy. And Crampas has a talent for disencumbering himself of his wife. He always finds some way of leaving her at home.'

'But she was there today.'

'Yes, today. There was no way round it. But I've arranged a visit to Ring, the senior forester, with him, Gieshübler, and the Pastor for the twenty-seventh, and you should have seen how cleverly he managed to prove that his wife had to stay at home.'

'Is it a men-only party?'

'Not at all. If it were, I'd say no thanks. You're invited and two or three other ladies, not counting those from the estates.'

'But then that's horrible of him, I mean of Crampas; there's always a price to pay for that kind of behaviour.'

'Yes, one day there will be. But I think our friend is one of those who doesn't lose any sleep over what's to come.'

'Do you think he's a bad man?'

'No, not bad. Almost the opposite, or at least he has his good side. But he's half Polish, you can't really rely on him, not in anything, least of all with women. A gambler. He doesn't gamble at the gaming-table but he's constantly taking chances in life, and you have to keep a close eye on him.'

'It's good of you to tell me that. I'll take care with him.'

'Do that. But not too much; then it won't be any use. Behaving naturally's always best, and of course the very best is strength of character and, if I may use such a strait-laced word, a pure soul.'

She looked at him, wide-eyed. Then she said, 'Yes, of course. But now don't say any more about all these things that don't cheer me up. D'you know, I feel I can hear the dancing upstairs. Strange that it keeps coming back. I thought you were only joking with all that stuff.'

'I wouldn't say that, Effi. But, either way, you just have to have a clear conscience and feel no need to be afraid.'

Effi nodded, and all at once what Crampas had said about her husband's passion for education came back to mind.

*

Christmas Eve came and went much as it had the previous year; presents and letters arrived from Hohen-Cremmen; Gieshübler presented his respects in a little poem, and Cousin Briest sent a card: a snowy landscape with telegraph poles and a little bird hunched up on the wire. And a tree was decorated for Annie, with candles that she reached out for and tried to grasp. Innstetten, relaxed and cheerful, seemed to be enjoying his domestic bliss and spent a lot of time with their child. Roswitha was amazed to see the master so tender and at the same time light-hearted. Effi too talked a lot and laughed a lot, but it didn't really come from the heart. She felt depressed and didn't know who to blame, Innstetten or herself. There was no Christmas-card from Crampas; on the one hand she was glad about that, on the other not; his attentions filled her with a certain apprehension, his indifference put her in a bad mood. She could see that things were not the way they ought to be.

'You're so restless,' Innstetten said after a while.

'Yes. Everyone's been so nice to me, you most of all; that depresses me because I feel I don't deserve it.'

'You shouldn't torment yourself like that, Effi. At the end of the day, the fact of the matter is that you get what you deserve.'

Effi listened closely to that, and her guilty conscience made her ask herself whether he had deliberately put it in such an ambiguous way.

Late in the afternoon Pastor Lindequist came to wish them a happy Christmas and to ask about the excursion to Uvagla Forest. It just had to be a sleigh-ride, of course. Crampas had offered him a seat in his sleigh, but neither the Major nor his servant, who would do the driving, as he did everything else, knew the way, therefore it would perhaps be a good idea to drive out in convoy with the Landrat's sleigh leading and Crampas's following. Probably Gieshübler's as well, for Mirambo, to whom their friend Alonzo had inexplicably decided to entrust the driving, was probably even less well acquainted with the route than the freckled Treptow uhlan. Innstetten, who was amused by these minor problems, was happy with Lindequist's suggestion and arranged that he would drive across the market square punctually at two and, without stopping, take the lead of the procession.

When the day came they proceeded according to that arrangement, and when Innstetten crossed the market square on the dot of two Crampas waved to Effi from his sleigh and then followed Innstetten's. The pastor was sitting beside him. Gieshübler's sleigh, with Gieshübler himself and Dr Hannemann, followed; Gieshübler was wearing an elegant buff-leather coat with marten trimmings, while the doctor had a bearskin coat that was thirty years old and showed its age. In his younger days Hannemann had been a ship's surgeon on a Greenland whaler. Mirambo sat in front, somewhat nervous because of his lack of experience in driving a sleigh, as Lindequist had suspected.

Two minutes later they were past Utpatel's mill.

Between Kessin and Uvagla (where, according to legend, there had once been a Wendish temple) there was a strip of woodland that was only about a thousand yards wide but must have been getting on for seven miles long; to the right of it was the sea, to the left a large, very fertile and well-cultivated piece of land stretching as far as the horizon. It was on this landward side that the three sleighs were now flying along, with, in front of them, a couple of old carriages that were most likely taking others who had been invited to the senior forester's house. One of these carriages was clearly recognizable by its old-fashioned high wheels as the one from Papenhagen. Of course, Güldenklee was considered the best speaker in the district (better than Borcke, yes, even better than Grasenabb), and his presence was essential on all festive occasions.

They drove quickly—the local gentry's coachmen were making a great effort as well and didn't want to be overtaken—and they had reached the senior forester's house by three. Ring, an imposing figure with a military look, who had fought in the first Schleswig campaign under Wrangel and Bonin* and distinguished himself at the storming of the Danewerk,* stood in the doorway to greet his guests who, after they'd taken off their coats and greeted his wife, first sat down at a long coffee-table on which there stood elaborate pyramids of cakes. Frau Ring was a very timorous, or at least very diffident, woman and showed these characteristics in the way she performed her duties as hostess, which visibly irritated the forester, for whom self-assurance and verve were of the utmost importance. Fortunately his irritation didn't lead to an outburst, for what his wife lacked, his daughters, pretty young girls of fourteen and thirteen who took after their father, had more than their fair share of. The older one in particular, Cora, immediately started flirting with Innstetten and Crampas, who both played along with her. Effi was annoyed at this, and then felt ashamed at being annoyed. She was sitting next to Sidonie von Grasenabb, and said, 'Strange, that was what I was like too when I was fourteen.'

Effi expected Sidonie to dispute that or at least express some reservations. Instead she said, 'I can well imagine.'

'And the way her father indulges her!' Effi went on, slightly embarrassed and only for the sake of saying something.

Sidonie nodded. 'That's the problem. No discipline. It's the mark of our age.'

Effi said nothing more.

They'd soon finished their coffee and stood up to take a half-hour walk in the surrounding woods, at first towards an enclosure where deer were fenced in. Cora opened the gate, and hardly had she gone in than the deer started coming towards her. It was actually delightful, just like in a fairy-story. But the young girl's vanity, her awareness of making a tableau, spoilt the impression, at least for Effi. 'No,' she said to herself, 'I wasn't like that. Perhaps I also lacked discipline, as this awful Sidonie just suggested, perhaps other things as well. At home they were too indulgent towards me, they loved me too much. But one thing I can say, I never put on airs. That was always Hulda's way. That's why I didn't like her when I saw her again this summer.'

On the way back from the woods it started to snow.

Crampas joined Effi, and said he was sorry he hadn't had the opportunity to say hello to her properly yet. Then, pointing to the large, heavy snowflakes that were falling, he said, 'If it goes on like this, we'll be snowed in here.'

'That wouldn't be the worst thing that could happen. For ages I've associated being snowed in with something pleasant, with a sense of protection and support.'

'I've never heard that before, Frau Baronin.'

'Yes,' Effi went on, trying to laugh, 'there's something odd about these ideas you get. You don't just get them from things you've experienced personally but also from something you've heard some-where or happen to know by chance. You're very well-read, Major, but it seems to me there's one poem I know—not one by Heine, of course, not "Sea-ghost", not "Vitzliputzli"—that you don't. It's called "God's Wall",* and I learnt it off by heart many many years ago, when I was quite small, with our pastor in Hohen-Cremmen.'

' "God's Wall", ' Crampas said. 'A nice title. What's it about?'

'It's a little story, a very short one. There was war somewhere, a winter campaign, and an old widow who was terribly afraid of the enemy prayed to God that He would "build a wall round her", to protect her from the enemy. Then God had the house snowed in and the enemy moved on past it.'

Crampas was visibly disconcerted by this, and changed the subject.

By the time it was getting dark, they were all back in the forester's house.

CHAPTER 19

They went to table as soon as the clock struck seven, and they were all delighted to see that the Christmas tree, a fir decorated with numberless silver balls, was lit again. Crampas, who had not been to the Rings' house before, was full of admiration. The damask cloth, the wine-coolers, the silver cutlery all looked as if it belonged to some grand family, well above the usual circumstances of a forester; the reason was that Ring's wife, shy and embarrassed though she was, came from the family of a rich Danzig corn merchant. That was also where most of the pictures hanging on the walls all round were from: the corn merchant and his wife, the refectory of Marienburg Castle,* and a good copy of the Memling* altarpiece in St Mary's in Danzig. Oliva Abbey* was represented twice, once in oils and once carved from cork. As well as these, there was over the sideboard a very much darkened portrait of old Nettelbeck* that came from the modest furnishings of Ring's predecessor, who had died only eighteen months ago. At the usual auction no one had wanted the picture of the old man until Innstetten, annoyed at this lack of respect, had made a bid. That had awakened Ring's patriotic feeling, and the man who had helped to organize the defence of Kolberg had remained in the forester's house.

The Nettelbeck picture was in a pretty poor state, but otherwise everything, as indicated, spoke of easy circumstances bordering on opulence, and the meal that was served was in line with that. Everyone enjoyed it to a greater or lesser degree, apart from Sidonie. She was sitting between Innstetten and Lindequist, and said, when she saw Cora, 'There's that insufferable brat again, that Cora. Just look at the way she's handing out the little wine-glasses, Innstetten, she's got it down to a T, she could become a waitress right away. Truly unbearable. And the looks your friend Crampas is giving her! You can see the path she's on already. I ask you, where will it lead?'

Innstetten, who actually agreed with her, found the tone in which it was expressed so offensively harsh that his reply was an ironic, 'Where will it lead, my dear Fräulein? I don't know that *either*,' at which Sidonie turned away from him and addressed Lindequist, who was on her left. 'Tell me, Pastor, does that fourteen-year-old coquette attend your classes?'

'Yes, Fräulein von Grasenabb.'

'Then you must forgive me for saying that you haven't been strict enough with her. I know that it's pretty difficult nowadays, but I also know that those who have responsibility for the young often don't take their task seriously enough. There's no two ways about it, it's the parents and teachers who are largely to blame.'

Lindequist, adopting the same tone as Innstetten, replied that that was all well and true, but the spirit of the times was too powerful.

'The spirit of the times!' Sidonie said. 'Don't start going on about that. I can't stand it, it's the expression of the worst kind of weakness, a declaration of moral bankruptcy. I know what it means: never wanting to seem too harsh, always avoiding uncomfortable issues. For duty is uncomfortable. Thus it's all too easy to forget that the time will come when the talents we have been given will be demanded back from us. Take action, my dear Pastor, discipline. The flesh is weak,* of course, but . . .'

At that moment an English-style roast loin of beef arrived, of which Sidonie took a substantial helping, without noticing Lindequist's smile as she did so. And since she didn't notice that, it was no surprise that she continued unabashed where she'd left off. 'And that's why everything you see here is the way it has to be; everything is on the wrong track from the very start. Ring, Ring—if I'm not mistaken there was a king of that name in a saga in Sweden* or somewhere round there. Now look, isn't he behaving as if he were descended from him; and his mother, whom I knew, was a laundrywoman in Köslin.'*

'I can't see anything bad in that.'

'Anything bad? Neither can I. There are certainly things that are worse. But I must, at the very least, expect you, as an ordained servant of the Church, to accept the social order. A senior forester is only a little more than a forester, and a forester doesn't have such wine-coolers and silver; that's all unseemly, and the result is children growing up like this Fräulein Cora.'

Sidonie, ever ready to prophesy terrible happenings when the spirit came upon her and she poured out her wrath, would have worked herself up into a Cassandra-like* vision of the future if, at that very moment, the steaming bowl of punch—with which Christmas gatherings at Ring's house always ended—had not appeared on the table, accompanied by crinkly cracknel cleverly piled up, even higher than the pyramid of cakes that had been served with the coffee several hours ago. And now Ring himself, who had kept somewhat in the background until then, went into action with beaming ceremony and started to fill the glasses in front of him, large, cut-glass goblets, in curving jets, a virtuoso demonstration of how to fill a wine-glass that Frau von Padden, unfortunately absent that day, had, with her ready wit, once called 'glass-filling *en cascade à la Ring*'. The wine poured out in an amber curve, and not a drop was to be spilt—as was the case again that day. But at the end, when everyone was holding their due—including Cora, who, with her amber curls, had sat down on 'Uncle Crampas's' lap—old Güldenklee from Papenhagen rose, in order, as was usual at these festivities, to propose a toast to his beloved senior forester.

'There are many rings,' he began, 'growth rings, curtain rings, wedding rings, and as far as engagement rings are concerned—surely that is a topic we can broach—I am happy to say that it is guaranteed that one of them will be seen in this house in the very near future, adorning the ring-finger (and in this case a ring-finger in two senses) of a pretty little hand . . .'

'Outrageous,' Sidonie whispered to Lindequist.

'Yes, my friends,' Güldenklee went on, raising his voice, 'there are many rings, and there is even a story we all know called the story of the three rings,* a Jewish story that, like all the liberal poppycock, has done nothing but create confusion and mischief. May God put things to rights. And now, so as not to take up too much of your patience and forbearance, let me close. I am *not* for these three rings, my dear friends, rather I am for *one* Ring, for a Ring that is a real ring, the way a ring ought to be, a Ring that has gathered together at his hospitable table everything that is good in this old Pomeranian district of Kessin, everyone that still stands up with God for king and country—and there are still a few of those left' (loud cheers). 'I am all for *that* Ring. Three cheers for him.'

They all joined in and crowded round Ring, who for the moment had to hand over the task of glass-filling *en cascade* to Crampas; but the children's tutor got up from his place at the bottom of the table, rushed over to the piano, and played the opening bars of the Prussian national anthem, at which everyone stood up and solemnly joined in: 'A Prussian I am . . . a Prussian I will be.'*

'That is really beautiful,' old Borcke said to Innstetten after the first verse, 'other countries don't have anything like that.'

'No,' said Innstetten, who didn't have much time for that kind of patriotism, 'other countries have other things.'

They sang every verse, by which time the carriages had been brought round and they all immediately rose so as not to keep the horses waiting. In Kessin district this 'consideration for the horses' took priority over everything else. In the hall were two pretty maids—Ring was particular about that—to help the guests on with their furs. Everyone was in a merry mood, some more than that, and it looked as if getting into the various vehicles would go quickly and with no hold-ups, when it suddenly turned out that Gieshübler's sleigh wasn't there. Gieshübler was much too well-bred to show nerves or make a fuss; finally, however, because someone had to say something, Crampas asked what had actually happened.

'Mirambo can't drive,' Ring's groom said, 'when he was hitching up the horses the left-hand one kicked him on the shin. He's lying down in the stable, howling.'

They of course called for Dr Hannemann, who went out and returned five minutes later to inform them, with a true surgeon's impassiveness, 'Yes, Mirambo will have to stay here. For the moment all he needs to do is lie still and rest. It's nothing serious.' That was a relief, but it didn't solve the question of how Gieshübler's sleigh was to be driven back, until Innstetten said he would take Mirambo's place and see that the medical pair—doctor and chemist—got safely home. His offer was accepted, with laughter and all sorts of jokes about this most obliging Landrat who, in order to be of assistance, would even leave his young wife behind, and Innstetten, with Gieshübler and Hannemann in the back, once more headed the procession. Crampas and Lindequist followed immediately behind. Then, when Kruse drove up with the sleigh, Sidonie came over to Effi and asked whether she could travel with her, since there was now a free place. 'It's always so stuffy in our carriage; my father likes it like that. And anyway, I'd like to have a chat with you. But only as far as Quappendorf. I'll get out at the junction with the track to Morgnitz, then I'll have to get back into our uncomfortable carriage. And Papa smokes into the bargain.'

Effi was not terribly pleased at this request and would have preferred to do the drive alone; but she had little choice and so Sidonie Grasenabb climbed in, and hardly had the two ladies taken their seats than Kruse cracked his whip and they set off from the forestry ramp, which had a splendid view of the sea, down the fairly steep dune towards the shore-path that went, almost dead straight for four and a half miles, to the Beach Hotel in Kessin and, turning right into the Plantation, to the town. The snow had stopped falling a few hours ago, the air was fresh, and the dull light of the crescent moon fell on the darkening expanse of the sea. Kruse drove close to the water, sometimes cutting through the foam of the incoming tide, and Effi, shivering a little, wrapped her coat tighter around her. She remained silent, and that intentionally. She knew very well that all that about the 'stuffy carriage' was merely a pretext, and Sidonie had only joined her because she had something unpleasant to say to her. And that would come soon enough. As well as that, she was really tired, perhaps from the walk in the woods, perhaps also from Ring's punch, of which, urged on by Frau von Flemming who was sitting next to her, she had partaken freely. So she pretended to be asleep, closed her eyes, and leant her head more and more over to the left.

'You mustn't lean over so far to the left, Frau Baronin. If the sleigh goes over a stone you'll fly out. Your sleigh has no leather guard-flaps as it is, and, as I can see, not even the hooks for them.'

'I can't stand the guard-flaps, there's something so prosaic about them. And then I'd be quite happy to fly out, most of all straight into the waves. A rather cold bath, true, but so what . . . ? By the way, can you hear something?'

'No.'

'Can't you hear something like music?'

'An organ?'

'No, not an organ. I'd imagine it was the sea, but it's something different, an immensely soft sound, almost like a human voice . . .'

'They're hallucinations,' Sidonie said, thinking the right moment had come. 'You're suffering from some nervous disorder. You hear voices. God grant it's the right voices you hear.'

'I can hear . . . of course I know it's silly, otherwise I'd imagine I'd heard the mermaids singing. But, please, what's that? There's something flashing right up into the sky. It must be the Northern Lights.'

'Yes,' Sidonie said. 'You're behaving as if it were one of the wonders of the world, Frau Baronin. It isn't. And even if it were, we have to beware of nature worship. Though we are truly fortunate that we've avoided the danger of hearing our good forester, that most vain of all mortals, talk about the Northern Lights. I bet he'd imagine the heavens were doing him the favour of making his festivities even more festive. He's a fool. Güldenklee should have better things to do than laud him like that. And he makes a big thing of his support for the church, recently he donated an altar-cloth. Perhaps Cora did some of the embroidery. These false Christians are to blame for everything, for their worldliness is always on the surface and is also attributed to those who are serious about the salvation of their souls.'

'Yes, it's so difficult see into a person's heart.'

'Yes, it is. But with some people it's also quite easy.' And with that she gave her young companion a look that was almost rude in its insistence.

Effi said nothing and turned away impatiently.

'With some people, as I say, it's quite easy,' Sidonie repeated. She had reached her goal and went on with a quiet smile, 'And our senior forester is one of those easy puzzles. I feel sorry for anyone who brings up his children like that, but the good thing about it is that with him everything is clear to see. And as it is with him, so it is with his daughters. Cora will go to America and become either a millionairess or a Methodist preacher; in one way or another she'll be lost. I have never before seen a fourteen-year-old girl . . .'

At that moment the sleigh halted, and when the two looked round to see what was the matter, they saw that on their right, about thirty yards away, the two other sleighs had also stopped—Innstetten's farther away, Crampas's closer.

'What is it?' Effi asked.

Half turning round, Kruse said, 'The Schloon, Madam.'

'The Schloon? What's that? I can't see anything.'

Kruse shook his head from side to side, as if to say the question was more easily asked than answered. And he was right about that, for you couldn't say what the Schloon was in a couple of words. But help for Kruse quickly arrived from Sidonie Grasenabb, who knew about everything in the area, and that included the Schloon.

'Yes, Frau Baronin,' Sidonie said, 'that's pretty bad. It doesn't matter much for me, I'll get through easily when the carriages arrive. They have high wheels and, moreover, our horses are used to it. But it's different with these sledges, they'd sink into the Schloon, so you'll have to make a detour, whether you like it or not.'

'Sink! Please, Fräulein, I'm still not clear about what it is. Is the

Schloon an abyss or something, where you go down with all hands? I can't imagine anything like that around here.'

'And yet it is something like that, only in miniature, of course. This Schloon is actually just a sluggish little runnel coming down from Lake Gothen and creeping through the dunes. In summer it sometimes dries out completely, and you can easily drive across and not even notice it.'

'And in winter?'

'Well, in winter it's a different proposition; not always, but often. Then it turns into a slough.'

'My God, what words and names you have here!'

'. . . Then it turns into a slough, and is worst when the wind comes off the sea. Then the wind forces the seawater into the little runnel, but not so that you can see it. And that's the worst thing about it, that's where the real danger lies. All this is happening underground, and the sand on the beach is saturated with water to quite a depth. And if you try to cross one of these stretches of sand, that isn't sand any more, you sink in as if it were a swamp or a quagmire.'

'I know that kind of thing,' Effi said animatedly, 'it's like in the Marshes at home.' And for all her anxiety she suddenly felt a kind of wistful joy.

As this conversation went on, Crampas had alighted from his sleigh and gone over to Gieshübler's, that was farthest to the right, in order to discuss what was to be done with Innstetten. Knut, he told him, was all for attempting the crossing, but Knut was stupid and didn't understand the matter at all; the decision should be left to those who were at home here. Innstetten—very much to Crampas's surprise— was also for risking it; it definitely had to be attempted again . . . it was the same old story every time: people here had a superstition and that made them afraid, even though there was really nothing to it. Not Knut, he wasn't familiar with it, but Kruse should have a go, and Crampas was to get in with the ladies (there was a small dickey) to be at hand should the sleigh tip over. After all, that was the worst thing that could happen.

Crampas went over to the ladies with Innstetten's message, and once he had informed them, with a laugh, of this arrangement, followed orders and sat himself on the little seat—it was actually nothing more than a plank covered with cloth—and called out, 'Off we go now, Kruse.'

Kruse had already taken the horses back a hundred yards, and hoped by working up to a good speed to be able to get the sleigh across; but the moment the horses just touched the Schloon they sank up to their fetlocks in the sand, and it was only with great difficulty that they managed to back out again.

'Impossible,' Crampas said, and Kruse nodded.

Whilst all this was going on the carriages had finally arrived, the Grasenabbs' in the lead, and once Sidonie, with a brief word of thanks to Effi, had taken her rear seat, opposite her father, who was smoking his Turkish pipe, the carriage headed for the Schloon without further ado; the horses sank in deep, but the wheels allowed them to overcome the danger easily, and within half-a-minute the Grasenabbs were trotting along on the other side. The other carriages followed, and it was not without some envy that Effi watched them go. But not for long, for by this time a solution had been found for those in the sleighs; Innstetten had simply given up all idea of forcing a crossing and decided on the more tranquil alternative of a detour. That is, precisely what Sidonie had predicted from the start. From the right came the Landrat's clear instruction to stay on that side for the time being and to follow him through the dunes to a wooden bridge farther upstream.

Once both drivers, Kruse and Knut, had been given their instructions, the Major, who had got down from the sleigh with Sidonie in order to help her, came back to Effi and said, 'I cannot leave you by yourself, Frau Baronin.'

For a moment Effi was uncertain what to do, but then she quickly moved over to the other side and Crampas got in and sat on her left.

All this could perhaps have been misinterpreted, but Crampas knew women too well simply to feel flattered by it. He clearly saw that Effi's reaction was the only right thing to do, given the way things stood. It was impossible for her to refuse to allow him into the sleigh. And so they flew along behind the other two, always close beside the watercourse, with the dark mass of trees towering up on the other bank. Effi looked across, assuming that later on the ride would continue along the landward edge of the woods, that is, on the same track they had taken in the afternoon. But in the meantime Innstetten had formed a different plan, and immediately his sleigh had crossed the wooden bridge, instead of choosing the route outside the woods he turned on to a narrower track that went through the middle of the dense mass of trees. Effi started in fright. Until then there had been light and air all around, but now that was gone and the dark crowns of the trees were bending over her. She started to shiver and clasped her fingers tight together to keep herself under control. Thoughts and images flashed through her mind, and one of those images was the old woman in the poem called 'God's Wall', and just like the old woman she now prayed that God would build a wall round her. She muttered it two or three times, but all at once she felt they were empty words. She was afraid, yet at the same time was under a spell she didn't want to break.

'Effi.' The word was whispered softly in her ear and she could hear that his voice was trembling. Then he took her hand and released her fingers, that she was still clutching tight, and covered them with hot kisses. She felt she was about to faint.

When she opened her eyes again they were out of the woods, and not far in front she could hear the jingle of the sleighs racing along ahead of them. It became more and more audible, and when, just before Utpatel's mill, they turned off the dunes, the little houses with their snow-covered roofs were on either side of them.

Effi looked round, and one moment later the sleigh had stopped outside Innstetten's house.

CHAPTER 20

The next morning Innstetten, who had given Effi a sharp look as he lifted her out of the sleigh but avoided any reference to the strange ride the two had had together, was up early and tried as far as possible to get over his continuing bad mood.

'You slept well?' he asked when Effi came for breakfast.

'Yes.'

'Good for you. I can't say the same for myself. I dreamt you and the sleigh had fallen into the Schloon and Crampas was trying to save you; I have to call it that, but he sank down with you.'

'You're saying that in such an odd way, Geert. There's a reproach behind it and I suspect I know why.'

'Very strange.'

'You're not happy that Crampas came and offered to help us.'

'Us?'

'Yes, us. Sidonie and me. You must have completely forgotten that it was you who sent the Major. And once he was sitting opposite me on that wretched little plank, should I have thrown him out when the Grasenabbs arrived and the drive continued immediately? I'd have looked ridiculous, and you're so sensitive to that. Just remember that we've often been out riding together, with your agreement, and now I'm not supposed to go in a sleigh together with him? At home we were always told it's wrong to treat a noble gentleman with distrust.'

'A noble gentleman?' Innstetten said, emphasizing the first word.

'Is he not one? You yourself called him a gentleman, even a perfect gentleman.'

'Yes,' Innstetten said, his voice taking on a friendlier tone, though it still had a touch of mockery, 'a gentleman, he is that, and a perfect gentleman, he certainly is that. But a noble gentleman? My dear Effi, a noble gentleman is a quite different kettle of fish. Have you noticed anything noble about him? I haven't.'

Effi stared at the floor and said nothing.

'So we're of the same opinion, it seems. Though, as you said, it's my own fault; I wouldn't call it a *faux pas*, it's not a good word to use in such a context. So it's my fault and it won't happen again, if I have anything to do with it. But you too, if you'll take my advice, should take care. He's a man who can be ruthless and has his own views about young women. I know him from the old days.'

'I'll bear that in mind. But I will say that I think you misjudge him.'

'I do not misjudge him.'

'Nor me,' she said, making an effort and trying to look him in the eye.

'You neither, my dear Effi. You're a charming little woman but steadfastness is not your strong point.'

He stood up to leave. As he reached the door, Friedrich came in with a note from Gieshübler. It was addressed to the Frau Baronin, of course.

Effi took it. 'A secret correspondence with Gieshübler,' she said. 'Grounds for more jealousy from my stern lord and master. Or not?'

'No, not at all, my dear Effi. I am foolish enough to make a difference between Crampas and Gieshübler. They are not of the same carat—carat is used as a unit to measure the fineness of gold, and sometimes of people as well. And I might add that personally I much prefer Gieshübler's white cravats, even though no one wears them any more, to Crampas's ginger moustache. But I doubt whether that corresponds to women's taste.'

'You think we're weaker than we are.'

'A comfort that is, in practice, of exceptional insignificance. But let's leave that. Read your note instead.'

And Effi read it out:

'May I ask how you are, Frau Baronin? I do know that you safely avoided the Schloon, but there were dangers enough driving through the woods. Dr Hannemann has just returned from Uvagla and reassured me as to Mirambo's condition; yesterday, he said, he felt the matter was more serious than he liked to admit to us, but not now. It was a delightful drive.—In three days' time it will be New Year's Eve. We will have to do without a celebration such as we had last year, but there will be a ball, of course, and to see you there will delight all the assiduous dancers, not least your devoted servant,

Alonzo G.'

Effi laughed. 'What do you say to that?'

'Still the same: that I prefer to see you with Gieshübler than with Crampas.'

'Because you take Crampas too seriously and Gieshübler not seriously enough.'

Innstetten playfully wagged his finger at her.

*

Three days later it was New Year's Eve. Effi appeared in a delightful ball-gown that had been among the Christmas presents. She didn't dance, however, but took her place among the old ladies for whom armchairs had been put out close to the musicians' platform. None of the Innstettens' preferred acquaintances among the noble families was there, because of a little disagreement with the Club committee, who were based in the town and, according to old Güldenklee, had once more been guilty of 'destructive tendencies'; three or four other noble families, however, who were not members of the Club but always just invited guests, since their estates lay on the other side of the Kessine, had come, in some cases from a great distance away, across the frozen river, delighted to be able to attend the ball. Effi was sitting between the wife of old Ritterschaftsrat von Padden and a somewhat younger Frau von Titzewitz. Frau von Padden, a superb old lady, was an original in every respect and strove to compensate for what nature had made of her, especially with her pronounced cheekbones, on the heathen Wendish side, with a Teutonic strictness of Christian belief that made even Sidonie von Grasenabb look like a kind of freethinker. On the other hand, she was endowed—perhaps because she united the Radegast and Swantowit* lines of the family—with the old Padden sense of humour, with which the family had been blessed since days of yore, and which gave heartfelt pleasure to anyone who came into contact with them, even their opponents in matters of church and state.

'Now then, child,' Frau von Padden said, 'how are you actually?'

'Well, Frau Ritterschaftsrätin; I have an excellent husband.'

'I know. But that doesn't always help. I also had an excellent husband. How are things here? No temptations?'

Effi was alarmed and, at the same time, in a way moved. There was something uncommonly refreshing about the free and natural manner in which the old lady spoke, and the fact that it was such a pious woman made it even more refreshing.

'Oh, Frau Ritterschaftsrätin . . .'

'There you are. I'm familiar with that. It's always the same. Times never change as far as that's concerned. And perhaps it's a good thing too. For what's important, my dear young lady, is the fight you put up. One has to wrestle with the natural man inside one all the time. And when you've got yourself pinned down and almost feel like crying because it hurts so much, then the angels above rejoice.'

'Oh, Frau von Padden. It's often very difficult.'

'Of course it's difficult. But the more difficult, the better. You should be happy about that. All that with the flesh never goes away, it stays with us; I have children and grandchildren, so I see it every day. But to conquer yourself in faith, that's the important thing, that's the true victory. That's what our old Martin Luther, our man of God, made clear. Do you know his *Table Talk?**

'No, Frau Ritterschaftsrätin.'

'I'll send it to you.'

At that point Major Crampas came over to Effi and asked if he might enquire how she was. Effi blushed furiously, but before she could reply Crampas said, 'May I ask you, Frau Baronin, to introduce me to the ladies?'

Effi now did so. He, for his part, was already completely *au fait* and, chatting easily, went through all the Paddens and Titzewitzes he had ever heard of. At the same time he apologized for not having yet visited the families on the other side of the Kessine and introduced his wife to them; but it was strange, he concluded, the divisive power that water had. It was just the same as with la Manche Channel . . .

'What?' old Frau Titzewitz asked.

Crampas, clearly thinking there was no point in going into explanations that would get them nowhere, went on, 'Of twenty Germans who go to France there's not one goes to England. It's the water that does that; I repeat, water has the power to separate.'

Frau von Padden who, with her keen instinct, suspected there was something suggestive behind this, was going to speak up for water, but Crampas went on in full flow, drawing the ladies' attention to the beautiful Fräulein von Stojentin, who was 'without doubt the queen of the ball,' this said with an admiring glance at Effi. Then, with a bow that included all three, he quickly took his leave.

'A handsome fellow,' said Frau von Padden. 'Is he on visiting terms with you?'

'Occasional.'

'A really handsome fellow,' Frau von Padden repeated. 'A little too sure of himself. And pride comes before a fall . . . But just look there, he really is going to dance with Grete Stojentin. He's actually too old for her, at least in his mid-forties.'

'He'll be forty-four at his next birthday.'

'Indeed! You seem to know him well.'

*

It suited Effi very well that, right from the beginning, the new year brought all kinds of excitement. Since New Year's Eve a sharp northeasterly had been blowing, that in the days following increased almost to a gale, and on the afternoon of the 3rd of January word came that a ship had not made the entrance to the harbour and was stranded a hundred yards from the breakwater; it was, they said, an English ship, from Sunderland, with, as far as they could tell, seven men on board. Despite all their efforts the pilots couldn't get round the breakwater, and to launch a boat from the beach was out of the question. That sounded pretty sad, but Johanna, who had brought the news, had something reassuring to add: Consul Eschrich was already on the way with his life-saving equipment and rockets, and he'd surely manage to rescue them; the distance wasn't quite as far as in '75, when it had worked; they'd even saved the poodle then, and it had been

Effi Briest

really touching to see how happy the dog had been, how it had kept licking the captain's wife and the dear little child, not much bigger than Annie, with its red tongue.

'I've got to go out, Geert, I've got to see this,' Effi had immediately said, and both of them set off at once so as not to be too late. And they arrived just at the right moment, for as they came out of the Plantation on to the beach they heard the first shot and quite clearly saw the rocket with the line attached fly across below the storm-clouds and come down on the other side of the ship. All hands on board immediately got into action and used the line to pull up the heavy rope with the breeches-buoy, and it wasn't long before the buoy returned and one of the sailors, a slim, very attractive man in a sou'wester, was safely on the shore and being plied with questions, while the buoy set off again, bringing a second, then a third sailor, and so on. All were rescued, and as Effi went back home with her husband half an hour later she could have thrown herself down in the dunes and had a good cry. She felt light of heart once more and was immensely happy that that was so.

That had been on the third. And on the fifth there was already more excitement, though of a different kind, to be sure. Innstetten had met Gieshübler, who was, of course, a member of the municipal council, as he came out of the town hall, and had learnt from him that the Ministry of War had asked the town authorities how they would feel about a garrison being stationed there. If they were willing to cooperate, that is, prepared to build the stables and barracks, they could be allocated two companies of hussars. 'Well, Effi, what do you say to that?'—Effi seemed dazed. At once her mind was filled with the innocent joys of her childhood, and straight away she felt as if red hussars—for they were also red ones, like those at home in Hohen-Cremmen—were the true guardians of paradise and innocence. And still she remained silent.

'You're not saying anything, Effi.'

'Yes, strange, isn't it, Geert. But it makes me feel so happy, I can't say anything for joy. Will it really happen? Will they really come?'

'Well, there's a long way to go yet, Gieshübler even thought his colleagues, the elders of the town, didn't deserve it. Instead of simply being united in their appreciation of the honour or, if not the honour, then the advantage, he told me they were full of ifs and buts and niggling about the expense of the new buildings; Michelsen, the confectioner, even went so far as to say the hussars would corrupt the morals of the town, and anyone who had a daughter should be on his guard and install bars over their windows.'

'It's beyond belief. I've never seen such well-mannered people as our hussars; really Geert. Well, you know that yourself. And now this Michelsen wants to put bars over everything. Does he have daughters?'

'Yes. Three in fact. But they're all of them *hors concours*.'

Effi laughed more heartily than she had for a long time. But it didn't last long, and when Innstetten went out, leaving her by herself, she sat down by the child's cradle and her tears fell on the pillows. She was overcome with feelings of guilt again and felt as if she were imprisoned and couldn't escape.

They made her suffer and she wanted to free herself from them, but although she was capable of strong feelings, she wasn't a strong character, she lacked the persistence, and all her good intentions would fade away. So she just drifted on, at first because she couldn't change things, then because she didn't want to change them. Forbidden, secret desires had her in their power.

Thus it came about that Effi, free and open by nature, more and more came to live a life in which she was acting out a part. Only in one thing did she stay true to herself: she saw everything clearly and didn't try to gloss over anything. Once she went over to the mirror in her bedroom in the late evening. The lights and shadows flitted to and fro; Rollo barked outside, and at that moment she felt as if someone were looking over her shoulder. But she quickly recovered. 'I know what it is. It wasn't *him*,' she said pointing to the haunted room upstairs, 'it was something else . . . my conscience . . . you're lost, Effi.' But things went on as they were, the ball had started to roll, and what happened one day determined what was done on the next.

Around the middle of the month invitations arrived to visits out in the country. The four families who were the Innstettens' preferred company had come to an agreement about the order: the Borckes to begin with, then the Flemmings and the Grasenabbs, finishing with the Güldenklees; with a week between each. All four invitations arrived on the same day; the purpose was clearly to give the impression of an orderly and well-thought-out process, also presumably of a special bond of friendship.

'I won't be going with you, Geert, and you must excuse me right away because of the course of treatment I've been undergoing for weeks now . . .'

Innstetten laughed. 'Treatment. I'm to blame the course of treatment. That's the pretext, the fact is, you don't want to go.'

'No, it's more honest than you're willing to allow. You were the one who wanted me to consult the doctor. I did so, and now I must follow his advice. Oddly enough, the good doctor thinks I'm anaemic, and you know that I drink some of the chalybeate water every day. And then if you imagine a dinner at the Borckes' on top of that, perhaps with brawn or eel in aspic, it must make you feel it would be the death of me. And you surely won't want that to happen to your Effi. Though I have to say, I sometimes feel . . .'

'Please, Effi . . .'

'But the one good thing about this is that every time you drive out I can look forward to accompanying you for a short distance, certainly as far as the mill or to the churchyard or even to the corner of the woods, where the side-road to Morgnitz starts. Then I'll get out and stroll back. It's always nicest in the dunes.'

Innstetten was happy with that, and when the carriage was brought round three days later Effi got in and accompanied her husband as far as the corner of the woods. 'Get Kruse to stop here, Geert. You'll be going off to the left, I'll go to the right, as far as the beach then back through the Plantation. It's quite long, but not too long. Dr Hannemann is always telling me exercise is everything, exercise and fresh air. And I almost think he's right. Give my best wishes to everyone, only you needn't bother with Sidonie.'

The drives on which Effi accompanied her husband to the corner of the woods were repeated each week; but even on the days in between, Effi was conscientious in following the doctor's orders strictly. Not a day passed without her taking the prescribed walk, mostly in the afternoon, when Innstetten would immerse himself in the newspapers. The weather was fine, the air mild and fresh, the sky overcast. Usually she went alone, and would say to Roswitha, 'Roswitha, I'm going down the high-road now and then to the right at the square with the merry-go-round; I'll wait there for you to come and join me. We'll come back along the beech avenue or the Reeperbahn. But only come if Annie's asleep. If she isn't asleep, send Johanna. Or no, don't bother, it's not necessary, I can find the way myself.'

The first day that arrangement was made, they did actually meet. Effi was sitting on a bench against the side of a long wooden shed and looking across at a low, half-timbered building, yellow, with the beams painted black, an inn for the common people, who were having a glass of beer there or playing cards. It was hardly beginning to get dark but the windows were already lit, and a shimmer of light fell from them onto the piles of snow and a few trees on one side. 'Look, Roswitha, isn't it beautiful?' That went on for a few days, but then when Roswitha came to the merry-go-round and the shed there would be no one there, and as she entered the hall when she came back Effi would greet her with, 'Where have you been, Roswitha? I've been back for ages.'

So the weeks passed. The proposal about the hussars had as good as fallen through because of the difficulties the townspeople made; but since the negotiations had not yet been finally broken off and were now going through another department, the High Command, Crampas had been summoned to Stettin, where they wanted to hear what he had to say about the matter. On his second day there he wrote to Innstetten, 'Forgive me for taking French leave, Innstetten. Everything went so quickly. And to be honest, I'll try and spin the business out, I'm glad to get away for once. Give my best wishes to your charming lady wife.'

He read it out to Effi. She remained calm. Finally she said, 'It's much better like that.'

'How do you mean?'

'That he's away. He's always saying the same things. When he's back, at least for a while he'll have something new to tell us.'

Innstetten gave her a quick, sharp look, but he saw nothing and his suspicion subsided. 'I'm going away too,' he said after a while, 'to Berlin, even. Perhaps then, like Crampas, I can bring back something new. My darling Effi always wants to hear something new, she gets bored in our dear old town of Kessin. I'll be away for about a week, perhaps a day more. But don't be afraid . . . it will surely not come back again . . . you know, that up there . . . And if it does, you have Rollo and Roswitha.'

Effi smiled to herself, and there was a touch of melancholy about it. The day came back to mind when Crampas had first told her that Innstetten was acting out a part with the business of the ghost and her fear. The great educator! But was he not right? Was his play-acting not warranted? And all kinds of conflicting thoughts, good and bad, went through her mind.

Three days later Innstetten left.

He had said nothing about what he intended to do in Berlin.

CHAPTER 21

Innstetten had been away four days when Crampas returned from Stettin with the news that the powers that be had decided to abandon for good the idea of stationing two companies of cavalry in Kessin; there were so many small towns that would be keen to have a cavalry garrison, especially one of Blücher's Hussars,* that they were accustomed to such offers being met with a welcoming rather than a hesitant response. When Crampas informed them of this, the town council looked rather abashed; only Gieshübler was jubilant, but that was because he was happy to see the petty-bourgeois attitudes of his colleagues suffer a defeat. The news caused a certain amount of disgruntlement among the common folk, and even some consuls with daughters were unhappy with it for a while; in general, however, they quickly got over the matter, perhaps because the inhabitants, or at least the notables, were more interested in the question of 'what Innstetten was up to in Berlin'. They didn't want to lose the Landrat, who was well liked, but there were wild rumours about the matter that Gieshübler had, if not invented, then certainly embellished and passed on. Amongst other things, it was said that Innstetten was to lead a legation to Morocco, one with presents that included not just the usual vase with pictures of Sanssouci* and the New Palace but above all a large ice-making machine. The latter seemed so plausible, given the temperatures in Morocco, that the rumour as a whole was believed.

Effi heard it as well. The days when it would have amused her were not that far back, but the mood she had been in since the end of the year made it impossible for her to laugh uninhibitedly at such things. The expression on her face had changed completely, and the partly touching, partly roguish childlike aspect that she had retained as a woman had gone. The walks to the beach and the Plantation, that she had given up while Crampas was in Stettin, were resumed once he returned, and she wasn't even put off by bad weather. As before, Roswitha was supposed to go to meet her at the end of the Reeperbahn or by the churchyard, but they missed each other even more often than before. 'I could tell you off for not managing to find me, Roswitha, but it doesn't matter. I'm not frightened any more, not even at the churchyard, and in the woods I've never met a soul.'

It was the day before Innstetten's return from Berlin that Effi said that. Roswitha was not much concerned about it, and instead spent her time hanging garlands over the doors; the shark was given a spruce-twig as well and looked even odder than usual. Effi said, 'That's right, Roswitha, he'll be pleased to see all the greenery when he gets back tomorrow. Am I going out today? Dr Hannemann insists I do, he keeps saying I can't be taking it seriously enough or I'd look better. But I don't really feel like it today, it's drizzling and the sky's so grey.'

'I'll bring Madam's raincoat.'

'Yes, do that. But don't come for me, we won't meet anyway,' she said with a laugh. 'Really, you're not very good at finding me, Roswitha, and I don't want you to catch a cold, all for nothing.'

So Roswitha stayed at home, and since Annie was asleep she went to have a chat with Frau Kruse. 'Frau Kruse, my dear,' she said, 'you were going to tell me the story about the Chinaman. Johanna interrupted us yesterday, she always acts so superior, that kind of thing's not for her. But I think there was something to it, I mean between the Chinaman and Thomsen's niece, if it wasn't his granddaughter.'

Frau Kruse nodded.

'Either', Roswitha went on, 'it was a tale of unrequited love' (Frau Kruse nodded again) 'or his love could have been returned and the Chinaman simply couldn't stand the idea that it was all suddenly over. After all, the Chinese are human beings as well, and things will be the same with them as with us.'

'Everything,' Frau Kruse assured her, and was going to tell the story to confirm this when her husband came in and said, 'You could give me the bottle with the leather varnish, Mother; I have to get the harness bright and shiny for when the Master comes back tomorrow; he notices everything, and even if he doesn't say anything you can tell he's noticed.'

'I'll bring it out to you, Kruse,' Roswitha said. 'Your wife's just going to tell me something, but it won't take long and then I'll bring it out.'

A few minutes later Roswitha came out into the yard with the leather varnish and stood beside the harness Kruse had just hung over the garden fence.

'It's not much use now, dammit,' he said, taking the bottle, 'it's drizzling all the time and the shine will go. But my view is that everything has to be done right.'

'Yes it has to. But then, Kruse, it's proper varnish, I can see that, and proper varnish doesn't stay sticky for long, it dries out straight away. Then if it's misty in the morning or there's rain, it won't do any harm. But I have to say, all that about the Chinaman's a strange story.'

Kruse laughed. 'It's a piece of nonsense, Roswitha. And my wife's always telling such stuff instead of doing what needs to be done, and when I have to put on a clean shirt, there's a button missing. And that's the way it's been since we've been here. She's got nothing but those stories inside her head. And the black hen, but the black hen doesn't even lay eggs. And how could it lay eggs? It never gets out, and eggs don't come from just a cockadoodledoo. You can't expect that of any hen.'

'Now then, Kruse, I'll tell your wife that. I always thought you were a decent man, and now you've come out with something like that about cockadoodledoo. You men are always worse than we think you are. I ought to take that brush there and paint a black moustache on you.'

'Well, from you, Roswitha, I wouldn't say no.' Kruse, who usually stood on his dignity, seemed about to adopt a more and more flirtatious tone, when he suddenly saw his mistress, who that day was coming from the other side of the Plantation and passing by the garden fence at that moment.

'Good afternoon, Roswitha, you seem very cheerful. What's Annie doing?'

'She's asleep, Ma'am.'

But Roswitha blushed as she said that and, quickly breaking off, hurried into the house to help her mistress get changed. Was Johanna there, that was the question. She was often in the 'office' over the road, because there was less to do in the house and Friedrich and Christel were too boring and never had anything to say for themselves.

Annie was still asleep. Effi bent over the cradle, let Roswitha take her hat and raincoat, and sat down on the little sofa in her bedroom. She brushed her damp hair back, put her feet up on the low stool

Roswitha had pushed over, and said, visibly enjoying the comfortable rest after a fairly long walk, 'I must point out to you, Roswitha, that Kruse is a married man.'

'I know, Ma'am.'

'Yes, it's surprising all the things we know, and then still behave as if we *didn't*. Nothing can come of it.'

'But nothing's going to come of it, Ma'am . . .'

'For if you're thinking she's sick, then you're counting your chickens before they're hatched. Sick people live longest. And then she has the black hen. You beware of that, it knows everything and lets everything out. I don't know why, but it gives me the creeps. And I'm willing to bet all that stuff upstairs is to do with that hen.'

'Oh, I don't believe that. But it is terrible all the same. And Kruse, who's always against his wife, can't persuade me otherwise.'

'What did he say?'

'He said it's only mice.'

'Well, mice are bad enough. I can't stand mice. But I could clearly see that you were chatting with him and getting quite familiar. I even think you were going to paint a black moustache on him. That's going quite far in itself. And afterwards you'd be left in the lurch. You're still a nice-looking woman, and you have something about you. But just be careful, that's all I have to say. What was it like the first time with you? Is it something you can tell me?'

'Oh, I can do that. But it was terrible. And because it was so terrible, Madam needn't worry about Kruse. Anyone who's been through something like I did has had enough of it and is careful. Sometimes I still dream about it, and then I feel shattered the next day. Such awful fear . . .'

Effi had sat up and rested her chin on her hand. 'Well tell me. What can it have been like? As I remember from home, it's always the same old story with you people . . .'

'Yes, I suppose at first it's always the same, and I don't imagine it was something special with me, not in the least. But the way they went on and on at me about it and I eventually had to say, "Yes, it's true," yes, that was terrible. Mother, well, that was bearable, but Father, he was the village blacksmith, he was strict and quick-tempered and when he heard, he came at me with an iron bar he'd just taken out of the fire. He was going to kill me, and I screamed and ran up to the loft and hid and lay there trembling, and only went

down when they called to me and said I should come. And I had
a younger sister, and she kept pointing at me and saying, "Shame
on you!" And then, when the child was about to come, I went into
a barn nearby because I didn't dare have it at home. Some other
people found me there, half dead, and carried me to the house and
put me in my bed. And on the third day they took the child away,
and when later on I asked where it was, they told me it was in good
hands. Oh, Madam, may the holy Mother of God preserve you from
such misery.'

Effi started and stared at Roswitha. But she was more startled than
indignant. 'How can you say that? I'm a married woman, you can't say
something like that, it's impertinent, it's out of place.'

'Oh, Ma'am . . .'

'Tell me instead what became of you. They'd taken the child away
from you. That's where you'd got to.'

'Then, after a few days, someone came from Erfurt and asked the
burgomaster if there was a wet-nurse in the village. And the burgomaster, may God reward him for it, said yes, and the stranger took
me with him right away, and from then on things have been better for
me; even with Frau Rohde it was always bearable, and then eventually
I came to you, Madam. And that was the best, best of all.' And as she
said that, she came over to the sofa and kissed Effi's hand.

'You mustn't keep kissing my hand, Roswitha, I don't like it. And
take care with Kruse. In other things you're such a good and sensible
woman . . . With a married man . . . that's never a good idea.'

'Oh, Madam, God and all the saints guide us most wonderfully,
and the misfortune we meet with also has its good side. Anyone who's
not improved by it is beyond help . . . I actually quite like men . . .'

'You see, Roswitha, you see.'

'But if I had those feelings again—that with Kruse's nothing—and
I couldn't resist them, I'd throw myself in the water right away. It was
too terrible. Everything. And what's become of the poor mite? I don't
believe it's still alive; they let it die, but I'm the one who's to blame.' She
threw herself down by Annie's cot and rocked the child back and forth
and kept singing the cradle-song from her own childhood.

'That's enough,' Effi said. 'Stop singing, I've got a headache. Bring
me the newspapers. Or has Gieshübler perhaps sent some magazines?'

'He has. And the fashion magazine's on top. We leafed through it,
Johanna and I did, before she went across the road. Johanna always

gets annoyed that she can't have things like that. Should I bring the fashion magazine?'

'Yes, do that. And bring the lamp as well.'

Roswitha went out, and once she was alone Effi said, 'What we won't do to get by. A pretty lady with a muff and a semi-veil; fashion dolls. But it's the best way of taking my mind off things.'

*

In the course of the next morning a telegram arrived from Innstetten to say that he would be coming by the second train and so wouldn't reach Kessin before evening. Effi couldn't settle all day; fortunately Gieshübler came during the afternoon, which helped her get through one hour. Finally at seven the carriage arrived, and Effi went out to greet him. Innstetten was worked up, in a way that was unusual for him, and didn't notice how Effi's warm welcome was tinged with embarrassment. The lamps and candles were lit in the hall, and the tea things, that Friedrich had already set out on a little table between the cupboards, reflected the profusion of light.

'It looks just the way it did when we arrived here. Do you remember, Effi?' She nodded. 'Only the shark is less fierce today with his spruce-twig, and Rollo too is more restrained and doesn't put his paws on my shoulders any longer. What's up with you, Rollo?'

Rollo brushed past his master and wagged his tail.

'He's not quite happy, either with me or with someone else. Well, I'll assume it's me. At least let's go in.' He went to his room and sat down on the sofa, inviting Effi to sit next to him. 'It was so nice in Berlin, better than I expected, but for all the enjoyment, I kept longing to be back here. And how good you're looking! A little pale and a little changed, but it suits you.'

Effi blushed.

'And now you're blushing into the bargain. But what I say is true. There was something of the spoilt child about you, but all at once you look like a woman.'

'That's nice to hear, Geert, but I think you're just saying it.'

'No, no, you can take the credit for it yourself, if it's something good . . .'

'I'd have thought it was.'

'And now guess whom I bring greetings from.'

'That's not difficult, Geert. Moreover, we women, among whom

I can now count myself since you've got back' (and she held out her hand to him and laughed), 'we women are good at guessing. We're not so slow on the uptake as you men.'

'Well then, who from?'

'Well, from Cousin Briest, of course. He's the only person I know in Berlin, apart from my aunts, whom you won't have gone to see and who are far too jealous to send me their greetings. Have you not found that all old aunts are jealous?'

'Yes, that's true, Effi. And when you talk like that you're my old Effi again. You should know that the old Effi, the one that still looked like a child, was very much to my taste as well. Just as much as the Frau Baronin I see before me now.'

'Is that so? And if you should have to choose between the two . . .'

'That's a tricky question, I'm not going to even try to answer it. But here's Friedrich with the tea. How I've looked forward to this moment! And I even said as much to your cousin Briest, when we were drinking your health in champagne at Dressel's* . . . Your ears must have been burning . . . And do you know what your cousin said?'

'Something silly, I'm sure. He's very good at that.'

'That's the most ungrateful thing I've ever heard. "To Effi," he said, "my beautiful cousin . . . Do you know, Innstetten, most of all I'd like to challenge you and shoot you dead. For Effi's an angel, and you've deprived me of that angel." And when he said that, he looked so serious and melancholy you could almost believe he meant it.'

'Oh, I've seen him in that mood too. How many glasses had you had?'

'I can't recall at the moment—perhaps I couldn't even have said at the time. But I do believe he was quite serious about it. And perhaps that might even have been the right thing. Don't you think you could have lived with him?'

'Lived with him? That's not much, Geert. But I almost feel like saying that I couldn't even have lived with him.'

'Why not? He really is a nice, charming person, and he's also quite intelligent.'

'Yes, he is that . . .'

'But . . .'

'But he's silly. And that's not a characteristic we women like, not even when we're still half children, which is what you've always seen me as, perhaps even still do, despite my progress. Silliness is not for us women. Men have to be men.'

'A good thing you said that. Damn it all, I'll really have to pull myself together. And I'm in the happy position of being able to tell you that I've just come, more or less directly, from something that looks like pulling myself together, or at least means I'll have to pull myself together in future . . . Tell me, what does a ministry mean to you?'

'A ministry? Well, it can be two things. It can be people, clever, distinguished people who run the country, and it can be just a house, a palazzo, a Palazzo Strozzi or Pitti* or, if they're not right, some other one. As you can see, my trip to Italy wasn't in vain.'

'And would you be agreeable to living in such a palazzo? I mean, in a ministry like that?'

'Good Lord, Geert, they haven't made you a minister, have they? Gieshübler was saying something like that. And the Prince can do everything. My God, so he's put it through, and I'm still only eighteen.'

Innstetten laughed. 'No, Effi, not a minister, we're not that far yet. But perhaps I'll develop all sorts of talents and then it won't be impossible.'

'So not at the moment, not yet a minister?'

'No. And, to tell the truth, we won't even be living in a ministry, but I'll be going to the ministry every day, just as I go to our Landrat's office, and I'll report to the minister and travel with him when he goes on an inspection of the offices in the provinces. And you'll be a Frau Ministerialrat and live in Berlin, and in six months time you'll hardly remember that you were here in Kessin and had nothing but Gieshübler and the dunes and the Plantation.'

Effi didn't say a word, but her eyes opened wider and wider; there was a nervous tic at the corners of her mouth and her whole delicate body started to tremble. All at once she slid down off the seat beside Innstetten, put her arms round his knees, and said, as if she were praying, 'Thank God.'

Innstetten went pale. What was it? Some feeling that had gripped him, briefly, but again and again over the past few weeks, had returned and was so clear to see in his look that Effi drew back in alarm. She had allowed herself to be carried away by a happy feeling that was as good as an admission of her guilt, and had said more than she ought to have. She had to find something to make it plausible, she had to find a way out of this situation, whatever the cost.

'Get up, Effi. What's wrong?'

Effi stood up quickly. However, she didn't go back to sit on the sofa but pulled over a high-backed chair, evidently because she didn't feel she had the strength to sit up without support.

'What's wrong?' Innstetten said again. 'I thought you'd had happy times here, and now you're saying "Thank God," as if everything here had given you the horrors. Was I a horror for you? Or was it something else? Tell me.'

'You still don't know, Geert?' she said, making a great effort to control the trembling in her voice. 'Happy times! Yes, of course, some happy times, but others as well. I've never quite got over my fear here, never. There was never a fortnight when I hadn't sensed it looking over my shoulder, that same face, that same pale complexion. And it was back again during the nights when you were away just now, not the face, but the shuffling again, and Rollo barked again, and Roswitha, who'd heard it too, came to my bedside and sat by me and we only got back to sleep as dawn was breaking. It's a haunted house, and I was meant to believe it, all that about the haunting—for you're an educator. Yes, Geert, that's what you are. But be that as it may, this much I do know: I've been afraid in this house for a whole year and more, and if I can get away from here I think it will leave me and I'll feel free again.'

Innstetten hadn't taken his eyes off her and followed every word. What could it mean, 'you're an educator'? And the other thing that came before it: 'I was meant to believe it, all that about the haunting.' What was all that? Where did it come from? And he felt his faint suspicion return and establish itself more firmly. But he was old enough to know that all signs were deceptive, and in our jealousy, Argus-eyed though it is, we more often go astray than in our blind trust. It could be the way she said it was. And if that were so, why should she not cry out: 'Thank God!'

And thus, quickly going through all the possibilities, he controlled his suspicion and held out his hand to her across the table. 'Forgive me, Effi, but I was so surprised at all that. My own fault, of course. I've always been too preoccupied with my own affairs. We men are all egoists. There's certainly one good thing about Berlin: there aren't any haunted houses there. Where would they come from? And now let's go across so I can see Annie; otherwise Roswitha will be calling me an uncaring father.'

As he spoke Effi had gradually calmed down, and the feeling of having saved herself from a danger she herself had created allowed her to stand up straight once more.

CHAPTER 22

The next morning the two of them had a somewhat belated breakfast together. Innstetten had overcome his ill-humour and worse, and Effi was so full of the feeling of liberation that she was once more not only able to display a slightly forced good mood but had almost recovered her former uninhibited temperament. She was still in Kessin, but already she felt as if it lay far behind her.

'I've been thinking, Effi,' Innstetten said. 'You're not entirely wrong in what you said about our house here. It was good enough for Captain Thomsen but not for a young, pampered woman; everything old-fashioned and no room. We'll see that you have a better place in Berlin, with a grand drawing-room as well, and high, stained-glass windows in the hall and on the stairs, the Kaiser with his crown and sceptre, or even something religious, St Elizabeth or the Virgin Mary. Let's say the Virgin Mary, we owe that to Roswitha.'

Effi laughed. 'Yes, that's what we must have. But who's going to find an apartment for us? I can't send Cousin Briest out looking for one. Even less the aunts! They'll think anything's good enough.'

'Yes, finding an apartment. No one can do that for you. I think you'll have to go there yourself.'

'When do you have in mind?'

'The middle of March.'

'Oh, that's much too late, Geert, everything will be gone by then. The best apartments are hardly likely to wait around for us.'

'That's true. But I only got back yesterday and I can't say "go tomorrow". That wouldn't look very good and wouldn't suit me either; I'm just glad to be back home with you again.'

'No,' she said, rather noisily rearranging the coffee things in order to conceal a rising feeling of embarrassment, 'no, it's not to be like that, not today and not tomorrow, but in the next few days. And if I do find something, I'll be back soon. And one more thing, Roswitha and Annie must come too. Best of all would be you as well. But I can see that's not possible. And I don't think the separation will last long. I already know where I'm going to look for something to rent . . .'

'Which is?'

'That's my secret. I want to have a secret too. So that I can give you a nice surprise.'

At that moment Friedrich came in to hand over the post, most of it consisting of official correspondence for Innstetten and newspapers. 'Oh, there's a letter for you as well,' Innstetten said. 'If I'm not mistaken, that's your Mama's handwriting.'

Effi took the letter. 'Yes, from Mama. But that's not the Friesack postmark; look, it clearly says Berlin.'

'Indeed,' Innstetten said with a laugh. 'You sound as if it's impossible. Your Mama will be in Berlin and has written her darling a letter from her hotel.'

'Yes,' Effi said, 'that will be it. But it still makes me almost afraid to open it, and what Hulda Niemeyer always used to say, "It's better to be afraid than to hope," is no comfort at all. What do you think about that?'

'Not quite what I'd expect from a pastor's daughter. But read the letter. Here's the paper-knife.'

Effi opened the envelope and read the letter out:

'MY DEAR EFFI,

I've been here in Berlin for twenty-four hours now; an appointment with Dr Schweigger. As soon as he saw me he congratulated me, and when, surprised, I asked him why, he said Wüllersdorf had just been to see him and told him that Innstetten had been appointed to the ministry where he's head of department. I was slightly annoyed to have to hear this from a third party, but my pride and delight outweighed my annoyance and so the pair of you are forgiven. I always knew (even when I was still with the hussars in Rathenow) that he would make his mark in life, and now *you're* the one to benefit from it. You must find an apartment, of course, and have new furnishings. If you think you could use my advice, my dear Effi, then come as quickly as your time allows. I'm staying here a week for treatment, perhaps a little longer if it's not effective; Schweigger's been very vague about it. I have a room in a pension in Schadowstrasse; there are rooms free near mine. I'll tell you about my eye when you get here, at the moment all I'm concerned about is your future. Briest will be immensely happy, he always acts as if he couldn't care less about these things, though actually they mean more to him than to me. Best wishes to Innstetten and kiss Annie for me.

As ever, with all my love,

Luise von B.'

Effi put the letter down and said nothing. She had decided what she had to do, but she didn't want to say it herself. She wanted Innstetten to suggest it, then she would hesitantly agree.

And Innstetten did indeed fall into the trap. 'Well, Effi, you're sitting there so calm.'

'Oh, Geert, there are two sides to everything. On the one hand it would be lovely to see Mama again, perhaps even in a few days' time. But there are so many reasons against it.'

'For example?'

'Mama, as you well know, has very definite views and insists on getting her own way. She could get Papa to agree to anything. But I'd like to have an apartment that is to *my* taste, and new furnishings that I like.'

Innstetten laughed. 'Is that all?'

'It would be enough, but it's not all.' Summoning up all her strength, she looked at him and said, 'And then, Geert, I don't want to leave you the moment you've come back.'

'You little rascal, you're just saying that because you know my soft spot. But we're all vain and I'm happy to believe you. I'm happy to believe you and will make a heroic effort to renounce your company. Go as soon as you think necessary and your heart will allow.'

'You mustn't say that, Geert. You're more or less obliging me to put on a show of affection, and I have to say, out of pure coquetry, "Oh, Geert, in that case I'll never go." Or something like that.'

Innstetten wagged his finger at her. 'You're too subtle for me, Effi. There was me thinking you were a child, and now I see you're up to all the rest of them. But no more of that or, as your Papa's always saying, "That's too big a question." Tell me instead when you want to go.'

'Today's Tuesday. Let's say on Friday. By the midday boat, then I'll be in Berlin by the evening.'

'Agreed. And when will you be back?'

'Well, let's say Monday evening. That gives me three days.'

'No, that's too soon. You can't do it in three days. And your Mama won't let you go so quickly.'

'So for as long as necessary, then.'

'Yes.'

And with that Innstetten got up to go over to his office.

*

The days until she went simply flew past. Roswitha was very happy.
'Oh, Madam, Kessin, well yes . . . but it's not Berlin. And the horse-
drawn trams. And the way they ring and you don't know whether to
go to the right or the left, and sometimes I've felt as if everything was
going right over me. No, there's nothing like that here. I think there
are some days when we don't even see six people. Just the dunes and
the sea beyond them. There's the noise of the waves all the time, but
that's all.'

'You're right, Roswitha. There's the noise all the time, but it's not
a proper life. And you get all kinds of silly ideas. You have to agree
that the business with Kruse wasn't right.'

'Oh, Ma'am . . .'

'No, I don't want to go into that any more. You'll only deny it anyway. And don't take too few things with you. Actually, you can take all
your things, and Annie's as well.'

'I thought we'd be coming back.'

'Yes, I will. The master wants me to. But you and Annie might be
able to stay there, with my mother. You'll just have to see that she
doesn't spoil little Annie too much. She was sometimes strict with
me, but with a grandchild . . .'

'And then Annie's such a little darling, you can't help loving her.'

That was on the Thursday, the day before their departure.
Innstetten was travelling out into the country and wasn't expected
back until the evening. In the afternoon Effi walked into the town, as
far as the market square, where she went to the pharmacy and asked
for a bottle of sal volatile. 'You never know who'll be on the train with
you,' she said to the old assistant, with whom she often had a little
chat and who idolized her as much as Gieshübler himself.

'Is Dr Gieshübler in?' she asked, after she'd put the bottle in
her bag.

'Of course, Madam. He's in his room there, reading the papers.'

'I won't be disturbing him, will I?'

'Oh, not at all.'

So Effi went in. It was a small room with a high ceiling and shelves all round with all sorts of flasks and retorts on them; just along the one wall there were boxes, with iron rings on them and alphabetically arranged, in which he kept the prescriptions.

Gieshübler was delighted and embarrassed. 'What an honour. Here among my retorts. May I beg you to take a seat for a moment, Frau Baronin?'

'Of course, my dear Gieshübler. But it really is only just for a moment. I've come to say goodbye.'

'But surely you're coming back, Frau Baronin. Just for three or four days, I heard . . .'

'Well, yes, my dear friend, I'm supposed to be coming back; in fact it's even been agreed that I'll be back in Kessin in a week at the latest. But it's possible I might *not* come back. Do I have to tell you how many things might happen . . . ? I can see that you're going to tell me I'm too young . . . young people can die as well. And there are so many other things too. So I'd rather say goodbye to you as if it were for good.'

'But my dear Frau Baronin . . .'

'As if it were for good. And I want to thank you, dear Gieshübler. You are the best thing there was here; because you are the best, of course. Even if I live to be a hundred, I'll never forget you. There were times when I felt lonely here, and sometimes I was heavy-hearted, more than you can imagine; I didn't always get things right; but, from the very first day, whenever I saw you I always felt happier and better, too.'

'But my dear Frau Baronin . . .'

'And for that I want to thank you. I've just bought a phial of sal volatile; on the train there are often strange people who won't even let you open the window; and if it should perhaps happen—it really goes to your head, I mean the smelling-salts—that the tears come to my eyes, then I'll think of you. Farewell, my dear friend, and send my greetings to your friend, Fräulein Trippelli. I've been thinking of her several times during the last few weeks, and of Prince Kotchukoff. It still seems a strange relationship, but I can understand it . . . And keep in touch. Or I'll write to you.'

With that Effi left. Gieshübler accompanied her out into the square. He was dazed, so much so that he didn't take in some of the mysterious things she had said.

*

Effi went back home. 'Bring me the lamp, Johanna,' she said, 'but to my bedroom. And then some tea. I feel so cold and can't wait until the master's back.'

Both were brought. Effi was already sitting at her little writing-desk, a sheet of paper in front of her, the pen in her hand.

'The tea on the table there, please, Johanna.'

Once Johanna had left the room, Effi locked the door, looked in the mirror for a moment, then sat down. And wrote:

'I am leaving on the boat in the morning and this is my letter of farewell. Innstetten expects me to return in a few days but I am not coming back . . . You will know why . . . It would have been best if I'd never seen this place at all. I beg you not to take this as a reproach, the guilt is all mine. If I look at your house . . . your actions may be excusable, not mine. I am heavily burdened with guilt but perhaps I can overcome it. That we have been called away from here I see as a sign that I may still find forgiveness. Forget what has happened, forget me.

Your Effi.'

She glanced again through what she had written. What struck her as strangest of all was the use of the formal *Sie*; but that had to be; it was to say that there was no way back. And she slipped the letter into an envelope and went to a house between the churchyard and the corner of the woods. A thin trail of smoke came from the ramshackle chimney. There she handed the letter in.

When she returned Innstetten was already home, and she sat with him and told him about Gieshübler and the sal volatile.

Innstetten laughed. 'Wherever did you get your Latin, Effi?'

*

The boat, a light sailing-boat (the steamboats only ran in the summer), left at twelve. Effi and Innstetten were already on board a quarter of an hour before that; Roswitha and Annie as well.

There was more luggage than seemed necessary for a trip that was only intended to last a few days. Innstetten was talking to the captain; Effi, in a raincoat and a light grey hat, stood on the afterdeck, close to the wheel, surveying the Embankment and the row of pretty houses along it. Directly opposite the jetty was Hoppensack's Hotel, a three-storey building with a yellow flag with a crown and cross on it, hanging down slackly from the roof in the still, somewhat misty air. Effi looked up at the flag for a while but then her gaze slid back down, finally coming to rest on a group of people standing around, full of curiosity, on the Embankment. At that moment the bell sounded. Effi had a very strange feeling; the boat started to move slowly, and when she surveyed the jetty again she saw that Crampas was in the front row. Seeing him gave her a start, but she was also pleased. Crampas though, his demeanour completely changed, was visibly moved, and raised his hand in a grave farewell, to which she responded, but with a very friendly wave accompanied by a look that had something pleading about it. Then she quickly went down to the cabin, where Roswitha had already settled with Annie. She stayed in the rather stuffy room until they had left the river and emerged into the broad estuary of the Breitling. Then Innstetten came and called her to come on deck to enjoy the splendid view. She did go up. Grey clouds were hanging over the surface of the water, with, just now and then, a half-veiled sun peeping through. Effi thought back to the day, exactly fifteen months ago now, on which she had driven in an open carriage along the bank of the Breitling. Such a short period of time, and her life often so quiet and lonely. And yet how much had happened since then!

Then they sailed up the waterway and were at the station, or at least quite close to it, by two. When they then passed the Prince Bismarck Inn, Golchowski was standing in the doorway again and insisted on accompanying the Herr Landrat and his wife as far as the steps up the embankment. The train not yet having been announced when they reached the platform, Effi and Innstetten walked up and down.

They talked about the question of their apartment; they were in agreement about the district, namely that it had to be between the area by the Tiergarten Park and the Zoo. 'I want to hear the finches singing and the parrots as well,' Innstetten said, and Effi agreed.

Now they heard the signal and the train arrived. The station-master was very obliging and Effi had a compartment to herself.

One last handshake, a wave of the handkerchief, and the train set off again.

CHAPTER 23

Friedrichstrasse Station was crowded, but despite that Effi spotted her Mama, with Cousin Dagobert beside her, from the window of her compartment. Great was their joy at seeing each other again, the wait in the luggage-hall didn't make too great a demand on their patience, and in less than five minutes the cab was driving along Dorotheenstrasse, beside the track of the horse-drawn tram, towards Schadowstrasse,* on the first corner of which the pension was. Roswitha was delighted, and enjoyed the way Annie stretched out her little hands to the lights.

Now they were there, and Effi was given her two rooms. They were not, as expected, next to Frau von Briest's, but still in the same corridor, and once everything was in place and Annie settled in a cot, Effi went back to her mother's room, a little parlour with a fire-place in which a fire was burning—a small fire, because the weather was mild, almost warm. Places for three had been set at the round table with the green-shaded lamp, and the tea things were on a little side-table.

'You've got a delightful room, Mama,' Effi said as she sat down opposite the sofa, only to get up immediately to busy herself with the tea. 'May I play the tea-lady again, Mama?'

'Of course, Effi dear. But only for Dagobert and yourself. I'm afraid I have to refrain, which I find almost too hard to bear.'

'I understand, because of your eyes. But tell me now, Mama, what's the situation with them? In the cab, clattering away as it was, we only talked about Innstetten and our great career, much too much, and it can't go on like that. Believe me, your eyes are more important to me, and in one respect I can see that they are quite unchanged, thank God, and still give me the same friendly look as always.' And she rushed over to her Mama and kissed her hand.

'You're so impetuous. Still the same old Effi.'

'Oh no, Mama. Not the same old Effi. I only wish I were. You change once you're married.'

Her cousin laughed. 'I can't see much of that, Cousin; you're even prettier, that's all. And I suspect the impetuosity's not gone either.'

'There speaks the cousin,' her Mama said, but Effi would have none of it and said, 'Dagobert, you're everything—apart from a judge of character. It's strange. You officers are never good judges of character, certainly not you young ones. You only have eyes for yourselves and your recruits, and those in the cavalry have their horses as well. They know absolutely nothing at all.'

'Whence all this wisdom, Cousin? You don't know any officers. Kessin, I read, has declined the hussars intended for it, a case unique in the annals of the world, by the way. Or are you harking back to the old days? You were still half a child when the hussars from Rathenow went over to Hohen-Cremmen.'

'To that I could say that children are the best observers, but I won't. That's all just idle chat. I want to know how Mama's eyes are.'

Frau von Briest told them that the eye specialist had said it was blood pressure on the brain. That caused the flickering. It had to be dealt with by dieting—beer, coffee, tea, all off the menu—and an occasional removal of some blood, then it would soon improve. 'He was talking about a fortnight. But I know doctors' estimates; a fortnight means six weeks, and I'll still be here when Innstetten comes and you move into your new apartment. I won't deny that that's the best thing about the whole business and reconciles me to the long treatment. Just find something really nice. I thought of Landgrafenstrasse or Keithstrasse, elegant and not over-expensive. For you'll have to tighten your belts. Innstetten's position is a great honour, but it won't bring in much. And Briest's complaining as well. Prices are dropping, and he tells me every day that if they don't introduce protective duties he'll be reduced to beggary and have to give up Hohen-Cremmen. You know how he likes to exaggerate. But now help yourself, Dagobert, and tell us something amusing, if you can. Reports on illnesses are always boring, and your nearest and dearest only listen because they have to. I'm sure Effi would like to hear something, perhaps a story from *Die Fliegenden Blätter* or *Kladderadatsch*,* though that's said not to be very good any more.'

'Oh, it's just as good as it used to be. They've still got Strudelwitz and Prudelwitz, and stories about them write themselves.'

'My favourites are Karlchen Miessnick and Wippchen von Bernau.'*

'Yes, they're the best. Though forgive me for saying so, my fair cousin, but Wippchen isn't from *Kladderadatsch* and he hasn't anything to do at the moment, since there are no wars for him to write his comic reports on. We'd like to have our turn and finally get rid of this terrible emptiness.' As he said that, he drew his fingers across his chest from the buttonhole to his arm.

'Oh, that's all mere vanity. Tell me something interesting instead. What's in vogue?'

'Well, it's strange, Cousin. It's not to everyone's taste. At the moment we have Bible jokes.'

'Bible jokes? What can they be? . . . The Bible and jokes don't go together.'

'That's what I said, they're not to everyone's taste. But acceptable or not, they're very popular. It's just a fashion, like plover's eggs.'

'Well, if it's not too outrageous, give us an example. Can you?'

'Of course I can. It starts with a question—all these jokes start in that way, this one with a very simple question: Who was the first house-guest? Come on, can you work it out?'

'The first house-guest? I've no idea. Who was it?'

'The first house-guest was sorrow. It says in the Book of Job,* "No longer shalt thou be visited by sorrow".'

Effi repeated the sentence, shaking her head. She was very much one of those fortunate people who have no appreciation of that kind of play on words, and her cousin got into more and more of a tangle as he tried to explain the joke.

'Oh, I see. I'm sorry, Dagobert, but I think that really is *too* stupid.'

'Yes, it is stupid,' Dagobert said, abashed.

'Stupid and unseemly; it's enough to spoil Berlin for me. I put Kessin behind me to have a social life again, and the first thing I hear is a Bible joke. Mama's kept silent too, and that says enough. But I'll help you get out of this awkward predicament . . .'

'Please do, Cousin . . .'

'. . . get you out of this awkward predicament by taking it seriously as a good omen that the first thing said to me here by my cousin Dagobert was, "No longer shalt thou be visited by sorrow." It's odd, my cousin, but however weak it is as a joke, I'm still grateful for it.'

Hardly was he out of the noose of his own making than Dagobert was trying to poke fun at Effi's earnest tone, but gave up as soon as he saw that she wasn't amused by it.

He left soon after ten, promising to come the next day to see how they were.

As soon as he had gone, Effi also withdrew to her room.

*

The next day the weather was fine, and mother and daughter set out early. They first went to the eye clinic, where Effi stayed in the waiting-room and leafed through a magazine, then headed for the

Tiergarten area, as far as the zoo, to see if they could find an apartment. And they did actually find something suitable in Keithstrasse, which was what they had been hoping for from the very first; the only problem was that it was a new building, not yet finished, and damp. 'It's not possible, Effi,' Frau von Briest said. 'It's out of the question for reasons of health. And then, a Geheimrat isn't the kind of person who takes a cheap tenancy while the apartment dries out.'

Even though she liked the apartment very much, Effi was more than happy to accept these considerations because she wasn't bothered about settling the matter quickly, on the contrary, 'more time, more choice', and putting off a decision was what suited her best. 'But we'll still keep an eye on that apartment, Mama, it's in such a lovely situation and is basically what I had in mind.' Then the two of them drove back to the city centre, dined in a restaurant that had been recommended to them, and went to the opera in the evening, to which the doctor had given his consent on condition that Frau von Briest went to hear more than to see.

The next few days were passed in a similar way; they were genuinely happy to be together again and to enjoy a good long chat with each other. More than once Effi, who, when she felt well, was not only a good raconteur and listener but also had a ready tongue when it came to scandal-mongering, was her old high-spirited self, and her Mama wrote home saying how happy she was to see the 'child' so cheerful and full of laughter again; it took them back to the days almost two years ago when they had bought her trousseau. Cousin Briest was the same as ever too. And that was indeed the case, though with the one difference: his appearances were less frequent, and when asked why he replied, apparently seriously, 'You're too dangerous for me, Cousin.' At that mother and daughter burst out laughing, and Effi said, 'You're still quite young, of course, Dagobert, but no longer young enough for that kind of flirtation.'

Almost a fortnight passed in this way. Innstetten's letters were more and more pressing and becoming rather caustic, almost towards his mother-in-law as well, so that Effi saw it wasn't possible to put off a decision any longer and she really had to take an apartment. But what about after that? There were still three weeks to go before the move to Berlin, and Innstetten was insisting she return soon. There was only one way out: she must put on an act again and pretend to be ill.

She didn't find that easy, and for more than one reason. But it had to be, and once she had decided that, she had also decided how the role was to be played, right down to the very last detail.

'Mama, as you can see, Innstetten's getting rather touchy about my continued absence. I think we'll have to give in and take an apartment today. Then I'll go home tomorrow. But, oh, it will be so hard for me to leave you.'

Frau von Briest agreed. 'And which apartment will you choose?'

'The first one, the one in Keithstrasse, of course. I liked it so well, right from the start, and so did you. It won't be entirely dried out yet, but it is the summer, which is a help. And if the damp is too bad and I get a bit of rheumatism, I've always got Hohen-Cremmen.'

'Don't tempt fate, child; sometimes you can get a touch of rheumatism and you've no idea why.'

These words suited Effi very well. She took the apartment that morning and wrote a card to Innstetten, telling him she'd be returning the next day. The cases were then immediately packed and all preparations made.

But the next morning Effi called her Mama to her bedside and said, 'I can't go, Mama. I've got such aches and pains, I feel sore right across my back. I almost think it must be rheumatism. I'd never have thought it was so painful.'

'You see? Now what did I tell you? You shouldn't tempt fate. Yesterday you were dismissive about it and today here it is. When I see Schweigger, I'll ask him what you should do.'

'No, not Schweigger. He's a specialist, and it's not on to consult him on something else, he might even take it amiss. I think the best thing is just to wait and see. It might pass. I'll live on tea and soda-water for the whole day, and if that makes me sweat, I may get over it.'

Frau von Briest agreed to that course of action, but insisted she must feed herself properly. To starve oneself, as used to be the fashion, she said, was quite wrong and simply weakened one; in that respect she was completely on the side of the new school: take in plenty of food.

All this was of no little comfort to Effi. She sent a telegram to Innstetten in which she spoke of the tiresome occurrence, causing an annoying, though only temporary, delay to her return; then she said to Roswitha, 'You'll have to fetch me some books now, Roswitha; it won't be difficult, I want some old ones, very old ones.'

'Of course, Madam. The lending-library's only just round the corner. What should I get?'

'I'll write them down, a selection, sometimes they haven't got the one you happen to want.' Roswitha brought pencil and paper and Effi wrote down: Walter Scott, *Ivanhoe* or *Quentin Durward*; Fenimore Cooper, *The Spy*; Dickens, *David Copperfield*; Willibald Alexis, *Herr von Bredow's Trousers*.*

Roswitha read through the list and cut off the last line in the other room; she would find it embarrassing, both for herself and for her mistress, to hand over the note in its original form.

The day passed without anything special happening. The next morning she was no better, nor on the third day.

'This can't go on, Effi. If something like that gets established, it's difficult to get rid of it again. It's these protracted illnesses doctors warn you about most strongly, and rightly so.'

Effi sighed. 'Yes, Mama, but whom should we consult? Not a young doctor; I don't know why, but I'd feel embarrassed.'

'A young doctor's always embarrassing, and it's all the worse if he isn't. But you can be reassured; I'll bring a very old one who treated me when I was still a boarder at Hecker's school, that was some twenty years ago. At that time he was close on fifty and had lovely grey hair, very curly. He was a ladies' man, but kept it within limits. Doctors who forget that never succeed, and quite right too; our women, at least society women, still have a sound core.'

'You think so? I'm always happy when I hear something good like that. For now and then you hear something different. And it must often be difficult. So what is the name of this Geheimrat? I assume your doctor has that title.'

'Geheimrat Rummschüttel.'

Effi laughed out loud. 'Rummschüttel—Dr Shake-it-all-about! And that a doctor for someone who can't move.'

'You do say some strange things, Effi. You can't be in all that great pain.'

'No, not at the moment. It's changing all the time.'

*

Geheimrat Rummschüttel appeared next morning. Frau von Briest welcomed him, and when he saw Effi, his first words were, 'Just like your Mama!'

Her mother tried to reject the comparison, saying that twenty years and more were a long time, but Rummschüttel stuck to his opinion, assuring them that while not every face imprinted itself on his mind, once the impression was there it stayed for good. 'And now, my dear Frau von Innstetten, what's the problem, how can we help you?'

'Oh, Herr Geheimrat, I find it difficult to tell you what it is. It's constantly changing. Just at the moment it seems to have disappeared. At first I was thinking of rheumatism, but I could almost believe it's neuralgia, pains down my back, and then I can't sit up. My Papa suffers from neuralgia, so I could observe what it's like when I still lived at home. Perhaps it's hereditary.'

'Very probably,' Rummschüttel said, after having felt her pulse and given his patient a brief but sharp scrutiny. 'Very probably, Frau Baronin.' However, what he was thinking to himself was, 'Acting sick to get off school, a virtuoso performance. A coquette *comme il faut*.' He didn't allow any of this to be seen, instead he said, as earnestly as any patient could desire, 'Rest and warmth is the best I can advise. Some medicine, nothing nasty, will do the rest.'

And he stood up to write the prescription: oil of bitter almonds, half an ounce; oil of neroli, two ounces. 'I would ask you to take half a teaspoon of this every two hours, my dear Frau Baronin. It will calm your nerves. And one more thing I must insist on: no mental exertion, no visits, no reading.' As he said that, he pointed to the book beside her.

'It's Scott.'

'Oh, there's no objection to that. Best of all is travel-writing. I'll call round again tomorrow.'

Effi had kept to her role wonderfully well, but despite that, once she was alone—her Mama was seeing the doctor out—she felt herself go bright red; she had very clearly seen that he had responded to her play-acting with some play-acting of his own. He was clearly a gentleman with great experience of life, who could see everything clearly, but didn't want to see everything, perhaps because he knew that such things sometimes had to be respected. But if there were pretences that shouldn't be respected, was not the one she was acting out of that kind?

Soon afterwards her Mama came back, and mother and daughter were full of praise for the refined old man who, despite the fact that he was nearly seventy, had something youthful about him. 'Send

Roswitha out to the pharmacy right away . . . but you're only to take a dose every three hours, he said to me outside. That's the way he was when I knew him before, he didn't often prescribe medicines and never a lot; but it was always invigorating and helped straight away.'

*

Rummschüttel came two days later, then just every third day, because he could see how embarrassed the young woman was at his visits. This endeared her to him, and after this third visit he had come to a firm opinion: 'There's something here compelling this woman to behave as she is doing.' He had long since stopped feeling irritated by such things.

At his fourth visit Rummschüttel found that Effi was up, sitting in a rocking-chair, a book in her hand and Annie beside her.

'Ah, my dear Frau Baronin. I'm delighted. I don't ascribe it to my medicine; this fine weather, these bright March days, illness just melts away. My congratulations. And your Frau Mama?'

'She's gone out, Herr Geheimrat, to Keithstrasse where we've rented an apartment. My husband will be here in a few days' time, and I very much hope to be able to introduce you to him once the apartment's in order. For I assume I can look forward to you taking care of me in future.'

He bowed.

'Our new apartment', she went on, 'has just been built, and I'm worried about it. Do you think, Herr Geheimrat, that the damp walls . . .'

'Not in the least, my dear Frau Baronin. Heat the place thoroughly for three or four days, keeping the doors and windows open, and you can risk it, I assure you. And as far as your neuralgia was concerned, it wasn't anything to be very concerned about, but I'm delighted your caution gave me the opportunity to renew an old acquaintance and make a new one.' He repeated his bow, gave Annie a friendly look, and left, giving his regards to her mother.

Hardly had he gone than Effi was at her desk writing a letter.

'DEAR INNSTETTEN,

Rummschüttel was here just now and has pronounced me recovered. I am now well enough to travel, tomorrow for example; but it's the 24th already and you're coming here on the 28th. And, anyway, I'm still suffering from the after-effects. I assume you'll understand if I give up the whole idea of making the journey. Our things are already on the way, and if I came we'd have to stay in Hoppensack's Hotel, like visitors. We must think about the cost as well, our expenses are going to pile up; amongst other things we'll have Rummschüttel's retainer to consider, if he's to remain our doctor. He's a delightful old gentleman. In medical matters he's not quite considered top-drawer, a "ladies' doctor" his jealous colleagues say. But that expression also contains praise, not everyone knows how to deal with us. The fact that I can't say farewell to the Kessiners personally doesn't really matter. I went to see Gieshübler. Frau Crampas always remained distant from me, distant to the point of rudeness; that only leaves the Pastor and Dr Hannemann and Crampas. Give my best wishes to the latter. I will be sending cards to the families out in the country; the Güldenklees, you tell me, are in Italy (I can't imagine what they're doing there), so that just leaves the three others. Make my excuses for me as best you can. You're the man who knows the proprieties, how to find the right word. I'll perhaps write a note to Frau von Padden—I really thought her delightful on New Year's Eve—expressing my regret. Send me a telegram to say whether you're in agreement with all that.

As ever,

your Effi.'

Effi posted the letter herself, as if by that she could make the answer arrive sooner, and the next morning the telegram she had requested from Innstetten arrived: 'In agreement with everything.' Her heart leapt with joy, and she hurried down the stairs to the nearest cab-rank. 'Keithstrasse 1c.' And the cab flew down Unter den Linden, then along Tiergartenstrasse, and stopped outside their new apartment.

Upstairs the things that had arrived the previous day were still lying around higgledy-piggledy, but that didn't bother her, and when she stepped out on to the wide balcony the Tiergarten Park lay there before her, on the other side of the canal bridge, all its trees already showing a shimmer of green. Above it the sun was shining brightly in a clear blue sky.

She quivered with excitement and took a deep breath. Then she stepped back into the room from the balcony, put her hands together, and looked up.

'And now, with God's aid, a new life. Things are going to be different.'

CHAPTER 24

Three days later Innstetten arrived in Berlin, fairly late, around nine. They were all at the station: Effi, her Mama, her cousin. He was warmly received, warmest of all by Effi, and a whole host of matters had already been discussed by the time the carriage stopped outside their new apartment in Keithstrasse. 'Oh, you've made a good choice, Effi,' Innstetten said as he went into the vestibule, 'no shark, no crocodile and, I hope, no ghost.'

'No, Geert, that's all over now. A new dawn is breaking and I'm not going to be afraid any longer, and I'm going to be better than before and live more according to your wishes.' She whispered all this to him as they made their way up the carpeted stairs to the second floor. Dagobert had given his arm to her mother.

Some things were still lacking upstairs, but they had made sure the apartment had a homely look and Innstetten said how pleased he was with it: 'You're a little genius, Effi.' But she rejected his praise and pointed to her Mama. She was the one who merited it, Effi said. She had been adamant with her 'This is where it has to go,' and had always been right, which had saved a lot of time, of course, and kept them all in a good mood. Finally Roswitha came to greet the master, adding 'Fräulein Annie begs to be excused for today'—a little joke of which she was proud and with which she made her point perfectly.

Now they sat down at the beautifully set table, and after Innstetten had poured himself a glass of wine and clinked glasses with everyone, 'to happy days', he took Effi's hand and said, 'But now tell me, Effi, what was all that about your illness?'

'Oh, let's forget that, it's not worth mentioning; a little painful and a real nuisance, because it frustrated our plans. But it wasn't more than that and now it's over and done with. Rummschüttel did his job; he's a delightful, refined old gentleman, as I think I told you in my letter. He's not supposed to be a leading light in medical science, but Mama says that's an advantage. And she'll be right about that, as she always is. Doctor Hannemann was just the same, but he could always put his finger on the problem. Now tell me, what are Gieshübler and all the others doing?'

'Who are all these others? Crampas sends his greetings to the Frau Baronin . . .'

'Oh, very courteous of him.'

'And the Pastor wants me to pass on his greetings too. The country gentry alone were rather chilly and seemed to blame me for your farewell without a farewell. Our good friend Sidonie was even rather caustic, and only dear Frau von Padden, to whom I drove across specially the day before yesterday, was sincerely pleased at your greetings and declaration of love. She said you are a charming woman, "but I should look after you well". And when I replied that you think me more of an educator than a husband, she said in a low voice, almost as if she were far away, "A little lamb, as white as snow." Then she broke off.'

Dagobert laughed. '"A little lamb, as white as snow." There you have it, Cousin. How does the nursery-rhyme go on?' He was going to tease her more, but gave up when he saw how she had gone pale.

The conversation, mostly concerning their former circumstances, went on for a while longer, and Effi finally learnt from bits and pieces that Innstetten let drop that of the household in Kessin only Johanna had been prepared to join them in the move to Berlin. She had stayed there for the moment, of course, but would arrive in two or three days' time with the rest of their things; he was glad, he said, that she had decided to come, for she had always been the most useful of the servants and had a certain urban chic. Perhaps a little too much. Christel and Friedrich had declared that they were too old, and from the outset there had been no point in discussing it with Kruse. 'What's the point of having a coachman here?' Innstetten said in conclusion. 'A horse and carriage, that's all *tempi passati*, that's a luxury we shall have to do without in Berlin. We wouldn't even have had anywhere to put the black hen. Or am I underestimating our apartment?'

Effi shook her head, and when there was a short pause in the conversation her mother stood up; it was almost eleven, she said, and she had some way to go, but she didn't need anyone to accompany her, the cab-rank was close by—a suggestion that Dagobert naturally rejected. Soon afterwards they left, having agreed to meet the next morning.

Effi was up fairly early and—the air having an almost summer warmth—had had the coffee-table moved close to the open balcony door, and when Innstetten appeared she went out onto the balcony with him and said, 'So what do you say to this? You wanted to be able to hear the song of the finches in Tiergarten Park and the parrots from the Zoo. I don't know if they'll both do you the favour, but it is possible. Did you hear that? It came from over there, from the little park over there. It's not the actual Tiergarten, but near enough.'

Innstetten was delighted and as grateful as if Effi had waved a magic wand herself to bring it all there. Then they sat down and Annie arrived as well. Roswitha insisted Innstetten should find the child much changed, which he then did. After that they chatted on, about the Kessiners and the people they would have to visit in Berlin, and finally about a summer-holiday trip. But they had to break off in the middle of their discussion to be at their rendezvous on time

*

They met, as agreed, at Helms's Restaurant, opposite the Red Castle,* went to various shops, had a meal at Hiller's and were home in good time. It had been a successful outing together, Innstetten really happy to be part of and enjoy city life once more. The next day, the 1st of April, he went to the Chancellor's Palace to add his name to the list of those congratulating Bismarck on his birthday (he didn't present his wishes personally, out of consideration for the Chancellor), then went to report to the Ministry. And he was received, even though it was a very busy day, both socially and as far as work was concerned—indeed, he was even honoured by a particularly amiable welcome from his minister, who said he knew what he had in him and was sure nothing would disrupt their congenial collaboration.

At home, too, everything was turning out well. Effi felt genuinely sorry to see her Mama return to Hohen-Cremmen, after her treatment, as she had suspected from the start, had taken almost six weeks. This feeling was only slightly offset by the fact that Johanna arrived in Berlin on the same day. That was at least something, and even if the pretty blonde did not have the same place in Effi's affection as the totally unselfish and good-natured Roswitha, she was respected both by Innstetten and her young mistress, because she was very adept and useful and showed a distinct and self-assured reserve towards men. A Kessin rumour had it that her origins went back to one of the leading lights of the garrison in Pasewalk, now long since retired, which, it was claimed, explained her superior attitude, her beautiful blond hair, and the particularly sculptural effect of her overall appearance. Johanna herself shared the general pleasure that was felt at her arrival, and was quite happy to assume her previous role as housemaid and Effi's lady's maid, whilst Roswitha, who in her time with them had picked up most of Christel's culinary skills, was put in charge of the kitchen. Effi herself was to take care of Annie, which made Roswitha laugh. She knew what young women were like.

Innstetten was entirely taken up with his work and life at home. He was happier than he had been in Kessin, because it didn't escape him that Effi was more cheerful and uninhibited. And that was because she felt freer. True, the past was still there, but it didn't frighten her any more, or at least much less often and only briefly, and the after-tremors that remained gave her whole being a particular appeal. There was a touch of remorse about everything she did, like a plea for forgiveness, and she would have been happy if she had been able to show all this more clearly. But that was out of the question, of course.

Social life in the big city was not yet over at the beginning of April when they made their first visits, but it was beginning to die down, so that she was never really part of it. It came to a final halt in the second half of May, and she was even happier than before that she could meet Innstetten in Tiergarten Park at midday, when he came out of the Ministry, or take an afternoon walk in the gardens of Charlottenburg Palace.* When she walked up and down the long façade, between the castle and the orange trees, she always looked at the numerous busts of the Roman emperors, seeing a strange similarity between Nero and Titus, would gather cones that had fallen off the weeping pines, and then go, arm in arm with her husband, to the lonely Belvedere over by the River Spree.

'They say that was haunted once as well,' she said.

'No, just apparitions.'

'That's the same thing.'

'Yes, sometimes,' Innstetten said. 'But actually there is a difference. Apparitions are always contrived—at least that's what's supposed to have happened here in the Belvedere, as your cousin Briest told me only yesterday—but a haunting isn't contrived, it's natural.'

'So you do believe in that?'

'Certainly I believe in it. Such things do exist. Only I don't really believe in what we had in Kessin. Has Johanna already shown you her Chinaman?'

'Which one?'

'Well, ours. Before she left our old house she peeled it off the arm of the chair upstairs and put it in her purse. I saw it when I asked her for change for a mark recently. She admitted it, though with some embarrassment.'

'Oh, you shouldn't have told me that, Geert. Now there's something like that in our house again.'

'Tell her to burn it.'

'No, I wouldn't want to do that, and it wouldn't help either. But I'll ask Roswitha . . .'

'What? Ah, I see, I can guess what you have in mind. She's to buy a picture of a saint and put it in her purse. Is that what it is?'

Effi nodded.

'Well, you do what you want. But don't tell anyone.'

Eventually Effi said she wouldn't bother and, chatting about this and that and, more and more, about their plans for the summer, they drove back to the big roundabout by the Tiergarten, then strolled home along the avenue there and the broad Friedrich-Wilhelms-Strasse.

*

They intended to take their holiday at the end of July and go to the Bavarian mountains, where the Oberammergau Passion Play* was to take place again that year. But that turned out to be impossible; Geheimrat von Wüllersdorf, whom Innstetten knew from earlier days and with whom he worked closely now, suddenly fell ill and Innstetten had to deputize for him. That situation lasted until the middle of August, and only then could they go on holiday. By that time it was too late for Oberammergau, so they decided on the Island of Rügen. 'First of all to Stralsund,* of course, with, as you will know, Schill,* who defended the town against Napoleon, and Scheele,* who, as you won't know, discovered oxygen, but it's not necessary to know that. Then from Stralsund to Bergen and Rugard Hill, from where, as Wüllersdorf told me, you have a view of the whole island; after that along the isthmus between the Greater and Lesser Jasmund Lagoons to Sassnitz. For to go to Rügen is to go to Sassnitz. Binz would be all right as well, but there—to quote Wüllersdorf again—the beach is covered in little stones and shells, and we want to go swimming.'

Effi agreed with all of Innstetten's plans, above all that the household should be split up for the four weeks, with Roswitha taking Annie to Hohen-Cremmen, while Johanna was to go and stay with her half-brother, who was somewhat younger and had a sawmill near Pasewalk.

Thus they all had somewhere to go where they would be well looked after. So at the beginning of the next week they set off, and reached Sassnitz that same evening. The sign above the place where they were staying said 'Hotel Fahrenheit'.* 'Their prices are in Celsius, I hope,' Innstetten said, reading the name, and they both set off in the best of moods for an evening stroll along the cliffs, and from a rocky ledge looked out over the calm sea quivering in the moonlight. 'Oh, Geert, that's Capri, that's Sorrento. Yes, we'll stay here. But not in the hotel, of course; the waiters are too superior, you feel embarrassed just asking for a bottle of soda water . . .'

'Yes, nothing but *attachés*. But I'm sure we'll be able to find a room somewhere.'

'I think so too. We'll start looking right away tomorrow morning.'

The weather in the morning was as beautiful as the evening before, and they breakfasted outside. Innstetten received a number of letters that had to be dealt with quickly, so Effi decided to use the hour she had to herself looking for somewhere to stay. She walked along a meadow fenced with hurdles, then past a few houses and fields of oats, finally turning into a sunken lane that led like a defile down to the sea. Where this lane came out on to the beach there was an inn standing in the shade of tall beeches; it wasn't so grand as the Hotel Fahrenheit, more just a restaurant that was still empty at this early hour. Effi sat at a table with a splendid view, and hardly had she taken a sip of the sherry she had ordered than the landlord came over, half out of curiosity, half out of politeness, to have a chat with her.

'We like it very much here,' she said, 'my husband and I; what a magnificent view out over the bay. Our only concern is finding accommodation.'

'Yes, Madam, that will be difficult.'

'But it's already late in the season.'

'Despite that. There'll not be anything to be found here in Sassnitz, I can guarantee that; but farther along the shore, where the next village begins—you can see the roofs shining from here—it might well be possible.'

'And what is the village called?'

'Crampas.'*

Effi thought she must have misheard. 'Crampas,' she repeated, having to make an effort. 'I've never heard of that as a place-name . . . Otherwise there's nothing else in the vicinity?'

'No, Madam, not round here. Farther up, to the north, there are more villages; they'll be able to give you information in the hotel right by Stubbenkammer Cliffs. People who would like to rent out rooms always leave their addresses there.'

Effi was glad she had had this conversation with the landlord by herself, and after she'd reported what he'd said to her husband, only omitting the name of the nearby village, he said, 'Well if there's nothing round here, the best thing will be to hire a carriage (you always impress a hotel when you do that) and move up there, towards Stubbenkammer Cliffs. I'm sure we'll be able to find some idyllic place with an ivy-mantled arbour, and if we don't, there's always the hotel itself. It all comes down to the same thing in the end.'

Effi agreed, and by midday they had already reached the hotel by Stubbenkammer that Innstetten had just mentioned, and ordered a light meal there. 'But in half an hour's time. We want to go for a walk first and have a look at Lake Hertha. I presume you have a guide?'

They did, and soon a middle-aged man came over to the two visitors. He looked so solemn and important that he could have been at least an acolyte in the service of the old Teutonic goddess Hertha.

The lake, surrounded by tall trees, was quite close. Bulrushes grew round the edge and there were countless yellow water-lilies floating on the surface.

'It really looks as if it could have been dedicated to Hertha,' Effi said.

'Yes, Madam . . . and the stones testify to that as well.'

'Which stones?'

'The stones of the sacrificial altar.'*

Continuing the conversation, the three of them went over to a wall of clay and pebbles that had been dug out, and against which several smoothly polished stones had been propped. All had a shallow depression and several channels running down.

'And what was the purpose of *those*?'

'So that it would run off better, Madam.'

'Let's go,' Effi said and, taking her husband's arm, went back with him to the hotel, where the light lunch they had ordered was waiting for them on a table with an extensive view of the sea. The bay below was bathed in sunlight, with occasional yachts gliding across it and the seagulls playing tig round the nearby cliffs. It was very beautiful, Effi thought; but when she then looked across the glittering expanse she saw, to the south, the brightly shining roofs strung out in the village, the name of which had given her such a shock that morning.

Innstetten, even though he didn't know, or even suspect, what was going on inside her, could see that all her pleasure, her enjoyment, had gone. 'I'm sorry you're not really enjoying being here. You can't forget Lake Hertha, and the stones even less.'

She nodded. 'It's just as you say. And I have to tell you that I've never seen anything in my life that's made me feel so sad. We won't bother looking for rooms; I can't stay here.'

'And only yesterday it was the Gulf of Naples and all sorts of beautiful places.'

'Yes, yesterday.'

'And today? Not even a trace of Sorrento any more?'

'A trace still, but just a trace; it's Sorrento as if it were about to die.'

'Right then, Effi,' Innstetten said, taking her hand, 'I don't want to torment you with Rügen, so we'll abandon the idea. That's settled. We don't have to cling on to Stubbenklammer or Sassnitz or places farther down the coast. But where shall we go, then?'

'I think we should stay here another day, then take the steamer that, if I'm not mistaken, comes from Stettin tomorrow and crosses to Copenhagen. They say there's so much to amuse one there, and I can't tell you how much I'm longing for some amusement. Here I feel as if I'm never going to be able to laugh again in my whole life, as if I never even had laughed, and you know how much I like laughing.'

Innstetten was very sympathetic towards her feelings, and that all the more as in many ways he agreed with her. Everything really was melancholy, however beautiful it was.

So they waited for the boat from Stettin, and two days later they arrived in Copenhagen early in the morning, where they took a room on Kongens Nytorv.* Two hours later they were already in the Thorvaldsen* Museum, and Effi said, 'Yes, Geert, that's lovely and I'm glad we made the journey here.' Soon afterwards they dined and made the acquaintance of a family from Jutland who were sitting opposite them at the residents' table, and whose beautiful daughter, Thora von Penz,* attracted the attention and admiration of both Innstetten and Effi. Effi couldn't stop looking at her big blue eyes and flaxen hair, and when they rose, an hour and a half later, the Penzes—who, unfortunately, had to leave Copenhagen that day—had expressed the hope that they would soon have the pleasure of the young Prussian couple's company in Aggerhuus Castle, three miles from Limfjord, an invitation that the Innstettens accepted with hardly a moment's hesitation. Thus the hours passed in the hotel. But that was not the end of their pleasure on that memorable day, of which Effi said it should be a red-letter day. To cap it all, in the evening there was a performance in the Tivoli Theatre: *Harlequin and Columbine*, an Italian comedy in mime. Effi was enraptured by all the roguish pranks, and when they got back to the hotel late in the evening she said, 'Do you know, Geert, I'm beginning to feel myself again. When I think—without mentioning the fair Thora—Thorvaldsen this morning and *Columbine* this evening . . .'

'. . . that you liked better than Thorvaldsen actually . . .'

'To be honest, yes. That kind of thing does appeal to me. Dear old Kessin was a disaster for me. Everything got on my nerves. Rügen almost did too. I think we should spend a few more days here in Copenhagen, with excursions to Frederiksborg and Elsinore,* of course, and then go across to Jutland. I'm really looking forward to seeing the fair Thora again; if I were a man, I'd fall in love with her.'

Innstetten laughed. 'You don't know what I'll do yet.'

'That wouldn't bother me. We'd fight over you, and you'd see I've still got my own powers.'

'You don't have to tell me that.'

*

Thus their holiday continued. Over in Jutland they sailed up Limfjord to Aggerhuus Castle, where they spent three days with the Penzes and then returned to Germany by many stages, with shorter or longer stops in Viborg, Flensburg, Kiel, and Hamburg (that they liked very much), but not to Berlin and Keithstrasse; rather, they went first to Hohen-Cremmen, where they wanted to enjoy a well-earned rest. For Innstetten that meant only a few days, since his leave was over, but Effi stayed one more week, saying that she only wanted to get back home on the 3rd of October, their wedding anniversary.

Annie had thrived in the country air, and Roswitha's plan for her to walk to her mother in little boots was a complete success. Briest played the affectionate grandfather and warned against showing the child too much love, but even more against being too strict; he was the same as ever in all things. But in fact all his affection was reserved for Effi, and she occupied his thoughts all the time, especially when he was alone with his wife.

'What do you think about Effi?'

'A dear, sweet child, as always. We can't thank God enough that we have such a delightful daughter. And how grateful she is for everything and always so happy to be home with us again.'

'Yes,' Briest said, 'that's a virtue of which she has rather more than I like. It actually seems as if this were still her home. But she has her husband and her child, and the husband's a jewel and the child's an angel, and yet she behaves as if Hohen-Cremmen were still the most important thing for her and husband and child don't get a look in. She's a splendid daughter, but for me a bit too much so. It frightens me a little. And it's also unfair to Innstetten. How are things between them?'

'What do you mean, Briest?'

'Well, I mean what I mean, and you know what as well. Is she happy? Or is there something getting in the way of that? From the very beginning it seemed to me she felt more respect than love for him. And in my view, that's a bad thing. Love doesn't always last for ever, respect certainly doesn't. Actually, women get irritated when they have to respect someone; first they're irritated, then they're bored, and finally they just laugh.'

'Are you talking from personal experience?'

'I'm not saying that. I was never highly respected enough for that. But let's stop this before we start getting on each other's nerves, Luise. How are things between them?'

'You're always going on about these things, Briest. We must have talked and exchanged our opinions about them more than a dozen times, and you keep coming back with your I-want-to-know-everything attitude, and put your question in such a naive form, as if there were no depths I couldn't plumb. What do you think a young woman, and more specifically your own daughter, is like? Do you think everything's out in the open? Or that I'm an oracle (I can't remember the name just at the moment), or that I'm in full possession of the truth once Effi has poured out her heart to me? Whatever people mean by that. What is "pouring out"? The main thing's always held back. There's no way she's going to tell me her secrets. And anyway, I don't know where she gets this from but she's . . . yes, she's a sly little woman, and her slyness is all the more dangerous because she's so very charming.'

'So you admit that . . . charming. And good as well?'

'Good as well. That is, she has a good heart. In other respects I'm not so sure; I think she has a tendency to take things as they come and hope the consequences won't be too severe.'

'You think so?'

'Yes, I think so. Moreover, I think she's improved in many respects. Her character is her character, but since they moved their circumstances have become much more favourable, and they're settling down more and more into life with each other. She said something like that to me and, what is more important, I found it confirmed, saw it with my own eyes.'

'What did she say, then?'

'She said, "Things are getting better now, Mama. Innstetten was always an excellent man, there aren't many like him, but I could never really get close to him, there was something alien about him. And he was alien in his tenderness. Yes, then most of all; there were times when I was afraid of it."'

'Too true, too true.'

'What do you mean by that, Briest? That I was afraid, or are you saying you were afraid? Both seem ridiculous to me . . .'

'You were going to tell me about Effi.'

'Well, then she told me this feeling of something alien had gone, and that made her very happy. Kessin hadn't been the right place for her, she said, the haunted house and the people there, some too pious, the others too dull. But since they've moved to Berlin she felt she belonged there. He was the best of men, she said, a little too old for her and a little too good for her, but now she was out of the woods. That's the expression she used, and it struck me.'

'Why? It's not the most elegant of expressions, but . . .'

'There was something behind it. And she wanted to hint at that.'

'You think so?'

'Yes, Briest. You always think butter wouldn't melt in her mouth. But you're wrong there. She's happy to drift along with the current, and if it's going in the right direction she's good. But swimming against the tide isn't her strong point.'

Roswitha came in with Annie and the conversation broke off.

*

This conversation between Briest and his wife took place on the day when Innstetten left Hohen-Cremmen to travel back to Berlin, leaving Effi there for at least a further week. He knew there was nothing she liked better than to be able to spend the time daydreaming, in a relaxed mood, with never a care in the world, never a harsh word, just the repeated assurance of how charming she was. Yes, that was what did her good, and this time again she gratefully enjoyed it to the full, despite the lack of any diversions: visitors were rare because, since her marriage, the house lacked real attraction, at least for the younger element, and even the parsonage and the schoolhouse were not what they had been in the past. The schoolhouse was half empty, in the spring the twins had married two teachers from the Genthin* area, a big double wedding with a report in the local paper, and Hulda had gone to Friesack* to care for a wealthy old aunt who, as was common in such cases, turned out to be living much longer than the Niemeyers had assumed. Despite that, Hulda kept writing contented letters, not because she really was contented (on the contrary), but to avoid giving even a hint that life could be anything but good for such an excellent person as herself. Niemeyer, a doting father, showed the letters with pride and pleasure, whilst Jahnke, whose life also centred entirely round his daughters, had worked out that the two young women would give birth on the same day, namely Christmas Eve. Effi laughed heartily and told the grandfather-to-be she would like to be asked to be godmother, but then dropped the subject of family news and told him about 'Kjöbenhavn' and Elsinore, about Limfjord and Aggerhuus Castle, and above all about Thora von Penz, whom she could only describe as 'typically Scandinavian', blue eyes, flaxen hair, and always wearing a red velvet dress with a tight waist. At this Jahnke became misty-eyed, and said again and again, 'Yes, that's the way they are, pure Teutons, much more German than the Germans.'

Effi wanted to be back in Berlin by the 3rd of October, her wedding anniversary. Now it was the evening before and, under the pretext that she wanted to pack and get everything ready for the return journey, she had withdrawn to her room relatively early. In fact, what she really wanted was to be alone; however much she liked chatting, there were times when she longed for peace and quiet.

The rooms she had on the upper floor gave on to the garden; Roswitha and Annie were sleeping in the smaller one, the door slightly ajar; in the larger one she walked up and down; the lower windows were open and the little white net curtains billowed in the breeze, slowly coming to rest over the arm of a chair until another breeze came and released them. It was still so light that the titles under the pictures hanging over the sofa in their narrow gilt frames could be clearly read: 'The Storming of Düppel,* Redoubt V', and beside it, 'King William I and Count Bismarck on the Heights of Lipa'.* Effi shook her head and smiled. 'The next time I come I'll ask for some different pictures; I can't stand all this martial stuff.' Then she closed one window and sat down at the other, leaving it open. How comforting it all was. The moon was beside the church tower, casting its light over the lawn with the sundial and the beds of heliotrope. Everything was a shimmer of silver, and there were strips of light alongside the strips of shade, like linen on the bleach-field. Farther away were the tall, giant rhubarb plants, their leaves an autumnal yellow, and she was reminded of the day, only a little over two years ago, when she had played there with Hulda and the two Jahnke girls. And then, when their visitor arrived, she'd gone up the stone steps beside the bench, and one hour later she'd been engaged.

She stood up and went over to the door and listened: Roswitha was already asleep, and Annie as well.

All at once, thinking of the child, all sorts of images from her days in Kessin came back to mind: their house with its gable and the veranda with the view of the Plantation, and she was sitting in the rocking-chair; and then Crampas came up to wish her a good morning, and then Roswitha with the child, and she took her and lifted her up and kissed her.

'That was the first day; that was when it began.' Musing on this, she left the room where Roswitha and Annie were sleeping and sat down at the open window again, and looked out into the quiet night.

'I can't rid myself of it,' she said. 'And what the worst thing about it is, what makes me doubt myself . . .'

At that moment the clock in the tower outside started to strike, and Effi counted the hours.

'Ten . . . And at this time tomorrow I'll be in Berlin. And we'll talk about it being our wedding anniversary and he'll say nice, friendly, perhaps even affectionate things to me. And I'll be sitting there listening to them and bearing this guilt inside me.'

She rested her head on her hand and stared into space, silent.

'And bearing this guilt inside me,' she repeated. 'Yes, I am. But does it weigh down on me? No. And that's why I'm horrified at myself. What does weigh down on me is something else—fear, mortal fear, and the constant dread that it will eventually come out after all. And then, apart from the fear . . . shame. I'm ashamed of myself. But just as I don't feel true remorse, I don't feel true shame. I just feel ashamed because of the eternal lies and deception; I always took pride in the fact that I couldn't lie and didn't need to lie; lying's so contemptible, and now I've had to lie all the time, to him and to the whole wide world, little lies and big lies, and Rummschüttel noticed and shrugged his shoulders; who knows what he thinks of me, certainly not very highly. Yes, I'm tormented by fear and shame at my deception. But shame at my guilt, that's something I *don't* feel, or not real shame, or not enough, and the fact that I don't feel it is killing me. If all women are like that, it's terrible, and if, as I hope, they're not like that, then I'm in a bad way, then there's something wrong inside me, then I lack a feeling for what is right. And old Niemeyer told me that, when I was still half a child: a feeling for what is right, that was the important thing, and if you had that then the worst would never happen to you, and if you didn't have it then you were in constant danger and what people call the devil would have you in his power. Merciful God, is that what things are like with me?'

And she put her head in her arms and wept bitter tears.

When she sat up again she had calmed down, and looked out at the garden again. Everything was so quiet, and a soft, gentle sound, like rain, came from the plane trees.

She stayed like that for a while. From the village street came the sound of someone bawling: Kulicke, the night-watchman, was calling the hour, and when he finally fell silent she heard the distant rattle of a train, two miles away as it passed Hohen-Cremmen. Then the sound died away until silence reigned once more, and there was just the moonlight on the lawn and just the rustle of the plane trees, like rain falling.

But it was only the night air stirring.

CHAPTER 25

The next evening Effi was back in Berlin and Innstetten was there at the station; Rollo was with him and trotted along beside the carriage as they drove, chatting, through Tiergarten Park.

'I thought you weren't going to keep your word.'

'But of course I'll keep my word, Geert, that comes before everything else.'

'Don't say that. To always keep one's word is asking a lot of oneself. And sometimes one can't. Just think back. I was expecting you back in Kessin while you were here looking for an apartment, and who didn't come? My Effi.'

'Oh yes, but that was something different.'

She couldn't bring herself to say 'I was ill,' and Innstetten passed over it. He had a lot of other things on his mind that concerned his work and his social position. 'Actually, Effi, our life in Berlin is only just beginning. When we moved here in April the season was coming to an end, there was just enough time for us to make our visits, and Wüllersdorf, the only one we were closer too—well, unfortunately he's a bachelor. From the beginning of June everything goes to sleep and the lowered blinds announce from a hundred yards off: "All gone away"—whether it's true or not makes no difference . . . What was there left for us to do? The occasional chat with your cousin Briest, a meal at Hiller's now and then, that's not real city life. But things are going to be different now. I've noted down the names of all the senior officials who are still socially active enough to keep open house. And we'll do that *as well*, keep open house, and when winter comes then the whole Ministry will be saying, 'Yes, the most charming woman we have now is Frau von Innstetten.'

'Oh, Geert, is that really you? You're talking like an admirer.'

'It's our anniversary, so you'll have to make allowances for me.'

*

Innstetten was seriously determined to exchange the quiet life he had led while he had been a Landrat for a socially much livelier one, for his own and, even more, Effi's sake. But it began slowly, with only an occasional outing, and the best part of their new life was exactly the same as in the preceding six months, life in their own home. Wüllersdorf often came, Cousin Dagobert as well, and once they were there they would send up to the Gizickis, a young couple that had the apartment above. Gizicki himself was a Landesgerichtsrat,* his bright and lively wife had been a Fräulein von Schmettau. Occasionally they made music, for a short while had even tried whist, but gave it up because they found chatting a pleasanter way to spend an evening. Until recently the Gizickis had lived in a little town in Upper Silesia,

and Wüllersdorf had even—though quite a few years ago, of course—
been in a variety of one-eyed places in Posen Province* and liked to
declaim the well-known mocking rhyme:

> Schrimm
> Is grim,
> You're lost in
> Kosten,
> But you really don't want to go
> To Ostrowo.

No one was more amused at this than Effi, and it usually led to an
abundance of stories about provincial life. Kessin, with Gieshübler
and Marietta Trippelli, Ring the forester, and Sidonie Grasenabb,
took its turn, and Innstetten, if he was in a good mood, was as frivolous as one could wish. 'Yes,' he would say then, 'dear old Kessin.
I have to say that it had a wealth of characters, first and foremost
Crampas, Major Crampas, quite the beau and a bit of a Barbarossa,*
to whom my wife—I don't know, should I say inexplicably or understandably—took a great liking . . .' 'Let's say understandably,'
Wüllersdorf interjected, 'for I assume he was chairman of the Club
and took part in plays, as a lover or a *bon vivant*. And perhaps there
was more, perhaps he was a tenor as well.' Innstetten confirmed his
guesses and Effi tried to play along with a laugh, but it took a great
effort, and when their guests left and Innstetten withdrew to his room
to work through a pile of papers, she was tormented by the past once
more and felt as if there were a shadow following her.

    She continued to suffer these alarms, but they became rarer and
milder, which was not surprising, given the way her life developed.
The love shown her, not only by Innstetten but by people who were
less close to her, and not least the almost affectionate friendship of the
Minister's wife, a young woman herself, at least reduced the worries
and fears of the past, and when, after a second year and on the occasion of the establishment of a new charitable institution, the Empress
chose the 'Frau Geheimrätin' as one of the ladies of honour on the
committee, and at the court ball the old Emperor addressed a few
gracious words to the beautiful young woman, of whom, he said, he'd
already heard, they gradually disappeared. It had happened, but far,
far away, as if on another planet, and everything dissipated like mist
and became a dream.

The Hohen-Cremmen family came to visit them from time to time, and were delighted to see their children so happy. Annie continued to develop—'as beautiful as her grandmother,' old Briest said—and if there was one cloud on the horizon, it was that it seemed almost certain that Little Annie would remain an only child; the Innstetten line (for there were not even others of that name) was therefore presumably dying out. Briest, who, being interested in the Briests alone, tended to take a rather casual attitude as far as the survival of other families was concerned, joked about it and said, 'Yes, Innstetten, if it goes on like this, when the time comes Annie will have to marry a banker (a Christian one,* I hope, if there are still some of those left) and then the Emperor, out of regard for the old baronial line of Innstettens, will enable Annie's high-finance children to live on in the *Almanach de Gotha** or, what is less important, Prussian history, under the name of "von der Innstetten".'—Comments to which Innstetten responded with a slightly embarrassed smile, Frau von Briest with a shrug of the shoulders, and Effi with amusement. She was proud of her noble birth, but only for herself, and she would definitely have had nothing against an elegant banker, who was a man of the world and, above all, very, very rich, as a son-in-law.

Yes, Effi, the way attractive young women are, didn't take the question of an heir too seriously; but after a long, long time—they were already in the seventh year in their new situation—Rummschüttel, who had a certain reputation in the area of gynaecology, was finally called in for advice by Frau von Briest. He prescribed a course at the mineral spa of Bad Schwalbach.* However, since Effi had suffered from catarrh since the previous winter and had even had her lungs checked, he said finally, 'So, first Schwalbach, my dear Frau Baronin, let's say three weeks, and then the same time in Ems.* The Geheimrat can be there with you in Ems. It does mean three weeks' separation, however, but that's the best I can do for you, Innstetten.'

That was agreed, and it was further decided that Effi should travel together with a Geheimrätin von Zwicker, 'as a chaperone for the latter', as Briest said, not without some justification, since Frau Zwicker, despite being well into her forties, had much greater need of a chaperone than Effi. Innstetten, who was once more very occupied with deputizing, complained that, never mind Schwalbach, he would probably have to forgo their time together in Ems as well. The date of departure was set for the 24th of June, and Roswitha helped her mistress pack and make a list of her underlinen. Effi loved her as much as ever; Roswitha was the only person with whom she could talk freely and uninhibitedly about the past, about Kessin and Crampas, the Chinaman and Captain Thomsen's niece.

'Tell me, Roswitha, you're a Catholic. Do you go to confession?'

'No.'

'Why not?'

'I used to go, but I never confessed to my real sins.'

'That's very wrong. In that way it can't help.'

'Oh, Madam, everyone in our village did that. And some of them even just giggled.'

'Have you never felt, if you have something weighing down on you, that it would be a relief if it could come out?'

'No, Madam. I was afraid when my father came at me with the red-hot iron bar; I was terribly afraid, but that was all.'

'Not of God?'

'Not really, Madam. If you're so afraid of your father, as I was, then you're not really that much afraid of God. I'd always thought God was good and would help a poor thing like me.'

Effi smiled and broke off the conversation. She thought it natural that poor Roswitha should say that, but still she said, 'You know, Roswitha, we'll have to have a serious talk about this when I get back. After all, it was a great sin.'

'That about the child, that it starved to death? Yes, Madam, it was. But that wasn't me, that was the others . . . And then, it was such a long time ago.'

CHAPTER 26

It was the fifth week of Effi's absence from home, and she was writing happy, almost over-exuberant letters, especially since she had arrived in Ems where, as she said, they could enjoy company again, that is, the company of men—the occasional one who had appeared in Schwalbach had been the exception to the rule. Geheimrätin Zwicker, her travelling companion, she went on, had questioned the value of such an additional ingredient for their cure and expressed strong disapproval of it, all of that, of course, with a look on her face that rather said the opposite. Frau Zwicker was delightful, Effi wrote, somewhat free and easy, probably even a woman with a past, but highly amusing, and there was a lot one could learn from her; never had she felt so much of a child, despite being twenty-five, as she had since making the acquaintance of this lady. And she was so very well read, in foreign literature as well, and recently, for example, when she, Effi, had talked about *Nana** and asked her whether it really was so terrible, Frau Zwicker had said, 'My dear Frau Baronin, what is terrible? There are much worse things.'

'She seemed', Effi said in conclusion, 'to want to make me acquainted with these "different things", but I declined the offer because I know that you blame the immorality of our times on these and similar things, and rightly so, I suspect. But I haven't yet felt any relief. One of the reasons is that Ems lies in an enclosed valley and we suffer very much from the heat.'

Innstetten had read that last letter with mixed feelings; he had been somewhat amused, but was also a little unhappy with it. Frau Zwicker wasn't the woman for Effi, who did have a tendency to let herself be led astray. But he abandoned the idea of writing to her along those lines, partly because he didn't want to upset her, but even more because, as he told himself, it wouldn't make any difference. At the same time, he was longing for his wife's return and complaining that in his case, now that all his colleagues were away, or intended to get away, 'the unvarying hour of duty'* had been varied, indeed doubled.

Yes, Innstetten was longing for some interruption to his life of work and loneliness, and there were similar feelings out in the kitchen, where Annie liked to spend most of her time once school was over, as was quite natural, since Roswitha and Johanna not only loved Fräulein Annie equally but continued to get on well with each other. This friendship between the two maids was a favourite topic of conversation for the various friends of the family, and Gizicki said to Wüllersdorf, 'I see in that a new confirmation of the old adage, "Let me have men about me that are fat."* Caesar was a good judge of character, and knew that qualities such as contentment and affability only come with *embonpoint*.' And that word could genuinely be used for the two maids, though with the difference that in the case of Roswitha it was something of a euphemism, whilst for Johanna it was, to use another unavoidable foreign expression, the *mot juste*. The latter couldn't actually be called corpulent, she was just buxom and shapely, and her blue eyes looked out on the world over her satisfyingly ample bosom with a particular expression of self-assurance that suited her well. With an innate sense of propriety and decorum, she was filled with pride at the idea of being the servant of a good family, and her feeling of superiority over Roswitha, who had retained something of her peasant origins, was such that her only response to the occasional preference shown to the latter was a quiet smile. This preferential treatment—well, if it had to be, it was just one of the Mistress's charming little foibles that one couldn't begrudge dear old Roswitha, with her eternal story of her father with the red-hot iron rod. 'If you have more self-respect that kind of thing can't happen.' That was something she thought but never said. It was a life of friendly collaboration. However, what particularly contributed to peace and harmony was the fact that there was an unspoken agreement to take separate roles in the treatment—one could almost say upbringing—of Annie. Roswitha had charge of the poetic department, telling fairy-tales and stories; Johanna, on the other hand, took care of decorum, a division of labour that was so deeply rooted on both sides that disputes over areas of responsibility hardly ever arose. This was helped by the fact that Annie had a decided tendency to accentuate the upper-class Fräulein, a role in which she could have had no better teacher than Johanna.

To recapitulate: both maids had equal status in Annie's eyes. However, during those days when they were preparing for Effi's return Roswitha was once again one step ahead of her rival, because the whole business of arranging the welcome home had fallen to her, as the competent authority. The welcome fell into two main parts: a garland with a wreath, and then, to finish off with, the recitation of a poem. Eventually the garland and wreath had—after they'd wavered between 'W.' and 'E. v. I.' for a while—caused no particular problem ('W.' woven in forget-me-nots was the preferred version), but the difficulties caused by the question of the poem might have remained unresolved had not Roswitha had the courage to corner the judge on the stairs as he was returning from a session in court and boldly request a 'poem' from him. Gizicki, a very amiable gentleman, had immediately agreed, and late in the same afternoon his cook had delivered the desired lines, which were as follows:

Mama, we've been waiting ages for you,
For weeks and days and hours,

Now we greet you with welcome true
And garlands woven with flowers.
Papa is laughing with joy, and says,
'Gone are those wifeless, motherless days
That left me so sad and alone.'
And Roswitha's laughing, Johanna as well,
And Annie jumps up with her poem to tell,
And cries out 'Welcome home, welcome home.'

Of course the little poem was learnt off by heart that very evening, but at the same time subjected to a critical review of its beauty—or non-beauty. At first, Johanna said, the emphasis on wife and mother had seemed correct, but there was something about it that might cause offence and, speaking personally, she would feel offended by 'wife and mother'. Annie, slightly concerned by this, promised to show the poem to her teacher in the morning, and came back with the comment that the teacher was perfectly happy with 'wife and mother', but all the more against 'Roswitha and Johanna'—to which Roswitha replied that the teacher was a stupid ninny and that was what happened when you spent too much time studying.

It was on a Wednesday that the maids and Annie had had this conversation and settled the argument about the line that had been criticized. The next morning—a letter from Effi setting the day when she would arrive home, probably not until the end of the next week, was expected—Innstetten went to the Ministry. It was nearly midday, school was out, and when Annie, her satchel on her back, came towards Keithstrasse from the canal she met Roswitha outside their house.

'Now let's see who can get up the steps first,' Annie said. Roswitha didn't want to race but Annie shot off, stumbled as she reached the top in such a way that she hit her head on the foot-scraper, and started to bleed badly. Roswitha, panting along behind, pulled the bell, and after Johanna had carried the somewhat frightened child in, they discussed what to do. 'We'll send for the doctor . . . We'll send for the Master . . . Lene from the porter's lodge must be home from school now.' Those ideas were abandoned because they'd take too long, something had to be done at once, so they laid the girl on the sofa and started to cool the wound with cold water. That went well, and they began to calm down. 'And now we must bandage her up,' Roswitha finally said. 'That long bandage the Mistress cut when she

sprained her ankle on the ice last winter must still be around somewhere . . .'—'Of course, of course,' Johanna said, 'but where? Oh
yes, now I remember. It's in the sewing-table. It'll be locked, but the
lock's child's play. Just get the chisel, Roswitha, we'll break the lid
open.' And they did force the lid up and started to rummage round
in the compartments, above and below, but the rolled-up bandage
wasn't to be found. 'But I know I saw it,' Roswitha said, and as, half
in irritation, they continued their search, everything they got their
hands on was chucked on to the broad windowsill: sewing things,
pincushions, reels of cotton and silk, little dried-up posies of violets,
cards, notes, and finally, a little packet of letters that had been right
at the bottom, under the third tray, tied up with a red thread. But
the bandage still wasn't there.

At that moment Innstetten came in.

'Oh, Lord!' said Roswitha, startled, and went over to the child.
'It's nothing, sir. Annie fell on the foot-scraper . . . God, what will
the Mistress say? Yet it's a good thing she wasn't there when it
happened.'

In the meantime Innstetten had taken the temporary compress off
and seen that it was a deep cut but otherwise not dangerous. 'It's not
serious,' he said. 'Still, Roswitha, we'll have to get Rummschüttel to
come. Lene can go, she'll have time now. But what on earth is all this
with the sewing-table?'

And Roswitha told him how they'd been looking for the rolled-up
bandage; but now she was going to give up and cut a new strip of
linen.

Innstetten was happy with that, and sat down by the child once the
two maids had left the room. 'You're so wild, Annie, you get that from
your Mama. Always dashing round like a whirlwind. But nothing ever
comes of it, or at best something like this.' And he pointed at the cut
and gave her a kiss. 'But you didn't cry, that's a brave girl, and for that
reason I'll forgive you for being wild. I imagine the doctor'll be here
in an hour; you do everything he tells you, and once he's bandaged it
up, don't you press and pull and tear at it, then it'll heal quickly and
everything will be all right again, or almost, by the time Mama comes
home. But it's a good thing that won't be until next week—the end of
next week, she wrote. I've just had a letter from her; she sends you her
best wishes and is looking forward to seeing you again.'

'Actually, you could read the letter out to me, Papa.'

'Of course I will.'

But before he could, Johanna came to say that lunch was served. Annie got up with him, despite her injury, and father and daughter sat down to lunch together.

CHAPTER 27

Innstetten and Annie sat facing each other without speaking for a while; finally, when he began to find the silence embarrassing, he asked a few questions about the headmistress and which teacher she liked best. Annie answered them, but listlessly, because she sensed his mind was elsewhere. Things only got better when, after the second course, Johanna whispered to her that there was more to come. And indeed, Roswitha, who thought she owed her little darling something on this day of misfortune, had gone to the trouble of making an omelette with apple slices.

Seeing this loosened Annie's tongue, and Innstetten's mood had also improved when the bell rang and Dr Rummschüttel came in. Quite by chance. He had just popped in, with no idea that he'd been asked to call. He was happy with the compresses that had been applied. 'Send out for some lead lotion and keep Annie at home tomorrow. Rest above all.' Then he asked about the Frau Baronin and what news they'd had from Ems; he'd come round and check the next day, he said.

*

When they'd finished lunch and gone into the adjoining room—the one where they'd searched for the bandage, so furiously and yet unsuccessfully—Annie was bedded down on the sofa again. Johanna came and sat with the child while Innstetten started to put away all the things that were still lying in a jumble on the windowsill. Now and then he didn't know where they went, and had to ask.

'Where were the letters, Johanna?'

'Right at the bottom,' she said, 'in that compartment there.'

And while he was asking he looked more closely at the little bundle tied together with a red thread, that seemed to consist more of a number of notes rather than letters. He ran his thumb across the side of the bundle, as if it were a pack of cards, and a few lines, actually only individual words, flitted past his eye. There was no question of clearly recognizing them, but he had the feeling he'd seen the handwriting somewhere before. Should he check?

'You could bring us the coffee, Johanna. Annie will have half-a-cup too. The doctor didn't forbid it, and anything that's not forbidden is allowed.'

As he said that, he undid the red thread and, while Johanna left the room, quickly leafed through the whole bundle. Only two or three letters had an address: 'Frau Landrat von Innstetten.' Now he recognized the handwriting; it was the Major's. Innstetten was unaware of any correspondence between Crampas and Effi, and his head started to spin. He put the bundle in his pocket and went back to his room. A few minutes later Johanna knocked on the door to tell him the coffee was ready. Innstetten replied, but otherwise everything remained quiet. A quarter of an hour later he could be heard walking up and down on the carpet. 'What can be the matter with your Papa?' Johanna said to Annie. 'The doctor told him it was nothing.'

*

The sound of Innstetten walking up and down went on and on. Finally he reappeared in the adjoining room and said, 'Keep an eye on the child, Johanna, make sure she stays resting on the sofa. I'm going out for a walk for an hour, perhaps two.'

Then he gave the child an intent look and left.

'Did you see what Papa looked like, Johanna?'

'Yes, Annie. There must be something that's annoyed him very much. He was quite pale. I've never seen him like that before.'

Hours passed. The sun had already set, leaving just a red glow over the roofs, when Innstetten came back. He took Annie by the hand, asked how she was, and then told Johanna to take the lamp to his room, which she did. In the lampshade were half-transparent ovals with photographs, all portraits of his wife; they had been taken in Kessin, when they had photographed all the various people who had acted in Wiechert's *One False Step*. Innstetten slowly turned the shade round and scrutinized every picture. Then he stopped that, opened the balcony door because it felt stuffy, and picked up the bundle of letters again. It seemed that when he had first gone through them he had taken out a few and put them on top. He now read these again in a quiet voice.

'Be at the dunes again this afternoon, behind the mill. We can talk undisturbed at old Adermann's place, the house is pretty isolated. You mustn't be so afraid of everything. We have a right *as well*, and if you keep telling yourself that, all your fear will fall away. Life wouldn't be worth living if all the rules we happen to have were truly valid. All that is best is beyond them. Learn how to enjoy it.'

' . . . Away, you write, let us escape. Impossible. I can't abandon my wife, abandon her to poverty into the bargain. It's just not possible and we have to accept that with a light heart, otherwise we're lost. A light heart is the best thing we can have. Everything is destined. It had to be. Would you want it any different, wish we had never met?'

Then came the third letter.

' . . . Be at the usual place again today. What are my days here going to be like without you! In this dreary dump. I'm in despair, but in just one thing you are right: it's our salvation, and when all is said and done we must bless the fate that has ordained our separation.'

Innstetten had put the letters aside again when the doorbell rang. Johanna immediately came to announce, 'Geheimrat Wüllersdorf.'

Wüllersdorf came in, and could tell at a glance that something must have happened.

'You must forgive me, Wüllersdorf, for having asked you to come round straight away. I don't like to disturb anyone's quiet evening, least of all that of an overworked Ministerialrat. But there was no other way. Please make yourself comfortable. Here, have a cigar.'

Wüllersdorf sat down. Innstetten was walking up and down again and, with the restlessness that was eating away at him, would have liked to remain in motion. But he saw that was not possible, so he took a cigar himself, sat down opposite Wüllersdorf, and tried to remain calm.

'There are', he said, 'two things I want to ask of you: firstly, to deliver a challenge, and secondly, to act as my second; the first is not a pleasant task, the second even less so. Your answer is?'

'I am, as you know, Innstetten, at your disposal. But before you tell me what it's about, permit me to ask a rather naive question: does it have to be? We're both of us too well on in years, you to pick up a pistol, me to support you. Now don't misunderstand me, that isn't a no. How could I refuse you? But now tell me what it is.'

'It's a lover of my wife who at the same time was my friend. Or almost.'

Wüllersdorf looked at Innstetten. 'That's not possible, Innstetten.'

'It's more than possible. Just read these.'

Wüllersdorf glanced through them. 'These are to your wife?'

'Yes. I found them in her sewing-table today.'

'And who wrote them?'

'Major Crampas.'

'Things, then, that happened while you were in Kessin?'

Innstetten nodded.

'So it was six years ago, or six-and-a-half?'

'Yes.'

Wüllersdorf remained silent.

After a while Innstetten said, 'It almost looks as if those six or seven years make some kind of impression on you, Wüllersdorf. Of course, there is a theory that a kind of statute of limitation operates in these cases, but I don't know if it comes into effect here.'

'I don't know either,' Wüllersdorf said. 'But, frankly, I have to say that seems to be the all-important question.'

Innstetten stared at him. 'You're saying that in all seriousness?'

'In all seriousness. It's not something about which one should indulge in witticisms or dialectical hair-splitting.'

'I'd be interested to know what you mean by that. Give me your honest opinion: what do you think of the matter?'

'You're in a terrible situation, Innstetten, and it's the end of your happiness. But if you shoot your wife's lover your happiness will be doubly at an end, so to speak; you will be adding the hurt done to others to the hurt done to you. Everything revolves round the one question: do you have to do it? Do you feel so hurt, insulted, outraged that one of you has to be done away with, him or you? Is that the way it is?'

'I don't know.'

'You must know.'

Innstetten jumped up, went over to the window, and tapped the glass, full of nervous agitation. Then he quickly turned round again, strode over to Wüllersdorf, and said, 'No, that's not the way it is.'

'What is, then?'

'The way it is, I'm desperately unhappy; I've been hurt, I've been shamefully deceived, but despite that I don't feel any hatred at all, and certainly not a thirst for revenge. And when I ask myself why

I don't, all that occurs to me is the years that have passed. People are always talking about guilt beyond redemption; in the sight of God I'm sure that's wrong, and for human beings as well. I'd never have thought that time, purely as time, could have that effect. And another thing is that I love my wife, yes, strange to say, I still love her, and however dreadful I think all that has happened is, I'm still so much under the spell of her appeal, of a vivacious charm that is all her own, that right down to the bottom of my heart I feel, despite myself, inclined to forgive her.'

Wüllersdorf nodded. 'I'm with you there entirely, Innstetten, I might well feel the same. But if that's how you view the matter and you tell me, "I love this woman so much, I can forgive her every-thing," and if we take that other aspect into account, the fact that it's all so far in the past, like something that happened on another planet, well, if that's the way it is, why then all this fuss, Innstetten?'

'Because, in spite of all that, it has to be. I've thought it through this way and that. We're not just separate individuals, we're part of a whole, and we must always consider the whole, we're entirely dependent on it. If it were possible to live in isolation, I could let it go. Then I would be the one bearing the burden I had taken up myself, true happiness would be a thing of the past, but many, many people have to live without this "true happiness", and I would have to do that too—and I'd be able to. You don't need to be happy, and in no sense do you have a right to be, and it's not necessary to eliminate the person who has taken your happiness away from you. If you're willing to turn your back on the world for the rest of your life, you can let him go. But there's a something that has developed in our social existence, it's there and we have become accustomed to judging everything according to its laws. And disregarding it's not possible; society would despise us, and eventually we would despise ourselves as well and be unable to bear it and blow our brains out. Forgive me for holding forth like this, when what I'm saying is something every-one's said to himself a hundred times. But who can say anything new, anyway? So, to recapitulate, it's not about hatred or anything like that, I don't want to have blood on my hands because of the happiness that's been taken away from me; but that—tyrannical, if you like—social something is not concerned with charm, nor with love, nor with the lapse of time. I have no choice. I have to.'

'I don't know, Innstetten . . .'

Innstetten smiled. 'You are to decide that yourself, Wüllersdorf. It's now ten o'clock. Six hours ago, this I will concede in advance, the decision was still in my hands, I could take one course or the other, there was still a way out. Not any more, now I'm stuck in a blind alley. If you want, you can say it's my own fault; I should have kept myself under control better, kept everything hidden inside me, wrestled with the problem in my own heart. But it came too suddenly, it was too strong, so that I can hardly blame myself for not exercising proper control over my nerves. I went to your house and left a note, and with that the decision was out of my hands. From that moment on there was a third party who was half-aware of my misfortune and, what carries more weight, the stain on my honour; and after our first exchanges here he is fully aware of them. And because that third party exists, there is no way back for me.'

'I don't know,' Wüllersdorf repeated. 'I don't like having recourse to a hackneyed expression but there's no better way to put it: Innstetten, your secret's safe with me.'

'Yes, Wüllersdorf, that's what people always say. But there's no such thing as absolute discretion. Even if you prove me wrong and are discretion itself, as far as others are concerned, you know about it and nothing can save me from you, who have just agreed with me, who have even said you're entirely with me. From this moment on I will be, and remain, an object of your sympathy (which in itself isn't very pleasant), and, whether you want to or not, you will be checking every word I exchange with my wife, and when my wife talks of fidelity or, as women do, sits in judgement on another woman, then I won't know where to look; and should it happen that in some discussion concerning an ordinary insult I speak in favour of letting it go, "because of the lack of any intention to hurt", or something like that, a smile will cross your face, or at least the corners of your mouth will twitch, and in your mind you'll be thinking, "Dear old Innstetten, he really has a passion for measuring the precise size of all insults but he never gets it right. Nothing has ever stuck in his throat" . . . Am I right or not, Wüllersdorf?'

Wüllersdorf had stood up. 'I think it's terrible that you are right, but you *are* right. I won't torment you any longer with my "does it have to be?" The world is the way it is, and things don't proceed the way we want them to but the way *others* want them to. People who pompously talk of a duel as referring the matter to the judgement of

God are talking nonsense, in fact it's the opposite, our cult of honour is worship of a false idol, but we have to submit as long as the idol rules.'

Innstetten nodded.

They stayed together for another quarter of an hour, and it was decided that Wüllersdorf should set off that very evening. There was a night train that left at twelve.

Then they parted with a brief, 'See you in Kessin.'

CHAPTER 28

As agreed, Innstetten set off the next evening. He took the same train as Wüllersdorf had the previous day, and soon after five in the morning he was at the station where the road to Kessin went off to the left. As always, as long as the season went on, the steamer set off once the train had arrived, and Innstetten could hear the first hoot of its siren as he reached the bottom of the steps down the railway embankment. It was only three minutes to the landing-stage. He went over to it and greeted the captain, who looked somewhat embarrassed, so must have heard about the business the previous day, and took a seat close to the helm. Immediately the boat cast off from the landing-stage; the weather was magnificent, bright morning sunshine, only a few passengers on board. Innstetten thought back to the day when, coming back from their honeymoon, he had driven along the Kessine here in an open carriage with Effi—it had been a grey November day then, but his heart had been full of joy. Now it was the other way round: the light was outside and the November day was inside him. He had come this way many, many times, and the peace over the meadows, the cattle in the enclosures that looked up as he drove past, the people at work, the fruitful fields had all been balm to his senses, and now, in contrast to those days, he was glad when some clouds drifted over and quietly started to cover the bright blue sky. Thus they sailed down the river, and once they had crossed the splendid expanse of the Breitling the church tower of Kessin came into view, and immediately after that the Embankment and the long row of houses with ships and boats moored in front. And now the steamer was tied up. Innstetten said goodbye to the captain and went to the gangplank, that had been pushed over to the boat to make disembarking easier. Wüllersdorf was already there.

Without a word they shook hands, then went across the Embankment to Hoppensack's Hotel, where they sat down under the awning.

'I took a room here yesterday,' Wüllersdorf said, not wanting to start on the business in hand right away. 'When you think that Kessin is just a little hole, it's astonishing to find such a good hotel here. I don't doubt that my friend, the head waiter, speaks three languages; to go by his hairstyle and his cutaway waistcoat, it wouldn't be too bold to make it four . . . Jean, would you bring us coffee and brandy, please.'

Innstetten understood perfectly why Wüllersdorf was adopting this tone and was happy to go along with it, but he couldn't quite control his agitation, and without thinking took out his watch.

'We've plenty of time,' Wüllersdorf said. 'An hour and a half, or as good as. I've ordered the carriage for a quarter past eight; it won't take us more than ten minutes.'

'And where?'

'At first Crampas suggested a corner of the woods, just past the churchyard. But then he broke off and said, "No, not there." Then we agreed on a place in the dunes. Close to the beach; there's a gap in the last dune with a view through to the sea.'

Innstetten smiled. 'Crampas seems to have selected a beauty-spot. That was always his way. How did he take it?'

'Wonderfully.'

'Arrogant? Flippant?'

'Neither the one nor the other. I have to confess, Innstetten, I was really shaken. When I gave your name he went deathly pale and had to struggle to maintain his composure, and I could see the corners of his mouth were quivering. But all that lasted just for a moment, then he had himself under control again and from then on he was all resigned melancholy. I'm quite sure he has the feeling he's not going to come out of this in one piece, and doesn't want to, either. If my assessment's correct, he enjoys life and at the same time is indifferent towards life. He makes the most of everything, but knows that there's not much to it.'

'Who will be his second? Or perhaps I should say, who's he going to bring along with him?'

'That was his main concern, once he'd recovered. He named two or three of the local gentry, but then dropped them, they were too old or too pious, he said, he'd send a telegram to his friend Buddenbrook in Treptow. And he came, a capital fellow, dashing and yet like a child. He couldn't calm down and strode to and fro, very agitated. But when I'd told him everything, he said just the same as we did, "You're right, it has to be."'

The coffee came. They had a cigar, and once more Wüllersdorf's aim was to direct the conversation on to less immediate topics.

'I'm surprised none of the Kessiners has come to greet you. I know you were very popular. And your friend Gieshübler, of all people . . .'

Innstetten smiled. 'You don't understand the people here on the coast; half of them are dull burghers, half of them sly dogs, not very much to my taste; but there's one virtue they have in common, they're all very well mannered. Especially dear old Gieshübler. Naturally everyone knows what it's about, but for that very reason they refrain from showing their curiosity.'

At that moment a chaise with its hood down appeared on the left, and, as it was before the arranged time, approached slowly.

'Is that ours?' Innstetten asked.

'I imagine so.'

Then the carriage stopped outside the hotel, and Innstetten and Wüllersdorf stood up.

Wüllersdorf went to the coachman and said, 'To the breakwater.'

The breakwater was on the opposite side of the beach, to the right, not the left, and the wrong instruction was simply given in order to avoid any incidents, which were, of course, a possibility. Anyway, whether they intended to keep to the right or the left farther out of the town, they would still have to drive through the Plantation, and that would inevitably take them past Innstetten's old house. It was quieter than it had been; the ground-floor rooms looked rather neglected, so what would it be like upstairs! And now Innstetten himself was overcome with the eerie feeling he had so often combated or smiled at in Effi, and he was glad when they were past it.

'That's where I used to live,' he said to Wüllersdorf.

'It looks odd, rather deserted and abandoned.'

'Could well be. In the town it was said to be a haunted house, and the way it looks now, I can't say the people are wrong.'

'What was it all about?'

'Oh, some stupid nonsense: an old sea captain with a grand-daughter or niece who disappeared one day, and a Chinaman who was perhaps her lover, and in the hall a little shark and a crocodile, both hanging on strings and always moving. A wonderful story to tell, but not now. I've got all kinds of other things going through my mind.'

'You're forgetting that everything can go well.'

'It won't be allowed to. And before, Wüllersdorf, when you were talking about Crampas, you were taking a quite different line yourself.'

Soon after that they were through the Plantation, and the coachman was about to turn right, to the breakwater. 'Turn left instead, we can leave the breakwater until later.' And the coachman turned left on to a wide highway heading behind the men's bathing beach straight towards the woods. When they were three hundred yards away Wüllersdorf got the coachman to stop, and the two of them walked, on crunching sand, along a fairly wide road that cut straight through the three rows of dunes. Everywhere alongside it were thick clumps of marram grass, with immortelles and a few blood-red carnations around them. Innstetten bent down and put one of the carnations in his buttonhole. 'The immortelles afterwards.'

They walked for five minutes. When they reached the fairly deep hollow between the two last dunes they saw the opposing party already there, on the left: Crampas and Buddenbrook and dear Dr Hannemann, holding his hat in his hand so that his hair was streaming in the wind.

Innstetten and Wüllersdorf went up the sandy defile, Buddenbrook came to meet them, they shook hands, and the two seconds went to one side for a short discussion on the arrangements. The result was that they should advance together and fire at ten paces. Then Buddenbrook returned to his place. It all went very quickly and the shots rang out. Crampas fell.

Innstetten took a few paces back and turned away from the scene. Wüllersdorf, however, had gone over to Buddenbrook, and the two of them waited for the doctor to speak, but he just shrugged his shoulders. At the same time Crampas waved his hand to indicate that he wanted to say something. Wüllersdorf bent down to him, nodded in agreement at the few, almost inaudible words from the dying man's lips, and went over to Innstetten.

'Crampas wants to speak to you, Innstetten. You have to comply with his request. He has three minutes to live at the most.'

Innstetten went over to Crampas.

'Will you . . .' They were his last words.

A look of pain, and yet almost of acquiescence, crossed his face, and then it was over.

CHAPTER 29

Innstetten was back in Berlin on the evening of the same day. He had driven straight to the railway station in the carriage he'd left at the crossroads in the dunes, without going through Kessin again and leaving it to the two seconds to report the matter to the authorities. During the journey (he had a compartment to himself) he mused over the events of the day, thinking everything through again; his thoughts were the same as two days previously, except that they proceeded in the opposite direction, starting with the conviction of his right and his duty and ending with doubts about it. 'Guilt, if it's anything at all, is not bound to time and place and cannot be wiped away from one day to the next. Guilt demands expiation, that makes sense. But a time limitation is neither fish nor flesh, it's feeble, or at best just banal.' And he took heart from this and told himself again that it had happened the way it had to happen. But even as he came to this conclusion, he rebutted it. 'There *must* be a time limit, a time limit is the only sensible way; whether that means it's banal as well doesn't matter; sensible things usually are banal. I'm forty-five now. If I'd found the letters twenty-five years later, I'd be seventy. Then Wüllersdorf would have said, "Don't be a fool, Innstetten." And if Wüllersdorf hadn't said it, Buddenbrook would have, and even if he hadn't, I would have done so myself. So much is clear. If you go to extremes, you go too far and just look ridiculous. No doubt about that. But where does it start? Where is the boundary? Ten years still requires a duel, and it's a matter of honour, and after eleven years, or even ten-and-a-half, it's a piece of nonsense. The limit, the limit. Where does it lie? Was it there? Had it already been crossed? When I see that last look of his again, resigned and yet a smile in his misery, it was a look that said, "Innstetten, still the stickler for principle . . . you could have spared me all that, and yourself." And perhaps he was right. There's something like that at the back of my mind. Now if I'd been full of murderous hatred, if there had been a desire for revenge deep in my heart . . . Vengeance is ugly, but there's something human about it, a natural human right. But then it was all just for the sake of an idea, an abstract concept, a made-up piece of business, almost play-acting. And I have to continue play-acting and send Effi away and ruin her life and mine too . . . I should have burnt the letters and never let the world outside know about them. And then when she came back, all unsuspecting, I should have said to her, "There is your place," and I should have separated from her inwardly. Not in full view of the outside world. There are so many lives that aren't real lives and so many marriages that aren't real marriages . . . then my happiness would have gone, but I wouldn't be haunted by his eye with its questioning look and its mute accusation.'

*

Shortly before ten Innstetten's carriage stopped outside his apartment. He went up the steps and rang the bell. Johanna came and opened the door.

'How's Annie?'

'Fine, sir. She's not asleep yet. If you would . . .'

'No, no, that will just excite her. I'd rather see her in the morning. Bring me a glass of tea, Johanna. Has anyone been?'

'Only the doctor.'

Now Innstetten was alone again. He walked up and down as he liked to do. 'They'll know everything already. Roswitha's stupid, but Johanna's a clever woman. And even if they don't know for sure, they'll have worked it out and know anyway. It's strange how many things can become a sign and give away matters, as if everyone had been there.'

Johanna brought his tea. Innstetten drank it. After all the exertion he was dead tired and fell asleep.

*

Innstetten got up early. He saw Annie, had a few words with her, praised her for being a good patient, and then went to the Ministry to report to his Minister everything that had happened. The Minister was very gracious. 'Yes, Innstetten, fortunate the man who can come out of everything life throws at us unscathed; you've been badly hit.' He was happy with everything that had been done, and left any further arrangements to Innstetten.

It was late in the afternoon when Innstetten got home, and he found a note from Wüllersdorf there.

'Back this morning. Seen a whole host of things; painful, touching, Gieshübler above all. The most delightful hunchback I've ever seen. He didn't say much about you, but your wife, your wife! He just couldn't calm down, and eventually the little fellow broke into tears. The things that be! It would be desirable if there were more Gieshüblers. But there are more of the other kind. And then the scene in the Major's house . . . terrible. Not a word about that. We've been taught a lesson again: watch out. I'll see you tomorrow. W.'

Innstetten was devastated when he read that. He sat down and wrote a few letters of his own. When he'd finished he rang. 'Post the letters, Johanna.'

Johanna took the letters, and was about to leave.

'. . . And one other thing, Johanna. Your mistress isn't coming back. You'll find out why from other people. Annie mustn't know anything, at least not now. The poor child. You must gradually get her to understand that she hasn't got a mother any more. I can't do it. But be careful how you go about it. And don't let Roswitha spoil everything.'

Johanna stood there for a moment, dazed. Then she went to Innstetten and kissed his hand.

When she was back in the kitchen she was filled with pride and a sense of superiority, indeed, almost with happiness as well. The Master had not only told her everything but added at the end, 'And don't let Roswitha spoil everything.' That was the most important thing, and although she was not without a kind heart and even sympathy for his wife, most important of all for her was the triumph of a certain intimacy vis-à-vis the Master.

Under normal circumstances it would have been easy to flaunt her triumph, but on that day it was unfortunate for her that her rival, despite not having been taken into the Master's confidence, should turn out to be better informed. The porter downstairs had called Roswitha into his little lodge and immediately handed her the page of a newspaper to read. 'There's something for you, Roswitha; you can bring it back to me later on. It's just the *Fremdemblatt*, but Lene's gone out to get *Kleines Journal*. I presume there'll be more in that, they always know everything. But who would've thought it, Roswitha?'

After this Roswitha, who was in general not very curious, had gone up the backstairs as quickly as possible and had just finished reading the article when Johanna came. She put the letters Innstetten had given her on the table, glanced at the addresses, or pretended to (for she knew well who they were for), and said with feigned calm, 'One's to Hohen-Cremmen.'

'I can imagine,' Roswitha said.

Johanna was more than a little surprised at this. 'Usually the Master never writes to Hohen-Cremmen.'

'Yes, usually. But now ... Just imagine, the porter downstairs gave me *this* only a few minutes ago.'

Johanna took the newspaper and read out in a low voice the place that had been marked with a thick line of ink: 'As we learnt from a well-informed source shortly before going to press, yesterday morning in the seaside resort of Kessin there was a duel between Ministerialrat v. I. (Keithstrasse) and Major von Crampas. Major von Crampas fell. There are said to have been relations between him and the Frau Ministerialrätin, a beautiful and still very young woman.'

'The things these papers write,' Johanna said, put out at seeing her news superseded.

'Yes,' Roswitha said. 'And now people will read this and say nasty things about my poor, dear Mistress. And the poor Major. Now he's dead.'

'What are you thinking of, Roswitha? Should he *not* be dead? Or should it be the Master who's dead?'

'No, Johanna, our Master should be alive as well, they should all be alive. I'm not in favour of shooting people dead, I can't even stand the bang. But just think, Johanna, that was all ages ago, and the letters—I thought they looked odd right away, with the red string wrapped round them three or four times and then knotted without a bow—they looked quite yellow, it was so long ago. We've been here over six years now, it's such an old business, how could they ... ?'

'Oh, Roswitha, you don't understand how these things are. And when you think about it, it was your fault. It's the letters that set it off. Why did you get the chisel and break the sewing-table open? That's something you should never do, open something someone else has locked.'

'That really is too bad of you, Johanna, to say it's my fault like that, when you know that it was *your* fault, that you came bursting into the kitchen as if you were going out of your mind and told me the sewing-table had to be opened, the bandage was in there, so then I came with the chisel and now it's supposed to be my fault. No, I say ...'

'All right, I didn't mean it, Roswitha. But you shouldn't come and say "the poor Major". What d'you mean, the poor Major? Your poor Major wasn't worth a fig; anyone who has a red moustache like that and is always twirling it is worthless and does nothing but cause trouble. When you've always had positions in the best houses . . . but you haven't, Roswitha, that's what you lack . . . then you know what's right and proper and what honour is, and you also know that when something like this happens there's no other way to it, you get what they call a challenge and one of them's shot dead.'

'I know that too; I'm not as stupid as you're always trying to make out. But when it was so long ago . . .'

'Yes, Roswitha, you and your never-ending "so long ago"; that's what shows that you know nothing about it. You're always telling us the story of your father with the red-hot iron rod and how he came after you with it, and whenever I put a red-hot heating iron in, it really does always make me think of your father, and I can see him trying to kill you because of the child that's dead now. Yes, Roswitha, you're always talking about that, and all we need now is for you to tell little Annie the story, and once she's confirmed then she's sure to hear it, perhaps on the very same day. And it annoys me that you've been through all that, when your father was just a village blacksmith who shoed horses or put a tyre on a wheel, and now you come along and expect the Master to accept all that just because it was so long ago. What is long ago? Six years isn't long ago. And the Mistress—she isn't coming back, by the way, the Master's just told me—will be just twenty-six on her next birthday, that's in August, and you're trying to tell me it's "a long time ago". And even if she were thirty-six, and I can tell you, at thirty-six you really have to watch out, and the Master had done nothing, then the grand folk would have "cut" him. But that's a word you don't know, Roswitha, you know nothing about it.'

'No, I know nothing about that, and I don't want to. But there is one thing I do know, Johanna, and that's that you're in love with the Master.'

Johanna gave a forced laugh.

'Yes, go on, laugh. I've seen it for a long time. There's something about you. And it's a good job the Master doesn't have an eye for that kind of thing . . . The poor woman, the poor woman.'

Johanna was happy to make peace. 'Never mind, Roswitha. You've had one of your funny turns again, that's all, but all the people from the countryside get them.'

'You may be right there.'

'I'll take the post out now, and while I'm down there I'll see if the porter's got the other paper yet. You said Lene'd been sent out for it, didn't you? There must be more in it, there's next to nothing here.'

CHAPTER 30

Effi and Geheimrätin Zwicker had been almost three weeks in Ems, where they had the ground floor of a delightful little villa. Between their two living-rooms was a shared parlour with a view out into the garden; it also had a rosewood piano, on which Effi would play a sonata now and then, Frau Zwicker now and then a waltz; she was completely unmusical, her interest in the art being restricted to her passion for Niemann as Tannhäuser.*

It was a splendid morning; the birds were twittering in the little garden and, despite the early hour, the clack of billiard-balls could be heard from the building next door, in which there was a 'saloon'. The two ladies had taken their breakfast not in the parlour itself but on a little veranda, strewn with gravel and built up a few feet above the garden, to which three steps led down; the awning had been rolled up to allow them full access to the fresh air, and both Effi and Frau Zwicker were busy at their needlework. Just now and then they exchanged a few words.

'I can't understand', Effi said, 'why I haven't had a letter for four days now; he usually writes every day. I wonder if Annie's ill? Or he is?'

Frau Zwicker smiled. 'You'll see that he's in good health, my friend, in perfectly good health.'

Effi found the tone in which this was said distasteful and seemed about to reply, but at that moment the housemaid came out onto the terrace to clear the breakfast table. She was called Afra, came from Bonn, and was accustomed to measure all the manifold phenomena of life against Bonn students and Bonn hussars.

'Afra,' Effi said, 'it must be nine by now; hasn't the postman been yet?'

'No, not yet, Madam.'

'What's the problem?'

'The postman, of course. He's from the country out by Siegen and just has no dash. I've told him before, it's nothing but sloppiness. And have you seen his hair? I think he's no idea what a parting is.'

'You're being too severe again, Afra. Just think: delivering mail, day in, day out, in this heat . . .'

'Right enough, Ma'am. But there are others who can do it; when they've got what it takes, they can manage it.' And while she was still talking she went down the steps, balancing the tray on the tips of her five fingers, to take the shorter route through the garden to the kitchen.

'A pretty woman,' Frau Zwicker said. 'So nimble and lively, I'd almost say with natural grace. Do you know, my dear Baronin, that this Afra . . . a wonderful name, by the way, there's even supposed to have been a St Afra, though I don't think ours is descended from her . . .'

'You're going off at a tangent again, my dear Geheimrätin. This time it's called Afra and it's made you forget what you were actually going to say . . .'

'No it hasn't, my dear, or at least I'll find my way back there again. I was going to say that this Afra reminds me very much of the well-built young woman I saw in your house . . .'

'Yes, you're right, there is a similarity. Only our housemaid in Berlin is much prettier, in particular she has much more beautiful and fuller hair. I've never seen such beautiful flaxen hair as our Johanna has. You see a bit of it now and then, but never so full . . .'

Frau Zwicker smiled. 'It's truly rare to hear a young woman speak with such enthusiasm of her housemaid's flaxen hair. And especially of its fullness. Do you know, I find that touching. Choosing a maid is a constant problem. They should be pretty, since any visitor, especially male, is put off at seeing a beanpole with a coarse complexion and dirty fingernails when the door's opened; it's a good thing that corridors are mostly quite dark. But then, if you pay too much attention to making the right first impression and even give a pretty woman like that one little lacy apron after another, then you can't rest easy any longer and, if you're not *too* vain and don't have *too* much self-confidence, you start to wonder whether you shouldn't find some redress for the situation. "Redress" was one of Zwicker's favourite words, he often used to bore me with it; but then he was a senior civil servant, and they all have favourite words like that.'

Effi listened to this with mixed feelings. Had the Geheimrätin been slightly different she could have found all this charming, but being the way she was, Effi's reaction to something that would otherwise perhaps simply have amused her was one of distaste.

'What you say about senior civil servants is right, my dear. Innstetten's got into that habit too, and always laughs when I give him a look and then apologizes for the official jargon. Of course, your husband had been in the civil service longer and was presumably older . . .'

'A little,' Frau Zwicker said tartly.

'And all in all, I cannot understand the kind of fears you are expressing. What people call the proprieties are surely still in force . . .'

'You think so?'

'The fact is, I cannot imagine that you of all people, my dear, should suffer such worries and fears. You have—forgive me for being so open about this—precisely what men call "charm". You are merry, captivating, stimulating, and, if it's not being indiscreet, given all those qualities, I would like to ask whether what you say is derived from painful experiences you have had yourself?'

'Painful experiences?' Frau Zwicker said. 'Oh, my dear Frau Baronin, "painful experiences", that really is going too far, even if one has actually been through certain things oneself. "Painful" is simply too much, far too much. And then, one has one's own strategems and countermeasures. You mustn't take that kind of thing to heart.'

'I can't form a clear idea of what you're suggesting. It's not that I don't know what sin is, I do know that; but surely there's a difference whether you start indulging in all kinds of bad thoughts or whether such things become an occasional or even a regular habit. And then, in your own home . . .'

'That's not what I'm talking about, that wasn't what I was saying, although, to be honest, I do have my suspicions in that respect as well or, as I must now say, had; for that's all in the past. But there are outside areas. Have you heard of country outings?'

'Of course. And I wish Innstetten were more of a mind to enjoy them . . .'

'Think carefully about that, my dear. Zwicker was always going to Saatwinkel.* And I can tell you, when I hear that word it still hurts. All these places round our dear old city of Berlin where people go out to enjoy themselves! In fact the very names of these places are enough to fill you with fear and concern. You're smiling. But you tell me, my dear, what can you expect of a big city and its morals, when right at its gates (for there's no real difference between Berlin and Charlottenburg any more) there's a Pichelsberg, a Pichelsdorf, and a Pichelswerder—three villages happy to include a word for 'booze' in their name within a thousand yards of each other? You can go round the whole world and not find anything like it anywhere.'

Effi nodded.

'And all of that', Frau Zwicker went on, 'happens under the greenwood tree on the banks of the Havel. That's all in the west, where you have culture and civilized behaviour. But now go to the other side, my dear Frau Baronin, up the Spree. I'm not talking of Treptow and Stralau, they're mere trifles, harmless, but if you have a look at the large-scale map you will find, beside names that are at least strange, such as Kiekebusch and Wuhlheide—you should have heard how Zwicker pronounced that word—names that are downright brutal, but I won't insult you by mentioning them. But of course, those are the places people prefer. I hate these country outings that are popularly seen as a trip in an open charabanc singing "A Prussian I am", but that in fact contain the seeds of a social revolution. And when I say a "social revolution", I naturally mean a moral revolution, everything else is already a thing of the past, as Zwicker said to me during his last days, "Believe me, Sophie, Saturn devours his own children."*And Zwicker, whatever faults and weaknesses he may have had, was of a philosophical turn of mind and had a sense of historical development, I have to give him that . . . But I can see that my dear Frau von Innstetten, however polite she generally may be, is only half-listening; of course, the postman has put in an appearance over there and her heart flies across to him, anticipating the words of love that are in the letter . . . Now then, Böselager, what have you got for us?'

By now the postman had reached the table and handed them the post: several newspapers, two advertisements from hairdressers, and, last of all, a large registered letter to Frau Baronin von Innstetten, née von Briest.

She signed for it and the postman left. Frau Zwicker glanced at the hairdresser's advertisements and laughed at the price-reduction for a shampoo.

Effi wasn't listening. She twisted and turned the letter she'd received and felt strangely reluctant to open it. Registered and sealed with two large seals, and a strong envelope. What could it mean? Postmarked 'Hohen-Cremmen' and addressed in her mother's hand-writing. The fifth day without a word from Innstetten.

She took a pair of embroidery scissors with mother-of-pearl handles and slowly cut open the envelope. And now there was another surprise in store for her. The sheet of paper, yes, that was a closely written letter from her mother, but wrapped up in it were banknotes, with a strip of paper round them on which the amount enclosed was written in red pencil and in her father's hand. She put the bundle back in the envelope and started to read, leaning back in the rocking-chair. But she didn't get very far, the letter dropped from her fingers, and her face went pale. Then she bent down and picked it up again.

'What's the matter, my dear? Bad news?'

Effi nodded but said no more, just asked if she would give her a glass of water. When she'd drunk it, she said, 'It'll pass, my dear Geheimrätin, but I'd like to retire for a moment . . . If you could send Afra to me.'

And she stood up and went back into the parlour, where she was clearly glad to find something to hold on to and felt her way along the rosewood piano. She reached her room, that was on the right, and, after groping and searching, managed to open the door and get to the bed against the wall, where she collapsed, unconscious.

CHAPTER 31

Minutes passed. When Effi had recovered, she sat down on a chair by the window and looked out at the quiet street. If only there'd been some noise and arguing; but there was just the sunshine on the macadamized surface of the road and the shadows thrown by the railings and the trees. She was overwhelmed by a feeling of being alone in the world. Only an hour ago a happy wife, the favourite of everyone who knew her, and now cast out. She had only read the opening of the letter, but it was enough to make her situation clear. Where could she go? She had no answer to that, yet she was filled with longing to get away from everything around her, that is, away from this Geheimrätin, for whom all of this was just an 'interesting case' and whose sympathy, if it existed, would certainly not reach the level of her curiosity.

'Where can I go?'

The letter lay before her on the table, but she didn't have the courage to read on. Finally she said, 'What am I still afraid of? What else can be said that I haven't already said to myself? The man for whose sake all this happened is dead, there's no possibility of a return home, in a few weeks the divorce will be granted and the father will be given custody of the child. Of course. I am guilty, and a guilty woman can't bring up her child. And what with, anyway? I'll presumably be able to manage for myself. I'll see what Mama has to say about that.'

With that she picked up the letter to read the rest.

'. . . and now to your future, my dear Effi. You will have to fend for yourself and, as far as finance is concerned, you can rely on our support. It will be best if you live in Berlin (that kind of thing is easiest to conceal in a large city), where you will be one of the many whose actions have deprived them of open air and bright sunshine. You will lead a lonely life, and if you don't want to, then you will probably have to go down the social ladder. The world in which you have lived will be closed to you. And what is the saddest part for us and for you (for you too, from what we believe we know about you), your parental home will also be closed to you; we cannot offer you a quiet corner in Hohen-Cremmen, a refuge in our house, for that would mean shutting the house off from all the world, and we are definitely not inclined to do that. Not because we are too much attached to the world and would find saying farewell to what is called "society" absolutely unbearable; no, not because of that, but simply because we must nail our colours to the mast and show to all the world—I'm afraid I can't avoid the word—our condemnation of what you did, you, our only and much-loved child . . .'

Effi couldn't read any more; her eyes filled with tears, and after she had struggled in vain to hold them back, her heart overflowed as she finally burst out sobbing and crying.

*

Half an hour later there was a knock at the door, and at Effi's 'Come in,' the Geheimrätin appeared.

'May I come in?'

'Of course, my dear,' Effi said. She was now lying on the sofa, hands clasped and with a light blanket over her. 'I'm exhausted, and I've made myself as comfortable as I could. May I ask you to get a chair for yourself?'

Frau Zwicker sat so that the table with a bowl of flowers on it was between Effi and herself. Effi showed no trace of embarrassment and didn't change her position at all, not even her clasped hands. All at once she couldn't care less what the woman thought; she just wanted to get away.

'You have received some sad news, my dear Frau Baronin . . .'

'More than sad,' Effi said. 'At least, sad enough to require a rapid end to our journey together. I have to leave today.'

'I don't want to seem intrusive, but is it something to do with Annie?'

'No, not with Annie. The news didn't come from Berlin, the letter was from my Mama. She's worried about me and I feel I need to reassure her, or at least to be there with her.'

'I find that only too understandable, however much I regret having to spend these last days in Ems without you. May I offer you any assistance I can give?'

Before Effi could answer, Afra came in and announced that the guests were gathering for lunch. The ladies and gentlemen were very excited, she said. The Emperor was coming for three weeks, and at the end there would be a large-scale military exercise and the Bonn Hussars were coming too.

Frau Zwicker immediately considered whether it would be worth staying until then, came to a definite 'yes', then went to apologize for Effi's absence at lunch.

When, after she'd gone, Afra was about to leave as well, Effi said, 'And then, Afra, when you're free, would you come for a quarter of an hour to help me pack? I'm leaving by the seven o'clock train this evening.'

'Today? Oh, that is a pity, Madam. The good times are just starting now.'

Effi smiled.

*

It was only with difficulty that Frau Zwicker, who hoped to hear some juicy titbits, was persuaded not to accompany the 'Frau Baronin' to the station. One always got so distracted at a station, Effi had assured her, all one could think about was one's seat and one's luggage; she particularly liked to say farewell to people she was fond of beforehand. Frau Zwicker expressed agreement with that, even though she clearly sensed it was just a pretext; she had spent her life listening at doors, and could immediately distinguish what was genuine from what wasn't.

Afra accompanied Effi to the station and made the Frau Baronin give a firm promise that she would return next summer; anyone who'd been to Ems always came back. Ems was the best place of all, apart from Bonn.

In the meantime Frau Zwicker had sat down to write some letters; not on the rather wobbly rococo writing-desk in the parlour, but outside on the veranda, at the same table where she'd breakfasted with Effi hardly ten hours ago.

She was looking forward to writing the letter, that was to be for the benefit of a friend of hers from Berlin, a lady who was staying in Reichenhall at the moment. Their two minds had long been as one in the profound scepticism with which they regarded the male of the species; they agreed that men fell far short of what could legitimately be expected of them, most of all the so-called 'dashing' ones. 'Those who are so embarrassed they don't know where to look are still, after a brief preliminary course of instruction, the best, but the real Don Juans always turn out to be a disappointment.' This was the kind of wisdom the two friends exchanged.

Frau Zwicker was already on her second page, and continued to pursue her more than rewarding subject, which of course was 'Effi', as follows:

'All in all, I liked her very much, charming, apparently open, completely free from aristocratic arrogance (or very good at concealing it), and always interested when she was being told something interesting, of which, as I have no need to assure you, I made full use. To recap, then: a delightful young woman, twenty-five, or not much more. But I still have my suspicions, especially at this moment, yes, perhaps now most of all. The business with the letter today—there's a real story behind it. I'm as good as certain of that. It would be the first time I've been wrong in such a matter. The way she liked talking about the fashionable Berlin preachers so much and measured the degree of piety of each one, that and her occasional look of innocence, each time assuring us butter wouldn't melt in her mouth—all these things confirmed me in my . . . But there's our Afra coming, I think I told you about her, a pretty girl, and she's put a newspaper on the table that, she says, our landlady gave her to bring to me; the article marked with a blue pencil. Forgive me if I read it first . . .

PS. The newspaper was pretty interesting and came just at the right moment. I'll cut out the marked passage and put it in with this letter. When you've read it, you'll see I wasn't wrong. Who can this Crampas be? It's incredible—to write notes and letters yourself in the first place, and then to keep the man's letters! Why do we have stoves and fires? Such things should never happen as long as this nonsense with duels continues; future generations will perhaps be free to indulge in this passion for writing letters, if it no longer presents a danger. But we're nowhere near that at the moment. I have to say, I have great sympathy with the young Frau Baronin and, vain as one is, my only comfort is that I wasn't mistaken about the matter. And it wasn't such a straightforward case. A less gifted diagnostician would perhaps have allowed the wool to be pulled over her eyes.

Yours as ever
Sophie.'

CHAPTER 32

Three years had passed, and for almost all of that time Effi had lived in a small apartment in Königgrätzerstrasse,* between Askanischer Platz and Hallesches Tor; one front room and one back room, with a kitchen and maid's bedroom behind it, all as average and ordinary as possible. And yet it was a distinctively nice apartment that struck everyone who saw it as pleasant, most of all, perhaps, old Geheimrat Rummschüttel, who dropped in now and then, and had long since forgiven the poor young woman her play-acting with rheumatics and neuralgia, and everything else that had happened since then, that is, if any forgiveness were necessary on his part. For Rummschüttel had come across much worse. He was now in his late seventies, but whenever Effi, who had been in poor health for some time, sent a letter asking him to call, he would be there next morning and wave away her apologies because the apartment was so high up. 'No need to apologize, my dear Frau von Innstetten; in the first place it's my job, and in the second I'm happy and almost proud that I can still manage the stairs so well. If I weren't afraid I'd be a nuisance—for I come as a doctor and not as an enthusiastic admirer of nature and landscapes—I would probably call more often, just to see you and to spend a few minutes sitting at your back window. I think you don't appreciate the view enough.'

'But I do, I do,' Effi said. However, Rummschüttel took no notice of that and went on, 'Please, dear lady, come over here to the window, just for a moment, or allow me to give you my arm. Really splendid again today. Look at all the railway embankments, three, no, four, and the constant gliding to and fro . . . and now the train's disappearing again behind a cluster of trees. Really splendid. And the sun shining through the white smoke! If it weren't for St Matthew's churchyard right behind it, it would be perfect.'

'I like to see churchyards.'

'Yes, you can say that. But we doctors? We doctors are always faced with the inevitable question: could there not perhaps be one or two fewer buried here? Otherwise, my dear Frau Baronin, I'm happy with you, and my only complaint is that you won't hear of Ems; with your tendency to catarrh, Ems would work . . .'

Effi remained silent.

'Ems would work wonders. But since you won't hear of it (and I can accept that), then take the waters here. You can be in the garden of Prince Albrecht's Palace* in three minutes, and though it lacks the bands and the elegant outfits and all the usual diversions of a regular promenade at a watering-place, it's the waters that are the main point.'

Effi agreed and Rummschüttel took his hat and stick. But he went back to the window again. 'I hear they're going to terrace the Kreuzberg.* God bless the City Council, and once that bare patch has more green on it . . . A delightful apartment. I could almost envy you . . . Oh, and there's one thing I've been meaning to say for a long time, my dear lady, you always write me such a charming letter. Well, who wouldn't be delighted to receive one of those? But it takes an effort every time . . . Just send Roswitha round.'

Effi thanked him, and they parted.

*

'Just send Roswitha round . . .' Rummschüttel had said. Was Roswitha with Effi? Was she in Königgrätzerstrasse and not in Keithstrasse? She certainly was, and had been there for a long time, for just as long as Effi herself had been living in Königgrätzerstrasse. Three days before she moved in Roswitha had come to see her beloved mistress, and that had been a big day for both. So much so that it must be examined in retrospect.

When her parents' letter had arrived telling her she couldn't return to Hohen-Cremmen, and she had gone back to Berlin on the evening train, Effi had not looked immediately for an apartment of her own but tried rooms in a boarding-house. And it had been reasonably successful. The two ladies who ran the boarding-house were well educated and considerate, and had long since given up being inquisitive. They had so many people under their roof that any attempt to find out the secrets of each individual would have been much too time-consuming. That kind of thing was bad for business. Effi, still remembering Frau Zwicker's gimlet-eyed cross-examinations, was very pleased at the restraint shown by the two ladies; but after two weeks she felt that the overall atmosphere, both physical and psychological, was not bearable. There were mostly seven of them at table, and they were, apart from Effi and one of the ladies in charge of the boarding-house, two English girls who were studying at the Academy, a titled lady from Saxony, a very pretty Jewish woman from Galicia, of whom no one knew what she was doing in Berlin, and the daughter of a church organist from Polzin in Pomerania, who wanted to be a painter. That was an unfortunate combination, and the reciprocal assertions of superiority, in which, strangely enough, the two English girls did not rule the roost but had to compete with the girl from Polzin, full of her sense of being an artist, were tedious. Yet Effi, who kept aside from all this, might have been able to tolerate such an atmosphere, had it not been for the additional physical burden of the guest-house air. What the component parts of this were was perhaps beyond definition, but what was only too certain was that it made it difficult for Effi, who was very delicate, to breathe properly, and so for that reason she was very soon forced to look for other accommodation, which she then found in the same area. This was the apartment already described, in Königgrätzerstrasse. She was to move in at the beginning of the autumn quarter, had already acquired what was needed, and during the last days of September was counting the hours until her release from the boarding-house.

On one of these last days—she had withdrawn from the dining-room a quarter of an hour previously with the intention of having a rest on a sea-grass sofa upholstered in a woollen fabric with a pattern of large flowers—when there was a quiet knock at her door.

'Come in.'

One of the housemaids, a sickly-looking woman in her mid-thirties, who, from constantly standing around in the corridors, carried the atmosphere pervading them everywhere in the folds of her dress, came in and said, 'Excuse me, Madam, but there's someone wants to speak to you.'

'Who?'

'A woman.'

'And did she give a name?'

'Yes, Roswitha.'

And, lo and behold, hardly had Effi heard the name than she shook off her sleepiness and jumped up and went out into the corridor to grasp Roswitha with both hands and pull her into her room.

'Roswitha. You. What joy! What have you got for me? Something good, I'm sure. Such a dear old face can only bring good things. Oh, I'm so happy, I could give you a kiss; I'd never have thought I could feel such joy again. How are you, my dear old friend? Do you remember the time when the ghost of the Chinaman haunted the house? Those were happy days. At the time I thought they were unhappy, but that was before I knew how hard life can be. Since then I've found that out. Oh, a ghost is far from being the worst thing. Come, dear Roswitha, come and sit down here with me and tell me . . . Oh, I feel such longing. What's Annie doing?'

Roswitha could hardly speak, and stared round the strange room with the grey walls, that looked as if they were dusty and were framed with thin gold mouldings. Finally, however, she found her tongue and said that the Master was now back from Glatz;* the old Emperor had said that six weeks' confinement in a fortress was enough in a case like that, and she'd been waiting until the day when the Master would be back because of Annie, who needed someone to keep an eye on her. Johanna was a decent woman, but she was too pretty and too preoccupied with herself and perhaps had God-knows-what kind of ideas. But now that the Master could look after her again and see to things, she'd thought she'd make the effort to go and see how the Mistress was doing . . .

'Quite right too, Roswitha . . .'

. . . and see if there was anything she lacked and whether she perhaps needed her; if that were so, she'd just stay there and help her and do everything and see to it that the Mistress was properly looked after again.

Effi had leant back in the corner of the sofa and closed her eyes. But all at once she sat up and said, 'Yes, Roswitha, what you say there is an idea, a good idea. I should tell you that I'm not going to stay here in this boarding-house, I've leased an apartment and furnished it and I'm moving in in three days' time. And if I could go there and say to you, "No, Roswitha, not here, the wardrobe should be over there and the mirror here," yes, that would be something, I'd like that. And when we're tired from all the toil, I'd say, "Now, Roswitha, go across and get us a jug of Spatenbräu, for when you've been working hard you need a drink, and if you can, bring us something good from the Habsburger Hof as well, you can always take the dishes back afterwards . . ." Yes, Roswitha, when I think of that, it's as if a weight were lifted from my heart. But I have to ask you, have you thought all this through? I'm not talking about Annie, though I know how fond of her you are, almost as if she were your own child—but still, Annie will be taken care of, and Johanna's fond of her too. No, it's not that. But just think how everything has changed, if you want to come back to me. I'm not the way I was; I've taken a very small apartment, and the porter will probably not do as much for me and you. And you'll have a very small household to cook for, always like what we used to call our Thursday meal, because that was the day the cleaning was done. Do you remember? And do you remember when Gieshübler came and had to join us at table and said he'd never tasted anything so delicious? Surely you remember, he was always so terribly polite, yet he was the only person in the town who knew something about food. The others all thought everything was nice.'

Roswitha was delighted at all this, and had assumed everything was going ahead when Effi repeated, 'Have you thought all this through? For many years—I have to say this, even though it was my own house—you've been spoilt, money didn't matter, we never had to economize. But now I do have to economize, for I'm poor and only have what I'm given, you know, from Hohen-Cremmen. My parents are very good to me, as far as they can be, but they're not rich. So now tell me, what do you think?'

'That I'll turn up with my case next Saturday, not in the evening but first thing in the morning, and that I'll be there when you start moving in. I can set to work in a way that you, Madam, can't.'

'Don't say that, Roswitha. I can do that as well. You can do anything, if you have to.'

'And then, Ma'am, you've no need to worry about me—as if I could think, "That's not good enough for Roswitha." Everything she has to share with Madam is good enough for Roswitha, especially if it's something sad. Yes, I'm really looking forward to that. Then you'll see that I know about that. And if I didn't, I'd learn soon enough. For I haven't forgotten when I was sitting in the churchyard, all alone in the world, thinking it would be best if I were in the row of graves with all the others. Who was it who came along? Who kept me alive? Oh, I've been through so much. When my father came at me with the red-hot iron rod all those years ago . . .'

'Yes, I know, Roswitha . . .'

'Yes, that was bad enough. But when I was sitting there in the churchyard, so poor and abandoned, that was even worse. And then Madam came. May I never go to Heaven if I forget that.'

At that she stood up and went to the window. 'Look, Madam, you have to see *him* as well.'

Effi went over to her.

There, on the other side of the road, Rollo was sitting looking up at the guest-house windows.

*

A few days later Effi, aided by Roswitha, moved into her apartment in Königgrätzerstrasse, which she liked from the very beginning. She lacked company, of course, but during her time in the boarding-house she had derived so little pleasure from her association with other people that being alone didn't bother her, at least at the beginning. It was, of course, impossible to have a conversation about artistic matters with Roswitha, not even about what was in the newspaper; but if it concerned simple, human affairs and Effi started with an 'Oh, Roswitha, I feel frightened again . . .' the devoted soul always had a good answer ready, and comfort and, usually, advice.

Things went excellently until Christmas, but Christmas Eve was really sad, and when the new year arrived Effi started to grow quite melancholy. It wasn't cold, just grey and wet, and when the days were short that meant the evenings were all the longer. What could she do? She read, she did embroidery, she played patience, she played Chopin, but his nocturnes were not such as to bring light into her life, and when Roswitha came with the tea things and also put two little plates with an egg and a Wiener schnitzel cut up into little slices on the table, Effi would say, as she closed the piano, 'Come and take a seat, Roswitha. Keep me company.'

And Roswitha did. 'I can tell that Madam has been playing too much again; you always look like that then, and have red blotches on your face. Dr Rummschüttel forbade you to.'

'Oh, Roswitha, it's easy for Dr Rummschüttel to forbid something and it's easy for you to repeat it. But then what should I do? I can't spend all day sitting by the window, looking across at the Christuskirche. I always look at it on Sundays, during evening service, when the windows are lit up; but even that doesn't help, it always makes me feel even sadder at heart.'

'Well, Madam, then you ought to go in. You've been over there once.'

'Oh, several times. But I didn't get much out of it. He preaches quite well and he's a very clever man and I'd be happy if I knew a hundredth of what he knows. But it's all just as if I were reading a book; and then when he starts speaking very loud and waving his hands about and shaking his black locks, then that's the end of my devout mood.'

'The end?'

Effi laughed. 'You mean there wasn't even a beginning. And that will be the case. But whose fault is that? Not mine. He always talks so much about the Old Testament. And even if it's quite good, I don't find it at all uplifting. And all that listening anyway, it's not the right thing. Look, I really ought to have so much to do that I'm at my wits' end. That would be something for me. There are associations where young girls learn housekeeping, or sewing schools or kindergartens. Have you ever heard of things like that?'

'Yes, I have heard of them. Little Annie was to go to a kindergarten once.'

'There you see, you know better than I do. And I'd like to join such an association where you can make yourself useful. But there's no point even thinking about it; the ladies wouldn't accept me, and couldn't even if they wanted to. And that's the most terrible part of it, the world's so closed to you that you're even forbidden to help to do good. I can't even give poor children some private tuition . . .'

'That wouldn't be anything for you, Ma'am; the children are always wearing greasy boots and when it's wet—then there's so much smell and smoke, Madam wouldn't be able to stand it.'

Effi smiled. 'You're probably right there, Roswitha, but it's not a good thing that you're right, and it tells me that there's still too much of my old self in me and that life is still too good to me.'

But Roswitha would hear nothing of that. 'Life can never be too good for someone who's as good as Madam. And you shouldn't always play those sad things, and sometimes I think something will turn up and everything will be all right again.'

And something did turn up. Despite the church organist's daughter from Polzin, whose artist's arrogance she still recalled with horror, Effi decided to become a painter; and although she laughed at the idea herself, because she was well aware she would never be more than an amateur, she still pursued her goal passionately because it gave her an occupation and one that, being calm and quiet, was very much after her own heart. She enrolled with a teacher, who was very old and well versed in the Brandenburg aristocracy; at the same time he was so pious that he took a great liking to Effi from the very start: here, he presumably thought, was a soul to be saved, and so he treated her with particular kindness, as if she were his own daughter. Effi was delighted at this, and from the day of her first lesson her life took a turn for the better. Her empty life was no longer so empty, and Roswitha was jubilant that she had been right and something had turned up after all.

This went on for a year and more. But since she once more had contact with people that made her happy, it sparked off a desire for these contacts to be renewed and multiplied. At times she felt a passionate longing to go back to Hohen-Cremmen, and even more passionate was her longing to see Annie again. She was her child, after all, and when she pondered on that, at the same time recalling what Marietta Trippelli had once said—'the world is so small, you could be sure of suddenly meeting an old acquaintance in the middle of Africa'—she was quite rightly surprised she had never run into Annie. But that was about to change. Coming home from her painting lesson close by the Zoo, she got onto a horse-drawn tram going down the long Kurfürstenstrasse. It was very hot, and the curtains, that had been let down and were billowing in the strong draught, did her good. She leant back in the corner facing the front platform, and was scrutinizing several sofas, blue with tassels, etched on a pane of glass, when—the tram happened to be going very slowly—she saw three schoolgirls, satchels on their backs and wearing little pointed hats, jump on, two blond and high-spirited, the third dark and serious. It was Annie. It gave Effi a shock. A meeting with her daughter, which she had so long desired, now filled her with consternation. What should she do? Quickly making up her mind, she opened the door on to the front platform, where there was no one but the driver, and asked him to let her get off from there at the next stop. 'It's forbidden, Miss,' the driver said, but she gave him the coin with such a pleading look that the good-natured fellow changed his mind and muttered to himself, 'She shouldn't really, but once won't hurt.' When the tram had stopped, he opened the railing and Effi jumped off.

She was still very agitated when she got home.

'Just imagine, Roswitha, I've seen Annie!' And she told her about the encounter in the horse-drawn tram. Roswitha was unhappy that mother and daughter had not had an emotional reunion, and it took a long time to convince her that had been out of the question in the presence of so many people. Then Effi had to tell her what Annie looked like, and when, with maternal pride, she had done that, Roswitha said, 'Yes, she's half and half. She gets her pretty looks and, if I may put it that way, her distinctive nature from her Mama; but her serious side, in that she's quite her Papa. And when I think about it, she's probably more like the Master.'

'Thank God,' Effi said.

'Well, that is the question, Ma'am. And I'm sure there are some who'll be more for her Mama.'

'You think so, Roswitha? I don't.'

'Oh come now, I'm not that easily fooled, and I think Madam knows very well the way things are and what men like best.'

'Oh, don't start on about that, Roswitha.'

With that the conversation broke off and wasn't taken up again. But although Effi avoided talking about Annie with Roswitha, she couldn't get over her encounter with her, and was distressed at the idea that she had run away from her own daughter. It tormented her so much she felt ashamed, and her desire to see Annie reached almost morbid proportions. To write to Innstetten and ask permission to do so was impossible. She was well aware of her guilt, indeed, she nurtured the feeling with an almost passionate zeal; but, on the other hand, for all her sense of guilt she felt a certain revolt against Innstetten. She told herself he was right, but however right he was, ultimately he was wrong. Everything that had happened was so far in the past, a new life had begun—he could have let it die away, instead it was poor Crampas who'd had to die.

No, writing to Innstetten was out of the question; but she still wanted to see and talk to Annie, to clasp her to her breast, and after she'd thought it over for several days she knew how best to go about it.

The very next morning she dressed carefully in respectable black and headed for Unter den Linden to call on the Minister's wife. She sent in her card, which simply said: 'Effi von Innstetten, née von Briest.' Everything else had been left out, even the Baronin. 'Her Excellency will see you now,' and Effi followed the servant into an anteroom where she sat down and, despite her agitation, scrutinized the pictures on the walls. There was Guido Reni's* *Aurora*, but opposite it some English etchings after Benjamin West* in the well-known aquatint style with a lot of light and shade. One of the pictures was of King Lear* in the storm on the heath.

She had hardly finished her scrutiny when the door of the neighbouring room opened and a tall, slim lady with an engaging expression came in and held out her hand to the petitioner. 'My dear Frau von Innstetten,' she said, 'what a pleasure it is to see you again . . .'

As she said that, she went across to the sofa and, as she sat down, drew Effi down beside her.

Effi was moved by the kindness of heart that came out in all this. Not a trace of haughtiness or reproach, just fine, human sympathy. 'What can I do for you?' she went on.

The corners of Effi's mouth twitched. Finally she said, 'What brings me here is a request, the fulfilment of which might be possible with Your Excellency's help. I have a ten-year-old daughter whom I have not seen for three years, and would like to see again.'

The Minister's wife took Effi's hand and looked at her with a friendly expression.

'When I say I haven't seen her for three years, that isn't quite correct. I saw her three days ago.' And Effi gave a vivid description of her encounter with Annie. 'Running away from my own child. I know that once you've made your bed, you must lie in it, and I don't want to change anything in my life. The way it is, is the way it has to be; I knew what I was doing. But with the child, that's too hard, I want to see her now and again, not secretly and surreptitiously but with the knowledge and consent of all concerned.'

'With the knowledge and consent of all concerned,' the Minister's wife repeated. 'That means with the consent of your husband. I see from this that his method of bringing up the child involves keeping her away from her mother, a procedure it is not my place to judge. Perhaps he's right, if you'll forgive me for saying so, my dear.'

Effi nodded.

'You yourself have come to accept your husband's attitude, and are simply asking that a natural feeling, perhaps the most beautiful of feelings (at least we women would agree on that), be allowed to express itself. Is that correct?'

'Entirely so.'

'And so I am to obtain permission for occasional visits to your house where you can attempt to win back your child's heart?'

Effi nodded her agreement again as the Minister's wife went on, 'I will do what I can, Frau von Innstetten. But it won't be easy. Your husband—forgive me for continuing to call him that—is a man who acts not on mood and impulse but according to principles, and he will find it hard to discard them, or even just lay them aside temporarily. If that were not the case, his attitude and way of bringing up the child would have long since been different. What your heart finds hard to bear, he regards as right.'

'So Your Excellency thinks it would perhaps be better if I withdrew my request?'

'Not at all. I just wanted to explain your husband's actions, not to justify them, and at the same time to indicate the difficulties we are likely to encounter. But I think we can do it, despite that. We women can get all sorts of things done, if we go about them in the right way and don't overdo it. Moreover, your husband is one of my particular admirers and is unlikely to refuse a request I make. We're having a little gathering tomorrow, at which I will see him, and the morning after you will have a note from me telling you whether I have gone about it in the right way, that is, successfully, or not. I think we will bring this off and you will see your child again and take delight in her. She's supposed to be a beautiful girl. Not surprisingly.'

CHAPTER 33

Two days later, as the Minister's wife had promised, a note arrived and Effi read:

'I am delighted, my dear Frau von Innstetten, that I have good news for you.

Everything went as we wanted; your husband is too much of a gentleman to refuse a lady's request. However, at the same time—I feel I have to say this—I could see that his "yes" did not correspond to what he really thought was sensible and right. But let's not quibble when we should be happy. The arrangement we made was that your Annie should come around midday; may Heaven look kindly on your reunion.'

The note came with the second post, which meant there were probably only two hours until Annie would arrive. A short time, but still too long, and Effi walked restlessly round the two rooms and then back into the kitchen, where she talked about all sorts of things with Roswitha: about the ivy on the Christuskirche, next year the windows would probably be completely overgrown; about the porter, who hadn't turned the gas tap off properly again (next thing they'd all get blown up); and that she'd do better to get the paraffin from the big lamp-shop on Unter den Linden again rather than from Anhalterstrasse—she talked about all sorts of things except about Annie, because she didn't want to allow the fear she harboured despite, or perhaps because of, the Minister's wife's note, to surface.

Now it was midday. Finally there was a shy ring at the door and Roswitha went to look through the spyhole. Yes, it was Annie. Roswitha gave her a kiss, but didn't say a word, and quietly, as if there were someone who was sick in the house, led the child from the corridor first into the back room, then to the door to the front room.

'In you go, Annie.' And with these words—she didn't want to be in the way—she left the child and went back to the kitchen.

Effi was standing at the other end of the room with her back to the pier-glass when the child came in. 'Annie!' But Annie stayed by the door, without closing it, half in embarrassment, but also half deliberately, and so Effi rushed over to the child, lifted her up, and kissed her.

'Annie, my sweet child, I'm so delighted to see you. Come and tell me about yourself.' Saying that, she took Annie by the hand and led her over to the sofa to sit down there. Annie stood upright and, while still looking shyly at her mother, took the corner of the tablecloth, that was hanging down, in her left hand. 'Do you know, Annie, I saw you once?'

'Yes, I thought so too.'

'Now tell me all about yourself. How big you've grown! And there's the scar, Roswitha told me about that. You were always so wild and boisterous when you were playing. You get that from your Mama, she was like that too. And at school? I imagine you'll always be top of the class, you have that look about you, as if you're a model pupil and always come home with top marks. I've also heard that Frau von Wedelstädt praised you for that. That's the way it should be; I was also ambitious, but I didn't go to such a good school. I was always best at Mythology. What's your best subject?'

'I don't know.'

'Oh, I'm sure you do. People know that. Which do you get your best marks for?'

'Religion.'

'There you are, you do know. Yes, that's excellent; I wasn't so good at that, but that was probably the fault of the teaching. We just had a probationer.'

'We had a probationer as well.'

'And he's left?'

Annie nodded.

'Why did he leave?'

'I don't know. We have the pastor again now.'

'Whom you all love.'

'Yes. Two from the top class want to convert.'

'Oh, I understand; that's nice. And how's Johanna?'

'Johanna came with me as far as the house.'

'And why didn't you bring her up with you?'

'She said she preferred to stay outside and wait by the church over there.'

'And that's where you're to meet her afterwards?'

'Yes.'

'Well I hope she won't get impatient out there. There's a little garden at the front and the windows are half overgrown with ivy, as if it were an old church.'

'But I don't really want to keep her waiting.'

'Oh, I see, you're very considerate and I suppose I must be pleased about that. You just have to know how to apportion it properly . . . And now tell me, how's Rollo getting on?'

'Rollo's fine. But Papa says he's getting very lazy; he's always lying in the sun.'

'I can believe that. He was like that when you were still little . . .

Now tell me, Annie—today was just a chance to see each other again—will you come and visit me quite often?'

'Oh, certainly, if I'm allowed.'

'Then we could go for walks in the garden of Prince Albrecht's Palace.'

'Oh, certainly, if I'm allowed.'

'Or we'll go to Schilling's* for some ice-cream, pineapple or vanilla flavour, I've always liked that best.'

'Oh, certainly, if I'm allowed.'

This third 'if I'm allowed' was the last straw; Effi jumped up, and there was a flash of indignation in her eyes as she looked at the child. 'I think it's high time, Annie; otherwise Johanna will be getting impatient.' And she rang the bell. Roswitha, in the neighbouring room, came in at once. 'Roswitha, accompany Annie as far as the church. Johanna's waiting there. I hope she hasn't caught cold. I'd be sorry about that. Give Johanna my best wishes.'

At that the two of them left.

Hardly had Roswitha closed the door behind them, however, than Effi, who felt she was suffocating, tore open her dress and burst out into convulsive laughter. 'So that's what a reunion's like!' With that she rushed to the window, opened it wide, and looked for something to relieve her distress. And she found something. There was a bookshelf beside the window with a few volumes of Schiller and Körner,* and on top of these books of poetry, that were all the same height, were a Bible and hymn-book. She picked them up, because she needed something at which she could kneel down and pray, and placed the Bible and hymn-book on the edge of the table, just by where Annie had been standing. Then she threw herself down before them and said, in a low voice, 'O, Lord in Heaven, forgive me for what I've done; I was a child . . . But no, no, I wasn't a child, I was old enough to know what I was doing. And I did know and I don't want to lessen my guilt . . . but this is too much. For all this with the child, that isn't you, God, who are punishing me, it's him, him alone! I thought he had a noble heart and always felt small beside him; but now I know that it's him, he's the one who is small-minded. And because he's small-minded, he's cruel. Everyone who is small-minded is cruel. He taught the child that, he was always a schoolmaster, Crampas called him that, in mockery, but he was right. "Oh, certainly, if I'm allowed." You *can*, there's no "allowed" about it. I don't want any of you any more, I hate you, even my own child. Too much is too much. He just wanted to get on in the world, that's all.—Honour, honour, honour . . . and then he shot the poor man dead, a man whom I didn't even love and whom I'd forgotten because I didn't love him. It was just a piece of stupidity, and then blood and death. And my fault. And now he sends the child to me because he can't refuse the request of a minister's wife, and before he sends the child off he trains her like a parrot and teaches her to say, "if I'm allowed". I loathe what I did, but what I loathe even more is your virtue. Away with you. I have to have a life, but it won't last for ever anyway.'

When Roswitha came back, Effi was lying on the floor, her face turned away, as if she were dead.

CHAPTER 34

When Rummschüttel was called, Effi's condition caused him no little concern. The feverishness, that he had observed in her for some time now, seemed more pronounced than ever, and what was worse, there were also the first signs of a nervous disorder. His calm, friendly manner, which he could combine with a touch of whimsical humour, did Effi good. When he finally left, Roswitha went with him to the entrance hall and said, 'God, I'm so worried, Herr Doktor; what if it should come back, and it could. God—I can't get a moment's peace. That with the child was just too much. My poor Mistress. And still so young, at the age when some are only just starting out.'

'Don't take on so, Roswitha, she can always recover. But she has to get away from here. We'll see. Different air, different people.'

Two days later a letter arrived at Hohen-Cremmen that said:

'DEAR FRAU VON BRIEST,

My long-standing friendly relations with the Briest and Belling families and, not least, the great affection in which I hold your daughter, will be sufficient justification for these lines. Things cannot go on as they are. If something doesn't happen soon to pull your daughter out of the loneliness and joylessness of the life she has been leading for some years now, she will quickly waste away. She was always susceptible to consumption, for which reason I prescribed a visit to Ems years ago; a new disorder has now joined this old one: her nerves are wearing away. A change of air is needed to stop that continuing. But where should she go? It would not be difficult to find a suitable place among the Silesian spas, Salzbrunn would be good and, with the complication of the nerves, Reinerz even better. But the only place it can be is Hohen-Cremmen. For, my dear Frau von Briest, it is not air alone that will help your daughter recover; she is wasting away because she has no one but Roswitha. A faithful servant is fine, but loving parents are better. You must forgive an old man for interfering in things that are outside his medical competence. But then that is not entirely the case, for it is the doctor who is speaking here and doing his duty in making—please forgive the expression—demands . . . I have seen so much of life . . . But enough of that. Please give my regards to your husband,

> your obedient servant,
> Dr Rummschüttel.'

Frau von Briest had read the letter out to her husband. The two of them were sitting on the flagged path, with their backs to the garden room and facing the circular flowerbed with the sundial. The Virginia creeper winding round the windows fluttered in the breeze and there were a few dragonflies hovering over the pond in the bright sunshine. Briest remained silent, drumming his fingers on the tea-tray.

'Please stop drumming like that; say something instead.'

'Oh, Luise, what can I say? Drumming my fingers says it all. You've known what I think for years now. Back then, when Innstetten's letter came like a bolt from the blue, I agreed with you. But that's ages ago now; must I spend the rest of my life sitting here like the grand inquisitor? I've been fed up with it for a long time now, I can tell you.'

'Don't you start reproaching me, Briest, I love her as much as you do, perhaps even more, everyone has their own way of showing it. But we're not here to be weak and tender-hearted and show consideration for everything that is against the laws of God and man and that people condemn and, at least for the moment, rightly condemn.'

'Oh, come now. One thing is more important.'

'Of course. One thing is more important; but what is that one thing?'

'Parents' love for their children. And when you only have one child . . .'

'Then that's the end of the catechism and morality and the demands of "society".'

'Oh, Luise, you can go on about the catechism as much as you like, but don't go on about "society".'

'It's difficult to get by without society.'

'Without one's child as well. And, believe me, Luise, "society" is very good at turning a blind eye if it wants to. My view on all this: if the Rathenow Hussars come over, that's fine, and if they don't, that's fine too. I'll simply send a telegram: "Come, Effi." Do you agree?'

She stood up and gave him a kiss on the forehead. 'Of course I do. You won't have anything to reproach me for. It's not an easy step to take. Our life will change from the moment she comes.'

'I can put up with that. The rape is doing well and in the autumn I can go and hunt a hare. And I still enjoy a glass of red wine. And once I have the child back in the house again, it'll taste even better . . . And now I'll send off that telegram.'

*

Now Effi had been in Hohen-Cremmen for six months; she had the two first-floor rooms she used to have when she was on a visit there; the larger one had been set up for her personal use, Roswitha slept in the neighbouring room. Rummschüttel's expectations of this stay and the good things associated with it had been, as far as possible, fulfilled. Her cough got better, the touch of bitterness, that had robbed her kindly face of much of its charm, disappeared, and there were days when she could laugh again. They didn't talk much about Kessin and the past, with the sole exception of Frau von Padden and, of course, Gieshübler, for whom old Herr von Briest had a particular liking. 'That Alonzo, that operatic Spaniard who keeps a Mirambo at home and brings up a Trippelli—yes, I think he must be a genius, and no one's going to persuade me otherwise.' Then Effi was forced to act out Gieshübler to the life, with his hat in his hand and his endless polite bows, which, given her gift for imitation, she could do very well, though unwillingly, because she always felt it was doing the dear, kind man an injustice.—Innstetten and Annie were never mentioned, even though it was settled that Annie would inherit Hohen-Cremmen.

Yes, Effi found a new lease of life, and her mother who, as women do, was not disinclined to regard the whole business, however painful it still was, as an interesting case, vied with her husband in showing her love and affection.

'It's a long time since we had such a good winter,' Briest said, and Effi got up from her seat and stroked the hair out of his forehead. But however pleasant all that was, as far as Effi's illness was concerned it was all just outward appearance, the truth was that the illness was still there, quietly eating away at her life. When Effi—she was once more wearing a blue-and-white striped pinafore dress with a loose belt, as she had done on the day she got engaged—came with quick, supple steps to wish her parents a good morning, they looked at her with joyful amazement, with joyful amazement but also with sadness, because they could not but be aware that it was not the brightness of youth but a kind of transfiguration that gave her slim figure and shining eyes this particular expression. Everyone who looked more closely could see that, only Effi herself couldn't and was entirely filled with the happiness of once more being in this place where she could find kindness and peace, reconciled with those whom she had always loved and by whom she had always been loved, even in the years of her misery and banishment.

She busied herself about the house, seeing to little improvements and embellishments. Her feeling for beauty meant she always made the right decision. However, she had completely given up reading and, above all, occupation with the arts. 'I've got so much out of them that I'm glad to be able to sit back and relax.' Presumably they also reminded her too much of her sad days. Instead she developed the art of quietly delighting in nature, and when the leaves fell from the plane trees, when the sun's beams glittered on the ice on the little pond, or when the first crocuses came into flower in the round bed when winter still wasn't quite over—it did her good, and she could spend hours looking at all that, forgetting what life had denied her or, to be more precise, what she herself had deprived herself of.

They were not entirely without visitors, not everyone was against her; her main intercourse, however, was with the schoolhouse and parsonage.

The fact that the two daughters of the schoolhouse had flown the nest didn't really matter, it would have been awkward with them anyway; but with her old friend Jahnke himself—who regarded not only the whole of Swedish Pomerania but also the area round Kessin as an offshoot of Scandinavia and was constantly asking questions about it—she got on better than ever. 'Yes, Jahnke, we had a steamboat and, as I've already told you in a letter or a conversation, I believe, I once almost crossed over to Visby. It's odd, but there's so many things in my life about which I can say "almost".'

'Pity, pity,' Jahnke said.

'Yes, a pity indeed. But I really did drive round Rügen, and that would have been something for you, Jahnke. Just imagine, Arkona* with a big campsite of the Wends. They say it's still visible, though I didn't get to see it; but not far away is Lake Hertha with white and yellow water lilies. It made me think of your Hertha . . .'

'Well, Hertha, yes . . . But you were going to tell me about Lake Hertha . . .'

'Yes, I was . . . And just imagine, Jahnke, close by the lake were two big stones, a sacrificial altar, smooth and still with the channels the blood ran down. From that time on I've felt a revulsion towards the Wends.'

'Oh, forgive me, Frau von Innstetten, but that wasn't the Wends. The business with the sacrificial altar was much, much earlier, before the birth of Christ; pure Teutons that we're all descended from, the Jahnkes certainly and perhaps the Briests as well . . .'

After that she dropped the topic of Rügen and Lake Hertha and asked about his grandchildren, and which ones were his favourites, Bertha's or Hertha's.

Yes, Effi got on well with Jahnke. But despite his intimate knowledge of Lake Hertha, Scandinavia, and Visby, he was a simple man, and it was inevitable that the lonely young woman much preferred her conversations with Niemeyer. And there had been an abundance of those during the autumn, as long as it was still possible to walk in the park, but they were interrupted for several months once winter came, because she didn't like to go to the parsonage itself. Frau Niemeyer had always been a very unpleasant woman, and now she really got on her high horse, even though in the opinion of the congregation she wasn't entirely irreproachable herself.

It was like that throughout the winter, much to Effi's dismay. But when, at the beginning of April, the bushes had a flush of green and the paths in the park dried out quickly, the walks started again.

Once, when they were taking a walk, they heard the cuckoo in the distance, and Effi counted how many times it called. She had taken Niemeyer's arm and said, 'There's the cuckoo. I don't want to take it as an omen. But tell me, my friend, what do you think of life?'

'Oh, my dear Effi, there's no point in asking me a question like that. You'll have to find a philosopher or send a request to a university. What do I think of life? A lot and not very much. Sometimes it's quite a lot and sometimes it's not very much at all.'

'That's right, my friend, I like that. I don't need to know any more.'
As she was saying that, they came to the swing. She jumped up on it
as nimbly as when she'd been a young girl, and before the old man,
who was watching her, could recover from the shock, she was sitting
between the two ropes and had set the seat moving by adroitly swinging her body to and fro. It was only a matter of seconds before she was
flying through the air and, holding on with just one hand, she pulled
off a little silk scarf she had round her neck and chest and waved it, as
if she were full of happiness and high spirits. Then she let the swing
slow down and jumped off and took Niemeyer's arm again.

'Effi, you're still the way you used to be.'

'No. I wish I were. But that's quite far back in the past, and I just
wanted to try it again. Oh, it was lovely, and the air did me good; I felt
as if I were flying up to heaven. Do you think I'll get there? Tell me,
my friend, you must know. Please, please . . .'

Niemeyer took her head in his two old hands, kissed her on the
forehead, and said, 'Yes, Effi, you will.'

CHAPTER 35

Effi spent the whole day out in the park, because she needed fresh air;
old Doctor Wiesike from Friesack was also happy with that, however,
in this he gave her too much freedom to do as she liked, with the
result that during a chilly spell in May she caught a bad cold; she had
a temperature, coughed a lot, and the doctor, who usually came every
third day, now came daily and was at his wits' end how to deal with the
situation, since the sleeping-pills and cough medicine Effi asked for
couldn't be given her because of her high temperature.

'What's going to come of all this, Doctor?' old Briest asked. 'You
know her from when she was little, you delivered her. I don't like all
this, she's losing weight visibly, and the red patches and the way her
eyes shine when she suddenly gives me a questioning look. What do
you think? What's going to happen? Is she going to die?'

Wiesike slowly shook his head from side to side. 'I wouldn't say
that, Herr von Briest. I don't like this temperature she has. But
we'll get it down again, then she'll have to go to Switzerland or to
Mentone. Pure air and a pleasant environment, that'll help her forget
the past . . .'

'Lethe, Lethe.'*

'Yes, the water of Lethe.' Wiesike smiled. 'Pity our old friends the Greeks only left us the word and not the spring itself . . .'

'Or at least the prescription for it; spa waters can be copied nowadays. Good Lord, Wiesike, we could make a packet if we could establish a sanatorium for that here: Friesack as a spring of oblivion. Well, for now we'll have to try the Riviera. Mentone is on the Riviera, isn't it? The price of corn's very low at the moment, but what must be, must be. I'll talk to my wife about it.'

He did that, and his wife immediately agreed; his suggestion fell in with her desire to see the south which—presumably because of the secluded life they led—had recently grown very strong. But Effi would hear nothing of it. 'You are good to me. And I'm selfish enough to accept your sacrifice, if I thought it would do me any good. But I'm convinced it would just make me worse.'

'You're only imagining that, Effi.'

'No. I've become very irritable; everything annoys me. Not here with you. You spoil me and keep everything out of my way. But that's not possible when you're travelling, unpleasant things can't just be swept away; it'll start with the conductor and end with the waiter. I only have to imagine their smug faces and I come out in a hot flush. No, no, let me stay here. I don't want to go away from Hohen-Cremmen again, this is where I belong. I prefer the heliotrope round the sundial in the flowerbed down there to Mentone.'

After this they dropped the plan, and Wiesike, who had had great hopes of Italy, said, 'We must respect that, it's not just a caprice; people with that kind of illness are very sensitive and seem to know with a remarkable degree of certainty what is beneficial for them and what isn't. And what Frau Effi said about conductors and waiters is actually quite right, and there's no air that has sufficient healing power to make up for the irritation in the hotel—if you do get irritated by it. So let's keep her here; if it's not the best thing for her, it's certainly not the worst.'

That turned out to be the case. Effi recovered, put on a little weight (old Briest was a fanatic about weighing yourself), and lost much of her irritability. However, her need for fresh air was constantly growing and she spent many hours out in the open, especially when there was a west wind and grey clouds scudding across the sky. On such days she would go out over the fields and the Marshes, often for more than two miles, and when she was tired would sit on a wooden fence and look, lost in dreams, at the buttercups and the red docks waving in the breeze.

'You always go by yourself,' Frau von Briest said. 'With our people you're safe; but there's a lot of riff-raff from outside prowling round.'

That made an impression on Effi, who had never thought of danger, and when she was alone with Roswitha she said, 'I can't really take you with me, Roswitha; you're too fat and not very sure-footed any more.'

'Oh, Madam, it's not *that* bad. I could still get married.'

'Of course,' Effi laughed. 'One can always do that. But, you know, Roswitha, if I only had a dog to go with me. Papa's hunting-dog isn't attached to me at all. Hunting-dogs are so stupid and they only get up when the huntsman or the gardener takes his rifle off the hook. I often think of Rollo.'

'Yes,' Roswitha said, 'they haven't got one like Rollo here. But that's not to say anything against "here". Hohen-Cremmen is very good.'

*

It was three or four days after this conversation that Innstetten went to his study an hour earlier than usual. The morning sun, which was very bright, had woken him, and since he felt he wouldn't get back to sleep again he had got up in order to start on a task that had been waiting on his desk for some time.

Now it was a quarter past eight, and he rang. Johanna brought the breakfast tray on which, beside the *Kreuzzeitung* and the *Norddeutsche Allgemeine*,* there were two letters. He glanced at the addresses and recognized from the handwriting that one was from the Minister. But the other? The postmark was smudged, and 'The Honourable Herr Baron von Innstetten' betrayed a happy unfamiliarity with the customary modes of address. That corresponded to the writing, that was very crude. But then the apartment was designated with remarkable precision: 'W. Keithstrasse 1c, second floor.'

Innstetten was enough of a civil servant to open the letter from 'His Excellency' first. 'My dear Innstetten, I am delighted to be able to inform you that His Majesty has deigned to sign your appointment, and I offer you my sincere congratulations.' Innstetten was delighted at the Minister's personal note, almost more than at the appointment itself, for as far as climbing the ladder was concerned, he had taken a somewhat critical view of that kind of thing since the morning in Kessin when Crampas had said farewell to him with a look of which he was constantly aware. Since then he saw things in a different light. An honour, what was it, after all was said and done? During what had become an ever more cheerless existence he had thought more than once of a half-forgotten civil-service anecdote from fifty years ago about Ladenberg, who had been a minister.* When, after a long wait, he had been granted the Order of the Red Eagle, he had flung it down furiously, crying, 'Stay there until you turn *black*.' It had probably eventually turned into a Black Eagle, but much too late and certainly not to the satisfaction of the recipient. Everything that should give us pleasure is bound to time and circumstance, and something that makes us happy one day is worthless the next. Innstetten was deeply aware of this, and, clear as it was that honours and marks of favour from the monarch were, or at least *had been*, important to him, it was clear now that these glittering prizes didn't mean much, and that what people called 'happiness' was, if it existed at all, something quite different from that glittering show. 'If I'm right, happiness consists in two things: on the one hand in being in a place where you belong (but what civil servant can say that of himself?), on the other, and best of all, in a comfortable course of daily life, that is, having a good sleep and a new pair of boots that aren't too tight. If the seven hundred and twenty minutes of a twelve-hour day pass without any particular vexation, you can call it a happy day.' That day Innstetten was again in the kind of mood that led to such mournful reflections. Now he picked up the second letter. After he had read it he passed his hand over his brow, with the painful sense that there was a happiness he'd once had but had no longer, nor could ever have again.

Johanna came in and announced, 'Geheimrat Wüllersdorf.'

He was already in the doorway. 'Congratulations, Innstetten.'

'From you I can believe it; the others will just be annoyed. Moreover . . .'

'Moreover. Surely you're not going to cavil at a moment like this.'

'No. I feel shamed by the favour His Majesty has shown me. And, if anything, even more by the good opinion of the Minister, whom I have to thank for all this.'

'But . . .'

'But I've forgotten how to take pleasure in things. If I were to say that to anyone else but you, then it would be taken merely as a manner of speaking. But you, you will know what I mean. Just look round here; how dreary and desolate everything is. I dread it when Johanna, a so-called jewel, comes in. This putting on a show (and Innstetten copied Johanna's posture), this half-comical flaunting of the bosom that seems to be making a particular demand, whether on me or on humanity in general I don't know, but I find it all so dismal, so dreary, it would be enough to make one blow one's brains out, if it weren't so ridiculous.'

'My dear Innstetten, you're going to become head of department in a mood like that?'

'Pooh! Can it be any other way? Read this, it's just arrived.'

Wüllersdorf took the second letter, the one with the illegible postmark, grinned at the 'Honourable', and went over to the window, where it was easier to read.

'DEAR BARON,

You will be surprised to receive a letter from me, but it's about Rollo. Last year little Annie told us that Rollo had got very lazy now, but that doesn't matter here, here he can be as lazy as he likes, the lazier the better. And the Mistress would like it so much. She keeps on saying, when she goes out into the Marshes or over the fields, "Actually, I'm afraid, Roswitha, because I'm so alone out there, but who can go with me? Rollo, yes that would be fine; he doesn't bear me a grudge. That's the good thing about animals that they're not concerned about that kind of thing." That is what my Mistress said and I've nothing to add, I'd just like to ask you to give my greetings to little Annie. And to Johanna as well.

From your most faithful servant,
Roswitha Gellenhagen.'

'Yes,' Wüllersdorf said as he folded the letter up again, 'we're no match for her.'

'I think so too.'

'And that's the reason why all the rest seems so questionable to you.'

'That's right. It's been going round in my mind for a long time now, and with these simple lines and their unintended or even intended reproach, my mind is in turmoil. It's been tormenting me for ages and I'd like to be free of this whole business, I can't enjoy anything any more; the more distinctions I receive, the more I feel that all that's nothing. I've made a mess of my life, and so, thinking about it, I've come to the conclusion that I ought not to have anything more to do with all this striving and vanity, and should exercise my schoolmasterly talent, which is probably my most essential self, as a kind of moral authority. That sort of person has existed. If that were to work, I'd have to become a terribly famous figure, like that Doctor Wichern* in the Rauhes Haus in Hamburg, that miracle-worker who could tame all criminals with his look and his piety . . .'

'Hm, there's no objection to that; that would be possible.'

'No, it's not possible. Not even that. The fact is, everything's closed to me. How could I get a killer to see the error of his ways? To do that, you have to have a clean bill of moral health yourself. And if that isn't the case, and you yourself are tarred with the same brush, then you must at least pretend to be madly repentant and put on a colossal act of remorse.'

Wüllersdorf nodded.

'You're nodding, you see. But I can't do any of that any more. I can't manage to do the man in the hair-shirt any more, and certainly not the dervish or fakir who dances himself to death while emitting self-accusations. And since none of that is possible, what I've worked out as the best solution is: to get away from here and mingle with pitch-black fellows, who know nothing of civilized behaviour and honour. Those happy ones! For it's precisely all that nonsense that's to blame for everything. You don't do that kind of thing out of an overflow of feeling, which might, after all, be acceptable, but because of an abstract idea . . . Ideas! . . . and then one man is done for and you're done for too. Only worse.'

'Oh, come on, Innstetten, those are just fancies, notions. What's all this nonsense about going to darkest Africa? That's something for a lieutenant with debts, but not for a man like you. Are you going to wear a red fez and preside over a conclave of natives, or become a blood-brother of a son-in-law of King Mutesa?* Or are you going to inch your way along the Congo, in a solar topee with six holes in it, until you reappear in the Cameroons* or thereabouts? Impossible!'

'Impossible? Why? And if it is impossible, then what can I do?'

'Simply stay here and resign yourself to the inevitable. Who is free of care? Who doesn't say every day, "A very dubious business, actually." As you know, I have my own cross to bear, not quite the same as yours, but not much less heavy. All this about crawling round the jungle or sleeping in a termite mound's nonsense. If someone enjoys that kind of thing, then let them do it, but it's not for the likes of us. Stand in the breach and hold out until you fall, that's best. But until then, make the most you can of the tiniest little detail, and have an eye for when the first violets appear or the flowers round the memorial to Queen Luise are blooming or the little girls in their lace-up boots are skipping. Or you could go to Potsdam and visit the Friedenskirche where Emperor Friedrich* is buried and they're just starting to build a mausoleum for him. And once you're there, think about his life, and if that doesn't calm you down, then nothing will.'

'All right, then. But a year's a long time and every single day . . . and then the evenings.'

'Those are the easiest to occupy. There's *Sardanapalus* and *Coppélia* with Antonietta dell'Era* at the ballet, and after them you can have a beer at Siechen's. Not something to be sneezed at. Three glasses always calm you down. There are still many, a great many, who have the same attitude to the whole business as we do, and one of them, for whom a lot of things had gone wrong, said to me, "Believe me, Wüllersdorf, life's completely impossible without jury-rigged expedients." The man who said that was a seaman so must have known what he was talking about. And he was right. A day doesn't pass when I'm not reminded of those "jury-rigged expedients".'

Once he had got that off his chest, Wüllersdorf took his hat and stick. But Innstetten, who at his friend's comments had recalled his own previous reflections on 'minor happiness', nodded his partial agreement and smiled to himself.

'And where are you off to now, Wüllersdorf? It's still too early for the Ministry.'

'I'm taking the day off today. First an hour walking along the canal as far as the Charlottenburg lock and then back again. Then I'll drop in to Huth's on Potsdamer Strasse, taking the little wooden steps carefully. There's a flower-shop at the bottom.'

'And you enjoy that? That's enough for you?'

'I wouldn't go so far as to say that. But it helps a little. I meet various regulars there, early birds as far as a glass of wine's concerned—I think it would be prudent not to mention their names. One will talk about the Duke of Ratibor,* another about Prince-Bishop Kopp,* and a third probably about Bismarck. There's always a bit that's worth hearing. Three-quarters is wrong, but as long as it's amusing, you don't waste time finding fault with it but are glad to listen.'

And with that he left.

CHAPTER 36

May was beautiful, June even more so, and Effi, once she'd overcome a painful feeling Rollo's arrival had initially aroused in her, was overjoyed to have the faithful animal with her again. Roswitha was praised, and old Briest went on and on to his wife with words of praise for Innstetten, who was a gentleman, not petty, his heart had always been in the right place. 'Pity that silly business should have come between them. They would have been a model couple, actually.' The only one to remain calm at the reunion was Rollo himself, either because he had no sense of time or regarded the separation as a muddle that had now simply been sorted out. That he had grown old was presumably also part of the explanation. He was sparing with his signs of affection, as he had been with his manifestation of joy at seeing Effi again, but his faithfulness had, if possible, grown even stronger. He never left his mistress's side. He was gracious towards the hunting-dog, but treated it as a being on a lower level. At night he lay on the rush mat outside Effi's door, in the morning, when breakfast was taken outside, by the sundial, always quiet, always sleepy; only when Effi got up from the table, went into the hall, and took first her sunhat and then her parasol from the stand, did his youth return and, unconcerned whether his strength was to be put to a hard or an easy test, he would race up and down the village street, and only calm down when they came to the first fields. Effi, for whom fresh air was more important than the beauty of her surroundings, avoided the little woods and mostly followed the wide street, that was lined with ancient elms and, where the high-road began, with poplars, to the railway station, a good hour's walk. She enjoyed everything, happily breathing in the scent coming over from the rape- and clover-fields or watching the larks rising, counting the wells and troughs where the cattle went to drink. As they did so a soft tinkling sound reached her ear, and she felt as if she should close her eyes and pass into sweet oblivion. Near the station, close by the road, was a road-roller. That was her daily resting place, from which she could watch what was happening on the railway embankment; trains came and went, and sometimes she saw two trails of smoke that coincided for a moment, then separated to the right and left until they disappeared behind villages and woods. Then Rollo would sit beside her, sharing her lunch, and when he caught the last morsel he would dash, presumably in a show of gratitude, furiously up and down some furrow or other, only pausing when a couple of partridges he had disturbed flew up from the eggs they'd been sitting on in one of the adjoining furrows.

*

'What a lovely summer! A year ago I'd never have thought I could be so happy again, Mama dear.'—Effi said that every day, walking round the pond with her mother, or breaking an early apple off the branch and boldly biting into it. For she had excellent teeth. Then Frau von Briest would stroke her hand and say, 'First of all just get well again, Effi, really well, and happiness will come; not your old happiness, but something new. There are, thank God, many kinds of happiness. And, you'll see, we'll find something for you.'

'You're so good to me, yet I've changed your life and made you into old people before your time.'

'Oh, don't say that, Effi dear. When it happened, I thought the same. Now I know that our quiet life is better than all the noise and hurly-burly we had before. And if you continue to get better, we could still travel. When Wiesike suggested Mentone you were unwell and irritable, and because you were unwell, you were quite right with what you said about conductors and waiters. But once you have stronger nerves again, then it will be possible, then you won't get irritated any more, you'll just laugh at their grand manner and curled hair. And then the blue sea and white sails and the rocks overgrown with red cactus—I haven't seen it yet, but I imagine it like that. And I'd like to see it some time.'

Thus the summer passed, and the clear August nights with shooting stars were already gone. During those nights Effi had sat at the window until after midnight and never wearied of watching. 'I was never a very good Christian, but I wonder whether we do come from up there after all and, once things are over here, will return to our heavenly home, to the stars up there, or even beyond? I don't know and I don't want to know, I just feel this longing.'

Poor Effi, you spent too long looking up at the wonders of the heavens and thinking about them, and the result was that the night air and the mist rising from the pond brought on a recurrence of her illness and when Wiesike was called, he took Briest to one side and said, 'She won't recover; prepare yourselves, the end will come soon.'

What he had said was only too true, and a few days after—not late, it wasn't quite ten o'clock—Roswitha came down and said to Frau von Briest, 'Madam, the Mistress upstairs is in a bad way; she's talking very quietly to herself all the time, and now and then it's as if she were praying but won't admit it, and I don't know, but I feel it could be over any moment now.'

'Does she want to speak to me?'

'She didn't say so, but I think she would like to. You know how she is; she doesn't want to disturb and worry you. But I think it would be a good idea.'

'That's all right, Roswitha,' Frau von Briest said, 'I'll come.'

And before the clock struck, Frau von Briest was going up the stairs and went to Effi's room. The window was open and she was lying on a chaise-longue beside it.

Frau von Briest pushed across a little chair with three gold slats in the ebony back, took Effi's hand, and said, 'How are you, Effi? Roswitha says you're very feverish.'

'Oh, Roswitha gets so worried about everything. I could tell she thought I was dying. Well I don't know, but she thinks everyone should be as worried as she is.'

'Are you so calm about dying, Effi dear?'

'Very calm, Mama.'

'Are you sure about that? Everyone is attached to life, young people above all. And you're still so young, Effi.'

Effi remained silent for a while. Then she said, 'You know that I haven't read very much. Innstetten was often surprised at that and wasn't really happy about it.'

It was the first time she had mentioned Innstetten's name, and that made a great impression on her mother, showing her clearly that the end had come.

'But I think', Frau von Briest said, 'you were going to tell me something.'

'Yes, I was, because of what you said about me being still so young. Of course I'm still young, but that doesn't matter. It was in the happy days when Innstetten used to read to me in the evening; he had very good books, and in one it said: a man was called away from a merry banquet and the next day he asked what had happened after he'd left. And he was told, "Oh, all sorts of things happened, but you didn't really miss anything." And those words have stuck in my mind, Mama—it doesn't really mean very much when you're called away from the banquet a little earlier.'

Frau von Briest said nothing. But Effi pushed herself up a little higher and said, 'And since I've been talking about the old times and Innstetten, there's something else I have to tell you, Mama dear.'

'You'll be making yourself overwrought, Effi.'

'No, no; getting something off my chest won't make me overwrought, it'll calm me down. I just wanted to tell you: I'm dying reconciled to God and the world, also reconciled to *him*.'

'Were you, then, so full of bitterness towards him in your heart? Forgive me for saying this now, Effi, but actually you yourself were the cause of your suffering.'

Effi nodded. 'Yes, Mama. And I'm sad that was the case. But when all the awful things happened, last of all that with Annie, you know what I mean, then, if you'll excuse the silly expression, I played him at his own game and quite seriously made myself think he was to blame, because he was so detached and calculating and, in the end, cruel as well. Then I really did curse him.'

'And that weighs on you now?'

'Yes. And I want him to know that it has become clear to me, here in these days of illness, that have been almost my best days, that he was right in everything he did. In the business with poor Crampas— after all, what else could he do? And then the thing he did that struck deepest: that he has brought up my child to keep her distance from me—however hard I find it and however much it hurts to admit it, he was right there as well. Tell him that, tell him I died convinced of that. It will comfort, hearten, perhaps reconcile him. There was much that was good in his nature, and he was as noble as anyone can be who lacks true love.'

Frau von Briest could see that Effi was exhausted and seemed to be asleep, or was trying to get to sleep. She stood up quietly and left. However, hardly had she gone than Effi also stood up and went to sit by the open window in order to suck in the night air once more. The stars were twinkling and not a leaf was moving in the park. But the longer she listened, the clearer she could hear again the soft sound, like fine rain falling on the plane trees. A feeling of liberation came over her. 'Peace, peace.'

*

It was a month later, and September was coming to an end. The weather was fine but the foliage in the park was already showing a lot of red and yellow, and since the equinox, that had brought three days of gales, leaves were strewn all over the ground. There had been a small change in the round flowerbed: the sundial had gone and in its place there had been, since the previous day, a white marble stone with just 'Effi Briest' on it and a cross underneath. That had been Effi's last request, 'I'd like to have my old name on my gravestone; I brought nothing but dishonour to the other one.' And that had been promised.

Yes, the stone had come and been set up the previous day, and now Briest and his wife were sitting facing the spot and looking at it and at the heliotrope, that had been carefully left there and now framed the stone. Rollo was lying beside it, his head on his paws.

Wilke, whose gaiters were getting fatter and fatter, brought their breakfast and the post, and old Briest said, 'Have the chaise brought round, Wilke. I want to go out for a drive with my wife.'

By this time Frau von Briest had poured the coffee and looked across at the flowerbed. 'Look, Briest, Rollo's lying by the stone again. He feels it more deeply than we do. He's not eating, either.'

'Yes, Luise, dumb animals. That's what I always say. We're not so great as we think. We're always talking about instinct; in the end it's probably what's best.'

'Don't go on like that. When you get one of your philosophical turns . . . Don't take it amiss, Briest, but you're really not up to that. You have your common sense, but when it comes to that kind of question, you can't . . .'

'Not really, no.'

'And if there are questions that should be asked, they're quite different ones, Briest, and I can tell you that not a day passes since the poor child's been lying there when I haven't been asking myself those questions . . .'

'What questions?'

'Whether it wasn't perhaps our fault?'

'Nonsense, Luise. Why do you say that?'

'Whether we shouldn't have brought her up differently, more strictly. We ourselves, that is. Niemeyer's actually no use at all, because he leaves everything in doubt. And then, Briest, much as it pains me to say so . . . your constant double entendres . . . and finally, something I reproach myself for, since I don't think I should come out of this without blame: was she not perhaps too young?'

Rollo, who woke up as she said this, slowly shook his head from side to side, and Briest said calmly, 'Oh, Luise, don't . . . It's too big a question.'

EXPLANATORY NOTES

3 *Hohen-Cremmen*: Kremmen is a town near Potsdam, south-west of Berlin; Fontane has moved it a little further to the west. The Briests are a historically attested family from the Havelland, which died out in the early nineteenth century. The daughter of its last male heir married Friedrich Baron de la Motte Fouqué (1777–1843), a Romantic writer once famous for his historical dramas and his fairy-tale *Undine* (1811). The Briests lived at Nennhausen, some thirty-five miles from Berlin.

Georg Wilhelm: ruler of Brandenburg, the core area of Prussia, from 1619 to 1640. Until 1701, when Friedrich adopted the title of King, the rulers of Brandenburg were called Electors because they had the right to participate in electing the Holy Roman Emperor.

Canna indica: a shrub, often two metres tall, with bright red flowers.

Effi: probably short for Euphemie or Eva (cf. p. 24).

4 *Rathenow Hussars*: Rathenow is a town on the river Havel, west of Berlin and evidently close to Hohen-Cremmen; it contained the garrison of the Zieten Hussars, a light-cavalry regiment.

Colonel Goetze: Goetze is the name of a Prussian noble family.

5 *Jahnke*: not a local man, but a native of Mecklenburg, on the Baltic; his mention anticipates Effi's later removal to the distant port of Kessin. The name Jahnke occurs in *My Childhood*, Fontane's memoirs of his early residence in Swinemünde, on which Kessin is based.

Hanseatic League: a medieval association of north German commercial cities, including Hamburg, Lübeck, Rostock, Greifswald, and others.

Fritz Reuter: a novelist (1810–74) who wrote in an accessible Low German dialect and was popular throughout the German-speaking world. The identical twin girls Mining and Lining ('-ing' is a diminutive suffix) are characters in his novel *Ut mine Stromtid* ('From my Time as a Farm Manager', 1862–4).

Hertha: supposedly the name of a goddess worshipped by the ancient Germans, according to a misreading of the name 'Nerthus' provided by the Roman historian Tacitus (*c*.55–115 CE) in his *Germania*. It reappears with 'Lake Hertha' (Ch. 24).

Klitzing: the name of a well-known Prussian military family.

Gabriel: see Luke 1: 26–8. This is the first of several humorous and disrespectful allusions to passages from the Bible.

Schwantikow: an imaginary place.

Landrat: the chief administrator of a district (*Kreis*), who, as the local representative of the government, mediates between the district and the state.

6 *eve-of-wedding party*: it is a German custom to hold a *Polterabend* (lit. 'noisy evening') before a wedding and to smash crockery; the pieces are supposed to bring the couple luck.

7 *the fourth commandment*: the Lutheran Church, like the Roman Catholic Church but not the Church of England, follows the sequence of commandments in Deuteronomy 5, where the fourth begins 'Honour thy father and thy mother'. In the other sequence, in Exodus 20, this is the fifth.

Belling: an actual family, whose members included Wilhelm Sebastian von Belling (1719–79), a cavalry general under Frederick the Great.

Ritterschaftsrat: the title indicates that Briest helps to represent the *Ritterschaft*, i.e. the landowning nobility, in the parliament of his province.

8 *when war broke out*: the Franco-Prussian War, 1870–1. See the Introduction, p. xii.

Perleberg Lancers: a cavalry regiment stationed at Perleberg near Potsdam, south-west of Berlin.

Bismarck: Otto von Bismarck (1815–98), conservative politician, who became prime minister and foreign minister of Prussia in 1862. He successfully directed wars with Denmark (1864), Austria (1866), and France (1870–1). In 1867 he formed the North German Confederation, which brought the great majority of the German states under German leadership and prepared the way for the establishment of the German Empire in 1871. Besides continuing as Prussian prime minister, Bismarck became Imperial Chancellor, and was known popularly as the Iron Chancellor. He received the title of Prince in 1871. He remained in office until his dismissal by the new Emperor, Wilhelm II, in 1890.

Kessin: an imaginary town, but closely based on Swinemünde (now Świnoujście in Poland) on the Baltic island of Usedom, where Fontane lived from 1827 to 1832. However, Fontane has transferred it to Eastern Pomerania (Hinterpommern), a region on the Baltic coast stretching from Kammin almost to Danzig (now Gdańsk), now entirely in Poland, and in Fontane's day a byword for 'the back of beyond'.

10 *figleaf*: an allusion to the figleaves with which Adam and Eve covered their nakedness (Genesis 3: 7).

13 *Luise*: Frau von Briest bears the evocative name of Luise, Princess of Mecklenburg (1776–1810), the wife of King Friedrich Wilhelm III. Queen Luise's support for Prussian resistance to Napoleon, together with her early death, made her into a national icon.

15 *Hotel du Nord*: a first-class hotel, situated on the boulevard Unter den Linden.

mesquineries: Fr. 'meanness'.

Spinn & Mencke, Goschenhofer: prestigious furniture dealers which advertised themselves as supplying the Court.

Tsar Alexander Guards Regiment: a grenadier-guard regiment named after Tsar Alexander I of Russia (Prussia's ally against Napoleon), garrisoned in Berlin.

Die Fliegenden Blätter: a humorous illustrated weekly which ran from 1844 till 1928.

16 *Café Bauer*: a café opposite Kranzler, which in the afternoons and evenings attracted a less respectable clientele and which, therefore, the Briests could not visit at such times.

Island of the Blest: a mythological painting by Arnold Böcklin (1827–1901), actually entitled *The Island of the Living*, showing a paradisal scene with nymphs bathing and a centaur standing in the water with a nymph on his back; Dagobert is making a strong sexual allusion, which Effi's father repeats a few pages later. The painting's erotic content aroused controversy when it was first displayed in 1878.

Princess Maria Anna: the wife of Prince Friedrich Karl of Prussia (1828–85) who served as a field-marshal in the Franco-Prussian War.

Demuth's: a smart shop, also on Unter den Linden, supplying travel equipment.

17 *sketches*: Effi intends her 'Polterabend' to include performances or charades involving fancy dress. Her prohibition on dressing as a mousetrap seller alludes to the common superstitious association of mice with death: see Hanns Bächtold-Stäubli, *Handwörterbuch des deutschen Aberglaubens*, 10 vols. (Berlin: de Gruyter, 1927–41), vol. 6, cols. 44–5.

18 *"Late ye come, but ye have come . . ."*: a very familiar, indeed stale, quotation from the opening line of the play *The Piccolomini* (1799) by Friedrich Schiller (1759–1805).

Käthchen von Heilbronn: in this play (1810) by the Prussian dramatist Heinrich von Kleist (1778–1811), the middle-class Käthchen falls in love with the noble Count Wetter von Strahl and follows him about devotedly. In Act IV, scene 2, Käthchen lies sleeping under an elder tree (where, according to superstition, one will dream of one's future partner) and talks in her sleep to the Count, calling him 'my lord' and confessing her love to him.

Innstettens: the name is Fontane's invention, but may have been inspired by the noble family Innhausen, with which he was personally acquainted.

19 *by-blow*: an allusion to the popular dramatist Ernst von Wildenbruch (1845–1909), whose father was an illegitimate son of Prince Louis Ferdinand of Prussia (1772–1806).

Cinderella: a comedy based on the story of Cinderella by the prolific dramatist Roderich Benedix (1811–73), first performed in 1867. Fontane reviewed a production favourably in 1873.

20 *Sedan Day*: 2 September, the anniversary of Prussia's decisive victory in 1870 in the Franco-Prussian War.

21 *Lot*: nephew of Abraham, notorious for sleeping with his own daughters when he was drunk (Genesis 19).

26 *in that sign*: an ironic allusion to the story that the Emperor Constantine, before the Battle of the Milvian Bridge in 312, saw a cross in the sky with the words: 'In this sign you shall conquer'; after his victory he made Christianity the official religion of the Roman Empire.

Hövel's: an elegant confectioner's shop on Unter den Linden.

garter: it was once customary to end a ball with a game of forfeits, one of which was a lady's garter.

27 *Kögel*: Rudolf Kögel (1829–96), Court preacher in Berlin from 1863 on and spiritual adviser to King Wilhelm I.

Valhalla: a classical building established by King Ludwig I of Bavaria and completed in 1842 as a German hall of fame, with plaques and busts commemorating famous Germans from ancient times to the present; it stands on a hill overlooking the Danube near Regensburg.

30 *Pinakothek*: the Alte Pinakothek, a famous art gallery in Munich; the *other one* may be the nearby Glyptothek, a collection of sculptures.

31 *Four Seasons*: a distinguished hotel in the Maximilianstrasse in Munich.

Palladio: Andrea Palladio (1508–80), architect who worked from Greek and Roman models and designed many classical buildings in Vicenza and villas in the surrounding countryside.

"In Padua there he buried lies": quotation from Goethe, *Faust, Part I*, line 2925. By quoting this relatively trivial line, Innstetten shows his conventional reverence for German cultural icons.

32 *St Privat panorama*: a large picture by Emil Hünten, on public view from 1881, depicting the Prussian capture of St Privat, one of the turning-points in the Franco-Prussian War. A panorama is 'a large circular painting, housed in a rotunda and viewed from a raised central platform': Andrew Cusack, '"Civibus aevi futuri": Panoramic Historiography in Fontane's *Wanderungen durch die Mark Brandenburg*', *Modern Language Review*, 104 (2009), 746–61 (at 747).

Klein-Tantow: an actual place in the extreme north-east of Germany, with a station on the railway-line between Berlin and Stettin (now Szczecin in Poland).

33 *Varzin*: now Warcino in Poland. The hunting-lodge there was given to Bismarck by the nation in 1867, and remained in the possession of his family till their expulsion in 1945.

starosta: a Polish term meaning the head of the local community.

34 *Kashubs*: speakers of a West Slavonic language closely related to Polish. Their territory is around Danzig (Gdańsk), much further east than Swinemünde.

35 *Macpherson*: based on Macdonald, a Scottish engineer whom Fontane mentions in *My Childhood* as living in Swinemünde.

Beza: suggested by Beda, the mayor of Swinemünde mentioned in *My Childhood*.

General de Meza: Christian Julius de Meza (1792–1865), a Danish general of Portuguese extraction.

Flying Dutchman: according to a legend, retold by Heinrich Heine and made famous by Richard Wagner (1813–83) with his opera *The Flying Dutchman* (1843), the Dutchman is punished for blasphemy by having to sail his ship round the world until a woman can be found to redeem him by her sacrificial love.

Black Flags: the Black Flag army consisted of Chinese bandits who, after the defeat of the Taiping Rebellion in China in 1864, moved south into Vietnam and helped the Vietnamese army to resist French invaders. They also harassed European vessels trading on the Red River; this must be where the Kessin captain practised his piracy. The Black Flag army was disbanded after the Sino-French War of 1884–5, which left the French in effective control of *Tonkin* (northern Vietnam).

36 *Rollo*: or Rolf, a Scandinavian leader who was granted the fief of Normandy in 913; his descendants were called Dukes of Normandy.

39 *Alonzo Gieshübler*: the humorous device of giving a character a forename incongruous with his surname occurs elsewhere in Fontane's novels (e.g. Dr Niels Wrschowitz in *The Stechlin*), and was adopted by his admirer Thomas Mann for such misfits as Tonio Kröger in the story of that name.

Small and cramped is my cottage: the first line of an anonymous folk-song.

42 *Bottegone*: a cafe in Florence.

Wrangel: an evocative name borne by many famous soldiers in both Germany and Sweden; here it refers to the field-marshal Friedrich Heinrich Ernst von Wrangel (1784–1877), who in 1848 led Prussian and other German troops in support of the revolutionaries seeking to detach Schleswig-Holstein from Denmark, and in 1864 was supreme commander of the Prussian troops in the Dano-Prussian War.

43 *good people but poor musicians*: a proverbial phrase, taken from the Romantic comedy *Ponce de Leon* (1804) by Clemens Brentano (1778–1842).

consuls: the Roman Republic was governed by two consuls, each elected for a year at a time; Lucius Junius Brutus (85–42 BCE), the assassin of Julius Caesar, was one. The consuls in Kessin are local businessmen who act as representatives of foreign countries. Similarly, in Thomas Mann's *Buddenbrooks* (1901) Jean Buddenbrook has the office of Consul and is generally referred to as 'the Consul'.

44 *black-and-white flags*: the Prussian flag showed a black eagle on a white ground; the flag of the German Empire, used from 1871 to 1918, had three horizontal bars, black, white, and red.

49 *Preziosa*: an opera (1820) with text by Pius Alexander Wolff (1782–1828) and music by Carl Maria von Weber (1786–1826).

49 *Fehrbellin*: a battle fought on 28 June 1675 in which the Prussian army decisively defended a stronger Swedish force. A member of the Briest family did indeed distinguish himself in the battle. Three days before the battle, a contingent of Prussian troops led by Major-General von Goetze drove the Swedes out of the town of Rathenow which they had occupied.

Froben: a patriotic legend tells how Emanuel von Froben (1640–75), master of the horse under the Elector Friedrich Wilhelm, on learning that the Elector intended to ride into battle at Fehrbellin on a conspicuous white horse, persuaded him to exchange horses and thus saved his monarch's life but lost his own.

Luther: Martin Luther (1483–1546), asked at the Diet of Worms in 1521 to withdraw his criticisms of the Church, is said to have replied: 'Here I stand. I cannot do otherwise. God help me. Amen.'

50 *Borckes*: an actual noble family called Borcke lived near Swinemünde in Fontane's youth.

Grasenabbs: an invented name, based on the actual name Glasenapp, borne by an acquaintance of Fontane; Glasenapp was not pleased to find an unpleasant fictional character with a name so close to his, and Fontane wrote him an apologetic letter.

Güldenklee: the name of an actual family, which, as Fontane knew, was extinct, so that his use of the name could convey authenticity without giving offence.

Crown Princess: Victoria (1840–1901), eldest daughter of Queen Victoria and wife of Prince Friedrich Wilhelm (1831–88), who reigned briefly as the Emperor Friedrich III.

Stiefel von Stiefelstein: an invented name, meant to sound comical; *Stiefel* means 'boot'.

51 *2nd of December*: on 2 December 1851 Louis Napoleon, who affirmed that he was the son of Napoleon Bonaparte's brother Louis, overthrew the French Second Republic and seized power, ruthlessly shooting down the Parisians who objected, and on 2 December 1852 he proclaimed himself Emperor Napoleon III.

Saarbrücken: in the first skirmish of the Franco–Prussian War the French won a victory at Saarbrücken, for which Napoleon III gave credit to his son Louis; Innstetten mistakenly calls the father, not the son, the conqueror of Saarbrücken. For details, see Michael Howard, *The Franco-Prussian War* (London: Hart-Davis, 1961), 79–85.

Eugénie: the Empress Eugénie (1826–1920), originally the Countess of Montijo and Teja, wife to Napoleon III; she was alleged to have a relationship with the banker Baron Alfons de Rothschild (1827–1905).

52 *Nobiling's attempt*: Karl Eduard Nobiling (1848–78), an anarchist who tried on 2 June 1878 to assassinate Emperor Wilhelm I.

Le Bourget: a town north-east of Paris, captured by the Prussians on 30 October 1870.

boston: a card game resembling whist, popular in nineteenth-century Europe; the players have 'chips' or counters of various sizes and values to keep their score.

53 *Graditzers*: horses from the stud farm at Graditz in Saxony.

54 *Bayreuth*: town in northern Bavaria where the Festspielhaus for the performance of Wagner's music-dramas was completed in 1876.

55 *"white woman"*: the ghost of Countess Kunigunde of Orlamünde, who lived around 1300, is said to have appeared several times in various northern Bavarian mansions.

"maudit château": 'accursed castle'.

58 *Verona*: the northern Italian city which provides the setting for the rivalry between the Capulet and Montague families in Shakespeare's *Romeo and Juliet*.

64 *Mirambo*: an African trader who became rich enough to raise his own army and become king of Urambo (in present-day Tanzania) from 1860 to 1884. Fontane read about him in Henry Morton Stanley's *Through the Dark Continent* (1878).

68 *Viardot*: Pauline Viardot-Garcia (1821–1910), a pianist and opera-singer.

69 *Lissa*: a town now called Leszno and located in central Poland; in Fontane's time it belonged to the Prussian-ruled province of Posen and had three squadrons of a hussar regiment in its garrison.

71 *souls*: before the abolition of serfdom in 1861, Russian landowners counted their wealth by the number of serfs or 'souls' they owned.

72 *Bock & Bote*: a leading music business in Berlin.

Gluck: Christoph Willibald Gluck (1714–87), composer of the opera *Orpheus and Eurydice* (1762).

73 *Orpheus . . . Chrimhild . . . Vestal*: Orpheus refers to Gluck's opera *Orpheus and Eurydice* (1762); Chrimhild is a leading female character in *The Nibelungs* (1854), an opera by Heinrich Ludwig Dorn (1804–92); the Vestal is a leading figure in the opera *The Vestal Virgin* (1807) by Gaspare Spontini (1774–1851).

"Erlkönig": ballad by Goethe, set to music by Franz Schubert (1797–1828) and Carl Loewe (1796–1869).

Die schöne Müllerin: poem cycle by Wilhelm Müller (1794–1827), set to music by Schubert.

"Die Glocken von Speier": 'The Bells of Speyer', a ballad by Maximilian von Oer (1806–46), set by Loewe.

"Ritter Olaf": a poem by Heinrich Heine (1797–1856), published in his *New Poems* (1844); translated as 'Sir Olaf' in *The Complete Poems of Heinrich Heine: A Modern English Version*, trans. Hal Draper (Oxford: Oxford University Press, 1982), 370–2.

Zampa and 'Heideknabe': *Zampa* is an opera (1831) by Louis Joseph

Ferdinand Hérold (1791–1833); 'Heideknabe' is a poem by the well-known dramatist Friedrich Hebbel (1813–63), set by Robert Schumann (1810–56).

74 *psychograph*: a device for writing down messages supposedly received at spiritualist seances.

75 *Torquemada*: Tomás de Torquemada (1420–98), Grand Inquisitor of Castile and Aragon.

76 '*Madame . . . Monsieur le Baron*': 'Baroness von Innstetten, née von Briest. Arrived safely. Prince K. at the station. More smitten with me than ever. A thousand thanks for your kind welcome. Heartfelt compliments to the Baron.'

81 *Eugen Richter*: Richter (1838–1906) was a liberal politician and a vigorous opponent of Bismarck.

Jewish question: Wagner was an outspoken anti-Semite, most strikingly in his pamphlet *Judaism in Music* (1850).

83 *Wilms*: Robert Friedrich Wilms (1824–80), a distinguished surgeon, whom Fontane knew personally.

Count Gröben: Count Georg von der Gröben (1817–94), a major-general in the Prussian army.

Swedish Pomerania: a territory on the Baltic coast, including the cities of Stralsund, Greifswald, and Stettin (Szczecin) and the island of Rügen, acquired by Sweden in 1630, during the Thirty Years War, and assigned to Prussia by the Congress of Vienna in 1815.

86 *Biliner mineral water*: water from the spa Bilin (now Bílina) in Bohemia.

Bornholm: an island in the Baltic, belonging to Denmark

Visby: Swedish city on the island of Gotland, in medieval times an important commercial town and a member of the Hanseatic League.

Wullenweber: Jürgen Wullenweber (1492–1537), a mayor of Lübeck who led a campaign against the Danes before being captured and executed.

Stockholm Bloodbath: in 1520 King Christian II of Denmark regained control of Sweden and executed over 600 opponents of Danish rule.

88 *Eichsfeld*: a strongly Catholic district in Thuringia in southern Germany.

Giebichenstein: a village near Halle in Saxony.

90 *Reeperbahn*: literally 'street of rope-makers', but it is difficult now not to associate the name with the Reeperbahn, a well-known red-light district, in Hamburg.

91 *Battle of Königgrätz*: the decisive Prussian victory in the Austro-Prussian War of 1866.

92 *Napoleon's birthday*: the birthday of Napoleon Bonaparte in 1769.

Bible: Sidonie is thinking of Revelation 3: 16: 'So because thou art lukewarm, and neither hot nor cold, I will spew thee out of my mouth.'

rock of St Peter . . . rocher de bronze: Jesus' words to Peter, 'thou art Peter, and upon this rock I will build my church' (Matthew 16: 18), have traditionally been interpreted as founding either the Christian Church generally, or (as here) the Roman Catholic Church specifically. King Friedrich Wilhelm I of Prussia, receiving a petition in 1716, wrote in the margin, in a mixture of German and French, 'I will make sovereignty as stable as a rock of bronze (*rocher von bronze*)'. The 'rock' here refers to Bismarck.

Justizrat: title given to a senior judge.

94 *Blücher*: Gebhard Leberecht von Blücher (1742–1819), the Prussian commander at the Battle of Waterloo in 1815.

98 *Heinersdorf*: Günther Schulz von Heinersdorf, a multi-millionaire and owner of several landed estates.

Pluto: the god of the underworld, but here seemingly confused with Plutus, the god of wealth.

Chinese dragon: in the late 1870s China was at war with Japan and Russia with Turkey.

99 *Vionville*: a town near Metz in north-eastern France where the Prussian army defeated the French on 16 August 1870.

100 *War in Peace . . . Euphrosyne*: *War in Peace*, a comedy (1881) by Gustav von Moser (1825–1903) and Franz von Schönthan (1849–1913); *Monsieur Hercules*: a farce (1863) by Georg Belly (1836–75); *Youthful Love*: a comedy (1871) by Adolf Wilbrandt (1837–1911); *Euphrosyne* (1877), a play by Otto Franz Gensichen (1847–1933). 'Euphrosyne' is an elegy by Goethe, written in 1797–8 to mourn the death of the nineteen-year-old actress Christiane Becker.

Castalian spring: a spring at the foot of Mt Parnassus, symbolizing poetic inspiration.

104 *Liancourt . . . Beauvais*: northern French towns occupied by Prussian forces during the Franco-Prussian War. The bishop of Beauvais who condemned Joan of Arc in 1431 was not called 'cochon' (= 'pig') but Cauchon.

106 *Basedow*: Johann Bernhard Basedow (1723–90), a prominent educationalist, who founded a progressive school called the Philanthropinum.

Pestalozzi: Johann Heinrich Pestalozzi (1746–1827), a Swiss educational reformer.

Schnepfenthal or Bunzlau: Christian educational institutions.

cherub with the flaming sword: alluding to the angelic guardian placed by God to prevent Adam and Eve from re-entering the Garden of Eden after the Fall (Genesis 3: 24).

108 *Vineta*: a mythical sunken city, supposed to be situated somewhere in the southern Baltic and to become visible at certain times; the Swedish author Selma Lagerlöf retells the story in *The Wonderful Adventures of Nils* (1906–7).

108 *Heine's poem*: the poem 'Seegespenst' (1827), translated as 'Sea Appar-
     ition' in Draper, *The Complete Poems of Heinrich Heine*, 141–3.

109 *Charles Stuart*: Crampas is confusing Heine's poem 'Charles I' from
     Romanzero (1851) with another about Marie Antoinette which follows it in
     the collection. See Draper, *The Complete Poems of Heinrich Heine*, 575–7.

     Vitzliputzli: a gruesome poem by Heine, also from *Romanzero*, about
     Spanish captives being sacrificed to the Aztec deity Huitzlipochtli. See
     Draper, *The Complete Poems of Heinrich Heine*, 599–614.

110 *Pedro the Cruel*: the story Crampas now tells comes from Heine's poem
     'Spanish Atrides' in *Romanzero*. See Draper, *The Complete Poems of Hein-
     rich Heine*, 619–26.

111 *Elizabeth's mother*: Anne Boleyn (1507–36), the second wife of Henry
     VIII. Fontane usually spells the name 'Bulen', which makes it look and
     sound like 'Buhle', an illicit lover.

     Black Eagle and the Pour le Mérite: high-ranking Prussian decorations,
     founded respectively by Friedrich I, to mark his coronation in 1701, and
     Friedrich II, to mark his accession in 1740.

112 *King of Thule*: in Goethe's ballad 'Der König in Thule', from *Faust,
     Part I*, the King is deeply attached to a goblet which was a present from
     his deceased lover.

113 *Friedrichsruh*: Bismarck's residence near Hamburg.

114 *'Buhküken von Halberstadt'*: a nursery-rhyme about the medieval Bishop
     Burkhard or Buko of Halberstadt (1009–56), who was famous for being
     fond of children.

     One False Step: a comedy (*Ein Schritt vom Wege*, 1873) by Ernst Wichert
     (1831–1902). Although the title sounds ominous, it refers only to the deci-
     sion of Ella von Schmettwitz, a newly-wed woman already bored with
     her conventional husband Arthur, that they should both depart from the
     norm by concealing their identity for three days while staying in a spa. As
     the local Prince is present incognito, and is said to have a liaison with an
     opera singer, much comic confusion of identity results.

115 *Kammergerichtsrat*: Ernst Wichert was born in Insterburg in East Prus-
     sia and studied at Königsberg (both now in Russia, the latter known as
     Kaliningrad), before becoming a judge, first in Königsberg, later attached
     to the supreme court (Kammergericht) in Berlin. Innstetten alludes to the
     oddity of a judge writing a comedy and also to the incongruity of Königs-
     berg's association both with Wichert's comedy and the rigorous moral
     philosophy of Immanuel Kant (1724–1804).

     seven charms: 'Every woman has seven charms' or 'seven beauties' is
     a common German saying.

119 *Wrangel and Bonin*: for Wrangel see note to p. 42. Eduard von Bonin
     (1793–1865) commanded a Prussian brigade in Schleswig-Holstein in
     1848.

Danewerk: (Dan. *Danevirke*), a fortification intended to secure Schleswig from German attack, which fell to the Prussian army on 23 April 1848.

120 *"God's Wall"*: a poem ('Die Gottesmauer') written in 1816 by Clemens Brentano (1778–1842); the event, accurately reported by Effi, takes place during an earlier war in Schleswig.

121 *Marienburg Castle*: a fortress of the medieval Teutonic Knights, situated in northern Poland, some thirty miles west of Danzig (Gdańsk), and known in Polish as Malbork.

Memling: Hans Memling (*c.*1430/40–94), painted an altar-piece, *The Last Judgement*, which was captured at sea in 1463, taken to Danzig, and displayed there in St Mary's Church.

Oliva Abbey: a Cistercian monastery founded about 1278 near Danzig.

Nettelbeck: Joachim Nettelbeck (1738–1824) helped to defend the Pomeranian town of Kolberg (Polish Kołobrzeg) when it was besieged by Napoleon's troops in 1806–7.

122 *The flesh is weak*: Matthew 26: 41.

saga in Sweden: Sigurd Ring was a legendary Swedish king mentioned in many sagas.

Köslin: (Polish Koszalin), a town in Pomerania, some miles east of Swinemünde.

Cassandra-like: in Greek legend Cassandra was a daughter of Priam, king of Troy; Apollo gave her the gift of prophecy but ordained that her prophecies would not be believed.

123 *three rings*: in the Enlightenment drama *Nathan the Wise* (1779) by Gotthold Ephraim Lessing (1729–81), the wise Jew Nathan, asked by the Sultan Saladin which of the three Abrahamic religions is the true one, tells how in ancient times a man had a ring which made its possessor beloved of God and man; he bequeathed a ring to each of his sons; wanting to know which was the genuine ring, they consulted a judge who told them to pursue active virtue and piety and thus make themselves beloved. The parable is famous as a plea for religious toleration.

'A Prussian I am . . . I will be': a patriotic song, often regarded as a Prussian national anthem and referred to as the 'Preussenlied', written in 1830 by Bernhard Thiersch (1794–1855).

132 *Radegast and Swantowit*: names of gods supposedly worshipped by the Wends, the first symbolizing reason, the second victory. Fontane discusses the Wendish pantheon in *Wanderings Through the March of Brandenburg*, ii. 28.

Table Talk: the sayings of Martin Luther (1483–1546), both serious and jocular, were collected and published in 1566.

138 *Blücher's Hussars*: a Pomeranian regiment, named after the Prussian victor at Waterloo.

Sanssouci: it was common for German embassies abroad to give presents in the form of china from the royal manufactory in Berlin, with pictures of the palaces in Potsdam. Sanssouci was built for Frederick the Great in 1745–7, the New Palace in 1763–9.

144 *Dressel's*: a smart restaurant in Berlin at Unter den Linden 50.

145 *Palazzo Strozzi or Pitti*: palaces in Florence.

154 *Dorotheenstrasse . . . Schadowstrasse*: streets in the centre of Berlin, close to Unter den Linden.

155 *Kladderadatsch*: a humorous weekly, founded in 1848, whose comic characters included Strudelwitz, Prudelwitz, and Karlchen ('Charlie') Miessnick.

   Wippchen von Bernau: a comic character from another periodical, *The Wasps*.

156 *Book of Job*: this quotation appears to be Fontane's invention. The original joke asks: 'Who was the first coachman?' and the untranslatable answer is 'Sorrow' because of the pseudo-biblical sentence 'Leid soll mir nicht widerfahren', 'Sorrow shall not afflict me' or 'Sorrow shall not drive me again'.

159 *Walter Scott . . . Herr von Bredow's Trousers*: *Walter Scott*, the Scottish historical novelist (1771–1832), whose work was also hugely popular on the Continent and inspired Fontane's first novel, *Before the Storm* (1878). *Ivanhoe* (1819) is set in medieval England, *Quentin Durward* (1823) in fifteenth-century France. *Cooper*: James Fenimore Cooper (1789–1851), whose adventure novels include *The Spy* (1821), set during the American Revolution. *Dickens*: *David Copperfield* (1850) by Charles Dickens (1812–70). Effi's tastes in fiction are quite conventional. *Willibald Alexis*: the pseudonym of Wilhelm Häring (1798–1871), who wrote novels inspired by Scott on Prussian history. *Herr von Bredow's Trousers* (1846–8), set in sixteenth-century Brandenburg, is his best-known work.

165 *Red Castle*: not actually a castle, but an imposing building containing shops.

166 *Charlottenburg Palace*: a palace built in 1699 for the Elector Friedrich, who in 1701 assumed the title King Friedrich I.

167 *Oberammergau Passion Play*: a drama about the arrest and crucifixion of Jesus, performed every ten years to commemorate deliverance from the plague in 1634.

   Stralsund: an important and historic city on the coast of the present German province of Mecklenburg-Vorpommern, the normal departure-point for visits to the island of Rügen.

   Schill: Ferdinand von Schill (1776–1809), who led an unsuccessful uprising against Napoleon but was killed in street-fighting in Stralsund. He is famous for saying to his followers: 'Better an end with horror than a horror without end,' which has become proverbial.

   Scheele: Karl Wilhelm Scheele (1742–86), born in Stralsund; the priority in discovering oxygen is disputed between him and the English scientist Joseph Priestley (1733–1804), who made the discovery three years later but published it before Scheele did.

168 *Fahrenheit*: the hotel in Sassnitz was actually called the Hotel zum Fahrnberg; Fontane changed the name for the sake of the joke (letter to Friedlaender, 29 August 1894).

'*Crampas*': a fishing village on Rügen, merged in 1906 with the village of Sassnitz.

169 *sacrificial altar*: there are photographs of these stones in James N. Bade, *Fontane's Landscapes* (Würzburg: Königshausen & Neumann, 2009), 139.

170 *Kongens Nytorv*: the largest square in the centre of Copenhagen; literally 'King's New Market'.

Thorvaldsen: the Danish neoclassical sculptor Bertel Thorvaldsen (1770–1844).

Penz: a family with many branches in Germany and Denmark; it is the name of a prominent character in Fontane's novel *No Way Back* (1891), set in Denmark.

171 *Frederiksborg and Elsinore*: Frederiksborg is a palace built for King Christian IV of Denmark between 1602 and 1620; Elsinore (Dan. Helsingør) is a town north-east of Copenhagen with a castle, Kronborg, which forms the setting of Shakespeare's *Hamlet*.

174 *Genthin*: a town in Saxony-Anhalt, south-west of Brandenburg and hence a long way away.

Friesack: a town in the Havelland, therefore near Hohen-Cremmen.

175 *Düppel*: the site of the main Danish entrenchments in the Dano-Prussian War; their capture by Prussian troops on 18 April 1864 was the turning-point in the war.

Lipa: a hill captured by the Prussian Guards during the Battle of Königgrätz in the Austro-Prussian War of 1866.

177 *Landesgerichtsrat*: a judge attached to the district court.

178 *Posen Province*: the province (Polish Poznań) acquired by Prussia in the Second Partition of Poland in 1793.

Barbarossa: the nickname ('Redbeard') of the German Emperor Friedrich I (1125–90).

179 *a Christian one*: alluding to the prominence of Jewish bankers in Berlin, the best-known being Bismarck's banker Gerson Bleichröder, to whom Fontane alludes in the novel *The Poggenpuhl Family* (1896).

Almanach de Gotha: the standard handbook of the European nobility.

Bad Schwalbach: a spa in the Taunus hills, near Frankfurt am Main.

Ems: another spa, in the Rhineland near Koblenz. It was from here that Emperor Wilhelm I sent the Ems Telegram which triggered the Franco-Prussian War.

181 *Nana*: novel (1880) by Émile Zola (1840–1902), telling the life-story of a courtesan.

'the unvarying hour of duty': a quotation from Schiller's *The Piccolomini*, Act I, scene 4.

"Let me have men about me that are fat": from Shakespeare, *Julius Caesar*, I. ii. 192.

200 *Niemann as Tannhäuser*: Albert Niemann (1831–1917) was a well-known opera singer who had sung the title role in the Paris première of Wagner's *Tannhäuser* in 1861.

202 *Saatwinkel*: a village on the north-west side of Berlin, a popular spot for trips to the country. Before the days of motor traffic the coachmen of Berlin assembled here twice a year to enjoy themselves in the local pubs and restaurants. It may be its reputation for festivities like these that makes the Geheimrätin disapprove of her husband's trips to Saatwinkel.

203 *Saturn devours his own children*: the Roman god Saturnus was identified with the Greek Kronos, who devoured his own children until Zeus killed him and freed the rest from his stomach. During the French Revolution Saturn was used to symbolize revolutionary violence. Cf. Georg Büchner, *Danton's Death* (written 1834), Act I, scene 5: 'the revolution is like Saturn, it devours its own children.'

208 *Königgrätzerstrasse*: a modest location, named after the decisive battle of the Austro-Prussian War; since renamed the Stresemannstrasse.

209 *Prince Albrecht's Palace*: the residence of Prince Albrecht of Prussia (1837–1906), a general, related to the royal family by being the grandson of King Friedrich Wilhelm III (reigned 1797–1940).

Kreuzberg: an area on the south side of Berlin which was landscaped between 1888 and 1894.

211 *Glatz*: a town in Silesia (the province south-east of Prussia, conquered by Frederick the Great in the 1740s), now Kłodzko in south-western Poland. It has a fortress where Innstetten has been confined as a token punishment for killing his opponent in the duel.

217 *Guido Reni*: Italian painter (1575–1642).

Benjamin West: English painter of historical scenes (1738–1820).

King Lear: see Shakespeare, *King Lear*, III. ii.

221 *Schilling's*: a cake-shop on the Friedrichstrasse, hence in the smart central area of Berlin that Effi used to visit in happier times.

Körner: Karl Theodor Körner (1791–1813), famous for his patriotic poems and for his death in the war against Napoleon's troops.

226 *Arkona*: one of the ancient centres of the Wendish religion. For an account of the German crusade against Wendish paganism, see Richard Fletcher, *The Conversion of Europe: From Paganism to Christianity 371–1386 AD* (London: HarperCollins, 1997), 435–50.

228 *Lethe*: according to Greek mythology, a river in the underworld whose water induced forgetfulness.

229 *Kreuzzeitung . . . Norddeutsche Allgemeine*: conservative newspapers. The *Neue Preussische Zeitung* (New Prussian Newspaper) was known colloquially by the Iron Cross (*Kreuz*) which formed its emblem. Fontane was its correspondent on British affairs from 1856 to 1870. The *Norddeutsche Allgemeine Zeitung* (North German General Newspaper) was understood to express Bismarck's policies.

230 *Ladenberg, who had been a minister*: Philipp von Ladenberg (1796–1847), who was annoyed at receiving only the inferior decoration.

232 *Wichern*: Johann Hinrich Wichern (1808–81), a theologian who in 1833 founded the Rauhes Haus, an asylum for the mentally ill, in Hamburg.

Mutesa: Mutesa I (1837–84), king of Buganda, in present-day Uganda.

Cameroons: present-day Cameroon in West Africa; it became a German colony in 1884.

233 *Emperor Friedrich*: Friedrich III (1831–88) reigned for only ninety-nine days before dying of cancer of the throat on 15 June 1888. This reference shows that we are now in the 'Year of Three Emperors': Wilhelm I had died on 9 March; Wilhelm II ascended the throne immediately on Friedrich's death.

Sardanapalus . . . Coppélia . . . Antonietta dell'Era: *Sardanapalus* is a ballet by Paul Taglioni (1808–84), director of the Berlin Ballet; *Coppélia*, a ballet (1870) by Léo Delibes (1836–91); Antonietta dell'Era was a famous ballerina (1860–1945?), a favourite with Berlin audiences.

Duke of Ratibor: Viktor, Duke of Ratibor (1818–93), a prominent conservative politician.

Prince-Bishop Kopp: Georg Kopp (1837–1914), Prince-Bishop of Breslau, who played a mediating role in Bismarck's conflict with the Catholic Church in the 1870s.

MORE ABOUT **OXFORD WORLD'S CLASSICS**

American Literature

British and Irish Literature

Children's Literature

Classics and Ancient Literature

Colonial Literature

Eastern Literature

European Literature

Gothic Literature

History

Medieval Literature

Oxford English Drama

Philosophy

Poetry

Politics

Religion

The Oxford Shakespeare

A complete list of Oxford World's Classics, including Authors in Context, Oxford English Drama, and the Oxford Shakespeare, is available in the UK from the Marketing Services Department, Oxford University Press, Great Clarendon Street, Oxford OX2 6DP, or visit the website at www.oup.com/uk/worldsclassics.

In the USA, visit www.oup.com/us/owc for a complete title list.

Oxford World's Classics are available from all good bookshops. In case of difficulty, customers in the UK should contact Oxford University Press Bookshop, 116 High Street, Oxford OX1 4BR.

	Eirik the Red and Other Icelandic Sagas
	The Kalevala
	The Poetic Edda
LUDOVICO ARIOSTO	Orlando Furioso
GIOVANNI BOCCACCIO	The Decameron
GEORG BÜCHNER	Danton's Death, Leonce and Lena, and Woyzeck
LUIS VAZ DE CAMÕES	The Lusiads
MIGUEL DE CERVANTES	Don Quixote Exemplary Stories
CARLO COLLODI	The Adventures of Pinocchio
DANTE ALIGHIERI	The Divine Comedy Vita Nuova
LOPE DE VEGA	Three Major Plays
J. W. VON GOETHE	Elective Affinities Erotic Poems Faust: Part One and Part Two The Flight to Italy
JACOB and WILHELM GRIMM	Selected Tales
E. T. A. HOFFMANN	The Golden Pot and Other Tales
HENRIK IBSEN	An Enemy of the People, The Wild Duck, Rosmersholm Four Major Plays Peer Gynt
LEONARDO DA VINCI	Selections from the Notebooks
FEDERICO GARCIA LORCA	Four Major Plays
MICHELANGELO BUONARROTI	Life, Letters, and Poetry

ANTON CHEKHOV

About Love and Other Stories
Early Stories
Five Plays
The Princess and Other Stories
The Russian Master and Other Stories
The Steppe and Other Stories
Twelve Plays
Ward Number Six and Other Stories

FYODOR DOSTOEVSKY

Crime and Punishment
Devils
A Gentle Creature and Other Stories
The Idiot
The Karamazov Brothers
Memoirs from the House of the Dead
Notes from the Underground and
    The Gambler

NIKOLAI GOGOL

Dead Souls
Plays and Petersburg Tales

ALEXANDER PUSHKIN

Eugene Onegin
The Queen of Spades and Other Stories

LEO TOLSTOY

Anna Karenina
The Kreutzer Sonata and Other Stories
The Raid and Other Stories
Resurrection
War and Peace

IVAN TURGENEV

Fathers and Sons
First Love and Other Stories
A Month in the Country